OCCUPATIONAL HAZARD

Hanna heard the twigs snap under his feet. She smelled the mixture of his cologne and sweat before she felt him kick her in the ribs, sending her rolling down the embankment. He followed. Her jawbone snapped as his fist slammed into it, bringing a blinding pain like no other she had ever known.

Then she saw it gleam in the moonlight. The smooth, polished blade was slightly curved, with an unusual braid-like design skillfully forged into it. She heard a guttural laugh, followed by the sickening sound of his zipper lowering.

In a flash of steel, her clothes were in shreds. The razor-sharp knife left stinging ribbons of crimson over her thighs, her breasts. Her screams drifted into a welcome void. A void that saved her from knowing the other unspeakable things he did to her. . . .

Hanna was the first to question what the company was doing. Now Hanna was gone, and an equally brilliant scientist had come to take her job. JoAnn Rayburn did not know it, but she was about to fill Hanna's shoes in more ways than one. . . .

DEADLY COMPANY

DEADLY COMPANY

Jodie Larsen

AN ONYX BOOK

ONYX
Published by the Penguin Group
Penguin Books USA Inc., 375 Hudson Street,
New York, New York 10014, U.S.A.
Penguin Books Ltd, 27 Wrights Lane, London W8 5TZ, England
Penguin Books Australia Ltd, Ringwood, Victoria, Australia
Penguin Books Canada Ltd, 10 Alcorn Avenue,
Toronto, Ontario, Canada M4V 3B2
Penguin Books (N.Z.) Ltd, 182–190 Wairau Road, Auckland 10, New Zealand

Penguin Books Ltd, Registered Offices:
Harmondsworth, Middlesex, England

First published by Onyx, an imprint of Dutton Signet,
a division of Penguin Books USA Inc.

First Printing, September, 1996
10 9 8 7 6 5 4 3 2 1

For Mark, Amanda, and Jonathan

ACKNOWLEDGMENTS

This book would not have been possible without
the support and encouragement of a few special
people who dared to share my dream. I am forever indebted to my editor, Audrey LaFehr, and
to all my friends and family with special thanks
to Judy Olender, Linda Shreck, Lesley Jaggers
and Pat Larsen.

Most of all I am grateful to my agents, Sherrie
Dixon and Dwight Lada, of Esq. Literary Pro-
ductions, for their confidence and faith in my
work.

Prologue

Hanna Shore never had a chance.

Her workout at TechLab's ultra-fitness gym had exhausted her body but not her mind. Tension still throbbed in her temples and stung her eyes. Was it from stress or instinctive fear?

Sweat glistened on her forehead as she whipped the midnight-black Lexus into her driveway. The car was a reflection of the late summer night, its sleek, lustrous surface mirroring the beauty of the warm, clear sky. Even though years of hard work had earned the luxurious company car, driving it now only served to remind her how much she hated everything associated with TechLab.

Three times she pushed the remote control button on her automatic garage door opener. Three times nothing happened. In frustration she pulled the small black control box from the visor and aimed it directly at the door as she pushed. Still nothing.

Wait a few minutes. It could be a trick. Or just a dead battery. Quit being so damned paranoid! She shut off the engine of the car and waited in silence.

Every shrub now became suspect, every movement of nature a threat. Watching, she waited for what she thought was a long time, even though the clock on the dashboard ticked off less than two minutes. With one hand clutching a small canister of pepper gas and her keys wedged firmly between the fingers of her other hand, she unlocked the car door and ran to her porch.

Hanna's fingers trembled as she tried to force the

key into the lock. Then she smelled it. The faint, sweet odor of vanilla. She held her breath, stepped back to run, but it was too late. Like an ice sculpture, she froze, then crashed to the ground. The scream never crawled out of her throat.

Oddly, her first thought was of SynCur6, one of TechLab's top secret chemicals. Hanna remembered the statistical reports clearly. SynCur6 was a synthetic derivative of curare with a distinctive, pleasant odor like vanilla. Two seconds after exposure it caused total, temporary paralysis of voluntary muscles. Reported to the Pentagon as the perfect weapon, TechLab would make millions on it, if the right socio-economic situation ever arose. Biologically, its characteristics were equally impressive: after two hours it left no trace in the bloodstream, had no detectable side effects, and unlike most chemical warfare agents, it presented no danger to the environment.

Although Hanna's body was paralyzed, her mind raced. She never saw the man who drugged her, since he kept her face to the ground as he dragged her to his car. As she felt the car accelerate, a flicker of hope ignited. *Maybe they just want to scare me. This is probably a second warning. A much stronger warning. Stay calm.*

But her hopes quickly vanished. He began to talk, slowly at first, but then his words came faster. The familiar voice echoed through her mind as though it were merely a part of a nightmare. Loyalty was mentioned, and the Riverparks rapist. She willed herself not to hear any more of his lies, not to blame herself for being so naive for so long. She tried to think of other things, yet every sound he uttered burned her mind. He stopped the car, and as he hauled her into the bushes, she was thankful to be surrounded by the silence of the night instead of his despicable voice.

Even with her face in the dirt, she could tell from the fading crunch of gravel he was leaving. The furious beating of her heart began to slow, and for a few moments only the peaceful sound of the river surrounded her. She prayed he would not return. The chemical would wear off in two hours. She would walk home, take a shower, and remain quiet. Forever.

But he came back. Hanna heard the twigs snap under his feet as he approached. She smelled the mixture of his cologne and sweat on the gentle southerly breeze before she felt him kick her in the ribs, sending her rolling through the sandy weeds and down the embankment. He followed. Her jawbone snapped as his fist slammed into it, bringing a blinding pain like no other she had ever known.

Then she saw it gleam in the moonlight. Another time, she might have admired it for the work of art it was. The smooth polished blade was slightly curved, with an unusual braidlike design skillfully forged into it. A guttural laugh accompanied its disappearance from her sight, followed by the sickening sound of his zipper lowering.

In a flash of steel, her clothes were shreds. He smiled as the razor-sharp knife left stinging ribbons of crimson over her thighs, her breasts. Hanna's mute screams drifted into a peaceful, welcome void. A void that saved her from knowing the other unspeakable things he did to her before she finally bled to death.

Chapter 1

"I know you must still be in shock, Ms. Rayburn. Ms. Shore was a valuable member of TechLab's research team, and we are all deeply saddened by her death. I appreciate you meeting with me on such short notice." J. D. Cook's voice was cool and soothing, effectively covering his surprise. He sat behind his sleek mahogany desk, projecting the executive image he had practiced for years: aloof, yet compassionate and open.

Cook had expected JoAnn Rayburn to be falling apart, an emotional wreck in need of a shoulder to cry on. Instead, she appeared amazingly calm, strangely unaffected by the news of her immediate supervisor's untimely death. This was an important step for him, a golden opportunity he had no intention of missing.

All morning he had agonized over his decision, but in reality, he knew he had no other choice. Every report in JoAnn Rayburn's thick personnel file categorized her as a Code 4—a blindly loyal employee with virtually no social life. Dependable, but equally dependent on her job. Code 4's supposedly thrived in unchanging environments, routine assignments. They were excellent employees, the natural choice for lengthy laboratory research projects.

But two months ago Hanna Shore's performance evaluation of her subordinate was less than glowing. Although it included a handwritten note that outlined JoAnn's lab work as "beyond perfection," the report went on to criticize her interpersonal skills. It flatly stated, "At this time, JoAnn is still unacceptable to be considered for upper management promotion due to her inability to supervise subordinates as a result of her unbending work ethic."

By reading over years of various comments in JoAnn's file, most written by Hanna, it became apparent to J.D. that JoAnn Rayburn expected everyone to perform their jobs as precisely as she did her own. It was an admirable attitude, but one that could cause numerous conflicts with the support staff, most of whom thought dedication to their job meant just showing up each day.

J.D.'s right hand stroked the chin line of his salt and pepper beard as he stared at the woman across from him. She wore the standard TechLab research attire— a crisp, white lab coat over jeans and a T-shirt. At first he thought she was just plain homely, then he realized it was probably a lack of makeup that made her seem so unappealing.

JoAnn's God-given features were, for the most part, average. Straight brown hair contrasted with skin so pale he guessed it rarely, if ever, saw the light of day. She had big brown eyes with thick black eyelashes. He wondered if her eyes really were enormous, or if the heavy tortoiseshell glasses magnified them out of proportion. Her lips were full, but without the help of even the slightest touch of lipstick, they, too, lost their redeeming potential to light up her dreary face.

Instinctively, J.D. felt JoAnn could handle the job fate had just thrown her way. Technically, she could not be enlightened for a year, but he hoped to convince the Board to let her help much sooner. Of course, she would have to learn tolerance, but she was bright. Hell, with an I.Q. well over 160, bright was an understatement. Management skills could be learned. TechLab would send her to any special schools, pay whatever the cost. She was no different than Hanna had been eight years ago.

JoAnn cleared her throat, then looked directly at him and said, "We weren't told much this morning, Mr. Cook, only that Ms. Shore was dead. Could you please give me a few more details so I can end the speculation?"

"Speculation?"

JoAnn's gaze shifted to her own hands, which were busily working a loose strand of thread around a button on her lab coat. "Well . . . yes, sir. Several techs think she was . . ."

J.D. snapped, "What?"

"Murdered. They say she was acting very strange for the last few days, and that just before she left on Friday she was so nervous she dropped an entire tray of specimens."

His heart skipped a beat, but he managed to keep his voice level as he stated, "Ms. Shore was murdered, but it was a random act of violence." He tilted back in his chair, hesitated, then asked, "Did Ms. Shore routinely work directly with specimens?"

"No, that was why everyone thought something odd was going on."

"Do you know what specimens were involved?"

"No."

"Could she have been smuggling samples to our competitors?"

JoAnn didn't immediately reply. Her stiff facial expression and those damned thick glasses made it impossible for him to tell what she thought of his insinuation of corporate espionage. Finally, she said, "Ms. Shore wouldn't do anything to hurt TechLab."

He leaned forward, removing his glasses as he asked, "And what did you think, JoAnn? Did you find her behavior unusual?"

"I wasn't in the lab last week. I was on mandatory vacation for five days."

J.D. nodded. He remembered reading in JoAnn's file that she only used her vacation time when the company forced her to, a policy he personally found ridiculous. If employees didn't feel the need for time away from work, then why force them to go? But the Board had adopted the policy recommended by their auditors in spite of his objections. Leaning forward, his eyes searched hers as he asked, "How did you spend your time off?"

"I revised the protocol for the next phase of Citrinol3 testing. I think the new inhalant format will be absorbed more evenly in the bloodstream and possibly solve some of our nervous system distribution problems."

He widened his eyes and nodded as he said, "Your latest Citrinol compound can be administered using an inhalant?"

"Yes, sir. The revised molecular structure lends itself quite readily to vaporization."

"And where did you do this work?"

"At home."

"Why?"

"Why not? It was theoretical work, sir," she said with a slightly defiant cock of her head. "I could have done it while hanging upside down from a skyscraper if I had wanted to. You don't have to be in a lab four stories underground to think."

J.D. started to answer, but hesitated instead. There was no use pointing out it was against TechLab's corporate policy to handle any confidential materials or data outside the building. He was certain she knew the rule as well as he did. Besides, his mind was already running through the vast testing benefits of an inhalant form of Citrinol3.

He continued, "As I said before, Ms. Rayburn, Ms.

Shore was murdered. She was the victim of a brutal attack last night. The police think she was assaulted by the rapist who has been terrorizing Riverparks. Her body was found in some shrubs between the Arkansas River and the main running trail. Apparently, she was brutally beaten, raped, and stabbed numerous times. I'm sure it will be on the news tonight, so you might want to call the lab staff together and brief them before they hear it from strangers."

JoAnn was visibly shaken as she muttered, "I can't believe she would go there. When the rapes began a few months ago, we all discussed how dangerous jogging alone could be. She told us she was going to start working out at the TechLab Physical Performance Center until the police caught the man. She even lectured me again last week for running alone."

"So you jog, too?"

JoAnn nodded. "Hanna . . . I mean, Ms. Shore convinced me to start a couple of years ago. It's a great way to relieve stress."

"You don't jog at Riverparks, do you?"

"No. I stay in my neighborhood."

He slowly shook his head. "Ms. Shore was right. You shouldn't run alone, it could be very dangerous right now. Until this man is caught, I think you should stop."

"I live in the house my grandparents built nearly sixty years ago by Swan Lake. It's an old, peaceful area. Besides, at four a.m., there aren't a lot of people awake, much less out stalking the streets. I do appreciate your concern, Mr. Cook. I will continue to be careful."

"Good. We can't afford to lose another Chief of Research."

"Excuse me?"

"That's why I called you here, JoAnn. May I call you JoAnn?"

"Of course."

"I've spent most of the morning meeting with the Board and going over your personnel records, and I must say I am very impressed with your background. Your work at TechLab has been exemplary. I understand you were the mastermind of the Citrinol experiments."

"Yes, sir. When I was hired, I was guaranteed the opportunity to conduct research that could help control or cure brain tumors."

"A personal vendetta?"

"Unfortunately. My father died only two months after being diagnosed at age fifty. I plan to eventually develop a drug that will control the rapid tumor growth that can be characteristic of certain cancers."

"But haven't you already developed such a drug? I understand Citrinol3 is in facility test phase six."

"It is, but there are several unfavorable side effects that must be eliminated before the compound can be tested on more advanced animals. Human testing is still years away. The problems with stunted cell growth and oxygen absorption have to be overcome."

"I've read the reports on the project's progression. However, Ms. Shore thought you were being overly cautious."

JoAnn was obviously stunned. "She did?"

"I am going to be totally honest with you, JoAnn. I think that perhaps Ms. Shore was trying to undermine your success here at TechLab."

"But . . . Hanna was my friend, as well as my colleague. I can't believe she would do anything that might negatively affect my career."

"Did the two of you ever discuss any work-related problems you might be having?"

"Such as?"

"Your inability to supervise the lab techs."

"No. We rarely talked about personnel. She always

introduced potential tech candidates to me and asked my opinion, but that was the extent of my involvement. Hanna hated what she called 'unproductive office gibberish,' so most of our conversations revolved around the technical aspects of my research."

"And private issues?"

"No. Hanna and I had what I would call a close business friendship. I admired her work and respected her very much, but we didn't meet after work or socialize together." She paused for several seconds, then added, "Except for two years ago when she convinced me to start jogging. She seemed to be nervous about something then."

"Did she confide in you?"

"No. Whatever it was, she must have dealt with it. After about a month, she said things were back to normal."

"Did you continue to run together?"

"No. She went back to her old routine. But I was hooked. I've been running ever since."

J.D. opened the manila file on his desk and removed JoAnn's latest performance review. Stretching across his mahogany desk, he handed the document to her. "Does this look familiar?"

JoAnn instantly recognized the annual review form. It was precisely completed in Hanna's meticulous handwriting. "We talked this over a couple of months ago."

"What about the 'Comments' section on the back?"

She flipped over the pages and quickly read the commentary. Her stomach knotted as she scanned the derogatory remark about her lack of management potential, which had obviously been written by Hanna. "This wasn't here when I signed the form. It doesn't make any sense."

"Why not?"

"Because I haven't had any direct contact with lab

techs for over four years. You know the level of security on the Citrinol3 experiment. When it was upgraded to Level 12 status, I assumed all responsibility for the actual protocol. I have one assistant who is in charge of disinfecting the test areas, equipment, and cages, but no one else works directly with me."

"What about research assistants?"

"I handle most of the testing alone. I'm sure you know that on Level 12 projects, my lab findings are blindly verified by the Pathology department. They don't even know which project's specimens they're examining, much less who is performing the research. Everything is coded and sent pneumatically." She paused, then added, "I do have contact with the techs in the adjoining labs. We share the equipment in the central analysis area, mainly the electron microscope and the centrifuge on Subfloor 5."

"How is your relationship with them?"

"I've never really given it any thought before. They came to me this morning when they heard about Hanna. I assume that means they trust me."

"How much do you know about the work Hanna performed as Chief of Research?"

"Very little. My own work has always consumed all my time and then some. Quite frankly, I'm not sure I'm the administrative type. I love what I do, and I think I'm close to a drug that may prove to be very beneficial, if not the cure for some people."

J.D. handed her an inch-thick black binder. "This is the handbook that outlines the job functions of Chief of Research. Don't worry, you could still continue your work on the Citrinol project, but in a supervisory fashion. You could handpick who you want to work for you. Of course, the job does require supervisory skills. Just let me know if you would like to attend any management training courses."

"This is very flattering, Mr. Cook, but . . ."

"Call me J.D. I don't need your answer right now. Take a couple of days."

"Yes, sir," she said as she slowly stood and headed for the door.

"Not 'sir,' JoAnn. It's J.D. Oh, yes, the job pays double your current salary, a company car, and a bonus based on annual corporate profit."

Her eyes widened, but she remained calm as she said, "Thank you. I'll let you know by Wednesday."

His smile faded as soon as she pulled the door closed behind her. Grabbing the phone, he quickly dialed the familiar extension. Slowly, deliberately, he said, "I've done what you asked. Don't expect my division to clean up your mistakes again."

"Just be at the meeting this afternoon, J.D. And lose the attitude before you wind up testing SynCur6, too."

Long after J.D. slammed the receiver down, his colleague's laughter rang in his ears.

JoAnn walked slowly down the hall, then took the elevator to the research facility four stories below ground level. She felt numb. The prospect of a new job with more money didn't excite her, even though her old house desperately needed renovation.

Tears threatened as thoughts ran through her mind. *Hanna really is dead. Why would Hanna betray me? Why write lies in my personnel file? What really happened to her?*

She stepped off the elevator into the sleek corridor. It had been a long time since she noticed the sterile, cold interior of the place where she spent most of her waking hours. Long fluorescent tubes ran down the ceiling of the arched passageway. Each side was blazoned with the TechLab trademark—burnt orange and black lines flowing like the sinuous rhythm of a heart on a monitor. The polished floor was color coded with glazed stripes leading to the three main wings.

The employees in the general research area followed what they called the "yellow brick road." The blue stripe in the middle of the corridor led to Pathology, which was connected to the entire underground facility by a sophisticated network of pneumatic tubes. The red stripe, the one JoAnn now methodically followed, ended at a computerized door marked "RESTRICTED AREA—BIOHAZARD."

This wing was reserved for top-secret projects and potentially hazardous chemicals and organisms. The back of the wing held the BioHazard Level 4 lab. JoAnn didn't envy the scientists who worked there. They dealt with deadly bacteria and viruses, wearing bulky space suits and protective gear at all times. One slip of a needle could mean death. Undetected exposure could spread a plague that would devastate the world.

JoAnn slid her identification badge through the slot on the door, then stepped into a small holding chamber. Once the massive door sealed behind her, she repeated the identification process, then pushed the green button to release the inner electronic door. She walked past the hallway of small offices to the central analysis lab.

Although each pretended to be diligently working, it was obvious the lab techs were waiting for JoAnn to return with news. Hanna had always treated them fairly, with respect for them not only as professionals but as individuals. They all stopped what they were doing, their eyes silently asking the question.

JoAnn cleared her throat and said, "Hanna was apparently attacked and killed by the Riverparks rapist last night. They found her body between the river and the jogging path."

Leanne Caldwell, the oldest of the women, said, "But . . ."

Before she could continue, JoAnn quickly held up

her hands and said, "I know what Hanna told all of us about being careful. God only knows what she must have been thinking to go out there alone late at night."

Leanne nodded, then said, "It must have been her time."

From the farthest corner of the lab, an apprehensive voice mumbled, "Like hell it was."

JoAnn recognized Amy's delicate voice. In any other environment, she would have been considered just an average soft-spoken, intelligent woman. But among the quiet lab techs, her tendency to bluntly vocalize her opinion on any subject made her a rebel. A five-foot-tall, ninety-five-pound rebel. JoAnn sighed and said, "I know how hard this is for everyone to accept. All we can do is continue Hanna's work the way we know she would want it done."

"Bullshit," Amy, one of the labtechs, said, her voice louder and stronger. She stood and walked toward JoAnn. All eyes watched and waited until she continued, "We all heard Hanna say she wasn't going back to Riverparks. I was at the gym last night."

"On Sunday night?" JoAnn asked.

"Sure. I either ride or work out seven days a week. Hanna did an hour on the StairMaster, then finished off a full program on the Lifecycle machines. She had to have been there more than two hours. There is no way she went for an evening jog after a workout like that. No way."

"Did you talk to her?"

"We walked to the parking lot together," Amy answered, her confidence obviously dwindling.

"Did she say where she was going?"

They could barely hear Amy as she muttered, "I'm dead tired. All I want is a nice long rest."

"What exactly is missing?" Gene Lemmond asked as he gazed out the window of his executive suite.

"Two canisters of SynCur6, two Priority One reports, and samples of both compounds," Mike Harper, TechLab's head of Security, replied nervously.

"Which reports?"

"Status updates on the final phases of both SynCur6 and NiAl2. They include complete details of test sites, surveillance procedures, project expenses . . ."

"Define complete," Lemmond demanded.

"Everything is spelled out. Basically who, what, when, where, and why the tests were performed. If those reports fall into the wrong hands, there will be no way to defend our actions. Even the ownership of the shell corporations is listed."

"What about the technical aspects? Did Hanna Shore get drug specifications? Formulas?"

"There's no way to tell. She had access to all the information, so it's very possible. Since there are samples of both compounds missing, it's probably irrelevant anyway. Any capable scientist could analyze the compounds and work forward."

"You realize how important it is to find them."

Shifting tensely from side to side, Harper answered, "Yes. We've covered her office, house, and car. We're going under the assumption that the samples she took were tagged with radioactive isotopes, so searching is relatively simple. She couldn't have gotten them out of the BioHazard wing without an alarm sounding. Obviously, nothing has turned up yet."

"Don't assume anything, much less that a security system is infallible. We're working with brilliant people, not idiots. Search again, and this time do it the old-fashioned way."

"Yes, sir." He hesitated for a moment before continuing, "Have you considered the possibility that our problem may not have been Hanna Shore?"

"Do you have a better suspect?"

"No, sir."

"Then don't waste my time. We both have a meeting to go to."

J.D. walked into the elegant conference room. He closed the double doors and sat down. A quick glance confirmed the entire Board was present, except for Hanna Shore, of course. The five other department heads all appeared to be as restless as J.D., their eyes downcast as they anxiously waited for the meeting to begin.

Gene Lemmond, TechLab's president and CEO, was seated at the head of the long oak table. Snow-white hair offset a golfer's tan, his lean build making him seem younger than his sixty-six years.

Twenty-seven years ago he founded TechLab hoping to build a company that could profit from the obvious long-range need for both civilian and military pharmaceuticals. An ex-Marine with Pentagon ties, he was not a man to be taken lightly. His foresight had paid off. TechLab was one of the largest research facilities in the world, employing over four thousand scientists in their central facility alone.

Gene stood and asked, "How did it go this morning, J.D.?"

"The techs are suspicious. Apparently Hanna had been acting strangely for a few days."

"Probably since our last meeting. It was pretty obvious she didn't approve of our plan to field-test Citrinol3 like we did SynCur6 and NiAl2."

Jeff Vance, the head pathologist, said, "She didn't have a problem with the other field tests a couple of years ago. Why object to Citrinol3? Especially with the impending FDA approval of NiAl2. Pretesting probably saved us six or seven years by helping us narrow our side effect issues . . ."

Gene interrupted. "The reason for her objection is no longer relevant. What is important is rebuilding the confidence of the staff. We can't have the BioHazard employees afraid of their own shadows. Damage control is essential. What steps were taken back in '85 when that pathologist, Ames, went UA with the sample of Cryogen5?"

J.D. recognized UA as the Marine Corps version of AWOL and answered, "The employees were told he was caught selling TechLab samples of deadly viruses to the highest bidder. It was implied a third world country was involved and that in all probability they eliminated him to keep from paying him the remainder of his money. The police found no trace of him, but one million in cash was found in a suitcase in the trunk of his car, along with his passport and a one-way ticket to Monte Carlo. As we hoped, his elimination was never tied back to us."

Gene shook his head as he spoke, "Obviously that strategy won't work in this situation. We need to come up with a way to discredit Hanna subtly."

J.D. said, "I planted enough doubt with JoAnn Rayburn when I offered her the position of Chief of Research this morning. I think we should do exactly the opposite from now on. Build up Hanna as if she were a saint. Openly talk about how much she'll be missed. We could offer grief counseling at company expense to the BioHazard group and build a memorial on Riverparks in her honor."

Jeff added, "Donating to the Call Rape hot line would look good."

J.D. continued, "Maybe even call a press conference to demand more police patrols until the Riverparks rapist is caught and present a check to the mayor to help defray the costs. I think we should support the random murder theory in every way."

Gene stood up and headed for the conference-room doors. Resting his hand on the doorknob, he looked around the room at the people gathered there and said, "TechLab will support the rapist theory. You've shown me once again why we're the number one contract research lab in the U.S. Barring any unforeseen problems, we'll meet in three weeks. By then, we may have some encouraging news on the Citrinol3 field-test site. I expect every one of you to heartily welcome Ms. Rayburn to our management team."

Staring directly at J.D., Lemmond opened the door and as he left added, "Cook, the ball's in your court. I wouldn't drop it this time if I were you."

J.D. gazed across the table, only a glint in his eyes defiantly answering the smirk on his colleague's face. The son of a bitch had won the first battle, but J.D. had no intention of losing to the bastard again.

Chapter 2

Stacey Fordman rushed down the stairs of her small apartment, trying to button her cream-colored jacket with one hand while cradling her high heels in the other. She groaned when she saw it was already ten after eight. If she hurried, and if traffic was light for the first time in six years, she might not be late for school.

Hanging her head upside down, she fiercely brushed her dark auburn hair. Standing up, it fell to rest on her shoulders and she pushed it away from her slender face with her fingers. Darting toward the door, she slipped on her heels, grabbed her purse from the counter, and froze as she watched the morning newspaper float to the floor.

"Shit!" she said, then mentally scolded herself for cursing as she gathered the scattered newspaper. Her summer job working at the photography studio had eased her language toward the colorful zone. Now that school was back in session, she couldn't afford to slip and have one of her first-grade students report home with a shocking new vocabulary word.

She grimaced as she thought how rowdy her class was this year. There probably weren't many words they didn't already know, and she suspected a couple of them could teach her a few things. Things six-year-olds had no business knowing.

As she plopped the jumbled newspaper back on the countertop, the bold title of an article on the back page caught her eye—SCIENTISTS DISCOVER BRAIN

TISSUE ABNORMALITY MAY CAUSE DYSLEXIA. Stacey stopped, her handbag hanging from her shoulder as she read. She studied every word of the article, searching for any clue that might be the breakthrough her special kids needed. The news was promising; another difference had been found in the way a dyslexic's brain cells carry sensory information. It was an exciting development, since understanding what caused their problems could eventually help them realize their potential.

When Stacey finally finished, she was disappointed. Help for the kids was still years away. As she glanced back up, the glowing green numbers on the microwave confirmed what she already knew. She was late.

"I can't go to school today, Dad. I just can't." Jonathan Lawrence sat on the oak bar stool, leaning over his uneaten breakfast as he clutched his stomach. The kitchen counter held a virtual smorgasbord of cereals, Pop-Tarts, and toast, none of which had been touched by the six-year-old. He brushed aside his light blond hair while his blue-green eyes pleaded for mercy. "I'm not kidding, Dad, I'm gonna be sick."

"We've been over this before, Jon. You need to eat something. Anything. You don't have a fever. You can't miss school just because you don't want to go. Sorry." Jess Lawrence's stomach ached, too, but not for the same reason Jonathan's did. As a single parent, he had no idea how to handle Jonathan's problem. Every day since school started he had hoped it would somehow mysteriously disappear. Instead, it seemed to be getting worse.

He walked over and pressed his son's head against his chest. "Is first grade that much harder than kindergarten?"

"No. The work is easy. Really easy."

"What about Ms. Fordman? Is she tough?"

"Sometimes. But she's nice, I like her. I don't know what it is, Dad. My stomach just hurts. Can't I go to the clinic with you? I'll just lay in your office. I promise."

"Maybe you're hungry. You haven't eaten anything."

"No!"

"Then I'm making an appointment for you to see Dr. Scott. We need to make sure there isn't anything physically wrong. This stomachache business has gone on long enough."

"Is he the one who made them take my blood last year when I had the flu?"

"Yep."

Jon's eyes narrowed. "Will he want to take my blood again?"

"Probably." Jess raised his hands in his best Dracula impersonation and in a Transylvanian accent slurred, "Doctors love to drink kids' blood, you know. It's sooo much sweeeeter than big people's because they eat sooo much mooore caaandy." He bent down and tried to bite his wiggling, shrieking son's neck.

After Jon finally stopped laughing he said, "I don't want to go to the doctor. I think I need to keep all my blood right now. Besides, I don't each much candy, so my blood won't taste so good." He hopped off the bar stool and grabbed his backpack from the kitchen counter trying his best to stand up straight in spite of the knot in his stomach. "I'll be all right, Dad."

Jess grabbed the car keys, tossed Jon over his shoulder in spite of his giggling protests, and said, "We'll see, son. We'll see."

The parking lot of East Elementary was an odd combination of order and chaos. Experienced parents pulled through the oval drive and children loaded with backpacks popped out of minivans and station wagons. One boy dragged a shaking puppy along the side-

walk, no doubt an unwilling show-and-tell partici-
pant. Parents new to the system inevitably stopped in
the wrong places, blocking traffic and infuriating the
rest of the crowd.

All this was watched with a calculated eye by the
man sitting in the light blue Dodge van. Although his
meeting with the principal, Grace Milliken, was
scheduled for well after nine, he purposely arrived
early enough to watch the morning turmoil.

Smiling, he realized it certainly hadn't been a disappointment. In fact, watching the general state of disorder strengthened his confidence that this was the
perfect site for the test. In an elementary school with
over two thousand children running rampant, he was
certain no one would notice a few subtle changes. And
even if they did, it would be too late.

⦁ Grace Milliken glared at the children as they slipped
through the door into Stacey Fordman's classroom.
She was a woman children naturally avoided, her face
a little too close to that of a fairy-tale witch for their
comfort. In her mid-fifties with only a touch of grey at
the temples of her dark hair, it was her eyes that first
warned them. Her face seemed to be shrinking away
from those dark eyes, making them conspicuously
menacing as she looked down at their tiny faces.

As principal, she believed it was important to maintain a strict demeanor at all times. Discipline ruled her
profession, with both the teachers and the students re-
quiring constant guidance. She watched the children
as they walked down the hall of the first-grade pod.
East Elementary was designed with classrooms along
central hallways, neatly arranged like peas in a pod.
Ms. Fordman's room was at the northwest end, closest
to the fire exit.

When Stacey rounded the corner, she instinctively
slowed her stride. Mrs. Milliken's irritation was more

than apparent from the way she was hovering at the entrance to the classroom, her angular nose pointing down at her wristwatch.

"You're late, Ms. Fordman."

"I'm sorry, Mrs. Milliken." Stacey knew better than to give an excuse. Instead, she said, "Is there something you need?"

"Yes. I just wanted to tell you that we have several people coming to observe your class this morning. Try to keep the kids in line."

Every muscle in Stacey's body tensed. She hated having her class observed. It made the children nervous and it made her nervous. Without looking in the room, she knew the children were hanging on her every word, so she took a deep breath and nicely asked, "Who will be visiting us?"

"Several people from the Board of Education and a representative of ITL, Independent Testing Labs."

"Independent Testing Labs?"

"The new superintendent thinks we should monitor classes on a trial basis to determine the adequacy of the curriculum. You realize our district's test scores were down again last year for both first and second grade. This is just a precautionary measure."

Stacey's heart continued to race. "You mean we'll be observed every day?"

"Of course not. The children will take a few extra standardized tests each semester. Other than today, there will be no classroom interruption. However, your lesson plans will be copied and submitted to the Board, so you might want to spruce them up a little."

Although Stacey was still apprehensive, she was relieved to know her class wouldn't be totally disrupted. "Why my class?" she asked.

"Your background working with special children was very persuasive. Using your class, we can monitor the requirements of both the average children and the children with learning disabilities. We've kept your class size at eighteen just in case this project was approved."

Last week when the class lists were distributed, Stacey had wondered why hers was smaller than the others. Now she knew. They were going to be guinea pigs.

Folding seats were pulled into Grace Milliken's office to accommodate the weary visitors. After spending the morning perched on tiny chairs fit only for the six and under crowd, they were ready for a break. The men's suits were wrinkled, their neckties loose under open collars. The one woman observer representing the School Board, Dorie Hughes, was still flushed and tiny beads of sweat dotted her forehead. Her male counterparts looked equally miserable.

Parker McDaniel, the representative from Independent Testing Labs, spoke first. "Ms. Milliken, do you realize how warm it is in Ms. Fordman's classroom?"

"Unfortunately, starting school in mid-August has its drawbacks. The rooms at the end of the pods tend to be warmer in the summer and colder in the winter. It drives the teachers crazy, but the kids don't seem to mind."

Dorie disagreed, "Such extremes could affect the test results. Maybe we should consider using a different classroom."

Grace shook her head. "Ms. Fordman has been in that room since she began teaching six years ago. I don't think she would want to switch now. The school is already over capacity. We don't have any open rooms. Plus, changing classrooms after only a week of school would be difficult for both the children and the teachers involved."

Parker said, "Would you mind if I contact my supervisor? We may have enough leeway in our budget on this project to install some sort of climate control unit. We could donate it to the school after the project is over." He glanced at the three representatives from the School Board and added, "If the Board gives final approval to the project, that is."

Dorie, the senior delegate of the team, enthusiastically said, "Just let me know what they say, Mr. McDaniel. We feel honored to have been chosen to participate in this project. It could save our district thousands of dollars."

"Pilot programs like this are beneficial to both sides. The school districts get free, impartial feedback, and our company has the chance to show how effective our programs can be. It's a win-win combination."

"How long has ITL been in business?" Grace asked.

"Over twelve years."

Dorie asked, "How many schools have you worked with?"

"This is our twenty-third district. I submitted the test result records to the supervisor's office about a month ago." Parker glanced at his watch and stood up. "I hate to cut our meeting short, but I have to be across town in fifteen minutes. It was a pleasure meeting you all, and don't hesitate to call if you have any questions."

Once he was gone, everyone in the room visibly relaxed. Grace asked, "Do you think we'll get approval?"

Dorie answered, "No doubt about it. Our report will recommend the program highly. Like Mr. McDaniel said, what have we got to lose?"

"Wonderful. I'll personally monitor things here."

"And you're sure Ms. Fordman is the right teacher for the job?"

"No doubt about it. She's conscientious, an enthusiastic teacher, and both the parents and kids love her."

"Then it's settled. We'll officially notify you as soon

as the Board votes." They all exchanged cordial hand-shakes and left.

Grace closed the door to her office and walked back to her desk. She sat for several seconds, her face resting on her hands. Once she gathered her strength, she opened her Rolodex, flipped it to the right number, and dialed.

She could picture him pulling out his pocket cellular phone. Those long, strong fingers pushing the tiny button as his muscular arm flexed to hold it against his handsome face. She actually jumped when the first ring ended with his quick response, "Yes."

"It's Grace. Everything went fine after you left."

"Is the committee going to recommend approval to the School Board?"

"Definitely. Tonight still possible?"

"You bet. But we have to be careful. Nothing in public yet."

"I understand. I'll fix dinner. Maybe rent a movie."

His low laugh ended as he throatily said, "Baby, we won't need a movie for entertainment."

JoAnn tried to focus on the cross section of brain tissue on the slide in front of her, but her thoughts were so scattered she couldn't concentrate. She leaned back in her seat, pinching the bridge of her nose to ease the pressure behind her eyes. She glanced down at her watch. Only seven hours ago she found out Hanna was dead. It seemed like days.

Looking at the bleak room filled with sophisticated lab equipment, she wished she were somewhere else, anywhere else. She closed her eyes and thought of where she could go. Somewhere above ground. Somewhere she could stare outside for a while or, better yet, feel the sun on her face. Somewhere she could tell what time of the day it was without constantly looking at her wristwatch.

All day her mind had pestered her with biting thoughts. *Would Hanna stab me in the back? If she did, why?*

She felt a hand gently touch her shoulder and without opening her eyes quietly said, "Yes?"

"Are you all right?"

JoAnn bolted upright, practically knocking the microscope over at the sound of J. D. Cook's voice. "I'm fine. I . . . just have a headache." She didn't remember ever seeing him in the lab before. But then again, with her one-track mind, he could have been there every day and she probably wouldn't have noticed.

"You really should take the rest of the day off. I could drive you home if you like. You look as if you could use a good meal, too. How about a quick dinner? My treat."

"I really do appreciate the offer, Mr. Cook. But my car is here, and I'm sure my headache will be better soon."

"Tell you what. Give me your car keys and I'll have one of the security guards drive your car home. We're having dinner together at Mia's. I'll be back in thirty minutes to get you."

"But . . ."

"I won't take no for an answer. Just be ready."

Stacey kicked off her high heels, thankful to be back home. The entire day had been a disaster, from the moment she saw Mrs. Milliken haunting the doorway to her classroom until Derek lopped off a substantial chunk of Tiffany's long blond hair with a pair of scissors he smuggled in his backpack from home. She wondered if Tiffany's parents would call her, or if they would wait until tomorrow so they could vent their fury in person.

For what seemed like an eternity, Stacey stared in the refrigerator. She didn't have the energy to cook, plus nothing looked good. Reluctantly, she grabbed a frozen dinner and stuck it in the microwave. Just as she was about to eat the first bite, the phone rang. Sighing, she debated whether to let the machine pick it up, then at the last moment grabbed it and said, "Hello."

"Ms. Fordman?"

"Yes."

"This is Jess Lawrence, Jonathan's father. I'm sorry to bother you at home. I hope you don't mind, I found your number in the directory."

Relieved, she said, "It's no bother, Mr. Lawrence. Is Jonathan having a problem at school?"

"Yes. I'd like to come talk to you about it. Would before or after school tomorrow work for you?"

"Either would be fine."

"How about eight o'clock in the morning?"

"Great. See you then."

She hung the phone up, then stared at it for a long time. Of all the children in her class, Jonathan was the last one she would have guessed was having a tough time adjusting to first grade. She was suddenly overwhelmed with sadness, not for Jonathan, but for a couple of the others. He was one of the lucky ones. Somebody cared about him.

Out of the corner of her eye, JoAnn watched every person who walked into the elegant restaurant. Even though J.D. had insisted her jeans and T-shirt were appropriate attire, she wanted to crawl under the linen tablecloth and hide.

J.D. rested his hand on hers and said, "JoAnn, don't you like your fettucini? You've hardly eaten a bite."

"It was very nice of you to take me to dinner. I suppose I'm just tired. This has been such a long day."

"Undoubtedly." He gently stroked the back of her hand with his thumb and smiled at her, weaving a strong undercurrent of desire around her melancholy mood. "Your work is your life, isn't it, JoAnn?" he asked.

She was silent for a few seconds, her fork endlessly twisting the long, thin strands of pasta on her plate. Whether it was the glass of wine or just his obvious compassion, she felt very comfortable with J.D., so she answered truthfully, "I went through a nasty divorce a few years ago. It really shook my confidence, in myself and in other people."

"Hasn't everyone?"

JoAnn smiled. "I wouldn't wish what happened to me on my worst enemy. I worked two jobs to put my husband through med school, and then he decided my best friend was the real love of his life. Sometimes, even after all these years, I still feel like I've got a couple of knives sticking out of my back. When I suddenly found myself alone, I felt like I had two choices. Try dating and making friends again, or bury myself in my work. Work won, no contest."

"But don't you get lonely? I mean, of all the people in the world I would be the last one who would want to see your work slide, but you should have something besides a career."

She laughed, then said, "Get a life, right?"

J.D. blushed. "That didn't exactly come out the way I intended."

"It's okay. I've heard the lectures a million times. 'So and so would be perfect for you, JoAnn,' 'Aren't you worried about starting a family before it's too late?' 'If you'd spend more time on your appearance, you could catch another husband,' 'Work isn't everything.' Well, for the last eight years, work has been everything. I eat, sleep, and dream about ways to improve Citrinol3. Even when I jog, I plan which tests to run next, how to improve the . . ." She looked down at her fettucini, then back at J.D. "I'm sorry, I didn't mean to get on my high horse."

"No offense. I appreciate how passionate you are about your work. And I want to help you keep that passion alive. Citrinol3 will be the wonder drug of the future. I have complete confidence in your ability, not only to finish revising the formula but to handle the Chief of Research job as well."

"I don't know . . ."

His hands reached over to hers once again. "You won't be alone on this. I'll be right there by your side the whole way. We can make it a gradual transition. I'll ease you into the administrative duties over the next year." Suddenly he leaned back in his chair, exhaling loudly with a look of self-disgust. "I'm sorry, JoAnn. I didn't intend for this dinner to be anything but that—dinner. It isn't fair of me to try to persuade you to take the position, and I want you to know there is no pressure. Your job is safe either way. Sometimes I think maybe I'm the one who should 'get a life,' as you said. TechLab takes up most of my waking hours, too."

"Why do you suppose that is? Hanna was the same way."

"I don't know, maybe it's the nature of the beast. So many people die every day from the diseases we're trying to stop. It makes the research so much more than just experiments. There are families depending on us, praying someone will find the answers they need in time. I just wish everything didn't take so damn long. The bureaucratic hoops we have to jump through before we can forward our work to the pharmaceutical companies are ridiculous, not to mention what they have to do to attain FDA approval . . . Sorry, I guess it was my turn to jump on my high horse."

"I don't think there's ever been a person who

worked in medical research who wouldn't give an arm and a leg to speed up the process. We both know the horror stories."

He raised his wineglass to toast her. "To the success of Citrinol3. May it prove to be another step closer to the cure for cancer, and JoAnn Rayburn will be awarded a Nobel Prize."

She clinked her glass against his, and as she sipped, she thought to herself, *Maybe he's right. God, how I wish he were right.*

Even though Stacey arrived twenty minutes early for her meeting with Jess Lawrence, he was standing by her classroom door when she came scrambling down the hall. His son, Jonathan, was beside him, a miniature version of his handsome father. Both had thick manes of blond hair and sharp, high cheekbones. Their faces were square, shoulders wide. Besides the freckles of childhood, only their eyes were different. While the father had pure cobalt-blue eyes, the son's blue was slashed with flecks of green and brown.

She smiled warmly at them and said, "Good morning. The two of you are certainly here bright and early."

Jess extended his hand, saying, "Thank you very much for meeting with me so soon. I really appreciate it."

Stacey spoke first to Jonathan. "Would you like to go play on the playground where we have recess while I get to know your dad?"

He nodded his head, and she continued, "You can, as long as you stay where we can see you out the window by my desk. Okay?"

"Okay," Jonathan said. In a flash his backpack was deposited at her feet with a loud thump, and he was gone.

As they walked into the classroom Jess said, "He really likes you. Since school started last week, you're practically all he talks about. You and the class pet, M. C. Hamster."

"He's a precious child. Bright and funny. He loves to play jokes on the other children. Quite frankly, I was shocked to find out Jonathan is having problems, Mr. Lawrence. He seems very well adjusted."

Jess stared at the floor, obviously uncomfortable. "I'm probably overreacting. Maybe there isn't really a problem, and this will blow over in no time. But since I've never been through this parenting business before, I felt it would be better to talk to you about it before it gets any worse."

"With a concerned father on his side, I'm certain whatever it is will work out fine. How can I help?"

Jess walked to the window and stared at his son, who was hanging from the top of a large piece of equipment. He didn't turn to face Stacey as he said, "I'm worried about his attitude toward school. He was always so enthusiastic about going to school before this year. Preschool and kindergarten were a breeze. But now he is so upset every morning he gets physically ill just before it's time to leave. For some reason, he's not adjusting."

"Now that you mention it, he is rather quiet right after he arrives. Some children just aren't morning people. He does fine on his daily work, and by morning recess he's the class leader. They all love him. I wish I had his level of energy."

"Me, too. He never stops. Even at night, he fights sleep. It's like he's afraid he's going to miss something."

"Is it possible he is just overly tired in the mornings? Sometimes the first few weeks back at school are tough. Schedules aren't set yet, routines haven't fallen back into place."

Jess shook his head. "Our schedule didn't change in

the summer. Instead of getting up and going to school, he would get up and go to the clinic with me."

Stacey had planned to pull Jon's records before his father arrived, but there hadn't been time. She was embarrassed that she didn't even know what Jess Lawrence did for a living. "You work at a clinic?"

"I'm a veterinarian. I have my own practice, and Jonathan loves to come help me. He's in charge of walking the dogs and snuggling the cats in the kennel. That is, the few cats who want to be snuggled."

Stacey laughed. "I'll bet the animals love him as much as he loves them." She smiled at him, and realized how attracted to him she was when he returned it so openly. "You may have just solved your own problem. Maybe he misses the animals. Where does he go after school?"

"Home. I have a housekeeper who watches him for a couple of hours in the afternoon until I get home from work."

"So school replaced something he loved. Not only did he get the attention of the animals, he got your attention, too. It's possible he misses the time the two of you have always spent together, and the blind love of the animals."

"You may be right. We lost his mother when he was only three, and we're pretty close. I could pick him up after school, and he could stay at the clinic with me until I close. It's worth a try. We'll give it a shot next week."

"If that doesn't work, let me know. Meanwhile, I'll keep an eye on him. You know, make sure there isn't some bully stealing his lunch money or anything."

"That still doesn't go on, does it?"

She smiled and nodded. "Unfortunately, it does, but I keep a pretty close eye on my kids. In a few weeks we'll talk about handling problems like those in class. Don't worry, Jonathan will do fine this year."

"He's lucky to have you." Jess stood up and tapped on the window, waving good-bye to Jonathan who was wildly swinging across the jungle gym. "Mind if I ask one more thing?"

"Not at all."

"Do they have some sort of school policy that makes it improper for a beautiful teacher to have dinner with the parent of one of her students?"

"Improper? No. *If* they knew about it, I'm sure it would discouraged based on possible complications to the delicate balance between teacher, student, and parent."

"So, what you're saying is, what they don't know won't hurt them?"

"As long as things are handled intelligently. We wouldn't want Jonathan to be upset. He still talks about his mother."

There was an awkward silence, then Jess said, "So can I call you sometime?"

"Sure."

"For an 'intelligent' date?"

"Based on my personal experience, I think that's a contradiction. Intelligent men should know better than to date."

Two days passed in a blur of work, worry, and excitement. JoAnn nervously stood in the ladies' room looking in the mirror one last time before her meeting with J.D. The makeup she was wearing felt oddly heavy against her skin, but she liked what she saw reflected. Her hair looked pretty, clean and bouncy, even though she knew it could use a good cut. She was pleased with the tailored grey suit and low heels she'd chosen to wear, although they were no match for jeans when it came to comfort. She turned sideways, admiring how the suit showed off her legs and tiny waist perfectly.

As she marched down the hall to J.D.'s office, she

felt more important, more mature than she had ever felt before. With her head held high, she knocked on his office door, slipped off her glasses, and walked confidently inside.

He stood up and said, "I'm sorry, miss. I have a meeting scheduled right now. Whatever it is you need will have to wait. Why don't you make an appointment with my secretary? Her office is right next door."

Luckily, she recognized his voice and mannerisms. Without her glasses he was just an interesting blur of color, so she slid them back on her face. "Mr. Cook, it's me, JoAnn."

He stared at her for several seconds, both stunned and impressed. "My, my. You must be exhausted, but you certainly don't look it. Did you have a hard time breaking out of your cocoon this morning?"

With a hand gesture fitting a model she said, "If you mean this transformation, a little makeup works wonders."

"That's an understatement. You look great. But why so formal?"

"I felt that accepting the position of Chief of Research deserved a more management-oriented presence."

A broad grin lit his face as he walked around the desk. J.D. shook her hand, then pulled her into a warm embrace. Stepping back he said, "This calls for a celebration." He walked over to his intercom and buzzed his secretary. "Marsha, I need reservations for two at eight tonight . . . Yes, the Warren Duck Club would be perfect."

JoAnn tried to interrupt, but he held up his hand and said, "I insist."

They spent the next two hours going over details. From the memo that would announce her promotion to the list of personnel who were now her direct responsibility, J.D. made everything appear to be part of a natural progression. His constant compliments on everything from her newfound beauty to her ability to quickly analyze the data he presented bolstered her confidence to an even higher level.

JoAnn left J.D.'s office anticipating not just her promotion but a totally new life. Although exposure to fresh challenges on a professional level promised exciting changes, it was a much more personal desire that lightened her step and made her heart dance.

The long journey back to the BioHazard lab was over before she knew it, her mind preoccupied with the promise the future held. She grabbed her long, crisp, professional white coat from a hook and slipped it over the suit. As the entered the central analysis area, she realized that first thing tomorrow the techs gathered around would report to her—to JoAnn Rayburn, Chief of Research.

But the looks on their faces made her spirits plunge. "What's wrong?" she asked.

Amy replied. "We were right."

"About what?"

She handed the morning newspaper to JoAnn. Next to a striking color photo of Hanna, the bold headline read: AUTOPSY REVEALS LATEST RIVERPARKS HOMICIDE NOT LINKED TO PRIOR ATTACKS—ANOTHER KILLER STALKS TULSA.

Chapter 3

Late yesterday, the County coroner's office revealed to the Tulsa Police Department the findings of the autopsy on Hanna Shore, whose body was discovered Monday morning near the jogging trail on Riverparks. Although specific conclusions of the autopsy have not been released, a police source who requested anonymity divulged several key elements that will strongly impact how the case is investigated by homicide detectives.

Specifically, it has been determined that Ms. Shore's murder was unlike the previous Riverparks rapist killings in several significant ways. She apparently did not struggle with her attacker, and although there were signs of rape, the coroner's office was not able to collect semen specimens from the body.

These new developments have led to many unanswered questions. According to City Hall, the mayor's hot line has been receiving numerous calls from frightened citizens. Police are reporting a sharp rise in 911 Emergency calls due to what one dispatcher calls "rampant fear."

According to Sgt. O. P. Cox, "The lack of a pattern to these murders makes them much more real to the average citizen. The victims were of different ages and races, and although the killings were all in the same general area, Riverparks stretches over ten miles. The only common thread seems to have been that the victims were at the wrong place at the wrong time. The Tulsa Police Department is doing everything it can to ensure the safety of our citizens, but they should be responsible enough not to take unnecessary risks until the killer or killers have been apprehended."

* * *

JoAnn laid the newspaper down, letting the information sink in. Amy interrupted her thoughts by
saying, "She knew the bastard who killed her. She
had to."

"Why do you think that?" JoAnn asked. She noticed
the other techs were already scattered back about the
room, resuming their work.

"No signs of a struggle. I called a friend of mine
who works in the morgue. She said it was the
strangest thing she'd ever seen. The cuts were like
surgical incisions. Straight and smooth through
muscle."

"So she must have been unconscious."

"But there was no brain trauma. None at all. No
chemical traces, like ether, or anything else. No skin
under her fingernails from scratching the bastard. No
fight. We both know Hanna would have knocked the
crap out of anyone who came close to her. She was one
hell of an athlete."

"Maybe her hands and feet were tied."

"No rope burns. No signs of tape residue. Even the
coroner said it was one of the more unusual cases he's
seen. He did have one good bit of information."

"What's that?"

"She bled to death relatively fast since the wounds
were razor clean."

"You call that good news?"

Amy said brusquely, "It's just if it were me, I'd want
to die fast."

"Maybe she didn't even know what was happening," JoAnn said as she stood up. Amy turned away,
but before she left JoAnn quickly asked, "Where was
her car?"

"They found it about a half mile down the path, in
the parking lot she always used to use."

"Have you talked to the police? Did you tell them you worked out with her the night she was killed?"

Amy shifted her eyes, avoiding JoAnn's questioning gaze.

JoAnn didn't press her, but merely said, "I understand," and walked away.

"Look, Ms. Fordman. I brought an obstacle illusion for show and tell. My dad can see it, but my grandma can't." Jonathan proudly held the multicolored poster in front of him. At first glance it was nothing but an attractive jumble of colors.

"I think you mean 'optical illusion,' Jon. An optical illusion is something that isn't what it first appears to be."

"No, it isn't one of those. This is hard to do. Like the obstacle course my soccer coach makes me run. It's an obstacle illusion. Can you see it? Can you?"

There was a loud crash in the back of the room and Stacey flipped the lights on and off twice. The class knew the warning signal well and they immediately quieted down. Everyone except Derek migrated silently back to their seats. Derek was in the back of the classroom wreaking havoc with his scissors. This time the object of his wrath was the laminated world map, which now had substantially less ocean than only a few moments ago.

"Jon, I'm sorry, I'll have to look at your poster a little later." Stacey walked to the back of the room and snatched the scissors out of Derek's hand. "I thought we cleared this up with Mrs. Milliken the other day."

He smiled slyly, his face more like a rebellious teen than a mere first-grader. "She said she never wanted to *see* me do anything like that again. Well, since she's not in here, she didn't *see* me do it, did she?"

Stacey felt the anger rising inside her, not just

because of his destructive behavior, but more over his obvious contempt of authority. She was much too irritated to deal with him now, so she said, "Go sit in the hall. I'll be out in a few minutes and we'll go talk to Mrs. Milliken together."

He glared at her, his brown-black eyes challenging. For an instant she was almost intimidated by him. She felt lucky he was only seven years old and, for now at least, still too short to carry out the threat his stare held.

It was seven p.m. when JoAnn heard the clank of the double locking doors. All the lab techs had been gone for over an hour. She tensed, wondering who would be coming in so late at night. Instinctively, she rolled her chair into the shadow of a nearby filing cabinet. If someone passed the lab, they wouldn't be able to see her unless they came inside. Footsteps clicked down the hall, two men in suits passed, but it was difficult to tell where they went.

The voices were impossible to distinguish, muffled by distance and intentional softness. She eased out of her chair and stepped silently to the door. Peeking out, she saw no one was in the hall, so she tiptoed closer to the sounds. As she drew nearer, the voices seemed to be coming from the corner office. Hanna's old office.

She gasped when she felt the weight of a hand on her shoulder. Whirling around, J.D.'s face was above hers, his eyes questioning as he whispered, "Why are we sneaking around?"

"I heard something. I think someone's in Hanna's old office."

He laughed. "They'd better be. I asked the computer jocks to make sure everything was ready for you bright and early tomorrow. I told them you usually arrive by six in the morning. They're supposed to be transferring your menu and files to that machine, and cleaning up files in general. I want your first day to be as trouble-free as possible. I'll go look in on them and be back in a minute. Meanwhile, why don't you check your desk? I think you'll find a pleasant surprise."

"Thanks, J.D., I don't know what I'd do without you." She watched as he disappeared into the office, and then she went back into her own. A dozen long-stemmed red roses were waiting there, beautifully arranged in a crystal vase. She tugged at the small white envelope, pulling out the note. It said, "JoAnn, To a future of progress, J.D."

He sauntered in, obviously pleased with himself. "I asked the computer guys to keep more regular hours. No use scaring our important lab personnel by lurking around at night."

"I guess I'm just jittery. The article in the newspaper this morning really upset everyone."

"About Hanna's murder?"

She nodded her head.

His eyes turned cold as he said, "I think employees who give information to the press should be fired. Whoever leaked that information from the coroner's office has frightened half of Tulsa for no good reason. Until the police are certain who killed Hanna, the de-tails should not be made public. Don't they have any respect for the dead?"

"They want to make sure no one else is harmed. You can't blame them for that."

He shook his head. "All they want is to sell news-papers. Flashy headlines about multiple murders based on sketchy details from informants aren't going to keep people safe. Smart people haven't been run-ning Riverparks at night for months. The few diehards like Hanna will still run there, no matter how dangerous the paper makes it out to be. They think they're invincible."

"We're almost certain Hanna wasn't running that night."

"We're?"

"One of the lab techs, Amy White, worked out with Hanna the night she was killed. When they left together, Hanna was exhausted and said she was going straight home. I suppose you could say she's my first personnel problem as Chief of Research. Amy is afraid to tell the police what she knows."

"Why?"

"I haven't had a chance to talk to her about it yet. I'm planning on asking her to lunch tomorrow. Maybe if I can get her out of here for a while, she'll open up to me."

He smiled. "I knew you could handle the personnel side of this job. Do you need any help moving your things down the hall?"

"No. Most of it is already there. I'll get the rest tomorrow." She slipped off her white lab coat and added, "If we don't hurry, we're going to be late for our dinner reservation."

They walked to the elevator together, her shoulder occasionally brushing comfortably against his. She felt exhilarated walking beside him, as though she could touch the confidence and strength he radiated. When they reached the main building, he said, "Would you mind waiting here for just a few seconds? I need to pick up a file from my office."

"I'll walk with you."

"No. Save your strength. I'll just be a second." He didn't wait for a reply, but instead raced off. Several minutes later he was back with his briefcase, slightly out of breath.

She smiled coyly at him. "You didn't have to run. I wasn't going to leave without you."

"I didn't want to miss a second more of this evening than I had to. This is an important day for TechLab, and tomorrow will be even better."

"Nothing like starting a new job on a Friday. People will be too tired to care if they have a new boss."

They walked through the nearly empty parking lot toward his Jaguar. "They're going to like you. Even if they don't, it won't matter."

"Why not?"

"Management isn't a popularity contest. Sometimes it's best if the workers aren't too comfortable with the boss."

"Uh-oh."

"What's wrong?"

"I'm getting awfully comfortable with you."

He laughed and opened the car door for her. "That, my dear, is an entirely different matter."

Every Tuesday and Thursday evening for the last five years Amy White arrived at the Circle N Ranch to ride. Horses were her passion, the one thing in her life she knew she could always count on. Even though the ranch was ten miles out of town, the city's heat still made the night steamy, miserable for both horse and rider. Sweat dripped off Amy as she dismounted. She walked the horse into her stall, stroking her damp mane and sinewy neck while she talked tenderly to her.

Amy brushed down the gentle chestnut mare for thirty minutes after her ride. It was well past dark, and she wasn't looking forward to the drive back into town. Since Hanna's death, she was as skittish as a colt, especially tonight.

Even the horses in the barn seemed restless. They whinnied and moved about their stalls, as though a storm were approaching. She wondered if a storm could be brewing. As often as the weathermen were

wrong about the weather, it wouldn't surprise her to
hear a clap of thunder any minute.

As she heaved the tenth pitchfork of hay into the
stall, her weary bones convinced her it was time to go
home. She scratched behind the mare's ears for a few
more seconds, then stepped out of the stall and
latched it closed with a wooden slat. A faint aroma
caught her off guard. She thought it was peculiar that
on such a sweltering night a sweet scent of vanilla
drifted over the stench of the barn.

The next instant her face slammed into the hay. In
horror, she realized her arms and legs were useless.
She wondered if she was having a stroke. She couldn't
turn her head or even scream for help. Nothing made
sense. Amy could *feel* her legs, her feet. Pieces of straw
poked painfully through her jeans. *Why can't I move?
God help me!*

The answer was clear soon enough. A man stepped
out of the shadows, his entire body cloaked in
camouflage. Only his eyes showed. Dark eyes. Cold
eyes.

Effortlessly he grabbed the back of Amy's shirt and
the waist of her blue jeans, hurling her over the locked
gate and into the mare's stall. Amy's eyes pleaded
with him, but his returned no sympathy. He picked
up the nearby pitchfork and jabbed repeatedly at the
mare. She reared and bolted around her narrow stall,
trampling everything in her path.

He didn't stop tormenting the horse until he was
certain the job was done. When he slipped out the
barn's side door, he blended perfectly back into the
sweltering starlit landscape. Only now, his eyes
seemed even darker.

On Friday morning Grace Milliken was still irritable.
She was tired of waiting by the phone. Tired of wondering if Parker McDaniel was ever going to call her

again. She had the door to her office closed, just in case. When the phone rang, her heart leaped and her answer was barely a whisper. "Hello."

"Mrs. Milliken?"

It was the voice she dreamed of day and night. "Yes, but you needn't be so formal. I thought after the other night . . ."

"Business first, Grace. Now that the school system has formally approved the project, I've scheduled the installation of the special air control unit for this weekend. Can you meet me early Saturday to unlock the door?"

"Certainly. Once you're finished, maybe we could have lunch or dinner, then . . . not rent a movie again."

"I wish I could, but I've got two more units to install this weekend. Maybe next week. See you Saturday."

She hung up the phone, staring at it while she thought. He'd sounded pleasant enough, and he probably was just busy. Saturday morning she'd make sure he got everything he needed.

The memo announcing the new Chief of Research was well received. The techs who now officially reported to JoAnn stopped by as they heard the news, all offering to help make the transition as smooth as possible. By nine o'clock everyone except Amy White had come by her office.

JoAnn circled the central analysis lab and walked down the narrow hall where the technicians' offices were located, hoping she could casually run into Amy and ask her to lunch. But when she stopped at Amy's door, she was surprised that her office light wasn't on.

One door down, she found Leanne diligently at work. "Excuse me, do you know where Amy is?" JoAnn asked.

"No. I'm really getting worried. She hardly ever calls in sick, and when she does, she always lets me know first thing in the morning."

"You mean she hasn't called?"

"No. I've left two messages on her machine. At first I thought maybe she just overslept, it being Friday and all ... But now, I don't know what we should do. Something must be wrong."

"She's single, isn't she?"

"Yes. She lives in a duplex not too far from here."

"Maybe she had car trouble. Why don't you run over and see if she's home. She could have fallen or ..."

Leanne grabbed her purse and headed down the hall. "I'll be back in a few minutes."

JoAnn walked slowly to her new office. It seemed ridiculously large and overpowering. Each time she walked in, the edge of her excitement dulled because she remembered Hanna so well. Hanna working at the conference table. Hanna studying specimens. She shook her head and pushed the memories down so she could get on with her own work, but constant interruptions made it almost impossible.

Several of the other department heads called to welcome her to the management team, some sent E-mail notes with open invitations to lunch. Most of them worked in what the BioHazard group called "Mt. Olympus"—the above-ground corporate offices where sun actually shines through glass things called windows. All the "cave dweller" managers stopped by in person.

She finally was ready to begin a new Citrinol3 test when the phone rang again and JoAnn curtly snatched it.

Leanne's voice cracked as she said, "The police are here."

❦ JoAnn leaned forward, resting her forehead on her hand. "What's wrong?"

"There was an accident. Amy's dead."

JoAnn didn't know how to answer, couldn't think at all. She could hear Leanne softly sobbing. Finally she asked, "How did it happen?"

"She was trampled by a horse."

"What? But . . . how?"

"Amy loved horses. She went riding last night. Something must have gone wrong. Terribly wrong. She was only twenty-eight, you know. Just a baby."

"I want you to go home, Leanne. I'll tell the rest of the techs."

J.D. tapped on her door and walked in just as she hung up the phone. She turned away from him long enough to brush the tears from her eyes.

He dangled a set of car keys directly in front of her. "I thought I should personally drop these by. Your midnight-black Lexus is parked in space 158 on level 2B of the parking garage." His voice deepened as he added, "Will you take me for a ride sometime?"

JoAnn was too disturbed to react to the double meaning of his question. She quietly said, "I appreciate you bringing them by personally. I'm afraid my first day isn't going as well as I'd hoped."

He moved closer. "You seem upset, what's wrong?"

"I just found out one of our techs was killed in a freak accident last night."

"Oh, my God. Who? What happened?"

"Amy White. She was killed by a horse."

J.D. stared at her in disbelief, the blood draining from his face. He was quiet for a few moments, as if he were groping for something to say.

JoAnn broke the awkward silence by adding, "I need to tell the rest of the staff. Do you know what the policy is for excused time off? I'm sure several of the techs who were closest to her will be too upset to work the rest of the day."

"Time off is at your discretion. Do whatever you think is right. Your goal is to pull the department back together as soon as possible. What did Amy do?"

"She was an X-ray protein crystallographer."

He stared at her.

"She prepares . . . I mean prepared protein samples for centrifuging. The process reduces the solutions to a concentrated form, enabling us to crystallize proteins for research."

"What was her background?"

"She was a Ph.D. with three years' experience."

"I know how crass this sounds, but you'll need to notify the Human Resources department right away. It can take weeks to find a qualified person, and we don't want to fall even further behind schedule. Experienced protein crystallographers are probably pretty tough to find. Get right on it, okay?"

JoAnn quietly said, "I understand."

J.D. walked around the desk and pulled her up, his strong fingers gripping her shoulders. "You can handle this. I know it's not the ideal way to start, but you need to use it to your advantage. Show the staff that you are tough, but compassionate."

It seemed so easy when he said it. His confidence poured through her. She believed she could do it, and she did.

The long walk back to his office cooled J.D. off a little, but not much. He slammed the door behind him, grabbed the phone, and furiously punched in the extension.

"Hello."

"What the hell are you doing? When I called last night to warn you about the White woman going to the police, all I expected was some damage control. Killing her is a bit extreme, don't you think?"

"Quit shooting your goddamn mouth off and tell me what the hell you're talking about, Cook."

"You know good and well what I'm talking about, you son of a bitch. Amy White was killed last night. Trampled by a horse, no less. Sounds like a textbook example of the powers of SynCur6 again."

"Coincidence, pure coincidence. I didn't have anything to do with it."

"Right. Then who the hell did?"

"How the fuck should I know? People do have accidents, J.D. You can't blame all the bad in the world on TechLab."

J.D. slammed the phone down. He knew it wasn't a coincidence, but he knew better than to ever mention it again.

Stacey was slipping on her earrings when the doorbell rang at exactly six o'clock. She opened the door to a huge bouquet of daisies and baby's breath.

"They're beautiful. Come in. You really shouldn't have."

Jess looked quite handsome in Dockers and a lightweight, boldly designed tennis shirt. "They aren't for my date. They're for my son's brilliant teacher, Ms. Stacey Fordman."

"And how did I earn such a distinguished title?"

"You were right about Jonathan. Since I started taking him back to the clinic with me after school, he gets up in the morning as happy as a puppy with a new bone."

Stacey gently arranged the flowers in a crystal vase as she said, "I'm glad I could be of service. Jon's a special child. I'm not supposed to tell you, but he did very well on a basic skills test we gave last week."

Jess watched as she stood back and looked at her floral creation. She quickly pulled several flowers out and snipped the ends off, then poked them back in. He was more than amazed at how professional the arrangement looked. "You handle flowers beautifully." When she blushed, he changed the subject by asking, "You're already testing?"

"Not the school, just our class. We're doing a special project, and we needed base test scores to determine the children's progress through the semester. Jon scored the highest in the class, in the ninety-eighth percentile compared to national statistics."

With pride Jess said, "He's a great kid."

"I'll bet you did well in school, too. I hear vet school isn't exactly a piece of cake."

"My grades were okay. I had my share of distractions. Sometimes I wish I'd had the sense to choose med school instead. The training is roughly the same, but there's no comparison when it comes to benefits. I look at my friends who practice medicine, and they're all driving high-dollar sports cars and living extravagantly, and I'm still trying to pay off my college loans. Financially, being a vet stinks."

"Sounds like being a teacher. Noble professions are known for the spiritual rewards, not the monetary ones. Unfortunately, a healthy dose of twenty-twenty hindsight makes it a little harder to choke down."

"Coupled with a bad day. I lost a young collie on the operating table this morning. She was hit by a car. The family was devastated. She ran out the front door behind one of the children. The poor kid feels so guilty. I just wish I could have saved her."

"I'm sure you did everything possible. You know, if this is a bad day we could have dinner some other time."

"And waste a perfectly good baby-sitter? No way."

"Does Jonathan know about this?"

He shook his head. "I didn't think it was a good idea yet. You know . . ."

Stacey laughed. "I know how unpredictable and frustrating dating can be if that's what you were thinking."

"Actually, I was thinking how nice it is to be going to dinner with such an intelligent lady. You'll have to excuse me, it's been a long time since I dated. Is it politically correct to compliment your date?"

"That depends."

"On what?"

"On whether you're dating a politically correct person or me." She grabbed her purse as they headed out the door. In the hall she stopped to twist her key in the dead bolt.

"So, you aren't into the latest in office manners?"

"Luckily, there are few comparisons between an office and a classroom. I get my share of office exposure in the summer. All the corporate games drive me crazy. Considering everyone works for the same company, it's amazing how much back-stabbing goes on. I guess I was meant to teach. I'm most comfortable in front of a class of children."

They walked into the warm night, and he opened the car door for her. "Speaking for both Jonathan and myself, I'm very happy you teach, and that you do it so well."

The two men sitting in the silver Ford Bronco across the street from the apartment building barely looked up as Jess and Stacey drove away. The driver of the car parked immediately in front of them tipped his hand and pulled into traffic to begin his surveillance. Ten minutes later the radio cracked to life. "They're inside the restaurant. You're clear."

Without speaking, the pair left the car, crossed

the street, and slipped into the apartment building. Their drab maintenance uniforms proclaimed them to be Joe and Bob from AAA Repair, and the silver tool chests they carried flaunted an assortment of grease-smudged wrenches and screwdrivers.

The door to the Fordman apartment took less than ten seconds to unlock. The next hour was spent cautiously placing six wireless remote listening devices so nothing appeared to have been disturbed. They saved the most dangerous job for last.

After studying the layout of the apartment, it was agreed that the bookcase headboard in the bedroom was the perfect spot. With utmost care, the two men lifted the mattress off the bed and laid it aside. Opening the small box, they took out the latest technological wonder, one guaranteed to drive the Fire Marshal crazy. Almost every part of the device would liquify at a low level of heat, then what little remained would be virtually eliminated by the ensuing blaze. Only a few tiny wires and a watch battery would be left at the scene.

Two screws were all it took to firmly attach the small incendiary bomb they had nicknamed "Sparky" to the underside of the headboard. To make sure remote detonation was possible, one man used a voltage meter to test the device before the switch was flipped from OFF to ON.

After lifting the mattress back on, they tucked the sheets neatly in place. A quick inspection showed everything was just as they had found it, and they eased out the front door. After slipping off his rubber gloves, one man slid the pick effortlessly back into the dead bolt. He froze at the sound of the elevator, pulling the pick out just before he could coax the tumbler back into place.

By the time the elderly couple emerged from the

elevator, the two men had disappeared. Three minutes later, with their coveralls and toolboxes neatly tucked inside gym bags, they emerged from the stairway as inconspicuously as they had arrived.

Chapter 4

"I could have sworn I locked this dead bolt."

"You did."

"It isn't locked anymore." Stacey pushed the door open and peered in.

"Wait here. I'll check inside." Jess disappeared into the apartment and returned saying, "Looks fine. Maybe your landlord needed to change the air filters or the batteries in the smoke alarm."

"I guess so. Even after all these years, knowing maintenance people can come in whenever they want still gives me the creeps. I wish I could afford a house. Living in an apartment is definitely getting old." She laid her purse on the counter and opened the refrigerator. "Can I offer you a drink? I've got sparkling water, wine coolers, and I think maybe one Coors hiding way in the back. I'll warn you, though, that Coors has been in there a long, long time. It might be able to walk over to you all by itself."

"A tempting offer, but I think I'll pass. Jonathan is probably waiting up for me."

"Where did you tell him you were going?"

"He didn't ask, so I didn't volunteer any information. I do plan to tell him I went to dinner with you, so you might want to prepare yourself for a barrage of questions."

"Questions I can handle. Are you sure you want to tell him so soon?"

Jess walked over and took her hands. "I had a great time. I think he'd figure out something was going on when we pick you up on Sunday for a picnic at the zoo, don't you?"

She smiled and said, "He's pretty bright. I think he might catch on. What time?"

"Noon?"

"Fine." She stood on her tiptoes to kiss him. "See you then."

Stacey closed the door and turned the dead bolt. From the window, she watched Jess get into his navy blue Jeep Cherokee and drive away. For the first time in years, she felt a growing sense of anticipation. Jess was handsome, polite, intelligent, and witty. She sighed, pushing down her excitement. Judging from her past experiences, he was obviously too good to be true.

It was eight o'clock on Saturday morning when JoAnn's doorbell rang. She ignored it the first two times, since she routinely ignored solicitors and uninvited guests. But whoever it was this time wouldn't give up. Finally, she laid down her checkbook and rolled away from her desk. She peeked out the peephole, only to see a small basket sitting on the front porch.

Warily, she opened the door. The basket was tied with a huge red bow. A piece of white paper was pinned to the bow. She reached down and plucked the note, reading it aloud, "*Everyone needs someone. See you tonight at seven. Dinner and dancing. J.D. P.S. His name is Rocket, as in scientist. Hers is Nobel, as in prize.*"

The basket rocked gently as JoAnn reached down and picked it up. Inside, two balls of black fur nervously wiggled about. They whimpered when she tugged on them, both frantically trying to free themselves from her grip. Holding them to her chest, she closed the door and sank down to the floor. The puppies squirmed and licked her face as tears mixed with her laughter and amazement.

Grace Milliken slid in the key, then propped open the heavy orange door with a chair. Disappointment still throbbed through her veins. Parker was waiting outside the first-grade building when she arrived, with two other men at his side. She led them into the pod and stopped at Stacey Fordman's room to unlock the door. "Do you need anything else?" she asked.

Parker answered, "No. We brought all our own equipment. The unit is relatively small, so it won't take long to install." He flashed his killer smile at her and said, "Why don't I stop by your office in a few minutes while the boys are wrapping things up here?"

Grace blushed and said, "That would be great. Be sure and pull both doors closed when you're finished, they lock automatically."

"We will."

She walked slowly down the empty, dark hallways, unlocked the door to her office, and went inside. It was a small inner room, and for once, she was glad there were no windows. In a matter of seconds, she cleared almost everything off the top of her desk and sat down to wait.

Almost thirty minutes later the phone startled her out of her daydream. After digging around she finally found where she had moved it and answered, "Hello."

"Grace, it's Parker. I'm sorry I didn't get a chance to stop by before we left. My boss called and . . . well, you know how it goes."

"I understand," she said curtly.

"I'll be back in town in a month to evaluate the first stage. Can we get together then?"

"I'll have to check my calendar. Why don't you call when you get in town?"

"I will. And, Grace, thanks for helping so much with the project. I know you'll keep close tabs on everything while I'm gone."

She hung up, as depressed as she had ever been. A month of waiting and wondering if he was still interested would make her crazy. But a smile slowly emerged as she rearranged her desk and locked the door to her office. Of course, if the unit were to malfunction before then, Parker might just have to fit an unplanned trip into his busy schedule.

"I still can't believe you gave me two puppies."

"Why? Do I seem like some sort of monstrous dog hater to you?"

"No, don't be silly. It's just . . . you shouldn't have."

"Listen, JoAnn, I know we don't know each other very well yet, but I think we're friends. Right?"

She nodded as she habitually pushed her glasses back against her face.

"When I see a friend who's lonely, I do something about it."

"Why do you think I'm lonely?"

He stared at her and smiled.

"Okay, so I didn't use to get out much. Lately, I've been quite a socialite, thanks to you."

"And hopefully, that will continue. The dogs are for when I'm not around. They're Yorkshire terriers, you know. They won't stay black for long. They'll turn silver or tan, and end up around five pounds each. I hope you don't mind, I snooped behind your house the other day. I chose Yorkies because you have a small backyard. They are very loving, and need little room to roam."

"Why two?"

"You work such long hours. They'll keep each other company while you're at the lab. You will keep them, won't you?"

She was overwhelmed by the thoughtfulness of his gift. He seemed to have considered everything. "I'll keep them under one condition."

"Name it."

"You come over sometimes and walk them with me."

"Done. But I have a condition, too."

"What?"

"I'd like to understand more about your work. I've tried reading the monthly progress reports, but I guess it's just not sinking in. I want to be able to present an upgrade for the project level of Citrinol3 to the Board at the next meeting, but I'll need to understand its potential better, as well as its drawbacks. I like to know my subject backward and forward before I risk my reputation on it."

JoAnn was thoroughly impressed. "What kind of an upgrade are you going to ask for?"

"Upgrades are one of the perks of my job. I can request shifts in the budget if I feel a particular project has both medical and financial advantages. Hanna and I had been talking about Citrinol3 for several months. In fact, we were supposed to meet on it about six weeks ago, but we kept running into scheduling conflicts."

"What happens if the Board approves an upgrade?"

"An entire team is assigned to study the drug. The testing process speeds up considerably. It's like having ten JoAnns working on it instead of one. Have you heard of NiAl2?"

"Of course. Everyone at TechLab knows about NiAl2. It's the wonder drug for treatment of migraine headaches. TechLab's stock skyrocketed when the rights were sold."

"FDA approval is only days away now. Five years ago only one scientist was working on it. It was Chang Barker's dream, like Citrinol3 is to you. Within the first six months after we upgraded the project, the major side effect problems were isolated. A year later a slight twist in the proteins created the drug as it is today. Upgrading probably cut anywhere from ten to twenty years off the project."

"Does Chang work in the BioHazard wing? I don't think I've ever met him."

"Unfortunately, Chang was killed in a car wreck about two years ago, not too long after the upgrade. He didn't live to see his dream come true, but millions of people will live richer, fuller lives because of his diligence."

"TechLab employees certainly seem to have a high death rate."

J.D. laughed. "After the week you've just been through, I can see why you would feel that way. But when you look at the big picture, we're just like the rest of the world. We employ around five thousand people worldwide. That includes everything from Ph.D.'s like yourself down to the tribal medicine men in the rain forests. They collect rare herbs and plants for us."

"You're joking, right?"

He held up his hand and said, "I swear on a stack of Bibles. We charter flights into parts of the world you wouldn't believe. The tribal leaders were tough at first, but they quickly learned the power of bartering. We exchange everything from chocolate to diamonds for roots, sticks, bark, and sap."

"Chocolate?"

"Not even the good kind. It melts too easily in the tropical climate."

"You're making this up, aren't you?"

"I'll make you a deal. You educate me on Citrinol3, and I'll enlighten you on the diversification required to manage a world-class research firm. Of course, you'll be sworn to secrecy."

"I work in BioHazard, remember? Security Level 12."

"Level 12 security is nothing compared to what I'm talking about. Hell, if they even knew I was thinking about discussing it with you I'd probably be out in a matter of days. Competition in this business is unbelievable."

"Is there really an espionage problem?"

He laughed. "Think about it. Research and development of a drug can take years. All that time, we're shelling out money for salaries, state-of-the-art equipment, test animals, international contacts . . . not to mention maintaining an underground lab built to withstand a small nuclear war. By the time we're ready to market a product, we've got tens, maybe even hundreds of millions of dollars invested in it. If one of our competitors registers the same compound the day before we do, then everything we've done is worthless."

JoAnn stared at her food for a second, then asked, "You don't really think Hanna was involved in anything like that, do you?"

"We'll never know, JoAnn. It's possible she was going to sell out and changed her mind. These guys play hardball. If she backed out, they may have made sure she didn't decide to talk to anyone ever again."

"But Hanna had a great job. Why would she even consider such a thing?"

"Greed does strange things to people. A friend of my mother's worked in the accounting department of a large corporation for thirty years. She had a secret bank account set up where she funneled money the whole time. If she had stopped after twenty years when they computerized, she would still have gotten away with over two million dollars and no one would have ever figured it out. But she kept it up. The FBI came in and hauled her off. Pure greed. There's no other way to explain it."

JoAnn shook her head. "I just don't believe Hanna would even think of it. She wasn't a materialistic person."

"Sometimes it's more a matter of power than money. *They* probably approached *her*. Who knows what they promised her? I only wish we could have known she was really in trouble."

"Really in trouble?"

"I shouldn't tell you this, but the corporate psychologist reported Hanna's behavior as unstable for the last year. She was acting more and more paranoid. The psychologist thought it was just job-related stress. Apparently he was wrong."

"Why was she seeing the corporate psychologist?"

"It's required for all top security positions. Biannual personality profiles and evaluations are submitted to the Board. To tell you the truth, no one has ever paid much attention to them. I suppose they will now. Human Resources will contact you when it's your turn."

"This is horrible. They could have saved her life."

"We'll never know. So, let's get back to business. When can I have my first Citrinol3 lesson?"

JoAnn was uncomfortable with the ease J.D. changed the subject, but said, "Is Monday soon enough?"

"Sure, but I have meetings scheduled out of the office all day. Will you be working late?"

She stared at him.

"Excuse me, madam. I forgot who I was talking to for a second. Why don't I stop by the lab around seven Monday night?"

"That would be perfect. There shouldn't be any interruptions. I'll whip up some tuna salad and we can have sandwiches while I turn you into a proto-oncogene expert. If you're a brave soul, that is."

"Your cooking is that bad?"

"No. To put it mildly, the lab refrigerator we keep our lunches in has some rather exotic specimens in it as well. If you grab the wrong container, you might have quite a surprise in store. Some of the techs are notorious for playing Russian roulette with harmless molds and fungi. At least, we all hope they're harmless."

"And I thought you cave dwellers had no sense of humor."

"Everyone needs something to make the time pass. After all, we don't get to play up in the clouds every day like you lucky souls do."

"I'll be there at seven, as long as you let me bring dinner."

"Chicken."

"If that's what you want."

"No, I mean *you're* a chicken."

"Damn right."

"Come on, Jason, we're gonna be late for class," Jonathan yelled as his friend disappeared around the corner of the building.

"This is too perfect!" Jason cried. "Check it out!"

Jonathan rounded the corner in time to see Jason jump up on the three- by four-foot metal box that had mysteriously appeared outside their classroom window over the weekend. It was a bland mechanical fixture most adults would probably never notice, but an addition a child could hardly pass by. Jason dug in his backpack, withdrew a pencil, and began wielding it like a sword.

Jonathan's eyes widened. "Cool! We can defend it like a fort. Won't that be awesome? Those dragons will never penetrate our shields."

Jason picked up his notebook, thrusting it forward like a coat of armor. "This is great!"

Suddenly Jonathan called to him from the side of

the metal box. "Wow! Jason, look at this! I think there's something back there!"

"No way!" Jason replied. "Where?"

"Right here. Look!" Jonathan pressed against the scratchy bricks and slid between the wall and the metal box.

Jason jumped down and tried to squeeze into the small space beside Jonathan. Jason was two inches taller and fifteen pounds heavier than Jonathan, but he finally managed to edge along the wall until he was alongside his friend. Both boys ran their hands over the strange thing, wondering what it could be. The circular glass embedded in the metal was colder than ice. Red digital numbers flashed rhythmically within it, generating a hypnotizing glow through the polished lens.

Jason elbowed Jonathan. "Swear you won't tell anyone?"

"Why?"

" 'Cause this is our ticket."

"Ticket to what?"

Jason glared at Jonathan, his size alone a threat. "Geez. Just swear, will you?"

"Okay."

Suddenly the unit began to vibrate, a strange hissing sound emerging from deep inside the glass. Jonathan was long gone by the time Jason freed himself and scrambled breathlessly into the classroom. The two boys sat wide-eyed and shaking for several minutes before they calmed down enough to begin their work.

Jonathan reached into his desk and pulled out his daily workbook. He kicked Jason under the table, a signal for his friend to start his work before they both got in trouble. By the time Ms. Fordman slowly walked by to check their progress, both boys were almost finished with their morning assignment. When she was well out of earshot, Jonathan leaned over and whispered, "Can you smell that?"

Jason's nose twitched as he sniffed the air. "I don't smell anything."

"I do. Kinda like that stuff they put in the bathrooms at the mall. Lemon-orangy."

"If you say so, dude. Let's meet at our secret place right after lunch."

Jonathan nodded, even though he had a funny feeling it wasn't such a great idea.

JoAnn was shocked to realize how unproductively a day could slip by. All morning she was trapped in a management meeting, and most of her afternoon was spent looking over résumés sent by Human Resources. Now, she was rushing through a job that required utmost care. But she was happy. For the first time since Hanna's death, she was doing some of her own research again, even if it was rushed.

After putting one set of specimens in the centrifuge, she reluctantly returned to her office. She began pulling out dyes in preparation to read a series of hematology slides extracted from the latest test animals. Just as she finished preparing the work area, J.D. poked his head in the door saying, "I know I'm a little early. Mind if I interrupt?"

Her heart skipped a beat, but she managed to appear calm. "Please do. I was just going to check the fourth-generation Citrinol3 samples I collected this afternoon."

"Would you mind showing me?"

"Not at all." JoAnn took a deep breath, hoping it would steady her hand before she reached for the double-headed teaching microscope. All night while the puppies cuddled around her, she thought of J.D., even though she knew it was a hopeless situation. He was only concerned with business.

J.D. stepped over to the microscope and sat opposite JoAnn. Their knees almost touched underneath the narrow table. She put her eyes to one eyepiece and focused, then nodded for J.D. to look. Immediately she recognized the blood specimen still showed signs of cell damage. Even though X rays showed the tumor had actually decreased in size, the hematology results made her heart sink.

Before she could speak, J.D. reached under the table and caressed JoAnn's thigh just above the knee. The tingling sensation crept up her leg like fire, and she froze, the edge of her glasses still glued to the eyepiece. For a few seconds she didn't even breathe. Finally, she tried to voice her disappointment in the specimen, but her concentration faltered. J.D.'s hand remained on her thigh, his fingers teasing her as he asked, "What exactly are we looking for?"

JoAnn remained silent for several seconds, then finally mumbled, "Signs that the Citrinol3 has stunted the growth of the tumor without adverse side effects."

"Has it?"

"No, it appears to have also damaged the red blood cells. See how the edges of the cells are thicker than normal?"

"If you say so." J.D. pulled away from the microscope, walking around to the other side of the table. He gently pulled JoAnn out of her chair, holding her lightly against him. "You just don't get it, do you?" he asked, his voice gentle.

"Get what?" she asked timidly.

"Your work is brilliant. You've succeeded in slowing the growth of brain tumors. Your first-generation studies conclusively proved that. I had a break in my meetings this afternoon, and I spent the time rereading the studies you've submitted. Citrinol3 will be one of the most successful drugs we market. Just wait and see."

"But healthy cells are adversely affected . . . not just the red blood cells, but brain tissue as well."

"Only after a long period of heavy medication. And then it appears their functioning slows. Maybe that isn't such a bad side effect. In fact, it may be useful."

"How could it be useful?"

"Think about it. Slowing down cell growth may also slow down cell aging. Maybe you've run across the fountain of youth and you don't even realize it."

"The test animals show a significant decrease in intelligence. Are you suggesting it would be all right to live to be a hundred and twenty with an I.Q. of fifty? Or that decreased oxygen absorption by the blood won't adversely affect the quality of life of the patient?"

He buried his head in her hair, his lips against her ears as he said, "I thought the test results were inconclusive because of the intelligence level of the animals involved. Isn't it impossible to predict exactly how humans would react?"

Unsteadily, she managed to say, "Of course, but it is far too soon to try." She stepped back, forcing herself to concentrate.

J.D.'s voice was husky as he said, "What about the results on the younger test animals? I thought they showed more promise."

"They do, but the normal cells are still affected. It's just harder to gauge the degree of damage when the test animal's entire body is undergoing rapid growth. Besides, children are not the prime target for this type of cancer research. Most of the patients we're targeting are adults."

"You're too critical of your work. Chang Barker had the same kind of concerns with NiAl2. Once he broadened his viewpoint, everything began to fall into place. Let's throw away logic and reality and talk hypothetically for a moment. Can you shut off the rigid scientific side of your personality long enough to imagine with me?" He stroked her cheek.

JoAnn knew she was fighting a losing battle, so she moved closer to him as she said, "I suppose. I'll warn you though, I'm pretty damned practical."

"No kidding. Okay, let's assume it's a hundred years from now. Human clones are used to test everything from drugs to how long it takes to wear out a pair of jeans."

"I suppose we can fly, too?"

J.D. laughed. "Of course. Now, you have a whole fleet of flying clones to run tests on to perfect Citrinol3. How would you start?"

"What stage of the experiment are we talking about?"

"That's an awfully technical question for a flying scientist, but let's assume we're at the stage you're currently at right now."

J.D.'s hands began gently caressing her shoulders, occasionally inching higher and higher as they talked until he was fondling her hair, her ears, her neck. It was becoming almost impossible to concentrate. JoAnn suppressed a giggle and said, "Can I have different ages of flying clones?"

"Anything you want."

"Then I'd use some old, some young. Since the inhalant formula is working well, I'd expose a control group to placebos, and the test groups to incremental steps of fifty milligrams a day. These clones have no feeling, right?"

"Right. You can dissect them, operate on them, do whatever your heart desires and they just smile stupidly at you."

"That's too bad. For the test to work, I'd want to do motor skills tests on a daily basis, plus constantly monitor brain function."

"Then they have feelings. This is your dream world, you can change it however you want."

"I'd stagger the test groups like I do the mice, so that the results overlap." His hands were making her crazy, so she pulled away and said, "This is really a waste of time, you know."

He pulled her back saying, "No, my dear, it isn't. It allows you to see a much bigger picture."

"An unrealistic picture."

"Not necessarily. I admit, flying clones are ridiculous, but thinking big isn't. Remember, more money plus more staff equals faster results."

"Faster in some ways, but you can't speed up the aging process."

"We can evaluate the initial tests and project future results. It worked on $NiAl_2$."

His hand reached down to stroke her inner thigh causing her voice to tremble as she said, "It's too soon to know what the long-term effects will be."

"Then let's worry about the short-term effects you're having on me instead."

To JoAnn, he was moving in slow motion, a fantasy come to life. One hand gently lifted her glasses from her face as the other hand cradled her cheek, tilting her head to meet his lips. His kiss was like a whisper, lips breezing over hers as he said, "Surely you know how I feel about working with a woman like you. It has been spectacular, so . . . exotic and exciting."

She arched her eyebrows in disbelief and moved almost imperceptibly into his embrace. "It has?"

He tightened his arms around her, smiling confidently as he realized she was not going to protest his advances. "Are all the lab technicians gone for the day?"

She nodded, her mouth raising to search for his. "I had no idea you felt . . . I'd dreamed . . ."

He kissed her hard. She responded with an intensity

he would never have anticipated. He explored her mouth with his own, her neck with his tongue, while pulling her toward the clear space at the end of the table. Her fingers fumbled with his belt, pulled on the buttons of his shirt. By the time they reached the zipper of his pants, he had managed to push the tight black skirt of her suit above her slender hips.

Stroking her breast with one hand, his other hand moved lower. JoAnn, obviously, needed no prolonged foreplay. With surprising agility and lust, she drew him toward her, driving her thighs until they tightly gripped his hips. She kissed him passionately as they simultaneously rocked.

"We work well together, JoAnn," he whispered as he plunged deeper and deeper.

"Yes, oh, yes . . ."

"We can help each other so much."

Her answer was veiled in a moan as she shuddered. J.D. felt his own distinctive rise toward orgasm as JoAnn began to rhythmically move under him once again. As the spasms ran through his body, he smiled down at her.

Some things in life are too damned easy, he thought. It had taken almost a year to get this far with Hanna.

It was midnight by the time JoAnn got home, but she wasn't the slightest bit tired. A feeling of total contentment wrapped warmly around her. She kneeled down, scooping the puppies into her arms and held them close as they wiggled and licked her face to welcome her home. When they finally calmed down, she grabbed the stack of mail from the kitchen table and went outside with them into the small backyard.

It was a beautiful fall evening; a radiant full moon cast enough light for her to sort through the mail while the puppies ran from bush to bush playfully nipping each other's tails and ears. She tossed unopened pieces of junk mail into a pile on the patio table, then ripped into the bills, barely glancing at the amounts. It was the last thing she came across that made her stop and shiver. A plain white envelope with no return address, but with handwriting she instantly recognized.

Slicing it open with her fingernail, she withdrew a smaller envelope from inside, along with a handwritten note. She held the note where the moonlight illuminated the beautiful handwriting that was so much like Hanna's. She slumped into the chair as she read:

Dear JoAnn,

I was sorting through Hanna's things when I came across this letter addressed to you. Since it was with her life insurance policy and other personal documents in her safety deposit box, I did not feel I should open it.

Hanna spoke very fondly of you. She often commented what a diligent coworker you were and that your work was brilliant. May God rest her soul,

Louise Shore

P.S. Please call me if I can help you in any way.

JoAnn's hand trembled as she held the envelope in her hand. Taking a deep breath, she sliced open the seal and pulled out the single sheet of paper.

Chapter 5

Dear JoAnn,

If you are reading this note, something has happened to me. I have tried to protect you, but since you are still the most likely candidate to take my position, I feel I should warn you.

Leave TechLab as soon as possible. Do not trust anyone who works there. I wish I could be more specific, but even now my actions are being closely monitored.

You have to trust me. I wish I'd had the courage to do it myself. Leave town as soon as you can, change your name, your life, and never look back. The cost of your lofty goals may be your life.

Hanna

JoAnn sat in the dark for over an hour, reading and rereading the letter. She desperately wanted to call J.D., to talk to him about Hanna. But the letter said to trust no one at TechLab.

She looked around the backyard. She'd lived in this house her entire life. Even when she was married to Bill, they'd stayed with her parents while he finished med school. How could she leave? She didn't know anything else. And worse, she didn't want to try. Yet Hanna's cryptic letter puzzled her. If she had the opportunity to write it, why hadn't she been more specific? Either she was afraid it would be intercepted, or her problems ran even deeper than J.D. had implied.

Pinching her eyes closed, she tried to remember Hanna at work. Those meaningless conversations they'd had while waiting for test results or jogging might now be important. Had she ever seen her with J.D.? No. Would she have noticed if she had? Probably not. *Damn it*, she thought, *why was I always so engrossed in my own work that I ignored everything and everyone around me?*

Stacey lay motionless in bed, the cold compress doing little to ease her nagging headache. Even though it was two a.m., yesterday's stack of papers to be graded still lay untouched beside her. Every time she tried to focus, the letters seemed to dance, making her a little more nauseous. Her mind toyed with calling in sick in the morning, but she knew she wouldn't. It was too important for her to be there.

She closed her eyes and tried to think of what might have made her sick. None of the kids in her class were ill. The salad at dinner couldn't have been the culprit. She'd felt fine until she'd gone to her step aerobics class, then halfway through she hadn't been able to catch her breath. Since then, her head had ached, sometimes mildly, other times viciously.

Great, she thought, *I'm probably allergic to exercise. What else could go wrong?* By three a.m. she finally fell into a fitful, restless sleep.

Several miles away two men were hard at work. They listened to the Fordman tape of her morning conversation with her mother, which they summarily deemed unimportant and erased. However, her evening phone conversation piqued their interest for two reasons. It was a lengthy discussion, lasting over an hour, with Jess Lawrence. A relationship was obviously developing, one that had the potential to jeopardize the entire project.

The other factor was even more important. She described, in detail, symptoms that could document the first side effects of the drug being field-tested in the Fordman classroom.

By six a.m. the recordings from all forty surveillance sites had been evaluated, and a copy of the Fordman/Lawrence conversation was on its way from TechLab Security to the executive wing.

JoAnn's work was an integral part of her life, something that filled every hour of every day with purpose. But now, it was becoming impossible. Three techs called in sick. Two major projects were falling dramatically behind schedule. She was supposed to interview six candidates for Amy's position as well as five others for the Citrinol3 project. Her own research was at a virtual standstill. Several Citrinol3 test animals that were healthy yesterday were suddenly dead when she arrived this morning. And last, but certainly not least, she was in the middle of an emotional storm where passion and confusion blinded logic and reason.

Yesterday she was certain she was in love with J.D.; today she wondered if she was crazy. Every day the news brought out more and more cases of sexual harassment in the workplace. But J.D. wasn't harassing her, he truly cared about her ... didn't he? It was a fine line that added even more turmoil to her already turbulent life.

JoAnn walked in the door of her office, quietly closing it behind her. Going to her desk, she sat down and laid her head on the cold wood surface. *One thing at a time*, she told herself. Picking up the phone, she dialed J.D.'s extension.

"J. D. Cook."

His voice still sent shivers of anticipation through her. "Hi. It's me. Do you have time for me to drop by for a couple of minutes?"

"Always. When did you have in mind?"

"Now?"

"Would you rather I come down to BioHazard?"

"No, I think the walk will do me good. I'll be there in fifteen or twenty minutes."

The walk did do her good. By the time she reached his office, she felt more confident about her decision. When she walked in, he quickly crossed the room and closed the door behind her. Embracing her, he kissed her, but she pushed him away, saying, "That's not why I came."

He feigned rejection and said, "Too bad. Last night's lesson was . . . exhilarating. I was hoping to learn more from you. Soon. You're not upset about how things turned out, are you?"

"No. Believe it or not, that has nothing to do with why I need to talk to you."

"Then, by all means, sit down and talk. The curiosity is killing me."

"I think you need to find someone else to handle the Chief of Research position. I'll help until you can find a qualified replacement, but then I'd like to go back to straight research."

He stared at her for several seconds, then walked over and took her hands. "JoAnn, after last night, I'd think you already know how I feel about you. I care deeply about you. I could say I love you, but words don't mean as much as actions. My definition of love is caring long-term about a person. Not just now, or in the heat of passion, but forever. I care about your future. I'll always act in your best interests. Do you believe me?"

JoAnn melted. She hugged him and said, "Of course I do. I just don't seem to be cut out for management. I was happy doing my research. Right now, I feel like I'm no good to anyone. Nothing is getting accomplished. The money and car are magnificent, but I've lived fine up till now, and I just don't think I'm the right person for the job."

"But this job is your future, JoAnn. It's too late to turn back. No corporation wants stagnant employees. You're a star. TechLab needs their stars to shine as bright as they can. We need your talents fully utilized. I swear, things will get easier. It is always hectic when you start a new position. There are so many things to comprehend, and the learning curve can be infuriating. But you can handle it, I know you can."

She decided to test him. "How did Hanna do at first? Did she have a hard time making the transition?"

"I don't know. My only exposure to Hanna was the last few years at Board meetings."

"I thought you were friends."

He turned and stared out the window as he said, "No. I barely knew her. I wasn't in charge of the Bio-Hazard wing until the reorganization three years ago. Even since then, I let Hanna handle things on her own. She didn't require much supervision. To tell you the truth, I didn't feel comfortable enough with my knowledge of the projects she was handling to do much hands-on management. That's one of the reasons I wanted you to teach me more about Citrinol3. I need to understand what your department is doing so I can perform my job better."

"I guess last night wasn't as educational as it could have been."

He took her in his arms. "I found it very educational. When's my next lesson?"

"I've been thinking about that. We really don't need to be in the lab for me to bring you up to speed on the projects. Why don't you come over to my house tonight?"

"I'd love to. I knew you were one smart lady. Office romances are risky. Keeping this under wraps is very wise. Shall we make a pact? At work, we're strictly professional. But outside TechLab . . ."

"I think that's wise." She turned to go, then hesitated and turned back to him. "J.D., do you think TechLab is a good place to work?"

"As opposed to what? The city dump?"

"No. As opposed to some other research facility. Does TechLab do anything illegal?"

"What on earth would make you ask that?"

"I got . . ." JoAnn suddenly felt uneasy. She turned around, twisted the doorknob, then opened the door.

"You got what?"

"Oh, it's nothing. I guess I just got a little worried about what happened to Hanna and Amy."

"Bad things happen to good people all the time. We're no better or worse than any other company. We're just bigger. Much bigger."

She smiled at him. "I know you're right. I'm just tired. In a couple of weeks, the puppies will settle down and work will fall into place. Getting some sleep will help, right?"

"I promise. If not, I will personally make it up to you."

"And how will you do that?"

"A gentleman has to have some secrets. See you tonight."

J.D. walked JoAnn to the elevator, then caught the next car up to the executive suites on the top floor. He headed toward the south end of the building, where Gene Lemmond's office, private library, and conference rooms were located. Janice Ross, Gene's personal secretary, smiled broadly when he approached.

"Is he in?"

"In a manner of speaking, yes. He's practicing his putting in the corner conference room."

"Alone?"

"Yes."

"Think I could barge in?"

"I'll check." She pushed the intercom and said, "Mr. Lemmond, Mr. Cook would like to see you."

Through the speaker, the husky voice barked, "Send him in."

J.D. walked slowly down the hallway. Even after all his years at TechLab, he never ceased to appreciate the exquisite artwork and furnishings that surrounded Gene Lemmond. The only place he had ever seen that was more impressive than the executive suite was Lemmond's personal mansion on the outskirts of town. J.D. shook his head as he remembered last year's Christmas party. The man's house was built on his own personal lake. A goddamn man-made lake. It was almost obscene.

The double mahogany doors were open, and Gene's white head was tilted down in concentration. He swung, nailing the twenty-foot putt easily. Without looking up, he maneuvered another ball into position with his putter and asked, "What brings you up here?"

As J.D. closed the doors he replied, "The Citrinol3 testing."

"Son, you don't have to worry about security up here. Arnold Schwarzenegger would have a tough time getting past the cameras and Janice."

"Of course."

"There a problem?"

"Possibly. Hanna may have been a bit too eager on this one. I'm working closely with JoAnn Rayburn to find out if we need to reevaluate our strategy."

Gene tapped the latest ball at his feet, which rimmed the cup and rolled back toward him. "Son of a bitch. Today's security report says you've worked your way in already. Says you scored big last night— in Hanna Shore's old office, no less. Must have been like déjà vu. That true?"

Angry blood rushed to J.D.'s face, but he managed to mumble a calm "Yes." He had completely forgotten about the security measures added to Hanna's office two months before she was killed.

"Hell, screwing your employees must be screwing up your brain. Don't you worry about corporate strategy, son. That's my job. We've already shelled out over a million on surveillance installation for the Citrinol3 test cases at the school and nursing home. Only an act of God could stop the project now."

Stacey's headache was finally easing up, a full two days after it had viciously attacked her. She walked slowly between the groups of desks, glancing over the children's shoulders as they silently worked. The room was calm and still. It dawned on her that it had been quiet for the last few days. Too quiet.

She stopped behind Amanda's desk, noticing how quickly the little girl was copying down the spelling words from the board. Since Amanda was one of her special kids, one with a learning disability, it didn't surprise her to see numerous reversals of b's and d's as well as some letter omissions. She bent down and whispered in Amanda's ear, "Did you forget something?"

Amanda grabbed the end of her long blond braid and began twisting. Alert blue eyes stared sweetly at Stacey as she said, "No, I didn't, Mrs. Fordman. I copied every word three times, just like you said."

Stacey bent down and pulled Amanda's special glasses out of her desk. Like many dyslexic children, the unique colored lenses helped her brain process the harsh fluorescent light. "You forgot your purple glasses. You need to go back and check which way the letters face and make sure all the letters are where they're supposed to be. Okay?"

Amanda slipped on the glasses and said, "Okay."

Without moving, Stacey watched Jonathan, who was seated in the desk next to Amanda. He was Amanda's reading buddy. When she had trouble deciphering words or reversing numbers, he was always willing to help. For several seconds Stacey watched him work. Usually, Jonathan would have been the first one finished with such an easy task. But this time he was writing so slowly that Amanda finished her corrections before he was close to being done.

Stacey walked around the room. All of the children with learning disabilities were done with the assignment, while the rest of the class seemed to be working at a snail's pace. She quickly dismissed it as a fluke and went to her desk to grade papers.

Fifteen minutes later, which is an eternity for any first-grade teacher, that eerie quiet still hung in the room like an iron curtain. She slid silently from her chair and eased out the door. The door to the room next door was closed, but she opened it and signaled for her friend and fellow teacher, Brenda Webster, to come out in the hall.

"What's going on?" Brenda asked.

"I just wanted you to verify that I'm not going crazy," Stacey said. "Look in my room."

Brenda cracked open the door and stared at the room full of children hard at work. "They're being angels."

"That's the problem."

She eased the door closed. "Some problem. Want to switch classes? I'll take a room full of angels any day over the mischievous crew I have."

"But they've been this good for two whole days. Doesn't that seem odd to you?"

"Have they only been good since you had your headache?"

Stacey thought for a second, then said, "Yes."

"Then that's your answer. They aren't going to push

you while you aren't feeling well. Count your blessings."

"So you think when they think I'm well, all hell will break loose?"

"I'd bet on it. The little beasties can only hold it in for so long."

Jess Lawrence scrubbed his hands, wiped them dry, then grabbed the chart from the back of the examining-room door. His clinic had three examining rooms, all of which had doors opening to the central hallway along the back, as well as in front where the patients entered. Everything in the clinic was ivory with pale blue trim. Ivory walls, ivory cabinets, and blue-striped ivory tile added to the customary gleaming hospital look, yet the atmosphere was warm and welcoming.

He quickly scanned the information for the new patients waiting in Room 2, then opened the door, expecting to greet a client. Inside, a young woman was sitting on the floor facing away from him, her shoulder-length brown hair tied back with a white ribbon that matched her T-shirt. He peeked over the treatment counter to confirm she was playing tug-of-war with two tiny Yorkie puppies. Each puppy had one end of an old sock that was knotted in the middle. The slick tile floor made their paws slip each time they tried to wrestle the sock free.

As soon as she saw him, JoAnn jumped up as if she'd been caught with her hand in a cookie jar. As she brushed off the seat of her blue jeans she extended her hand and said, "Excuse me, I didn't hear you come in. I'm JoAnn Rayburn."

He shook her hand vigorously. "Jess Lawrence. Sorry I'm running a little late. Looks like you have your hands full with these two. They are adorable."

"Thanks." She bent down and herded them into a corner where she could catch them. "They are miniature balls of energy. I wish I could find a way to harness it in my lab. People would pay a fortune for it."

"I saw on your information sheet that you work at TechLab. I have several clients who work there. Is that how you heard about my clinic?"

"Yes. One of the lab techs who works for me, Diane Dunn, told me you were the best vet in town."

He blushed. "Her dog, Cashew, is a gorgeous sheltie. I'll have to thank her for referring me." He reached over and scratched behind the dog's ear. "Let's look at these little ones of yours." He gently took Nobel in his hand and began to examine her. A few minutes later they switched and he checked Rocket. When he was finished using the stethoscope, he pulled it back down around his neck and said, "Nobel and Rocket. Interesting names."

"A friend of mine gave me the puppies. He thought I needed companionship. Nobel is for prize. Rocket is for scientist. A little too clever for my taste, so I call them Bell and Rocky when he's not around." She snuggled the little girl and added, "I started to nickname her No, but that got way too confusing for all of us."

"I'll bet it did. They seem to be very healthy." He cradled them both in his arms and said, "A lot of Yorkies have leg problems, but their joints feel fine. I'll take them in the treatment room and give them their shots. It'll only take a couple of minutes."

When he returned, both puppies whimpered and struggled to go back to JoAnn. "They may be sore tonight, but by tomorrow they should both be fine. Rocket tipped the scales at a whopping one pound three ounces, and Nobel weighed in at fifteen ounces. They'll need their next shots in six weeks."

"Thanks. You know, I thought about becoming a vet, but I decided I'd get too attached to the animals."

"Believe me, it happens all too often. What do you do at TechLab?"

"I just became Chief of Research."

"Sounds fascinating. Do you work with orphan drugs?"

"Somewhat. My specialty is proto-oncogenes. Are you familiar with that field?"

"I know oncogenes are the substances in certain viruses that are believed to be the cause of cancer."

"Right. Proto-oncogenes disguise themselves as oncogenes, but prevent or retard the cancer. It is a fascinating field."

"Do you do the research yourself?"

JoAnn sighed. "I did until about a month ago. Since I got promoted, my own research has taken a backseat to all the bureaucratic mumbo jumbo. I really miss it."

"Remind me when we do any blood work on the puppies to take you in the treatment room with me. I'll show you what to look for under the microscope. Could save you some time and trouble later."

"Thanks, I appreciate that. I feel like I've spent half my life with my face glued to a microscope." She smiled and added, "It would be nice to know my skills are useful in real, everyday life, instead of just grand theories."

Jess opened the door and led her into the reception area. Jonathan was asleep on one of the couches, his head resting on his backpack.

"Is that your son?" she whispered.

"Yes, but you don't have to worry about waking him. Once he's out, a hurricane could hit and he'd never bat an eye. I don't know what's gotten into him lately. This is the third day in a row he's fallen asleep before we close the clinic. He's usually bouncing off the walls, playing with the dogs in the kennel or rollerblading in the parking lot. Maybe he's going through a growth spurt or something."

She laughed. "Or he got bit by a tsetse fly."

"Let's hope they haven't invaded the U.S."

"Only if they escaped from TechLab."

"You have tsetse flies?"

"Thousands. You wouldn't believe some of the things we use. The most bizarre creatures and plants can dramatically impact cell growth."

"I suppose you have bubonic plague and all those other horrible diseases, too."

"Some. Luckily, the Centers for Disease Control handles most of the really contagious things. We're more concerned with diseases that impact large numbers of people. But you know how business goes. If a cure for bubonic plague would be profitable, I'm sure we'd be working on it."

Jess held out his hand. "It's truly been a pleasure to meet you, Ms. Rayburn." He handed her a magnetic business card. "Thank you for choosing my clinic. This has both my home and office numbers. Feel free to call anytime."

"I wouldn't want to bother you at home."

He motioned to the walls around him. "Unfortunately, dogs and cats are just like children, they don't wait to get sick until office hours. If you think there is a serious problem, then call. If I'd wanted a job with regular business hours, I definitely would not have chosen this field."

"I know exactly how you feel."

JoAnn was still not used to the luxury of the Lexus, and she marveled at how comfortable it was as she drove home. The power steering made it easy to balance Bell in her lap as they drove, while Rocky twisted around her feet and disappeared under the seats. When she finally pulled into the driveway of her house, he was nowhere in sight. She carefully opened the door and kneeled down to look for him.

His furry black hind end wiggled out from under the back of the passenger seat, tail wagging furiously. He struggled with his feet firmly planted on the floor mat as he growled and pulled at something wedged securely under the car's beige leather seat.

"Okay, Rocket Scientist, what have you got there?" JoAnn asked playfully. He growled again, but lost his grip and tumbled backward against the backseat. She went to the passenger side, opened the door, and tossed Bell onto the front floorboard. Reaching under the seat, she felt the damp edge of what he had been tugging on.

Opening the glove compartment, she took out a small flashlight and stretched her body half in and half out of the luxurious car. Before she saw exactly what Rocky had been wrestling with, she noticed a neat slit in the rough black cloth underneath the passenger car seat. With one hand, she once again felt for the wet spot where Rocky had been tugging. Reaching inside the slit, she pulled out the object of his attention.

Sliding down, she sat on the concrete driveway. The sunlight flashed brilliantly off the elegantly embossed gold letters on the soft leather cover of the executive calendar she held in her hand.

"Oh, my God" was all she mumbled when she realized whose initials were branded there.

Chapter 6

Bell yelped when JoAnn accidentally touched the tender spot where her shot had been given. Balancing the struggling puppies, her purse, and the leather-bound calendar, JoAnn carried everything inside. She went straight through the house and out the back door, setting both puppies down in the soft grass of the yard before she slumped into one of the patio chairs. The puppies scampered off to play as JoAnn took a deep breath and slowly opened the leather cover of the small book.

Her suspicions were immediately confirmed. Gold initials—H E S—graced the outside of the calendar, while inside the front cover Hanna's unmistakable handwriting stated:

> Property of Hanna Elizabeth Shore. If found, please call 918 555-2620 or mail or deliver to 7135 South Florence. Generous reward for safe return.

Several pages inside, she had listed all her credit card numbers, as well as what JoAnn recognized was probably her alphanumeric BioHazard entry code.

JoAnn scanned the first few pages, noticing that in the "Comments" section of almost every single day there were some sort of codes listed. Additionally, entries for meetings throughout the days were written across from the calendar's printed hourly times. Each page seemed to come to life in her hands as JoAnn recognized the names and places Hanna referred to in her book. In the last month, JoAnn had attended many of the same meetings. She wondered if Hanna had hated sitting through them as much as she did.

Page by page, she watched as the winter entries flowed into spring. Hanna's entries for business meetings were becoming predictable, but the strange codes at the bottom still did not have any apparent rhyme or reason. Some codes appeared regularly: DC7/D/H, DC8/M. She noticed other codes were only written once or twice: EB2/SCR, FTM3/SWCR.

Toward the end of July, the codes began to be more frequent, plus almost every day had one or more of the following: TRP-NiAl2; TRP-SYNCUR6; TRP-CRYOGEN5; TRP-OZOPLAG2. JoAnn recognized the names of some of the projects, her heart pounding. *My God, J.D. must have been right. Hanna was taking samples of our compounds to our competitors.*

She began flipping through the pages more rapidly. The entire month of August was filled with references to TechLab's top secret compounds. She turned to September 1 and noticed a sudden change. The handwriting was stiff, the words pressed firmly into the paper as if written under extreme pressure. One of the last codes appeared on September 1—EB6/CONFRONT!! After that, the rest of the week contained only a few references to scheduled meetings, the type that JoAnn knew were arranged weeks in advance. The day of her death, September 10, had the last fiercely written entries referring to two meetings: a ten a.m. meeting with Dr. Calahan and a three p.m. meeting that merely said DC—end.

She sighed as she finished turning through the rest of the book, the clean, crisp pages almost shouting the reality of Hanna's death. Laying the book facedown on the table, she leaned back, pinching her eyes closed while she tried to sort through what she had just read.

Several seconds later the sound of J.D.'s voice made her bolt upright. She gasped, unexpectedly toppling onto the brick patio when the chair slid out from under her. Although she had done nothing wrong, she felt an overwhelming sense of guilt. Somehow, merely finding and reading Hanna's personal calendar was an insult to J.D., and to his loyalty to TechLab. The blood rushed to her cheeks, but she realized she still could not tell him about the letter or the book lying on the table.

"I'm so sorry, JoAnn. I didn't mean to scare you half to death." J.D. bent to help her up. "When you didn't answer the doorbell, I came through the south gate. I thought you might be back here playing with the puppies."

"It's okay, J.D. You just startled me." Rocky and Bell jumped playfully at JoAnn's feet, as if belatedly announcing the arrival of a guest. She crouched down and grabbed their little heads, playfully jiggling them back and forth as she said, "Some watch dogs you guys are. Next time bark or something."

"They might lick someone to death, but I think that's about the extent of the harm they could do." He pulled her to him, his lips brushing over hers as he asked, "Are you too tired to go to dinner, or were you just catnapping so you'd have plenty of energy for later?" His accent on the word "later" carried definite sexual connotations.

"I must have dozed off watching the puppies. What time is it?"

"Seven. Isn't that the time we agreed to this morning?"

"It's already seven?" She glanced down at Hanna's calendar, thankful it was facedown. Picking it up as casually as she could, she backed away from him as she said, "I'm sorry, J.D., I lost all track of time. If you'll excuse me, I'll run in and change. It'll just take a second."

He followed her inside, carrying on a conversation from the living room while she went upstairs to the bedroom to change. "Did the puppies check out okay?"

She raised her voice to answer, "The vet said they were as healthy as can be."

"I'm glad. I'd hate to have given you a couple of sickly runts. But then again, you probably could have found a cure for any disease they came down with."

"You give me far too much credit. I have a very, very narrow frame of reference when it comes to my work."

He silently opened the door, walking into the bedroom just as JoAnn was about to step into a sexy black slip. Her glasses were on the nightstand, so she did not see him from across the room. She wore only lacy French-cut black panty hose that matched her strapless black lace bra. Turning away from him, she bent over, grabbed the tight half slip, and wiggled her slender thighs into it.

J.D. cleared his throat and said, "Since I've met you, my own frame of reference seems to be getting very narrow. You're the only one I think about." He was walking slowly across the room, his eyes cloudy with lust, his pulsing erection obvious even through the dress slacks he wore. "I hate to admit it, but I've spent far too many hours imagining what you would look like in black lace." His voice had grown husky. "Turn around for me. Please."

JoAnn was more than just flattered by his arousal at her appearance. Never before had anyone made her feel so sexy, so alive, and so desired with just a stare. In an instant he was next to her, his hands trembling as they stroked the sheer black lace. She pulled him to her, whispering, "You don't have to imagine anymore, J.D. If you want something, all you have to do is ask for it."

He picked her up, his breath against her ear as he mumbled, "I want you. Only you." Laying her down on the bed, he showed her exactly how much. For the second time that day, JoAnn lost all track of time, all sense of any other life going on around her. She lived only in the moment, her entire being devoted to satisfying the intense sexual appetite that was such a welcome experience.

The expensive pile of black lace lingerie created a nest of sorts on the floor beside the bed. Rocky and Bell scratched at it until they were satisfied it was a warm and cozy spot to settle down and wait. They snoozed away as the bed beside them rocked, and moans of pleasure filled the room. Much later their slumber suddenly ended when J.D.'s bare foot came down directly on top of them, painfully catching their hair and startling them. Both yelped as though they'd been attacked by a ruthless giant.

To keep from completely crushing the dogs, J.D. pushed away, falling sideways. His head caught the sharp corner of the nightstand, inflicting a deep wound on his forehead. Splayed naked on the carpet, he grabbed his temple. When he felt blood oozing through his fingers he screamed, "Goddamn those goddamn dogs! Son of a fucking bitch."

JoAnn grabbed her puppies, comforting them against her naked breasts as they whimpered. "It's okay, babies. No one is going to hurt you. J.D. didn't mean to step on you."

"Maybe next time I will!" He stood up and stomped into the bathroom, viciously slamming the door behind him.

JoAnn had never seen anyone so angry. His eyes had practically burned a hole through her as he cursed. But it was something else that scared her, something unexplainable she felt deep inside. She nestled the shaking dogs, hoping he hadn't hurt them. With gentle hands, she examined each one until she was certain they were all right. Then she sat them on her pillow, grabbed the T-shirt she'd been wearing, and went to the bathroom door. Pulling the T-shirt over her head, she softly knocked and said, "Are you okay?"

"Define okay," he snapped indignantly.

"Can I come in?"

"Only if you aren't squeamish."

She slowly opened the door, gasping at what she saw. J.D. was leaning over the sink, his naked shoulders and chest splattered with drops of blood. The sink and countertop no longer resembled cream-colored marble, instead deep red stains made the room look ghastly. As he pulled the washcloth away so he could look at the wound in the mirror, a stream of blood poured down his cheek and dropped into the sink.

"I think I need stitches."

"No kidding. I'll bring you your clothes. Do you want me to get you some Tylenol to take the edge off the pain?"

"No. Is there a minor emergency center around here anywhere? I'd rather not sit in a damn hospital emergency room waiting for hours."

JoAnn handed him his silk boxer shorts and his slacks, then she held the compress to his head as he slipped them on. When she picked up his jacket and shirt, a small copper canister fell out of his inside coat pocket and rolled across the tile floor. She chased it and picked it up, asking, "What's this? Some sort of outrageously expensive breath freshener?"

He lunged at her and grabbed it. Sighing, he said,

"That's pepper gas mixed with Mace. Believe me, you wouldn't want to inhale it."

"And I thought you were one of those macho men."

"I'm macho enough to use my brains instead of my fists." He slipped the canister back in his pocket and patted it. "This just evens up the odds." He examined his wound again in the mirror and turned back to her saying, "Believe it or not, I'm really hungry."

She helped him slip into his shirt and began to button it for him. "How can you think about food at a time like this?"

The anger in his voice was finally beginning to ease up. "Haven't you ever heard that all men are interested in is food and sex? No, I said that backward. It's sex and food. Sex is always first. Always."

"I'll remember that." She ran water on a washcloth and wiped him clean thinking how true that had been when she was married. Consciously willing the depressing thoughts away, she said, "I have an idea. I'll drive you to the doctor, then while you're waiting I'll go pick us up a submarine sandwich. Sound good?"

"Only if you get me two. And some beer." He wormed his arms into the jacket she held up for him, then impatiently waited for her to button it. "I think we need some old towels. This one is soaking through fast."

JoAnn opened the cabinet and grabbed a handful of hand towels. She carefully wrapped one around his shoulders to catch any blood that might fall. When they were finally headed outside she asked, "You aren't planning on bleeding all over my new Lexus, are you?"

She opened the passenger door for him as he said, "Better your Lexus than my Jaguar. By the way, how do you like the company car?"

"It's beautiful, and it rides like a dream."

"Then it fits you perfectly."

"If that was a compliment as to my recently demonstrated abilities, then thank you. Do you know how the company cars are handled at TechLab?"

"What do you mean?"

"Do they rotate them?"

As he watched the passing scenery, he shook his head while still pushing the damp towel against the gash in his forehead. "You ask the strangest questions sometimes. I suppose they rotate the tires during regular maintenance. Is that what you want to know?"

"No. I mean do managers switch cars? For instance, will I drive this one for a few months, then get a different one, or will I have this one for the next few years?"

"You'll have this one until the corporate lease expires. That's usually three or four years. Why?"

"No reason. I just thought it was odd that this car already has twelve thousand miles on it. I thought big corporations like TechLab always bought everything brand-new."

"They usually do. Maybe this particular car was an exception." JoAnn watched as he tilted his head back against the headrest in frustration. She wondered if he was only trying to find a position that was a little less uncomfortable, or if the topic of conversation was irritating him. He continued, saying, "Or I suppose whoever it was originally issued to could have quit or been fired."

"Or maybe they died," she mumbled.

"What?"

"Nothing. Nothing at all."

"Be careful up there!" Jess shouted to Jonathan who was grinning down at him from high in the oak tree in the backyard.

"Bombs away!" Jon cried, just as he held tightly on

to one branch while jumping furiously up and down on another. A torrent of acorns came pinging down, some striking Jess while most bounced harmlessly as they struck the ground. Instinctively, Jess raised the pan of uncooked hamburgers over his head for cover and ran to the safety of the porch.

Stacey came out the back door of the Lawrence house, a load of paper plates, napkins, and condiments in her hand. When she saw the burgers, she picked an acorn off the top of one and said, "No wonder you wanted me to help with dinner tonight. Obviously, you have a lot to learn about seasonings."

"You mean you don't want to try a nut burger? The squirrels around here love them."

"I think I'll pass." She nodded toward Jonathan who was still high in the tree. "He seems to have more energy today."

"It's Saturday. I let him sleep till noon. It was eerie. He's never slept past seven o'clock until a couple of weeks ago. I kept going upstairs to make sure he was breathing." He held up his hands. "I know. I sound like a paranoid father."

"No. You sound like someone who cares." She lowered her voice so Jon couldn't hear. "I had a really strange visitor at school yesterday."

"Who?"

"Derek's mother."

"Is Derek the hair-chopping, ocean-eradicating maniac who gives grossly inaccurate sex education lessons in his spare time?"

Stacey laughed. "The very one."

"What did his mother want?"

"She wanted to know how I did it."

"Did what?"

"That's exactly what I asked her. I didn't have a clue what she was talking about. She wanted to know how

I changed Derek's behavior so drastically in only six weeks."

"So he's no longer the terror he was when school first opened? I couldn't believe some of the things Jon told me he did. Especially the obscenities he called you when you took him to the principal the first day."

"I suppose Jon repeated every word."

"Just repeated? I wish. He wanted definitions! Complete, accurate, anatomically correct definitions."

Stacey grinned. "Sorry about that. At any rate, I hadn't really thought about it until his mother came in yesterday, but Derek has changed. It's like he matured overnight. One day he was a cretin, the next an almost normal little boy. He actually said 'thank you' to his mother for fixing his breakfast. That's why she came in to see me. Surprisingly enough, his mother is a very nice woman. Apparently, they've been going to counseling for years trying to correct his behavior problems and nothing had helped. Now she thinks I'm some sort of miracle worker and I don't have a clue what really happened."

"Seems pretty obvious to me." Jess took her face in his hands and looked into her eyes. "You cast your spell on him, just like you did me."

He kissed her lips tenderly until Jonathan yelled, "Ooohh, gross, Dad!" They broke apart, laughing, but kept a discreet distance.

Stacey began spreading the plates and silverware on the table as she said, "You know, this has been a strange year. Most of the kids seem to have become almost . . . docile. Have you met the P.E. teacher, Judy Olender?"

Jess shook his head as he said, "No, but Jonathan loves her. He says she invents really awesome games and she plays with them instead of just telling them what to do."

"She is wonderful. The other day she told me that

my class did worse in the mile run than any other first-grade class—ever. Almost every one of them got so winded they had to sit down afterward. Don't you think that's strange?"

"You said most of them are docile. Which kids aren't?"

"Let's see. Amanda and Sloan. Oh, yes, and Meredith."

"Do those kids have anything in common?"

Stacey thought for several seconds. "They're my LD kids. Other than that, I can't think of anything else they have in common. Amanda lives in a house near school with her parents. Sloan lives in an apartment with his mother, and Meredith is being raised by her grandparents."

"LD kids?"

"Sorry. LD stands for learning disability. Amanda and Sloan are dyslexic. Meredith has an auditory processing disorder."

"Is she deaf?"

"No. Her brain doesn't process sounds in the normal way, so her lessons have to be tailored to her visual learning needs."

"Now that you mention it, I have a cousin who is exactly the opposite. He's an auditory learner, so he reads everything out loud. It's amazing how many different learning styles there are. How do you handle teaching special kids with all the others?"

"They go to lab classes in the morning, plus we have an inclusion teacher who comes to the class in the afternoon. As they get older, they'll only have an inclusion teacher."

"That must be Mrs. Stroud."

"Yes. Has Jonathan mentioned her?"

"He says she helps people read better. Apparently, she helps him, too, if he asks for it."

"That's the beauty of inclusion teaching. The special

kids aren't singled out. Inclusion teachers help every child in class who needs it. Unless someone tells the children who the inclusion teachers are specifically there to help, they'll never know."

"So why do you think these three kids haven't been tired like the rest of the class?"

Stacey sat down at the picnic table. "You make it sound like I'm working everyone else to death."

"I didn't mean to. It just seems like there has to be a reason why their behavior hasn't changed when everyone else's has."

"I read an article the other day about research that's being done on the brains of dyslexic people. Scientists now believe that dyslexics' visual and auditory processing is altered because the brain cells that transmit the signals are smaller than those in normal people." Stacey stood up and began pacing across the patio. "You know, this is getting a little scary. What if something is making the rest of the children tired?"

"Have any of the other teachers in your pod had any problems?"

"First of all, let me explain something. Most first-grade teachers would not classify having a room full of calm, quiet children as a problem."

"Excuse me. Have any of them noticed any behavioral changes in their classes?"

"No. They seem to think I'm being . . ."

"Paranoid? I don't. If this goes on much longer, I'm taking Jon in for a full physical. Lethargy could be a sign of something much more serious."

"But what could a whole class come down with that doesn't make them sick enough to stay home from school?"

"That's why I'm going to wait for a couple more weeks. If it is some mild form of the flu, then it will run its course and everything will be back to normal by the end of October. For now, I'll do a blood count on him at the clinic just to make sure he's not anemic. If he's not better soon, then he's going to the doctor. Period."

J.D. felt the bandage on his head and cringed. For some reason he couldn't keep from touching it, even though time after time it hurt when he did. He stared down at the Citrinol3 telephone logs and surveillance reports and tried harder to concentrate. More than half the children's parents had now voiced concern over the substantial drop in their children's activity level. Surprisingly, most of them seemed happy with the change.

The Lawrence boy was a concern, but nothing to worry about yet. On the other hand, Stacey Fordman, the teacher, was an interesting case. The drug's side effects seemed to hit her hard, then decrease slowly. She no longer talked to her relatives and friends about frequent headaches, and the surveillance team reported she was back to a full aerobic workout three times a week. Her oxygen absorption levels must have returned to normal. J.D. found it all quite fascinating.

The nursing home report held little interesting information. The six patients in the east wing were showing no apparent sign of any side effects of the compound, but their restricted activity levels made it almost impossible to tell. One man had a beagle that he walked three times a day, every day. The surveillance report indicated his walks had not changed, either in speed or duration.

J.D. had recommended that the Citrinol3 project be tested on several age levels, since the geriatric group's symptoms were too hard to gauge. The older people had other health problems that could mask the test results, plus some tended to suffer silently. The nursing home had been perfect for earlier project testing, but Citrinol3 wasn't like SynCur6, whose early side effect had been a quick death that perfectly mimicked a heart attack. As he read through the rest of the reports on the children, he was pleased that his foresight was paying off.

The knock on his office door made him quickly cover his current work with a stack of legitimate project status reports. "Come in," he called.

JoAnn shyly poked her head in the door. "Am I still welcome?"

"Of course you are. Why would you even ask?"

"When you left my house last night you weren't exactly in a friendly state of mind."

"I'm sorry. I guess my temper got the best of me." He reached up and touched the bandage again. "Plus, I had one hell of a headache."

"I'm sure you did. I want you to know how sorry I am that it happened."

"It was an accident. Don't worry about it."

"You just seemed so upset . . ."

"So you've found my flaw. I have a nasty temper, inherited it from my crazy Irish grandfather. But don't worry, it passes quickly and it's only verbal. I just tend to vent my anger long and loud. Did I scare you?"

"A little. To be honest, I was afraid you would hurt the puppies . . . or me. Your eyes were wild."

He walked over and hugged her. "I'd no sooner hurt the puppies than I would hurt you. The best thing you can do when I get mad is stay away from me for ten or twenty minutes. Give me time to blow off steam and then I'll be fine. I promise, it doesn't happen very often. Deal?"

"Deal. How's your head?"

"Great. I'll bet I end up with a nice rugged-looking scar. I hear women are crazy about men who look tough."

"Tough or battered? People will probably see us together and think I'm one of those husband beaters."

"So that's it." He grabbed her and started to tickle her. "You pushed me into the nightstand, didn't you! Admit it, or I won't quit!"

Laughing, she answered, "I didn't push you, you moron. I waited until you were sound asleep, then I smashed you in the head with a brick. Obviously, you don't know much about husband beaters."

"Probably because I'm not a husband."

"Touché. And never will be one?"

"I didn't say that. Although at my age some people would argue it wouldn't be a very wise idea."

"How ancient are you, anyway?"

"You first. And by the way, remember I have access to your personnel records, so lying isn't an option."

"Why would I lie? I'm thirty-six." She plucked a grey hair from his temple and after carefully examining it said, "Let me guess. Forty-six, give or take a year."

"Forty-five. How did you do that?"

"Your aura. It's kind of a pinkish-green. Men start mellowing after forty-five, the potency of their auras drops dramatically. You know, just like in *other* areas of their life."

He stepped back and looked at her as if she were a total stranger. Finally, he said, "Aura, my ass. You must have seen my driver's license or something."

"The memory really is the first thing to go. Remember? I filled out the form at the minor emergency center last night. It had your birthday on it. Having a photographic memory comes in handy every once in a while. By the way, I can't wait until January. You gave me two Yorkie puppies. I think giving you two Newfoundland puppies would be an appropriate payback."

"Aren't those the huge black beasts that look more like bears than dogs?"

"You bet. They'd be perfect companions for you."

"Sorry. My condo doesn't allow pets, or monster dogs for that matter." He moved back, grabbing her and whirling her around until her legs were trapped against his desk. "I already know what you can give me for my birthday."

"Now, now. Not here, remember?" she said.

"I remember. Who made up that stupid rule, anyway?"

"We both know it isn't stupid."

He suddenly wondered if his office was bugged. The last thing he needed was the guys in Security snickering through another one of his sexual encounters, then passing the tape up the corporate ladder. He backed away from her, his hands raised in surrender as he walked around to the other side of his desk. "You're right. Absolutely right, as usual, JoAnn." Picking up his pen he said, "Let's make it official. What time is good for you tonight?"

"How about eight?"

"Your place or mine?"

"Yours. I'd like to see what kind of elegant place doesn't allow pets. The first major cold front is supposed to be here today. You do have a fireplace, don't you?"

"Actually, I have three. One connecting the den and the kitchen. One in the living room, and one in the master bedroom."

"How exciting. I'll bring some marshmallows."

"I'll pick you up at eight, we can stop for a light dinner, then savor an evening of romance." J.D. winked and added, "Once mine gets roasted will you lick it off my stick?"

"We'll see," she said.

J.D. reached over and scribbled "JR/8/M" on his desk calendar. "Now it's official. Once you're on my schedule there's no backing out."

JoAnn's stomach tightened as she looked at the abbreviations. With great effort she asked as casually as she could, "Obviously the 'JR' stands for JoAnn Rayburn, and the '8' is for eight o'clock tonight. But what's the 'M' for?"

"My place."

"And if it was going to be at my house?"

"An 'H,' for hers, of course."

"Of course."

It was midnight when JoAnn got home, her feelings confused. Exhaustion mixed with sexual fulfillment was effectively stifling the warning signals her mind had been sending since she'd seen J.D.'s calendar that morning. She thought about pulling Hanna's book out again, but she knew it wouldn't do any good. Every letter in it had long ago been burned into her memory.

Coincidence. The calendar abbreviations have to be a coincidence. Hanna and J.D. must have attended the same supervisory school, learned similar time management techniques.

She stood shivering outside while Rocky and Bell took care of business, then grabbed them and ran upstairs. Throwing off her clothes, she dug through her bureau and found her favorite pair of flannel pajamas. Once she was under the covers, she snatched the telephone and dialed J.D.'s number while Rocky tried in vain to get Bell to play with him.

"Hello, JoAnn," he said.

"Hi. What if it hadn't been me?"

"I guess it could have been one of the other six women I'm stringing along right now. That could be quite embarrassing. From now on, I'll just answer 'Hello, gorgeous.' That way none of you will catch on to the others."

"Six, huh?"

"Used to be ten, but you know how us old guys start to lose our potency."

"I haven't noticed. Believe it or not, I actually have a reason why I called."

"Of course you do. You're mad about me and you can't stand to be away from my body longer than ten minutes. Right?"

"Wrong, Mr. Ego. I was wondering if your offer to take a management course is still open." She took a deep breath and lied, "I remember Hanna mentioning the one she attended was excellent."

"I'll see if I can find out which program she took. If it was when she first started, it probably isn't offered anymore. Our Human Resources department stays current. Only the latest and greatest techniques for TechLab, you know."

"And its VP's."

"Why thank you, gorgeous. Get some sleep. You have miracles to work tomorrow."

"I thought I worked miracles tonight."

"You did. Go to sleep."

"Good night," she said.

"Tomorrow," he said and hung up.

JoAnn felt the familiar curl of doubt run through her as she hung up the phone. *Could he be using me? How well did he really know Hanna? Why would Hanna warn me about TechLab unless something is gravely wrong there? Should I try to find another job, leave everything I've ever worked for behind? Maybe I should confide in J.D., tell him about the calendar and the letter. He might be able to explain things. Or he might be the one who killed her.* JoAnn turned over, smashing her fist into her pillow as if she could physically push the thoughts plaguing her away.

Hours later, JoAnn was finally sound asleep. Rocky was wrapped snugly around the top of her head like a warm furry hat, but Bell was restless under the covers at her side.

A cold, slimy sensation gradually brought JoAnn out of her dreams. When she managed to groggily switch on the reading lamp by her bed, she gasped at the pool of dark blood on the sheets beside her.

Chapter 7

"I'm sorry to bother you at this hour, Dr. Lawrence, but I think this is an emergency. This is JoAnn Rayburn. You said it was all right to call you at home."

"Of course, what's the problem?"

"Bell is bleeding."

Jess was instantly awake even though it was four a.m. "What kind of injury is it?"

"That's the problem. There isn't an injury. We were asleep and when I woke up there was blood on the sheets."

"Stay calm. Wrap her up and bring her to the clinic. I'll meet you there in ten minutes. Okay?"

"Thank you. I'll be right there."

Jess pulled on a pair of blue jeans and was halfway down the stairs before he remembered Jonathan. He bounded back up and scooped him into his arms. To his amazement, Jon stirred a little as he carried him downstairs and then laid him in the back of the Jeep, but he never woke up.

He was unlocking the back door to the clinic when JoAnn's sleek black Lexus pulled into the parking lot. He rushed over, gently taking the sick puppy from her. "Come in this way," he told her.

They entered the central hallway, and Jess pointed into his office. "Put Rocky in there until we're through examining Bell. I'll need to get blood and stool samples. I'm afraid I'll need your help holding her down. Are you squeamish?"

"In my line of work, I can't afford to be. You just tell me what to do."

They worked well as a team. After collecting the specimens, Jess took the slides into his office and asked JoAnn to join him.

"Let's see what we're dealing with here."

He removed the slide of Jon's blood he had worked on the day before and positioned the new sample. After focusing and studying it for several seconds he said, "Coccidia. She'll be fine. It's relatively easy to treat. Have a look."

"Thank God." JoAnn walked over and gazed at the slide for several seconds. "Is it a parasitic protozoa?"

"Excellent diagnosis. Usually found in the digestive epithelium of vertebrates. Quite common in dogs."

"How did she get it?"

"She was probably exposed at the kennel. We'll check Rocky, too. Most likely he was exposed at the same time, although some dogs are never adversely affected."

"I can't tell you how much I appreciate this."

"Times like these are exactly why I became a vet."

JoAnn glanced down and noticed the slide Jess had laid aside. It was marked "Jon L." with the date. "Is that a specimen of your son's blood?"

"I know it seems odd, but he's been so tired. I thought I'd do a blood count and see if he was anemic." He laughed and added, "You'd have thought I'd chopped off his arm when I pricked his finger."

"How did the test come out?"

"Normal red and white count. I've made him an appointment for a full checkup next week. Maybe some more sophisticated tests can turn up something."

"Mind if I have a look?"

"Not at all. I'm going to check on Jon. He's asleep in the back of the Cherokee."

JoAnn positioned the slide and stared at it for a few

seconds, certain she was imagining things. When Jess returned she said, "Why don't I pay back this morning's favor? We have the most sophisticated testing equipment in the world available at TechLab. I can run a few tests, maybe eliminate some possibilities for you."

"I wouldn't want you to get into any trouble."

"I won't. I have total discretion over the tests I run. I just wish I had more to work with."

"Jon hates being poked or having blood drawn."

"Then we'll see what we can do with what little we have."

"Fine. I'll be anxiously waiting."

"Is this an answering service?"

"Yes, ma'am. The lines at Independent Testing Labs must all be busy. Their phones automatically forward here. May I be of some assistance?"

"I'd like to speak to Parker McDaniel."

"I can get a message to him for you. I'm sure he'd be happy to return the call."

She took a breath, then said, "All right. Please tell him Grace Milliken called. I need to speak to him right away."

"I'll forward the message to him as soon as possible, Ms. Milliken. Have a nice day."

Grace hung up the phone. She hadn't planned to really go through with damaging the unit ITL had installed, but now she had no choice. Parker would be expecting her to have called for a good reason.

She slid open her drawer and took out a screwdriver. Late tonight she would come back and carefully do something to the motor that he would need to have repaired. No one else would ever know. After all, it was October and that particular classroom really didn't need special air-conditioning at this time of year.

Then it dawned on her. Kids were constantly setting off fire alarms and telling lies even though telling the truth got them in far less trouble. She put the screwdriver back in her drawer and smiled when she realized she could merely say the kids had tampered with the equipment. Finally, after twenty-seven years of teaching and administrative work, a childish, asinine stunt would come in handy.

◆ The thought of leaving Bell and Rocky home alone that day was too much for JoAnn to bear. She decided to take them to work with her, knowing that no one would ever know they were hidden in her office if she arrived early and left at her usual late hour. Bell snuggled in her lap as they drove over, while Rocky continued his investigation under the seats of the Lexus. JoAnn hoped he didn't uncover anything else.

Between the letter and the hidden calendar, she didn't know what to think of Hanna. Both actions could easily fall under the category of paranoia. What if Hanna had been ill? She certainly hadn't acted unstable at work, at least not in front of JoAnn. Besides, she was murdered. Maybe she had good reason to be paranoid. If so, then her warning was real and should be taken seriously . . .

JoAnn shook her head. She had too much work to do to waste valuable time worrying about a puzzle she couldn't solve. She parked the car and tucked the puppies inside her coat. They must have sensed her anxiety, because they held absolutely still as she walked past the security guard near the main door and onto the central elevator. When she was finally in the BioHazard wing, Rocky wiggled his head out and looked around.

"This is where I work," she said. "You guys have to be very quiet while you're here. Promise?" She looked into their eyes as if they actually understood and might miraculously answer, but their response came in soft, puppy-breath licks instead of words. Once inside her office, she shut the door and opened her briefcase. She took out two small plastic bowls, a fluffy towel, and two chew toys.

She wedged the towel in the corner behind her desk and said, "We'll pretend this is a bed, okay?" Bell circled around three times, then plopped down in the center and closed her eyes.

Rocky was too excited to sleep. He was jumping up and down, his toenails snagging JoAnn's hose. She tapped his nose and tried to sound mean when she scolded him. "Stop that!" After emptying a small plastic bag of dog food into one bowl, she filled the other with water, but Rocky was unrelenting. "Quit begging!" It was obvious he didn't want food or water, or sleep for that matter. He wanted to play, and his usual playmate was sound asleep in the corner.

In the Security surveillance room, Tom Cane was on his sixth cup of coffee, trying desperately to make it through the last hour of the graveyard shift. He had almost dozed off when JoAnn arrived. Now he was wide awake, eagerly hanging on her every word. Pushing the button on his lapel transmitter he said, "Jim! You gotta come hear this. Sounds like that Rayburn woman is gonna get it on again in her office."

"With Cook? McDaniel would probably pay for the tape this time! I'm just one floor up. I'll be there in twenty seconds."

JoAnn's voice came through loud and clear. "Don't you want to eat? Come on, Rocket Scientist, I'll show you one more time where the pretend bed is. Sometimes I wonder if there's anything between those two pointed ears of yours."

Tom cracked up. He choked on his coffee and was still trying to recover when Jim came rushing in. He grabbed a set of headphones and sat down, his face instantly reflecting total concentration.

"You hairy little beast, you're ruining my hose." There was a strange sound, like a whimper, then she said. "Lie still, I can't get my work done with you wiggling around. Can't you be more like your sister?"

Both men's eyes flew open. Jim whispered to Tom, "Now I know McDaniel will pay for it. She's doing his sister, too!"

"Lie still and be quiet or this isn't going to work!" This time they heard something like a snarl. "Quit pulling on my skirt." Her voice became almost childish as she added, "This is a brand-new, expensive silk suit. If you slobber all over it I'm going to be very upset. And being cute won't help you. You can look innocent all you want, I know the truth."

Both men jumped when a crisp, clear bark came through their headphones. They looked at each other, a mixture of confusion and speculation in their eyes.

"No barking today, understand? Pretend like you're human for a change." A pause. "If you do that again, I'll have to spank you. We can't let anyone know you're in here."

Another high-pitched bark. Tom leaned over and whispered, "This is the kinkiest thing I've ever heard." Jim nodded his agreement.

"I warned you!"

Silence.

"Okay, I'm sorry. Would you be happier in my lap?"

Silence.

"Damn it!" A whimper. "You win, you win. I've always been a sucker for big brown eyes. I'll play with you for a few minutes first, but then I have to get down to business. I have a million things to do today and I don't have time for this."

The next few minutes were more than interesting.

The men literally were on the edge of their seats as they listened. Something banged softly, then there was a guttural growling noise. A thump, a scrape, panting. Then finally, "Good boy! Give Momma a kiss." A pause, then, "I hope you're satisfied. My hose are ruined. Absolutely, totally ruined."

Stacey plugged in the iron and grabbed the remote control. For once, she had the entire evening to relax at home. No papers to grade, no aerobics class, nothing except peace and quiet, and a pile of laundry a mile high.

One of the television shows her kids were always talking about was coming on, and she wanted to watch it so she could see for herself if it was as funny as they said. Of course, what first-grade children considered amusing could prove to be hilarious, disgusting, or both. It was impossible to guess which extreme the show would fall in.

The overstuffed easy chair in the corner of the living room was piled with clothes to be ironed, so she grabbed a hand-painted blue-jean blouse and spread it on the ironing table. It was one of her favorites, the collar and yokes painted by a local Indian artist whose work was beautiful. After licking her finger, she tapped the bottom of the iron to see if it was hot, and was surprised to find it cold. She checked the setting, then followed the cord to the wall socket. Everything appeared to be working. On a hunch, she carried the iron across the room and plugged it into a different wall socket. It immediately began to hum and crackle as it heated.

From the bottom of her coat closet, she pulled out the pink toolbox her father had jokingly given her as a college graduation present. Using a screwdriver, she removed the cover from a wall socket in the kitchen that she knew worked and looked inside. Then she repeated the same process in the living room.

It didn't take an electrician to know that one of the wires had come loose inside the living-room socket. The one right beside the tiny silver thing that looked like a battery to a watch.

Stacey went back in the kitchen and looked once again at the wall socket that worked. Going back in the living room, she touched the small silver thing and was surprised when it came off in her hand. She slipped it in her pocket, then noticed it was time for the television show to start.

Tomorrow she would call maintenance and have them send an electrician. Even though she was pretty sure she could fix the problem herself, she had no desire to tempt fate or risk electrocution.

It was getting late, and JoAnn was emotionally and physically overwhelmed with disappointment, her arms and legs as heavy as her bleak mood. The series of tests she had run on the dead lab animals verified her suspicions. The inhalant format of Citrinol3 was somehow causing extensive tissue damage in the higher dosage research animals. The scheduled testing would have to be reversed and revised, a time-consuming, frustrating setback for both the project and JoAnn. She dreaded having to give the bad news to J.D. She was relieved he was out of town until late tonight. Too late for her to have to tell him.

Glancing behind her, she looked at the puppies. Bell had spent the day sleeping, obviously not back to her playful self yet. Rocky had given up hours ago on getting either of them to play with him. Now they were huddled together into balls of adorable black fur. Her spirits instantly lifted as she studied them. There was no doubt about it, they had filled a void in her life that she hadn't even realized existed.

JoAnn opened her attaché case and began stacking papers and puppy supplies inside. She was almost finished when she noticed the envelope holding the Lawrence child's specimen tucked into the upper storage pocket of her briefcase. She had been so busy, so obsessed with Citrinol3, she had forgotten all about it.

The surveillance technician practically ripped the headset off when the shrill feedback from the Fordman apartment ripped through him. Having done surveillance for twenty years, he knew exactly what had happened. Someone had just found a device.

He picked up the phone and called the emergency number listed. "Station one here. I'm looking at an apparent equipment breach."

"Location?"

"D-12. Fordman. Apartment."

"Activate Sparky."

"Yes, sir." He opened a slender grey box and withdrew the sender marked "Fordman." Pulling up the file on the computer, he printed the information and shoved it into his pocket. Jogging downstairs, he jumped into the black Ford pickup truck and headed to the address shown on the printout. As he passed the address, he held down the signal button. In his mind, he could hear the hissing, picture the small white-hot flare firing from Sparky. By the time he rounded the corner, he was confident that the mattress was smoldering, and what little was left of the incendiary device was rapidly disappearing. The rest would be washed away by the fire department or removed by the company's recovery team after things had settled down in the morning.

Sometimes he hated this job. The Fordman woman's curiosity may have just killed her, not to mention the other unfortunate people who lived nearby.

* * *

Stacey grumbled when she smelled something faintly burning. She was sure it was the iron overheating, so she turned it off and unplugged it. Obviously, tonight was not destined to be the night she caught up on her chores. The light smoky smell persisted as she collapsed the ironing board and stored it in the closet, but she was certain it was her imagination. The iron was cooling on top of the stove, there was no way it could hurt anything.

Although the television show was really pretty funny, she wasn't in the mood to just sit and idly watch anything. For some reason, she was tightly wound, a ball of nervous energy. Her jean jacket was hanging by the door, so she grabbed it and her keys and headed outside for a brisk walk. The evening air was crisp and clear, and the stiff breeze brought freshly fallen leaves with each gust. It wasn't long before she felt better, and she slowed her frantic pace, falling into a leisurely stride that helped clear her mind and settle her nerves.

Inside Stacey's empty apartment, the smoke detector beeped wildly. The small, white-hot flare had easily ignited the mattress, and now flames jumped effortlessly from the curtains to the carpet. Some crawled into the closet, while others headed for the living room.

Throughout the building, smoke detectors began to scream in unison. While some of the residents selfishly ran, others warned neighbors whose names they didn't even know as they fled. Some grabbed a few prized possessions on their way out, but most left without looking back. Outside, the group gathered solemnly together to watch their lives change forever. Some prayed, others gossiped, already trying to blame someone else for their misfortune.

* * *

Stacey heard the first fire engine pass nearby, the wailing of its siren winding down a few blocks away. When the second engine came flying right past her, she suddenly became anxious, a sense of alarm growing from deep inside. The light smell of smoke she'd left behind nagged at her, evolving into a compelling force. Hurried steps quickly became a jog, then an all-out sprint as she headed back toward her apartment.

Once she rounded the corner, she stopped dead in her tracks. There was no hurry. Flames poured from her living-room window and from the apartment above hers as well. The firemen worked quickly, hauling equipment and hoses into the smoke-filled belly of the building. The street was a display of organized confusion, the emergency personnel trying to perform their jobs around the gathering sightseers.

Stacey stepped back, leaning against a lamppost for support. She felt numb and confused, but most of all, she felt lost. Pushing herself, she headed down the street, away from the fire. A few blocks away, she found a pay phone near a convenience store and searched her pockets. She quickly realized she had no money, only the little batterylike thing she'd found in the wall socket. Tears sprang to her eyes when she realized she didn't even have a quarter to call her parents. Maybe the clerk inside the store would have pity on her and let her use his telephone.

Taking a deep breath, she forced the tears back. *Why upset them? They're five hundred miles away, they can't help tonight anyway. Let them get a good night's rest.*

I can handle this. Things will be back to normal in no time. Jess. Jess will help. Please, Jess, help.

By eleven p.m. JoAnn was so exhausted she wasn't sure she was seeing clearly. The first series of hematology tests she ran on Jonathan Lawrence's blood showed the same variable red cell damage her Citrinol3 tests had shown in the experiment animals. It was getting ridiculously late, but she ran the tests again.

She knew it was impossible, even absurd, yet nevertheless, every time she looked down, the test results practically screamed at her. Was she imagining things? Having stress-induced hallucinations? Had she worked on the Citrinol3 project so long that her judgment was impaired? Or was she just too damned tired to accurately perform the tests?

Walking slowly across the room, she pushed the button on the side of the small silver door. It slid open, and she pulled out a cylindrical pneumatic tube. Twisting the top of it sideways, she withdrew the protective foam casing, coded the specimens, and laid them gently inside. Covering them with the other half of the foam casing, she slid the protected specimens into the tube.

Moving back to her desk, she completed the carbonless Pathology form in triplicate, listing her personal Pathology code and the code for the Citrinol3 project. She automatically wrote STAT at the top and her old office code as the return site. At the last minute she realized her mistake. Scratching out the incorrect site code, she replaced it with her new office location. Keeping the pink copy for her files, she slid the form into the tube, snapped the top closed, and placed it in the transfer position. After closing the silver door, she entered the six-digit code for the maximum security section of Pathology, then pushed the SEND button. The characteristic *whoosh* sound followed as the tube was sucked away. Within seconds it would arrive in Pathology, just another anonymous test request among the hundreds they received every day.

Thanking God the day was finally over, JoAnn scooped up the sleeping puppies, stuffed them inside her coat, and headed home.

* * *

By the time Stacey walked back to the apartment building again, the fire was under control. The frantic activity had slowed, and the firemen were cleaning up their equipment. Reluctantly, she stepped up behind the group of people she recognized as her neighbors.

Before she could say anything, she overheard an elderly man say, "So it started in 404. Whose apartment is that, anyway?"

Stacey knew she should answer, but she was too embarrassed.

An old woman answered for her, one with a wrinkled, sour face and bitter eyes. "Isn't that where that young redheaded woman lives? No telling what someone like that was up to. I've seen her with men at all hours, if you know what I mean."

"There aren't any redheads on the fourth floor. You're thinking of the one on the third floor. They evicted her about a month ago. Found out she was dealing drugs I hear."

"Then it must be that auburn-haired one. You know, the one who wears the skimpy little exercise outfits on the elevator. I think one of these days my Henry is going to bite off his own tongue when the elevator comes to a stop. It's usually hangin' almost to the floor when she's in there. People today have no sense of decency."

Stacey blushed. She did have auburn hair, and once or twice when she was in a hurry she wore her aerobics clothes home without changing. She decided it was time to end the speculation. "Excuse me, I think you may be talking about my apartment, about me."

All eyes slowly turned to her, but no one said a word.

She found one sympathetic-looking man and stared into his eyes as she asked, "Does anyone know how it started?"

Instantly the bitter old woman answered, "I heard one of them say it looked like it was from smoking in bed."

Her accusing glare sent chills down Stacey's spine. "That's impossible. I don't smoke, and as you can see, I'm certainly not in bed, nor have I been this evening."

"Maybe it was a friend of yours."

"Listen, I know it's not any of your business, but none of my friends smoke, and none of them have been in my bed."

"Maybe it wasn't cigarettes being smoked. Things can smolder for a long time, dear. Days."

"I don't care if they can smolder for years. No one was smoking in my bed. Or anywhere else in my apartment for that matter. No cigarettes, no marijuana, nothing. Understand?"

"Then what started it? I don't know about anyone else, but I'd like to know why everything I own is now ruined. What isn't burned in that building will be either smoke- or water-damaged, and I don't have insurance. I live on a fixed income, you know."

Stacey was about to mention the iron when Jess came up behind her. She turned into him, burying her head in his chest to calm her temper. *How dare they blame me? It isn't my fault she isn't insured. Or is it? I smelled smoke, I could have stopped it.*

"You okay?" he asked. He glared at the woman, ending her vicious verbal assault. Pulling Stacey away from the group he said, "Let's go sit down. My car is just around the corner. I'm so glad you called me."

Stacey was grateful for everything about him. His presence, his warmth, his very being made her feel as though the world would no longer end before the sun had time to crawl over the horizon again. Once they were inside his car she looked at him and said, "What am I going to do? It was my fault."

"What makes you think that?"

"I was ironing. I smelled something burning so I unplugged the iron. Then I left . . . and when I came back . . ."

"Where did you put the hot iron?"

"On the stove."

"Could it have fallen off?"

She shook her head. "Even if it somehow managed to fall over, it would still have been on the metal part of the stove."

"Then this can't possibly be your fault. Don't let that old biddy get to you. She'll live off this fire for the next ten years. By the time she gets through telling all her friends, she'll have turned you into a drug-crazed lunatic with a flamethrower. People like that make up whatever story best suits their needs at the time."

"I think I should talk to the fire chief."

"Sounds like a good idea to me."

They walked back around the corner and immediately spotted the chief. He was the only one wearing white safety gear and a white hat. Jess led Stacey straight to him, ignoring the stares from the people across the street.

Stacey said, "Excuse me, could I have a word with you?"

He didn't look up from his clipboard, but mumbled, "Yes, ma'am. Do you live here?"

"Yes. Apartment 404."

That caught his attention. He stopped what he was doing and looked at her. "We think the fire started in your apartment. Do you have any idea what could have happened?"

Stacey ran through the story about the iron, and even backtracked and told him about the faulty wall socket.

"Where was that wall socket located again?"

"In the living room, on the north wall just as you enter the apartment."

He shook his head. "No, ma'am, that can't be our problem. This fire definitely started in the bedroom. Near or under the bed from what we can tell, center of the east wall. A typical cigarette-related fire pattern."

"Except that I don't smoke. And I wasn't in the bedroom all evening. No one was."

"Then we need to check the scene for more evidence. Don't worry, our investigators will be able to figure it out, but not before morning. If you'll give me a number where I can reach you, I'll contact you as soon as we know anything."

Jess immediately pulled out one of his business cards and handed it to him. "You'll be able to reach her at this number," he said.

Stacey raised her eyebrows and looked at Jess, relieved when he said, "Don't even think of staying anywhere else. I won't hear of it."

Stacey asked the chief, "Can I get some personal belongings before I go?"

"There really isn't much left, ma'am. I suggest you get a good night's rest and then come back tomorrow afternoon. By then, the investigators should be finished and you can sort through what's left. Don't expect much."

Jess put his arm around her and directed her to the car.

"Did you hear that?"

"Every word."

"He made it sound like everything I own is gone."

"What about your car? Where is it parked?"

"Behind the building. I guess it's okay."

"Do you have insurance?"

"Yes. It's even the kind that pays the replacement cost of the things you lost."

"Then you have a lot to be thankful for. You'll have new furniture, a new wardrobe . . ."

"My Indian shirt is gone. It was my favorite."

"The one with the feathers painted on the lapel?"

She nodded, then laughed. "It was the only thing I ironed tonight. What a waste of time. But there is a bright side to all of this."

"What's that?"

The laughter had turned to tears as she said, "I didn't bother to iron the rest of the pile."

JoAnn kicked off her high heels as soon as she came into the house. Before doing anything else, she took the puppies outside. As she walked across the brick patio, each step snagged her already ruined hose. Feeling slightly perverted, she purposely slid her feet along the crusty surface until her hose were a mass of snags and runs. For some reason, the feel of the brick on her almost bare feet made the silliness of her worries strike her.

I've started tests over before, and I'll start them over again. Citrinol3 still has a strong foundation to work with, it just needs a little more tweaking. I have more than I've had in years. The puppies love me and so does J.D. . . . well, maybe he does. I know he cares . . .

Going inside, she peeled off the shredded panty hose and dropped them into the trash can. She opened the cabinet and grabbed the dog food, but when she tipped the bag of Puppy Chow over only three tiny pieces plopped into the empty dish. Knowing the grocery store would be deserted at this hour, she quickly decided to get the dog food now instead of postponing the trip until tomorrow when she would have to wait in line. She let the puppies inside, locked the house, and drove the short distance to the store.

JoAnn parked the Lexus directly under the only streetlight even though it was in the middle of the practically empty parking lot instead of close to the main doors. She glanced around out of habit before she opened the car door. As she sprinted from the car to the grocery store, she pushed the ARM button on her key chain to engage the car's security system. The chirp that signaled it was operational was still new to her, a sound that both pleased her and embarrassed her if people were nearby. She was not the type to flaunt her possessions, and drawing attention to herself was the last thing she ever wanted to do.

Ten minutes later she emerged carrying the puppy chow and a loaf of bread. A large Dodge van the color of rusty nails blocked her view of the Lexus as she approached it, causing her to slow her bouncy stride. She noticed the van's tag was splattered with mud, obliterating the "Oklahoma is OK!" on the bottom and making the ZHS-666 on the plate hard to read. Cautiously, she glanced through the van's tinted back windows. It appeared to be filthy inside, but empty. She sighed with relief when she confirmed the backseat of the Lexus and passenger side were empty as well.

She waited until she was at the driver's door of the Lexus before she pushed the button to disarm the car alarm. Before she opened the door, she hesitated, checking one last time to be sure no one was lurking inside the car. It never dawned on her to look down.

Chapter 8

When the sudden sensation of liquid fire crawled up JoAnn's leg she never imagined it was caused by a razor-edged knife.

What in the world was that? My God, something stung me! She grabbed for the car just as her ankle buckled, her purse and the dog food dropping to the ground. The burning, stinging pain was so intense she fell to her knees. *A wasp? No, maybe a snake? Not in a parking lot.* It wasn't until she looked down that she realized what had happened. Her foot was hanging at a very unnatural angle, blood running from a straight line across the back of her ankle where it had been sliced with a knife. The same knife that now gleamed menacingly at her from under the van as her attacker slid out from under it, grabbing her purse on his way.

Terror filled her. Screaming, she lunged to the side, but he grabbed her other leg. A rush of adrenaline gave her enough strength to kick him hard in the shoulder with her good leg, breaking her partially free as she fell backward.

He was a big, powerful man and he effortlessly grabbed at her again, this time angrily dragging her back between the two parked cars. She kicked and tried to gouge his eyes with her fingers, but her hands slid off the hosiery that masked his face.

For an instant the lamplight illuminated him. Her assailant's face was a murky brown, his features contorted by the mask into a savage grimace. Even through the tightly stretched hose, she could tell his hair was dark, and his eyes, too, seemed as black as night. He swung the razorlike knife in a silvery arc and she slammed her body against the Lexus, desperately trying to avoid its path. But fiery pain, the same brand that had claimed her ankle, ran down her face as the knife slashed into her right temple.

• His other hand grabbed her left wrist, but she struggled and pulled almost free before his grip caught. She heard her middle finger snap as a new breed of pain joined the others. Bending her good leg, she blindly kicked out at him, landing her high heel full force in his groin. He grunted in pain and curled into a ball dropping the knife long enough for her to grab it and hurl it with all her strength over the Lexus.

Although blood was rolling over her left eye, she managed to find the bag of dog food. Grabbing it, she crawled to her knees and began to scream at the top of her lungs. While she screamed, she swung the ten-pound bag of dog food blindly in the direction of the man, landing blow after blow on what she hoped was his head.

She was still screaming and flailing the tattered bag of dog food when she realized the van was gone and people were rushing toward her in slow motion. Somewhere in the distance, a siren wailed.

JoAnn leaned against the cool, smooth surface of the Lexus, laid her face on the bag of puppy chow in her arms, and just before she passed out she thought, *I wonder if this is how Hanna felt at the end.*

Her ears were ringing when she floated back. She stayed conscious long enough to see a swarm of people in uniforms hovering above her. The one closest to her face was a fireman, and she whispered, 'Thank you," to him.

A man's voice was suddenly close to her ear saying, "Help us catch the bastard who did this to you. Do you remember anything that could help us?"

Opening her eyes she saw a pair of crystal-blue eyes slashed with gold, more like those of an exotic cat than a person. They were undoubtedly the prettiest eyes she'd ever seen, offset by lustrous jet-black hair. She wasn't sure if she was dreaming, since he seemed too handsome and perfect to be real, but she managed to whisper an answer before she faded back into the darkness.

"Dodge van, rusty. Filthy. Tag ZHS-666. Big man. Black."

At three a.m. the ringing phone sent J.D. from dead sleep to full awake with such suddenness that he felt overwhelmed with a sense of fear, as though his worse nightmare had come to life. For a second he had no idea what had awakened him, or where he was, until the phone rang again. He shook his head, trying to orient himself as he grabbed the receiver and mumbled, "Hello."

"Mr. Cook? J. D. Cook?"

"Yes. What is it?"

"This is Margaret Reynolds with Saint Francis Hospital. We've just admitted a Ms. JoAnn Rayburn and she asked that we contact you."

He yawned and rubbed his eyes as he came more awake. He asked, "Is she all right? What's wrong with her?"

"I'm sorry to say, she was attacked by a mugger in a parking lot a couple of hours ago. She didn't list any other next of kin or relatives on her admittance forms. Will you be able to come down?"

"Of course. Tell her I'll be right there." He paused

for a second, then hesitantly asked, "Was she temporarily paralyzed when she came in?"

There was a long pause, then the woman finally said, "I'm sorry, sir, I don't know anything about her admittance condition. I can tell you that she is out of surgery and is currently listed as stable. By the time you arrive, she will have been assigned a room. You'll need to check at the front desk to find out her room number."

"I appreciate the call. I'll be right there."

He hung up, then stared at the phone as he tried to absorb the news. Why would they target JoAnn? Had her office surveillance turned up something suspicious? If it did, then why didn't they contact him before taking action? Surely that son of a bitch wasn't killing people now for no reason. Or was he?

His stomach knotted as he realized the answer could mean a bigger problem. He, too, must be a suspect for some reason, or they would have included him in the plan to eliminate JoAnn.

Memories of the SynCur6 test videos ran through his mind. Accounts of those who'd been drugged recalling every sensation of pain they felt while the SynCur6 rendered their bodies totally useless. For the first time he could remember, J.D. felt vulnerable. He reached into the nightstand, withdrew the weapon, and laid it on the bed beside him. It was obvious he would need to start being more careful. Very careful.

Jess heard the squeak again, this time certain it wasn't his imagination. He checked the clock beside his bed. Four a.m. With every fiber in his being he lay still and listened. Whatever was making the noise was definitely upstairs.

Wearing only his boxer shorts, he went into the hall and grabbed a baseball bat that was beside the door.

He climbed the steps slowly, careful not to make a sound. Just as he rounded the corner at the top of the stairs, he ran into something, no someone, in the dark.

A scream followed. Even in the darkness and commotion, he recognized Stacey and dropped the bat to his side as he flipped on the hall light. "I'm sorry. I didn't know you were up."

Stacey was holding her hands to her chest. She looked tired, yet incredibly sexy in the pajama top he'd loaned to her. "You scared me half to death," she mumbled.

"I thought you were a burglar."

"I'm sorry. I couldn't sleep. I was just pacing back and forth. It helps me think."

"I'll remember that. I thought maybe we had a fifty-pound mouse. Did all that pacing help any?"

"I decided not to try and teach tomorrow. I'm going to take the day off. I need some basics. Toothbrush, makeup, clothes. I realized I don't even have a purse anymore, not to mention credit cards or money."

"I'll loan you whatever you need."

"You've been so nice. But I won't need a loan. All I need is my car. I have an extra checkbook in my glove compartment. At least I had my keys with me."

"I hate to burst your bubble, but what about a driver's license? How are you planning on writing checks without any ID?"

"Shit," she said.

"Damn," he mimicked.

"Nice outfit."

Jess looked down at his boxer shorts, then at her. "Ditto." He kissed her gently, then pulled away when he felt moisture on his cheek. There were fresh tears in her eyes as she asked, "Could you take me to get a new driver's license, too?"

"I'll do even better. I'll take the day off and be your

personal chauffeur. But first you need to get some sleep. You wouldn't want to buy a new wardrobe when your judgment is impaired, would you?"

"And make a fashion blunder? Heaven forbid."

"Then I'll take Jon to school and stop by the clinic first thing in the morning. I'll be back here by ten to pick you up. Promise me you'll try to sleep awhile. No more pacing."

"I promise."

Jess had just stepped off the last stair when she called down, "You left your bat up here."

He knew better than to go back upstairs. She looked too damn good and it had been hard enough turning away the first time. He called back, "Take it with you. You may have to fight me off with it."

● Nausea was the first proof JoAnn had that she was still among the living. The second was pain.

She tried opening her eyes, but barely managed a flutter before her heavy lids fell back in place. She could feel a hand tighten on hers. Then she remembered the sickening snap of a bone, but it was a red, cloudy memory that was too fleeting to catch. A monster's hand reaching for her, his face distorted and twisted as he stabbed wildly at her. A glint of steel floating in a white light. But it was dark, there was no light, nothing made sense.

"JoAnn. Wake up. You're okay."

The words floated through her as if she weren't really there. In fact, she wasn't even sure who this person, JoAnn, was. Besides, she really didn't give a damn.

"JoAnn, it's J.D. Can you hear me?"

She forced her eyelids up for a second, long enough to see a blurry shape hovering over her and remember who J.D. was.

"That's good. Try a little harder. The nurse is going to get the doctor so she can see you're doing better."

This time her eyes stayed open long enough to focus. When she tried to speak, her throat felt like someone had scrubbed it with sandpaper, but she managed to mutter, "What happened? Where am I?"

"Relax. You're going to be fine."

She blinked and glared at him, obviously wanting a better answer. "What happened?" she growled.

"You were attacked in the parking lot of the grocery store by your house. Do you remember anything?"

"Monster."

"Monster?" His voice was heavy with skepticism.

"Hose on face . . . Like monster . . . Knife?"

"Yes. He had a knife."

"Hurt me?"

"I'm afraid so. He cut your left Achilles tendon, broke your left middle finger, and you have a nasty wound on your head. They've already done surgery to repair the tendon, set the finger, and stitched your temple." He smiled and squeezed her hand as he said, "I suppose you arranged all this because you were jealous of my scar. If it makes you feel any better, it looks like mine will be bigger."

She rolled her eyes.

"Sweetheart, did you notice anything odd about the man who attacked you? Any particular odor or distinguishing marks?"

"Dirty."

"He was dirty?"

"Yes. Body odor. Van dirty, too." She coughed, grimacing from the pain it ignited everywhere from her dry throat to her sore toes.

"Did you smell anything besides body odor? Maybe a sweet smell, like vanilla?"

"No. He was big. Stunk." She smiled. "I won. Kicked him where it hurts."

"Is that why he left?"

"Dog food."

"What?"

"Too hard to explain. Can I still jog?"

"You're worried whether you'll be able to jog again?" He shook his head. "You amaze me. You're lucky to be alive and you want to know if you can run. The answer is, I don't know. But your doctor should be here soon, you can ask her."

"Purse?"

"The police found most of what was in it behind the store. Your wallet and credit cards are gone, of course, but he didn't take your TechLab ID. I guess he didn't care to get into the BioHazard wing."

"Smart guy." She raised her eyebrows and said, "Cancel credit cards?"

"Will I cancel your credit cards for you?"

She nodded.

"Sure. Do you have the numbers listed somewhere?"

"Home. Rolodex on rolltop desk in den."

"I'll do it as soon as I leave here. Don't worry about it. Is the key still in the same pot out front?"

She tried to nod, but winced in pain again. After catching her breath she whispered, "Puppies?"

"I'll feed them and let them out to play. You just get well. Promise?"

"Work. Need to work."

"Not for a while, pretty lady. You're only going to rest."

The room was beginning to spin, and her stomach was warning her to relax, but she fought long enough to say, "Can't. Know Citrinol problem now. Inhalant . . ."

"Shhh. We'll talk about it later. Right now, you relax."

JoAnn closed her eyes, not wanting to give in to sleep, yet thankful for the peaceful retreat it gave her from the pain.

It took J.D. a long time to make it from JoAnn's hospital room to her house. Even though the attack didn't sound like the work of a normal TechLab hired goon, he wasn't going to take any chances. At every stoplight, he watched his rearview mirror, his hand resting on the semiautomatic pistol lying on the passenger seat beside him. The feel of the canister of Syn-Cur6 in his jacket was even more comfort to him. No one seemed to be following him, but deep down he was smart enough to know he'd only see them coming if they wanted him to, which was crazy. Why make a scene? A little dose of SynCur6 sprayed within twelve feet of the target guaranteed two hours of paralysis. Plenty of time to creatively dispose of any evidence and the body. Or bodies, depending on the motive.

Pulling into her driveway, he was surprised to see JoAnn's house was well lit. The living-room lights glistened through the front windows as if she were home, making going inside seem eerie. J.D. found the key and unlocked the door. From down the hall he could hear something coming. He braced himself, his finger tightly gripping the trigger of the gun.

Then he saw them. The puppies were bounding toward him, excited balls of energy. When they reached his feet, they were jumping and barking playfully. He ignored them as he walked straight through the house to put them outside. Once he was alone, he went to the kitchen to find their food. After searching the cabinets to no avail, he realized JoAnn must have run out of dog food. That was probably what she was trying to tell him at the hospital about the attack. Her life was now in a state of total turmoil over a stupid bag of dog food.

He opened the refrigerator, grabbed a container of cottage cheese, a bowl of leftover rice, and dumped them into a dish. As soon as he put the food outside the door, Rocket and Nobel attacked it as if they'd never eaten a day in their lives. In less than two minutes they were licking the empty dish greedily, each trying to cheat the other out of the last tasty grains of rice clinging to the edge.

J.D. easily found the desk in JoAnn's den where she said her credit cards were listed. The Rolodex was on the top right corner, near the phone, so he sat down and pulled it to him. He flipped to the section marked "V," thinking he would find Visa, but there were no "V" cards at all. He tried "M" for MasterCard, and "D" for Discover with no luck as well. Finally, he looked through each letter, recognizing a few of the names from work. Under "E" was a card marked "Emergency Information." All her credit cards were neatly listed on one card, as well as the telephone numbers to call to cancel them.

J.D. sat down at the desk and began dialing. By the time the last credit card company put him on hold, he was getting impatient with the entire process. Out of boredom, he opened the top drawer of JoAnn's desk to look around. There were plenty of paper clips, postage stamps, pens, and mechanical pencils. To the back, he could barely see the edge of a leather-bound book.

Rolling the chair back, he pulled the drawer out as far as it would go. He didn't need to see the gold initials—H E S—to know what it was he had found. After all, he had special ordered it just last Christmas for Hanna.

* * *

The cheerful voices of the *Good Morning Oklahoma!* news team echoed through the kitchen of the Lawrence house as Jess pulled up the miniblinds so he could catch the sunrise. Moving slowly, he filled a container with cold water, measured exactly four tiny scoops of coffee grounds, then poured the water into the top of the coffee machine. As he did every morning, he plodded outside in his boxer shorts and grabbed the newspaper from the driveway. The crispness of fall was finally reaching Oklahoma, and he shivered as he ran barefoot back inside. He glanced up at the guest-room window, wondering if Stacey had ever fallen asleep.

The coffee was brewed when he returned, so he poured a cup and sat down to read the paper. There was a small story inside the City/State section of the *Tulsa World* about an unidentified woman who was attacked late last night, but he quickly scanned it and went on.

Just as he was about to start back into the master bedroom to shower and shave, the cheerful anchorwoman sobered and began the story of the midnight attack of a local woman at a grocery store that was only two miles from his clinic. He stared in disbelief as footage rolled of a woman being loaded into an ambulance filled the screen. The words "Midnight Mugging Victim" were superimposed below as the camera zoomed in to show her bloody face.

Even though the newswoman said they were waiting to release the victim's identity until notification of relatives, Jess knew exactly who it was. He instantly knew what he needed to do. Glancing down at his watch, he realized he would have to hurry.

When he came out of the shower, Jonathan was groggily standing at his bedside.

"You're not going to believe this, Dad. The guest-room door was closed when I walked by, so I opened it. Ms. Fordman is asleep upstairs." He grabbed Jess's hand and pulled him toward the door. "Really. I'm not making it up."

"I know you aren't, Jon. Ms. Fordman spent the night here last night. You were already asleep when she called me, so I had Mrs. Cox from next door stay here while I went to get her. Her apartment burned last night, so she needed someplace to stay. Is she asleep?"

"Yes. Did she get hurt?"

"No. She was very lucky."

"What about her stuff?"

"Pretty much all gone."

"That's sad. I wouldn't want to have my stuff burn up."

"Neither would I. That's why we'll be extra nice to her, okay?"

"Sure. You really like her, don't you, Dad?"

"I really do, Jon. Does that bother you?"

"Will she be my stepmom? Kids at school say step-moms are mean."

"Remember when we talked about lumping people all together?"

"I know. Everyone deserves a chance."

"Right. Not all stepmoms are mean, and not all stepmoms are nice, but everyone deserves a chance."

"She'd be nice, I can tell. So is she gonna be my step-mom or not?"

"I don't know yet, and I don't want you to ask her about it. She has enough things to worry about right now without us bugging her."

"Okay."

"Want a donut for breakfast?"

"Sure! Can I have a dozen donut holes instead?" His smile suddenly faded. "You aren't going to make me go to the doctor, are you?"

"Not today. We're going to go pick up some puppies who need a place to stay for a while. We can keep them here at the house if you'll promise to help take care of them."

"Awesome! Ms. Fordman *and* puppies staying with us. This is gonna be sooo cool."

The morning brought JoAnn back to harsh reality. Her doctor thoroughly outlined her course of recovery, pointing out the degree of pain and therapy involved in rehabilitating her severed Achilles tendon. JoAnn didn't wallow in self-pity as some patients do. Instead, she became determined to get back to the lab as soon as possible. Her work couldn't wait.

JoAnn was mentally outlining her plan to return when she was interrupted by a light knock on the door. "Come in," she called, her throat already feeling better.

Jess and Jonathan Lawrence walked cautiously to her bedside.

She smiled and quietly said, "My gosh, bad news really does travel fast. How in the world did you find out so quickly?"

Jess said, "You're the lead story on every local news program this morning. Are you all right?"

"I've definitely been better."

Jonathan held out a bouquet of flowers from the hospital's gift shop. "We brought you these to cheer you up," he said. He stared at the IV tube going into her arm. Shaking his head he said, "I'll bet that hurts. Dad does it to the dogs and cats who are really sick and they don't like it at all. I hope they never do it to me. It was gross enough when they took my blood. Did they do that to you, too? Take your blood, I mean."

"I'm afraid so. Of course, considering the condition I was in at the time, I really didn't even feel it."

"Why did that man hurt you?"

Jess nudged his son as he glared and said, "I thought we weren't going to talk about that, Jon."

JoAnn slightly waved her bandaged left hand. "It's okay. Kids need to ask questions." She took his small hand in her good one and said, "Jonathan, I don't know why he hurt me. I suppose he wanted the money in my purse, my credit cards, or maybe even my car."

"But you'd have given them to him without him hurting you, right?"

She thought about that for a second, then said, "I don't honestly know. I believe in right and wrong, and I probably would have instinctively fought for the right thing. He shouldn't have tried to steal someone else's money. What he did was very wrong."

"What's 'instinkily' mean?"

She laughed. "It means some things just come naturally to people. Like breathing."

"And rollerblading?"

"I suppose rollerblading is instinctive for some little boys. It certainly wouldn't be for me. I'm sure your dad has explained that there are good people and bad people in the world. Sometimes bad things happen for no apparent reason to good people."

"Like random acts of violence?"

Jess looked sideways at his son and asked, "How do you know about that?"

" 'Cause there's a sign in our school that says we should do a 'Random Act of Kindness' each day. The teacher told us a really nice guy started a very awesome campaign to get people to treat each other better. Doing something nice for someone else makes both people happy." He grabbed his father's hand. "Like why we came to the hospital, Dad."

JoAnn looked at Jess and said, "It was very nice of you to come by so early in the morning. The flowers are beautiful and I feel better already. Is Jon going to miss school this morning?"

Jess glanced at his watch. "No, we still have an hour. We came by to see if we could puppy-sit for you until you're better. We have a big house with a fenced backyard. I'm sure the Yorkies would have a great time playing with Jonathan, and I happen to know a little bit about caring for animals."

Tears came to her eyes. She barely knew them, yet they were there to help her. "I think that's the nicest thing anyone has ever offered to do for me." Looking at Jonathan she said, "You'd have to promise me something, though."

"What?"

"They like to sleep snuggled next to someone who loves them. Would you let them sleep with you?"

He looked up at his dad expectantly. When Jess nodded, Jon said, "You bet! I'll get Rocky and Bell each a pillow of their very own. It'll be awesome. Can I take them to show and tell one day?"

"Sure. There's a key in the flower pot next to the front steps. Just feel around for it. I can't tell you how much I appreciate it."

"It'll be fun, won't it, Jon?"

"Yep. I hope you get well soon, Ms. Rayburn. But not too fast. I want to have time to teach the puppies some tricks."

They were about to leave when JoAnn said, "Oh, by the way, I'll have the results from that blood sample of yours as soon as I get back to work. It's probably already in my office."

Jess smiled and said, "It can wait. You just get well."

He drove straight to JoAnn's house. Before he could

even open his car door, Jonathan had jumped out and was searching through the flower pot for the key. He shrieked and jumped up and down when he found the hidden treasure.

Together they walked up the brick stairs to the front door, admiring the meticulous landscaping. Jess instinctively pushed Jonathan behind him when he realized the key Jon so proudly held wouldn't be needed. The front door was standing wide open.

Chapter 9

Jess grabbed Jonathan by the shoulders and whisked him around. He sternly said, "Go wait in the car, Jonathan."

"Why?"

"Because I said so." He gave him a shove in the right direction and said, "Lock the car doors and wait. Call 911 on the car phone if you get scared. Don't open the door for anyone except me. Got it?"

Jon hung his head and slowly walked back down the stairs, repeatedly flashing a nasty glare at his father. When Jess was sure Jon was safely locked inside the car, he approached the open door and yelled, "Anyone here?"

Dead silence filled the air. Very slowly, he crept inside. The furniture was overturned and JoAnn's things were strewn across the room. With disgust he noticed her paintings were slashed, cushions and upholstery viciously ripped, and vases shattered. In the next room, the drawers of her large rolltop desk were strewn across the room and papers were scattered everywhere. Jess suddenly remembered the puppies.

"Rocky! Bell! Here, puppies." He whistled and tried again, "Rocket! Nobel!" Each time he entered a room, he was afraid he would find them. They were so small and fragile. Then he realized they could easily have escaped out the front door. They might be wandering lost around the neighborhood.

Jess found a telephone on the kitchen wall and dialed 911 to report the burglary, then continued cautiously through the house. Apparently, the thief wasn't in any hurry. The entire house was a mess. He was about to go back downstairs when he heard a weak whimper. Searching the room, he found Rocky and Bell hiding under the bed. Both were shaking frantically, obviously terrified.

"It's okay, babies. Come here." He lay on his stomach and wiggled his arms under the bed until he could reach them. One by one he pulled them out. Rushing into the bathroom, he grabbed a bath towel and wrapped them up, then raced downstairs.

By the time he reached the car, Jonathan was panicked, his shaking hand already dialing the cellular phone. "Dad. I was really scared. Are you okay?"

"I'm fine." He handed the puppies to Jon just as the first sound of a siren in the distance reached them. "You need to keep them warm."

"They're shivering, Dad."

"I know. They may be going into shock. As soon as I tell the police what happened, we'll get them to the clinic and check them over. Meanwhile, you make sure they feel safe and warm. Okay?"

"I will, Dad. I will."

Two police units arrived, and Jess greeted the officers at the bottom of the driveway. As they walked to the house Jess explained, "This is JoAnn Rayburn's house. She is the woman who was attacked last night at the grocery store not far from here. When we came to get her puppies, we found the front door open and the house vandalized."

The young officer answered, "Not surprising. Didn't the guy get her purse? He would have known her address from her driver's license, probably even had a house key. He knew he hurt her bad enough that she wouldn't be back home for a while. Unfortunately, burglaries are tied to muggings all too often. I'll call

dispatch and have them patch me through to Detective
Kent. I'm sure he'll want to check the place out."

Jess followed the officer inside as he placed his call.
Surprisingly, the detective responded almost immediately and Jess eavesdropped on their conversation.

"I'll be right over, but I don't think the burglary is
related to the attack."

"Really? Why not?"

"Ms. Rayburn gave us a description of the van her
attacker was driving. She even remembered the license plate. We arrested a guy matching the description she gave us less than thirty minutes after she was
assaulted. His clothes were bloodstained, and with
any luck his prints will match the ones we lifted from
the knife left at the scene. He was up north, just about
a thirty-minute drive from where he attacked Ms.
Rayburn. I don't see how he could have broken in and
made it there so quickly."

By the time Jess got back to his house it was almost
eleven o'clock in the morning. Stacey was waiting patiently, wearing the same jeans and sweatshirt she'd
had on when he picked her up last night. He walked
over to her and kissed her lightly on the cheek. A faint
smell of smoke still clung to her clothes, but he didn't
mention it.

Rocky and Bell were snuggled under his lightweight leather jacket. Bell's entire being seemed to be
trembling, but Rocky's eyes curiously scanned his surroundings and he squirmed to get down. "I'm sorry
I'm late. You wouldn't believe what kind of morning
I've had."

"After last night, I'd believe anything." She reached
out and stroked the puppies. "Who are these cuties?"

He handed her Rocky. "This is Rocky, and this is
Bell."

"Why is she shaking?"

"She's had a rough couple of days. I gave her a sedative a few minutes ago, so she should start calming down any minute."

"Are they part of your hectic morning?"

He nodded. "One of my clients, JoAnn Rayburn, was attacked last night. When Jonathan and I stopped by her house to pick up her puppies, her house had been vandalized."

"She got attacked and then her house was robbed?"

He nodded.

"And I thought I had a bad night."

"To make a long story short, we offered to puppy-sit until she's back on her feet."

"So I'm not the only one you rescue. And I thought I had my very own knight in shining armor."

"You do. This knight just has a soft spot for animals."

"And kids. And greasy hamburgers with acorn seasoning."

"True. All true." He took Rocky from her and said, "I'll put these guys in the laundry room so they can nap while we're gone. Are you ready to go?"

"It doesn't take long to get ready when you only have the clothes on your back. I never realized how much time I spend putting on makeup."

"You look beautiful without it. I have a feeling we'll set some sort of shopping record today."

"Probably not. My insurance agent says I have to submit a list of everything I lost before they can begin to process my claim. I guess his office needs to be our first stop. Then I need to go see the fire chief. I forgot to show him this." She pulled the small silver object out of her pocket.

Jess took it from her. "What is it?"

"I don't know. It was in the electrical socket in the living room when I removed the cover. It fell off in my hand."

"Why take it to the fire chief?"

"Because I want to know what it is. Maybe it means the wiring in the building is faulty. I'd feel a lot better if I knew the fire wasn't my fault. Besides, I'm curious."

"You certainly are handling all this well."

"I feel like I'm playing hooky from real life right now. Nothing around me is familiar or normal. It makes it all seem like it isn't really happening."

"But you do realize it is happening?"

"I know it is. Believe me, I know."

"Ms. Rayburn? I'm sure you don't remember me, but I was at the scene of your attack last night."

JoAnn remembered him quite well, she was just surprised he was actual flesh and blood. He looked even better in broad daylight, the epitome of tall, dark, and handsome. "Yes. Come in," she said, blushing as if he could read her mind.

He held out a tanned, muscular hand. "I'm Detective Chase Kent."

"Chase?"

"An old football nickname that stuck. My real name is Charles, but everyone calls me Chase. How are you feeling?"

"Better than last night."

"I'm sorry about your house being burglarized. An officer did come by earlier for a statement, right?"

"Yes, but without seeing it, I have no idea what could be missing."

"Just what you need, one more thing to worry about."

"When it rains, it pours, right?"

"Unfortunately. You were very helpful last night. Most people don't remember the license plate number at all, much less when they're so traumatized."

"That part was easy. It was a demon plate."

He shook his head and smiled. "Triple sixes. I should have known. What about the ZHS?"

"Simple. Zebras have stripes."

"What line of work are you in?"

"I'm a research scientist."

"You'd make a hell of a detective."

"I doubt it. I didn't see the attack coming. I should have known something was wrong when that van parked next to my Lexus. The parking lot was practically empty. Pretty stupid to fall into such an obvious trap."

"No. Trusting. Most people don't want to think like a potential target twenty-four hours a day. It's too stressful. Can you tell me what happened?"

"I was getting ready to open the door of my car when he slit my ankle. He was hiding under his van. Can you believe it? I looked around and inside, but not down and under. I won't make that mistake again."

"Unfortunately, severing the Achilles tendon is a quick, simple way to bring someone down. He was probably shocked when you fought back. Most victims don't."

She touched the bandage on her forehead with her broken finger. "Maybe I shouldn't have."

"Twenty-twenty hindsight. If you hadn't you might be dead right now. There's no way to know. What's important now is keeping him behind bars."

"You mean you caught him?"

He flashed the killer smile again. "With the help of your great memory. We even have bloodstains on the clothes he was wearing as evidence. Since he wasn't cut, we're hoping the samples match your blood."

"Can you nail him with DNA fingerprinting?"

"Let's hope so. Would you be able to pick him out of a lineup?"

She shook her head. "He had a pair of ladies'

stockings over his face." She hesitated, then added, "But you could match the heel of my shoe to a bruise he probably has in a very tender location."

"I like your style. The hose he had on his head was recovered from the van. What about the knife? Would you recognize it?"

She closed her eyes and thought. "I doubt if I'll ever forget it. I picked it up and threw it. I think it went over my Lexus, but I'm not sure. I just wanted to get it as far away from him as possible. I knew if I tried to use it on him he'd overpower me in a second."

"We have it. You must have quite an arm. It was a good thirty yards from the Lexus."

"Adrenaline does amazing things."

"Could you ID the van?"

"Absolutely. It had a mud-splattered blue tarp in the back end and a deep scratch just above the left brake light."

He looked up from the notebook he'd been scribbling in and eyed her as he said, "I'm impressed."

"Don't be. I'm beginning to think having a photographic memory is more of a curse than a blessing. When I close my eyes I can see the whole thing, over and over again. Especially the way that knife gleamed in the moonlight."

"Maybe we can replace those memories with ones of him being hauled off to prison. You get some rest. I'll be back by later to check on you."

JoAnn held out her hand and said, "Thanks for catching him."

Chase took her hand in his and held it for several seconds before he said, "That's my job. Mind if I come back later?"

When she finally said, "Not at all," he gently laid her hand down. Chase Kent left, leaving JoAnn with a new problem. If she cared so much about J.D., why was her heart still pounding over a total stranger?

* * *

J.D. spent the morning with the door to his office
closed and locked. For the first few hours he poured
over every detail of Hanna's calendar. She only began
referencing specific drugs toward the end, and she always referred to her meetings with him by using his
middle initial, D. From the beginning of their relationship, he had insisted she call him Dean, his middle
name. At least JoAnn could not have guessed that the
numerous references to evening meetings with "D.C."
were actually with him.

When he was finally finished, he realized with relief
how lucky they were to have stopped her when they
did. She was dangerously close to destroying the entire organization. It occurred to him that he should
feel something besides contempt for Hanna, but the
only other emotion that crept from inside was anger.
Anger that she hadn't kept up her end of the bargain.
Irritation that her actions were still impacting him
every day, and probably would for the next few years.

He wondered why JoAnn had the calendar. Had it
been left in Hanna's desk or in her office? Surely
the security team was more efficient than to leave such
evidence behind. He jotted a note on his calendar to
contact Dr. Calahan. JoAnn's first session with the
company shrink would be more revealing than she
knew, at least to TechLab's executive officers.

Next, he searched every crevice for hidden listening
devices and high-tech fiber-optic cameras. He had just
finished reassembling his phone and was considering
dismantling his computer when his phone rang. Relieved that it still worked, he grabbed it and said,
"Yes."

"Mr. Cook, Mr. Lemmond has called an Executive
Board meeting. It will be in the secured conference
room in one hour, at eleven. Will you be able to attend?"

He automatically jotted "EB11/SCR" on his desk calendar as he said, "I wouldn't miss it for the world."

Hanging up, he went back to his search, wishing he had a better idea of exactly what kind of technology he was up against. Tonight he would have to find a safe phone and place a call to an old friend of his who was better acquainted with the fine art of surveillance.

With disgust, he realized his palms were sweaty, so he grabbed several tissues and tried angrily to wipe them dry. His desk was covered with shreds of crumbled white fluff when the phone rang again. "What?" he barked into the receiver.

"Having a bad day, are we, Cook?"

"What's it to you?"

"Since we're such good friends, I thought I should warn you about the topic of the Board meeting. Your Citrinol3 tests aren't bringing in the results they should be, are they? Lemmond isn't thrilled."

"Since when are you worried about one of my projects?"

He laughed. "You mean *our* project? If you don't look good, then TechLab doesn't look good. Like it or not, we're in this together."

"And what do you suggest I do at this point? Offer myself as a sacrifice to the great corporate gods? Gnaw off my leg like a trapped animal and crawl away with my tail tucked between my legs?"

"You really are pigheaded, aren't you? Change your attack plan, you stupid son of a bitch. Originally, the Citrinol3 tests were simply to determine side effects for the cancer research angle so we can narrow the scope of the research, right?"

"I'm listening."

"We both know Lemmond is a sucker for the defense position. At the meeting today tell them you think the drug has more potential with the Pentagon market."

"Go on."

"Jesus, do I have to spell the whole thing out for you? Those test kids are as passive as can be. Tired, but more diligent about their work than before. It's like they become almost single-minded, very task-oriented. Think of how easy it would be to manipulate a society where . . ."

"I get the point." He thought for a second, then said, "It could even be used in schools with high dropout rates, inner city areas." He laughed. "Just imagine, gang members sleeping fifteen hours a day, then calmly doing whatever they're told to do."

"Now you're getting the picture."

"Not totally. Why didn't you wait and present the idea yourself at the Board meeting? You'd have come off as a star, and I'd have looked like an asshole."

"As happy as that would have made me, Cook, I have better things to do right now. See you at the meeting."

J.D. hung up the phone and stared out the window. The new angle just might salvage the project, but he was even more worried now than he was before. Parker McDaniel never did anything without a reason. Usually a damned selfish reason at that.

Parker McDaniel stretched out in his leather executive chair and propped his feet on the windowsill. The Board meeting had been downright entertaining. He had Cook right where he wanted him now. The Citrinol3 project was granted an extension of at least six months, possibly a full year. Plenty of time for him to collect the data he needed, as long as the Rayburn woman kept her ass in high gear.

The only part of the Board meeting that had been a surprise was Cook's report on the violent attack she'd suffered last night. Either fate had thrown them an unexpected twist, or one of their competitors was increasing their own odds of success by screwing TechLab. Whichever was the cause, her injuries could slow things down tremendously.

His secretary buzzed in, saying, "Mr. Harper is here to see you."

"Send him in."

As Executive Chief of Security, Mike Harper was expected to keep the Board informed of any aspect of a top secret project that could jeopardize its progress, yet he had not contacted anyone regarding the attack on the Rayburn woman. He walked confidently into the office, his tall slender body shrouded by the dull, accountant-grey suit he wore. McDaniel stood up and extended his hand. "Harper. How are you today?"

His cold grey eyes didn't yield any insight into his temperament as he responded, "Fine."

"We just had an Executive Board meeting and Lemmond asked me to meet with you about the breakdown."

"Breakdown?" His voice was flat, with no hint of either agitation or interest.

Parker smiled. He loved playing power games, it gave his usually boring desk job the savage flavor he enjoyed in other parts of his life. "Communications. To be more specific, Security's communications. You are aware of what happened to our new Chief of Research, aren't you?"

"Yes. We picked up the conversation from the hospital to Mr. Cook early this morning."

"Why didn't you immediately pass the information on to the Board?"

"Early this morning we were busy clearing the surveillance evidence left from the Fordman fire. I was planning on telling everyone myself, but I didn't make it back in time to be at the meeting. My staff assured me that Cook was fully aware of the situation. The

Rayburn woman is under his authority." He almost smiled when he sarcastically added, "Isn't she?"

Cocky son of a bitch. I'd like to knock his ass down a peg or two. "Only on an organization chart. From now on when there is a serious breach of our security, you need to notify Lemmond and myself, not just Cook. Understood?"

Harper narrowed his dark eyes and slowly said, "Define 'serious breach of our security,' McDaniel. I was unaware there had been such a breach."

"Any act of violence against one of our people is serious."

"I personally checked with my contact at the police department. The attack on the Rayburn woman was cut and dried. The guy was an ex-con crack addict. They had him behind bars in under an hour. Neither CCR no VTL would risk paying off a bastard like that. He'd sell his own soul for a buck or a hit."

"Nevertheless, we should have been informed directly. Consolidated Chemical Resources personnel have been known to use unconventional methods before, as have Virtual Test Labs. I want someone planted in the jail. We need to be absolutely certain neither CCR nor VTL could have been behind this. Understand?"

Harper got up to leave, adding with a blatant smirk, "Whatever you say, McDaniel."

McDaniel smugly watched Harper as he left, then propped his feet back on the windowsill behind his desk. His secretary brought in a stack of letters to be signed and a pile of message slips. Sorting through them, he tossed all but one in the trash can.

Taking a deep breath, he picked up the phone and dialed the number written on the pink slip of paper. His voice was nothing like it had been during his conversation with Harper. There was no longer any edge of threat present as he pleasantly said, "Grace Milliken, please."

"Hello."

"You rang?"

"Parker! Why ... yes, I called. How have you been?"

"Fantastic. What can I do for you?"

"Well, I just wondered how we're supposed to handle maintenance on the unit your company was generous enough to have installed."

"Is there something wrong with it?"

"Just a minor leak. I'm sure it's nothing to worry about."

Parker's mind raced through the official corporate damage control procedures, which ranged from sending out a repair team to burning down the entire school, if necessary. "Where is the leak, Grace?"

"I really don't know, Parker. It was reported by a student."

"I'm going to send a repairman over right this minute. Don't worry, ITL will keep the unit in working order. He'll come and go without bothering a soul."

"When do you think you'll be back in town?"

I'm in town, bitch. I just try to stay as far away from your ugly ass as possible. "A few more weeks. We'll get together then, I promise. I'm really looking forward to it."

"Me, too, Parker. Me, too."

He hung up and sighed. Closing his eyes, he pictured Grace Milliken stretched naked before him, her muscles frozen by a tiny whiff of SynCur6. In his imagination, he thought of the terror that would shine from her eyes as he exhausted his fury on her flesh, and how they would glaze over long before he was finished.

He was fully aroused when he finally opened his

eyes and leaned back in his chair. For a moment he wondered if this job was worth the quarter million a year TechLab paid him. The answer was simple. It was worth a hell of a lot more than that.

By the time the Board meeting was over, J.D. had experienced the gambit of emotional highs and lows. McDaniel had been right about Lemmond targeting the Citrinol3 project, and he struck hard and fast. Without the tip, the entire undertaking would have been immediately terminated and Citrinol3 would have joined the other experimental drugs that never progressed past Level 12. But after an hour of heated discussion, the defense angle McDaniel had suggested saved the day, just as he had predicted it would.

J.D. wanted nothing more than to just go home, have a stiff drink, and go to bed, but he knew that wasn't to be. Right now, the most important part of his job was to build his relationship with JoAnn. She held the key to Citrinol3, and he knew it was critical to get her back on the job immediately. If there was one thing he was good at in the world, it was manipulating people without them realizing it. It was his gift in life, and he used it faithfully. Getting JoAnn back in the lab in her condition might be tricky, but he already had a plan.

He dialed her room at the hospital and said, "Hi, baby. Are you feeling better? Sorry I haven't had time to come by to see you today."

"That's okay. I come and go, mentally that is. They have this wonderful invention that automatically gives you IV morphine when the pain is severe. It takes the edge off, but it makes you pretty woozy sometimes. Have you had a busy day?"

"Is there such a thing at TechLab as a boring day? We had an Executive Board meeting. Everyone hopes you get better as soon as possible."

"Are they worried about the Citrinol3 research?"

He wondered again if she knew more than she should. "No. They're worried about you. Screw the tests."

"I tried to call you earlier. Did you go by my house this morning?"

"Right after I left you. I fed Rocket and Nobel for you and canceled all your credit cards. You should get an award for being so organized."

"Was the house okay when you left?"

"Sure. I put the puppies inside and locked it up. I left the key in the flower pot so I could go back and feed them this afternoon. Why?"

"Apparently I got robbed. I asked a friend to take care of the puppies for me until I'm better and when he went over to get them, the house was a disaster area."

"Oh, my God, I'm so sorry, JoAnn. Is there anything I can do to help?"

"Not today. I get to go home in a couple of days if my tendon is healing properly. Maybe you could help me sort through what's left this weekend."

"I'd be happy to."

"I'm kind of groggy. I can't remember who I told what. Did I tell you they caught the guy who attacked me? Apparently, he needed a little quick cash, and thought I had more than my share."

Relief washed over him. He knew TechLab's goons never got caught. For the price TechLab paid, perfection was required. He cleared his voice and said, "The police caught him already?"

"Last night. Not long after the attack. Isn't that great?"

"It really is. I know you'll sleep better knowing he's behind bars." *And I'll sleep better knowing it wasn't planned by Lemmond or McDaniel.* "Who is taking care of the puppies for you? You know I would have gone over every day to feed them."

"I know, but my veterinarian offered to let them stay at his house. He has an adorable son who will play with them. I'll bet they love it there. I just hope they want to come back to me when I'm better."

"Who's your vet?"

"Jess Lawrence. His clinic is only a few miles from my house. He's a sweetheart."

He smiled at the irony. "Should I be jealous?"

"Maybe. But only if you still have six other girl-friends running naked through your condo."

"With your encouragement of my sexual prowess, I'm back up to ten. Seriously, I'll come by the hospital tonight. Do you need anything?"

"A new body would be nice."

"I like the old one. By the way, how's your head?"

"Sewn up. Why?"

"I just wondered if I could talk you into doing a little research while you're healing. I thought it might keep your mind off your troubles."

Her voice was drifting off as she said, "Troubles? What troubles? I think I'm falling asleep again. See you tonight."

J.D. hung up. He realized it was time to stop passively watching this particular corporate game. Answers to some of his questions were essential. *How much did JoAnn already know? Where did she get Hanna's calendar? What the hell does Parker McDaniel expect to gain from all this?*

All morning Stacey had imagined her apartment burned and black, but the reality of the devastation overwhelmed her. She stood where the front door had been just yesterday and stared at nothing. There was nothing left.

Where her furniture had been there was now only

blackened fragments of wood and cloth. The carpet had disintegrated into the slab flooring giving it a crusty black coat. She turned to leave, not wanting to see any more, when she noticed her purse still hung from one of the brass hooks by the front door. The leather was brittle and charred, and as she lifted it off, the strap crumbled in her hand.

Carefully, she pulled open the top, which came off as soon as she tugged on it. When she reached inside, her fingertips came back red. The lipstick had melted, coating everything inside. She pulled out her wallet, which was now decorated with slimy red blotches, and slowly opened it. "Look, Jess! My driver's license and credit cards are okay." She held them up. "A little stiff and yellow maybe, but better than nothing."

Jess came back into the living room. "That's great, Stacey. Come in here, there's someone you should meet."

Stacey tiptoed across the gunk and walked into what had once been her bedroom. She hadn't thought it was possible, but it was in even worse shape than the living room and kitchen had been.

"This is Stacey Fordman. Stacey, meet Joe Thompson. He's head of the fire department's arson squad."

Stacey held out her hand and as he firmly shook it she said, "Arson? You think someone set my apartment on fire . . . on purpose?"

"Right now, Ms. Fordman, that's the only thing that makes sense. The blaze started near the headboard of the bed. There were no electrical outlets or extension cords within a six-foot radius of the ignition point and you said no one had been in the room for at least an hour. Plus, I found these under the debris. We were lucky the force of the water didn't wash them away." He held up a clear specimen bag that contained one small black wire and a watch-size battery that was very charred. "Look familiar?"

"Not at all." She pulled the silver buttonlike object out of her pocket, but it was larger than the thing the firemen had recovered. "I found this inside the wall socket in the living room right before the fire started. Do you know what it is?"

He looked it over carefully, then took a Swiss army knife out of his pocket. Raising his eyebrows he said, "Do you care if I open it?"

"Be my guest."

The top easily popped off revealing what appeared to be an incredibly small circuit board. "Mind if I take this downtown to the central crime lab?"

"No, but can you tell me what you think it is first?"

"I don't think it's anything. I know exactly what it is. It's a bug."

Both Jess and Stacey simultaneously said, "You're kidding."

"Afraid so. A fine specimen, too. These babies are high tech. They don't come cheap. Someone was very interested in what you were doing."

Stacey said, "But I'm just a schoolteacher. Who would want to listen to what I have to say?"

"Seems pretty obvious to me, ma'am. The same person who burned down your apartment."

Chapter 10

Jess helped Stacey carry the vast array of shopping bags and boxes up to the guest room. After dropping everything loaded in her arms on the floor, Stacey plopped onto the white comforter as though she could actually make a snow angel on the soft down sewn inside. Jess set the packages he had carried down and eased himself onto the bed beside her.

Rolling over, he flipped on the clock radio and whispered over the music, "I know you're going to do it anyway, but I think you're being a little paranoid."

She turned to him, snuggling closer so he could hear as she murmured, "You'd be paranoid, too, if everything you owned had just gone up in flames and someone had been listening to your life."

"Did it ever dawn on you that the bug was there when you moved in? Maybe whoever lived there before thought their spouse was cheating on them. It may not have anything to do with you."

"I've lived there since I got out of college. Six years and seven months to be exact. Surely I'd have found out the place was bugged sooner."

"Okay, let's assume someone was listening to you. What if they knew you found that bug, and that was the reason they set your place on fire? I'd rather not come back from picking up Jon and find this house in flames. Maybe you were just lucky the first time."

"Good point. I'll look, but I won't touch."

"There won't be anything *to* touch, but knock yourself out anyway."

"You're just worried I'll find dust bunnies under your bed."

He nibbled on her ear. "We could look together when I get back."

She nuzzled against him. "What about Jon?"

"He sleeps like a rock these days."

"Lucky kid. I'll think about your proposition. But keep in mind, I'm still his teacher. I can imagine what kind of rumors are already flying."

"Who gives a damn about rumors?"

"I do."

"Then I'll start one. I'll ask Jon to tell the kids you're going to be his new stepmom."

"Not funny. Not funny at all."

He rolled away from her and smiled as he stood up. "I wasn't trying to be funny." He headed toward the door, still smiling as he said, "I'll take Rocky and Bell with me, just in case you find something interesting." She glared at him as though he had just endangered their lives, so he reluctantly added, "I'm sure you'll find many treasures among your majesty's purchases. I bid you farewell, my queen. Master Jonathan and I will return to court in approximately one hour. If it pleases her majesty, we will bring back meat of fatted calf wrapped in the finest bread in the kingdom for her dining pleasure—sans onions, of course."

Stacey groaned and said, "Hamburgers again?"

"You doubt my ability to vary the feast I hunt for milady?"

"Yes."

"I am truly dishonored. Will roast beast sandwiches satisfy your royal hunger pangs?"

"Sounds a little lower in cholesterol. Tomorrow I'll cook. Will Jon eat chicken breasts with mushrooms and wild rice?"

"Will he have to slay the feathered fowl himself, milady? Alas, he is young, and his arrows are sharp and fly true. Unfortunately, there are few fowl to be found in the neighboring forests these days."

"Get out of here! I have work to do." She grabbed a bag and threw it at him, realizing as it spilled lace bras and panties on its way that it was from Victoria's Secret.

Catching a bra, he dangled it and pleaded, "But, milady, 'tis just getting interesting! Have ye a chastity belt hidden under those fine silks? Dare I return with a locksmith in tow?"

Stacey hurled a shoe box at him as she shouted, "Out!"

Once he was gone, she curled up on the bed for a while, realizing how lucky she was not only to be alive, but to have found Jess. Finally, she removed all the things she'd bought from their sacks and spread them on the bed. With utmost care, she cut the tags off the clothes and hung them in the closet. Five complete outfits had seemed like an extravagant spending spree while they were shopping, but now that they were hanging alone in the closet they looked pathetically inadequate.

She went to the window and peeked out the frilly white curtains in time to watch a dark car pull slowly by the house. The sun was bright, and the warmth poured through the glass. Running her fingers along the delicate material, she wondered if Jonathan's mother had decorated the guest room before she died. For the first time, she realized the entire house was beautifully done, feminine yet comfortable and warm. An ache twisted with envy and sorrow ran through her. *Poor Jess, poor Jonathan. They must have loved her very much.*

Shaking off her melancholy mood, she headed downstairs. Even though it made her feel somewhat ridiculous, she went to the garage and found a screwdriver. Next, she scouted around until she located a flashlight under the kitchen sink. Her hands were shaking when she unscrewed the cover from the first wall outlet and shined the light inside.

Nothing but wires and a socket. She sighed with relief.

Half an hour later, she had checked fifteen different outlets throughout the house. Feeling silly but relieved, she tucked the flashlight back under the kitchen sink and put the screwdriver in the toolbox in the garage.

She never thought to check under the headboard of Jess's bed or inside a few strategically located air ducts.

J.D. awoke in a pool of sweat. Frozen in his bed, he listened for movement, for whatever it had been that jerked him so viciously from his sleep. Minutes passed, but nothing happened. No monsters came out of the shadows. He thanked God. He had a pretty good idea of what monsters were out there and he didn't have any desire to confront them, especially if they had SynCur6 on their side. Finally, he realized that the condo's sophisticated security system had not been triggered, so it was just his imagination working overtime that had ruined his night's sleep.

Rolling out of bed, he went to the bathroom to relieve himself. The skylight above the elegant whirlpool tub shed barely enough moonlight for him to see his own reflection in the large mirror over the sink. He appeared crushed inward on himself as if collapsing under the weight of enormous burdens. The image jolted him, and he flipped on the lights. Running his fingers through his disheveled hair, he suddenly realized the toll the last few months had taken. The grey that had once graced only his temples was quickly taking over his entire head. He looked old, and worse, he felt old.

When the phone rang, he simply stared at it. Some-how he knew who it was, and why he was calling at two a.m. It was all part of his perverted game, and he didn't care to play right now. Just as J.D. expected, whoever it was hung up, opting not to leave a message on the answering machine.

JoAnn hung up the phone when the answering ma-chine picked up the call. She had been scared and lonely and after an hour had gathered enough courage to wake J.D. in the middle of the night just to have someone to talk to. Now she was confused. Where was he at two a.m.? Maybe he did see other women. Lots of other women.

The pain from her Achilles tendon coursed up her leg and into her hip, but the IV had been removed and she didn't want to bother the nurse for another shot of painkiller. She wanted to talk to someone. Anyone. But at two o'clock in the morning, she didn't have many choices.

She suddenly realized who she really missed. It wasn't J.D. at all. It was Rocky and Bell. In such a short time, they had become her sounding board. They lis-tened at all hours, never criticized, loved uncondition-ally.

I really am turning into an old maid. J.D. has done so much for me and I miss my dogs more than I miss him. Why? Because I know he wants something, I can feel it when he's near me. Hell, I can feel it when he's miles away. But what does he want? Citrinol3? Maybe. Sex? He's rich and pretty good-looking, he probably does have ten other women at his beck and call. So why is he being so nice to me?

Hanna knew. She's tried to tell me, to warn me. I just wish I understood. Damn it, why can't anything in life be easy?

* * *

The sun was already creeping up the horizon when Jonathan peeked into his room, where his teacher was sitting cross-legged in the middle of his bed. "Have you seen it yet, Ms. Fordman?"

Stacey shook her head.

"They don't call them obstacle illusions for nothing. They're tough. But you'll see it. I know you will."

The wall behind his bed was covered with three-dimensional posters. Stacey had tried for the last twenty minutes to see what everyone else could see, but it was no use. The only thing she'd succeeded in doing was giving herself a headache.

"*Optical* illusions, Jon. Remember? Optical, not obstacle."

"Wrong. Obstacle is what I mean. I even looked it up in the dictionary at school like you told us to. It means something that hinders progress. The substitute told me that means something that makes things hard to do. All the colors make it hard to see the picture. Right?"

"Whatever you say. You do have a point. Most things people perceive as obstacles probably are only illusions. All they need is the confidence to overcome them."

"Huh?"

She pulled him into a hug, tickling him as she said, "Never give up, tiger. If you want something in life, you have to work hard to get it. Never, ever quit."

His face suddenly grew serious. "I want my momma back more than anything. Dad says some things can't happen. Mom can't come back."

Stacey pulled him closer. "Your dad's a smart man. You're lucky to have him. Do you remember your mom?"

"Sure. She was really pretty. And she kissed and hugged me all the time. But I didn't care. It felt good."

"She was a great mom, wasn't she?"

Jonathan smiled and nodded.

"A very wise person once said that it is better to have had a great mom for a short time than a bad mom for a lifetime."

"You mean like Jason's mom?"

Stacey felt as though she'd been kicked in the stomach, but managed to calmly say, "What do you mean?"

"She hits him really hard. My mom never, ever hit me. She would put me in time-out if I was bad, and if I did something really terrible she would put herself in time-out."

"How'd she do that?"

"She'd go in her room, close the door, and lock it. I hated that worse than anything."

"I'll bet you did." Stacey hesitated, weighing losing Jonathan's trust against her professional ethics, then asked, "How do you know Jason's mom hits him?"

"I'm not supposed to tell."

"Sometimes keeping secrets is fun, but every once in a while they can hurt people. Jason is one of my favorite kids in class this year." She ruffled his hair and squeezed him saying, "Just like you. I wouldn't let anyone hurt you, now would I?"

"I guess not."

"Does Jason have bruises?"

Jon looked away, but nodded.

"I'll keep an eye on him, Jon. And no one will ever know you told me. I promise. We'd better get going. School starts in an hour, and I can hear your dad cooking breakfast."

Jon managed to squirm away from her and shouted as he ran downstairs, "I bet I can climb the big tree in the backyard faster than you can."

Stacey ran after him, through the house, and into the backyard. Both of them ignored Jess when he shouted at them to slow down. By the time she reached the tree, Jon was two stories up. "No fair. You had a head start."

"You run like a girl!"

"What am I suppose to run like, an elephant?"

"That would be better than a girl!"

She began to climb the tree, careful not to tear her brand-new pair of jeans. "So you think girls can't do everything boys can do, huh? I guess I'll just have to prove how wrong you are."

Jonathan was giggling. "I'm not wrong. Girls can't do lots of things that boys can."

Stacey was as high as Jon now, and not at all comfortable with the height. She tried to keep her voice steady as she said, "Bull. I climbed this tree, didn't I? Name something else."

"Look at Rocky and Bell. She's afraid of everything. He's tough. See how he's watching that squirrel on the fence so he can catch it if it gets near him? If a squirrel came near Bell, she'd pee all over the place."

"Temperament doesn't count. There are boys who are shy and frightened and girls who are brave and strong. Tell me just one thing a boy can do that no girl in the world can do and I'll make your bed for the rest of the week."

His blue eyes sparkled in triumph. "I can name two things! A girl can't pee her name in the snow, and a girl can't be a dad."

Stacey tried to grab him, murmuring, "I'll get you, you little . . ."

Sensing his life was in danger, Jonathan scampered quickly down the tree. Once he was on the ground he yelled, "I like my sheets pulled really tight, and don't forget to fluff my pillow!"

"You'll pay later, you clever little beast!" Stacey yelled, but she was more concerned with getting out of the tree in one piece than anything else. Before she started down, she looked around. The view was spectacular. The oak trees had lost about half of their leaves, so it was easy to see into the neighbors' yards. She turned around slowly and realized that she could even see between the houses and into the spacious front lawns.

Just as she was about to climb down, she noticed a dark blue sedan pull slowly past the house. At any other time in her life, she would have ignored it, assuming it was just someone who was lost or interested in buying a house in the neighborhood. But since her world had been turned upside down, she looked longer and harder at things she had so recently taken for granted.

A car just like that passed the house yesterday. And come to think of it, there was one like it at the shopping mall, too.

"So what did you find?" J.D. asked. He was sitting in a corner booth at Goldie's, a juicy four-inch-thick burger and home fries in front of him.

The man with him was small and wiry, his hair cut in a bristly flat top that made him look like a wayward Marine. "Your house phones are tapped, but I'm sure you already knew that."

"I always suspected it. Any way around it?"

"You could use a scrambler, but they'd know you were on to them. Most people don't feel like tipping their hand. As long as you know they're listening, you can always be careful." He wiped the juice from his chin and added, "This place has great burgers. I'll have to remember it next time I'm in town."

"Find anything else?"

"Your car is wired, too." He took another bite and mumbled through his food, "And it had a locator on it."

"Really? Can you get rid of it?"

"I'd suggest you slip it off whenever you need some privacy. But most of the time, leave it alone. You don't

want *them* to know that *you* know, remember? I'll
show you how to put it back on when we leave."

"You took it off?"

"I didn't care for them to get snapshots of our little
meeting here."

J.D. nodded. "How soon do you have to leave
town?"

"Depends."

"Can you run a check on someone else without
them knowing?"

"It'll cost an extra five hundred."

"Fine." J.D. scribbled Parker McDaniel's name and
address on a napkin and slid it across the table.

"What do you want to know?"

"If there's a similar level of surveillance on this
man."

One thin lip curled up as he asked, "Afraid one of
the wolves is circling his own pack?"

"Exactly."

"You wanted to see me, Mr. Lemmond?" Although he
appeared to be the picture of calm, inside J.D. was
sweating bullets.

"Sit down, Cook." Lemmond ran a hand through
his hair and sat farther back in his chair. "I'm getting
more and more worried every day about the situation
in BioHazard. I hear you aren't working on a replacement for the Rayburn woman."

"No, sir. I have a plan that will minimize her absence."

"You know that if this thing comes apart at the
hinges, we stand to lose over a hundred million dollars."

"Yes, sir. But . . ."

"But, nothing. This is your responsibility. Rayburn
is under your command and I'll expect to see some

progress in spite of her recent attack. Security informs me it was an unrelated coincidence, by the way."

"So McDaniel wasn't behind this?"

"McDaniel? Why the hell would you think one of our own would do such a thing? McDaniel's one of our key people. He's in this for the long haul, just like you and me. You two having some differences of opinion?"

"Nothing I can't handle, sir."

"That's good. I'll expect a detailed plan of how you presume to maintain the BioHazard level without a middle manager while the Rayburn woman is on sick leave."

"It might take some rather unusual tricks."

"I don't care if you stand on your head and gargle peanut butter while humming 'My Country 'Tis of Thee.' Just do whatever it takes to keep this project in line. Understand?"

"Yes, sir."

Jonathan tugged on his father's jacket and whispered, "Is anyone coming?"

"Not a soul. You two make sure they stay hidden. I'll lead the way." He pushed open the stairway door and held it ajar until Jon and Stacey scurried past. They both looked as guilty as sin as they rushed down the hall trying to look as natural as possible. Jess caught up to them, easing back into the lead before they passed the nurse's station. He smiled and nodded at the two nurses, who were both too busy to care about the trio of nervous visitors.

After a hurried knock, they slipped into JoAnn's room just seconds before one of the smuggled puppies poked his head out and barked. Jon pulled Rocky out of his shirt, scolding him for speaking, but he was all smiles when he walked to JoAnn's bedside and said, "We brought you some special visitors to help you feel better, Ms. Rayburn. But it's a secret. The nurses might get mad, so we have to keep them extra quiet. They missed you a whole bunch." He handed Rocky to her.

Tears were in JoAnn's eyes as she snuggled the squirming puppy against her cheek. "I'll bet I missed them more," she said between loving licks and nips.

Stacey opened her jacket and withdrew Bell. She gently laid her beside JoAnn. Bell wiggled up to kiss JoAnn's face, her tail wagging wildly as she wet the bed. Stacey grabbed a handful of Kleenex from the nightstand and tried to soak up the mess.

Jon looked wide-eyed at his father, but before he could say anything JoAnn said, "It's okay. They'll just think I spilled my juice. I see Bell is her same brave, adorable self."

Jon said, "She pees if you even look at her funny. Maybe you should have named her Puddles."

Jess cast a mild warning glare at his son and said, "That's enough, Jon. Remember your manners? I'm sorry, it looks like I've forgotten my own. JoAnn Rayburn, this is Stacey Fordman. She's Jon's teacher, and a very good friend of mine."

JoAnn held out her hand, shaking Stacey's as she said, "Nice to meet you. I think we've both made headlines lately. Aren't you the one whose apartment burned?"

"Afraid so," Stacey replied.

"I'm so sorry. Believe me, I know how you feel."

"Jess said they caught the person who did this to you."

"Yes, but not the one who robbed my house."

Jess was shocked. "You mean it wasn't the same guy? I can't believe it."

She shook her head as she said, "The police say it couldn't have been, they arrested the creep not long after the attack. It must have been a bizarre coincidence, or he had an accomplice. Obviously, it wasn't my day. Superstitious people would tell me to watch out. Bad things supposedly come in threes."

Stacey ran her hands up and down her arms, trying to quiet the goose flesh that had suddenly crept up. She had no desire to have two more disasters plague her in the near future. "I think we can all live without any more bad things cropping up for a long, long time."

JoAnn laughed and said, "I agree," as two black balls of fur happily sniffed and inspected the pillows and anything else in their path.

Jonathan cheerfully stroked Rocky as he said, "Your puppies are really cute, Ms. Rayburn. It's been fun taking care of them."

"So they aren't too much trouble?"

"No way! Bell sleeps on my head and Rocky stands guard at the foot of my bed all night. I think he's waiting for you to come get them."

"That may be a while. I get out of here on Saturday, but I won't be staying at my house for a few more weeks." She shifted her gaze to Jess. "I hate to ask, but do you think you could keep them a little longer?"

Jonathan beamed at his father. "Could we, Dad? Please?"

"Sure. Under one condition."

"Just name it."

"You come over and visit them sometime."

"Your house will be one of my first stops when this place sets me loose. How about Saturday afternoon?"

"Only if you'll stay for dinner."

"I'd love to. All the jokes about hospital food seem to be based on good solid evidence."

Stacey poked Jess and said, "He'll have your cholesterol level up in no time, believe me. I think these two handsome men live on hamburgers and fries."

Jon added, "And pizza!" as he headed for the door. He peeked into the hallway, then crept back over to his father when he was sure the coast was clear. "If they catch us with the puppies in here, will we have to go to jail?"

"No, son. Jail is reserved for much worse offenses. I'm pretty sure dog smuggling isn't a felony. A felony is a big crime, something so bad everyone agrees the criminal should be put in jail."

"Is hurting someone like Ms. Rayburn a felony?"

"Yes."

"Is the bad guy in jail?"

"Yes."

"Forever?"

Jess looked profoundly at Stacey and JoAnn before he answered. "We can hope so, Jon."

"The man on the news said the guy who hurt Ms. Rayburn had been in jail before for doing the same thing. Why did they let him out of jail?"

"I guess they thought he deserved another chance."

"Another chance to hurt someone?"

Stacey said, "You ask good questions, Jon. Maybe when you grow up you can help change some of the laws. You could be a politician or a lawyer, maybe even make it to the Supreme Court."

"I already know what I'm going to be."

"What's that?"

"A male model. They make lots of money and get to hang around the prettiest girls."

Stacey shot a wicked glance at Jess, who immediately threw up his hands and said, "He didn't get that from me. I swear."

Jonathan smiled and said, "Of course not. I figured it out all by myself."

Stacey had been looking out the window, watching a line of dark clouds move closer and closer. "I think we need to get to school. It looks like the weatherman was finally right. We're in for a storm."

Stacey and Jon tried to tuck the puppies back inside

their coats, but they were too excited. Finally, they decided to just carry them. They had almost successfully made it past the nurses' station when the head nurse yelled, "Puppies! Aren't they adorable! Can I hold them?"

Fifteen minutes later the nurses went back to work while Jess, Jon, Stacey, and the dogs drove through the first huge drops of rain. By the time they reached school, black clouds were rolling across the fields from the southwest, and nervous children ran as fast as they could to get inside. A few others strolled steadily along, oblivious to the approaching sound of thunder or the threat of lightning.

"Mr. Cook, this is Betty Jean Simmons with Maid in America. You were trying to contact us about a cleaning job?"

"Of course. A friend of mine was recently burglarized and I need a crew to handle straightening out her house before she's released from the hospital. I understand you can work with interior decorators and repairmen. Is that true?"

"Yes, sir. We will do whatever we're asked to do."

"Fine. My decorator will be there promptly at eight o'clock in the morning. Can someone meet her then?"

"That's awfully short notice, sir. Was the house damaged badly?"

"There was quite a bit of vandalism. We've already replaced some furniture, repainted, and redecorated the living areas. We'll pay twice your normal fee if you can fit us into your schedule. It's important that the work be completed by Saturday."

"We'll be there with bells on, sir."

He gave her the address, hung up, then promptly dialed Security. "Mike Harper, please."

"Harper."

"This is Cook. I've arranged a rather large, unusual

delivery to be made to BioHazard on Friday. I thought one of your people might want to check it out."

"What delivery firm?"

"Our subsidiary, V.R. Services, of course."

"Authorization?"

"Mine. Who else would authorize a BioHazard delivery?"

"Since you're the originator, it would normally be your immediate superior."

"You want me to bother Gene Lemmond with such petty nonsense when you know he's already given me carte blanche on this project?"

"Depends on what kind of delivery there is going to be."

"Furniture. Some of Ms. Rayburn's furniture to be exact."

"Don't you think you're taking your little office romance a bit too far, Cook? Ever heard of sexual harassment?"

"Pull your head out, Harper. I'm doing what it takes to keep our projects on time, which is a hell of a lot more than you ever do. As far as I can see, Security has one of the biggest budgets, yet you don't produce a damn thing. Overhead, pure overhead."

"Funny, I seem to remember saving your ass a few times."

"And I'm working on saving all our asses."

The huge bouquet of exotic flowers arrived at the hospital not long after Jess and Stacey left. JoAnn dialed J.D.'s private extension and was relieved when he answered. "They're beautiful," she said. "But you shouldn't have. You've done more than enough already."

"They're a peace offering. I won't be able to come by tonight either. Without you here, things are getting a little wild in BioHazard."

"Such as?"

"Someone broke the electron microscope. Maintenance can't find the blasted replacement part anywhere in the States. They're ordering it from someplace like Hong Kong or Taiwan, so God only knows how long it will take before it's back on-line. The techs are fussing about the new security measures. A cleaning person was caught removing a drug sample. Normal management crapola."

"What drug sample was being taken?"

"CryoGen3."

"But that was outdated by CryoGen5. Why would someone want to steal an experimental drug that was in the testing phase? Why not go for the real thing?"

"No one said it was an intelligent move. She probably thought she could sell it to someone, or maybe she doesn't read well. Haven't you ever heard that criminals are stupid? Who knows? The attorneys will handle it from now on."

"You've implied the same things about Hanna, and she was far from stupid. As a matter of fact, she was brilliant."

Annoyance practically dripped through the telephone line until J.D. finally broke the silence. "There are exceptions to everything. Greed is a powerful emotion."

JoAnn let her own silence hang for several seconds before she moved on to safer territory. "What new level of security was installed?"

"None, really. Security briefed everyone on the latest state-of-the-art contraption that will be installed in a couple of weeks. Basically, it's to ensure samples can't be taken out of the lab, either on purpose or by accident. The techs overreacted. A couple of them are screaming that they don't want to be strip-searched every day. Don't those people ever listen during meetings?"

"You're going to strip-search the employees? My God, J.D., no wonder they're in an uproar! There has to be a certain degree of trust between an employer and an employee."

"Hold on. There won't be any strip searches, that was a ridiculous extreme that Harper used as an analogy in his speech. He may be head of our security team, but his management skills leave a lot to be desired. What it boils down to is that as employees leave, they'll walk through this new device Security spent a bundle on. Random top secret lab samples will be tagged with harmless radioactive isotopes. As people pass through the detection sector near the elevators or stairways, it will sound an alarm if one of the tagged isotopes is being removed from the building. We've had a similar device operating for years. We've just never told anyone before."

"So why are you telling them now?"

"Security thinks it will make everyone a little more hesitant about trying anything. This last incident with the cleaning woman was caught by the old system."

"Seems to me it would just make people be more devious about the methods they use."

"Why don't you tell Harper that next time you see him? I'm sure he'd love to know I'm not the only one who dislikes his techniques."

"The whole process sounds dangerous. Are the employees going to be exposed to low-level radiation on a daily basis? Who will tag the samples?"

"Pathology randomly inserts the isotopes. I've been assured the process is completely safe. Looking back, I think we should have kept this under wraps. It would have been much easier to just install the upgraded devices on the elevators going down to BioHazard and not tell anyone. When an isotope registered, the elevators would just lock up. It's really pretty simple, but the lab techs are blowing it out of proportion."

"You know they've been under a lot of stress lately. First Hanna, then Amy. I'm sure what happened to me doesn't help. They probably feel like they're sealed in a tomb all day."

"I hope you can bring morale up a notch or two."

"I can try."

"You trust me, don't you, JoAnn?"

JoAnn hesitated, then said, "Why? What are you up to?"

"You'll find out soon enough. I've taken care of everything."

"It's really nice of you to let me stay with you for a while. Did you move the things on the list I gave you to your place yet?"

"You've got to trust me. I'll pick you up tomorrow morning. Get a good night's rest, okay, baby?"

She hated being called "baby" so she coldly said, "I'll try."

"I'll always be here whenever you need someone. I promise."

"Thanks, J.D."

JoAnn hung up the phone, her thoughts coiling around her growing sense of uneasiness over everything associated with TechLab. A few months ago she would never have believed she would feel relieved that she wouldn't have to go to work for a while. She sighed, silently appreciating the fact that she still had a few weeks to rest before she had to return there.

Pulling the curtain aside, JoAnn watched the sky grow darker with rolling black clouds. She was thankful she was warm and safe inside, with no one expecting her to do anything. For the first time in her life, she felt drained, too tired to think clearly, much less work. Rest was all she cared about right now. In a few weeks she could decide exactly what she was going to do with her life. For the first time ever, she began to seriously consider leaving TechLab. Slowly, a smile emerged, and she was genuinely surprised that her world didn't come to an end at the very thought of throwing her life's dreams into the howling winds.

Stacey was growing more and more nervous. Having lived in Oklahoma her entire life, she had no fear of thunderstorms. What she did have was a healthy respect for their ability to turn violent, even deadly.

Although it had been steadily raining for over an hour, the latest wall of clouds towered black on the horizon. Veins of lightning shot down, followed by thunder so forceful you could feel it roll over the building. Windows rattled and a few of the children gazed up at her. She smiled reassuringly, and they went back to work. Her special children seemed to be the only ones concerned with the weather. They fidgeted and squirmed in their chairs, nervously watching the windows instead of working on their dictionary skills.

A few seconds later the civil defense sirens began to blow the tornado warning signal. The sirens were located on the corner of the school grounds and were ear-piercing in spite of the roaring storm. Over the loudspeaker, Grace Milliken's voice sternly instructed the children to do exactly what they had practiced in drills. The lights flickered and died, cutting the principal off in midsentence, which several children applauded.

Outside, a tree limb snapped in the rising winds and crashed through the classroom window. Had Stacey been seated at her desk, she would have been struck by the falling debris. But she was by the door, herding her children into the hall to relative safety away from the glass windows.

Without electricity, the halls were dark, except when briefly illuminated by a bolt of lightning. Outside, winds howled and a peculiar roaring grew closer and closer. If the children could have seen the tornado coming toward them, most of them would have been more fascinated than scared. The black, undulating column moved gracefully back and forth across the horizon, one of nature's most awesome spectacles.

As though alive, it touched the ground, slowing to painfully clear its path, throwing everything it collided with into a swirl of black wind. An instant later the funnel seemed to cringe, as if the soil held too many deadly secrets and it shrank back toward the protective sky to regain its strength.

The pressure in the building suddenly changed, causing rows of children kneeling in the hallways to scream as their ears popped and the building was pummeled by debris. Stacey kneeled alongside her class, her head raised so she could count each child for the third time. Everyone was exactly where they should be when the ceiling began to peel away from the brick walls.

Chapter 11

It was an eerie sound, the whining of roofing nails as they slowly pulled free of the wood. A sound no child or adult would ever forget. For the few who glanced upward, the sight of the roof twisting away would fuel nightmares for years to come.

One second the children and teachers were warm and dry, the next they were being soaked by torrential rains. Stacey noticed most of her kids were still huddled against the wall, their hands folded precisely over the back of their necks. Only her three special kids had moved next to her in all the commotion, and they were holding on to her for dear life. She looked down the hall and gasped. Children from the other classes in the pod were crying hysterically, some standing, others running frantically. Her fellow teachers were doing their best to control the frightened children, but they were rapidly losing ground. Stacey yelled to her kids to stay where they were, gave the three closest a reassuring hug, and went to help.

While she settled children back into their emergency positions, she kept an eye on her own class. They were perfect. A few sobbed quietly with their hands over their heads, but every single one stayed down. Even when dime-size hail began to pummel them, they remained still. Within minutes, the sounds of fire engines and ambulances filled the air.

The rest of the day was a blur of activity. Although only a few of the first-grade children suffered minor cuts from the debris and hail, the roof from their building had blown into the middle school a few blocks away. An entire section of seventh-graders had been trapped when a wing of their building collapsed.

Teachers gathered the elementary school children whose classrooms were destroyed in the gymnasium, while the National Guard was called to control crowds and direct traffic. Two hours later, when the skies began to clear, frantic parents were slowly being reunited with their children.

Stacey kept Jon at her side as she worked her way back to her classroom. "You're awfully quiet," she said.

"I'm worried about Dad."

"I'm sure he's fine. The fireman said the tornado hopped over the rest of the city. All the damage is southwest of here. That means both the clinic and your house are fine."

"Then why isn't he here to pick me up? Everyone else's parents came and got them."

"I don't know, Jon. But he knows I'd take good care of you. He may be caught in traffic."

"I'll bet some dogs and cats got hurt real bad in the storm. He's probably taking care of them. I'm glad. I wouldn't want them to die."

"I'll bet you're right. Do you know how to ride piggyback?"

"Sure."

Stacey leaned down and said, "Hop on."

"Why?"

She pointed at the ground. "See all the broken glass and sharp metal? I don't want you to step on anything or get cut. Besides, it'll be fun."

He hopped on and Stacey slowly maneuvered through the rubble. When they reached her room, she let him slide down. The desks were overturned and stood in about an inch of water. The sound of the wind inside the walls and the sun shining through what used to be a roof gave the whole scene an unreal appearance, and for a few seconds they both stood and stared. For some reason Stacey couldn't take her eyes off the streaked mess on the chalkboard that had been that morning's assignments.

"What a mess!" Jon finally said as he began sloshing boyishly around.

Stacey shook herself back to reality. "I'll say. Can you very carefully help me put all the kids' backpacks over by the door? I'll take them with us and dry them out over the weekend."

"Should I put the lunches over there, too?"

Stacey looked at the overturned laundry basket. All the sack lunches had spilled into the standing water so she said, "I think they're okay where they are." With glass crackling underfoot, she made her way to her desk and tried to slide the broken tree limb over far enough so she could slip open her top drawer. She reached inside and pulled out her purse, grateful that she at least had her car keys and wallet again.

First my apartment, now the school, what next? she thought.

Stacey sighed as she looked outside, noticing that the special air conditioner that had made her room the envy of all the other teachers was smashed under the weight of the tree limb. Beyond that, everything in sight was scattered with debris.

Beneath the tangled limbs, she couldn't see that the mysterious glass dial on the back of the unit was shattered. Although Stacey thought she heard something unusual, she never realized it was the wind blending with a strange hissing sound. Or that the breeze was swiftly carrying away the last few droplets of an orange-scented mist.

Mrs. Milliken walked around the campus, surveying the damage with a National Guardsman close on her heels. The Guard was there to prevent looting and assist in cleanup, and they were allowing no one on campus without permission. Although one neighborhood had been partially damaged by the storm, East Elementary and East Middle School were the Guard's top priority, and they took their jobs quite seriously.

The first-grade building sustained the greatest amount of damage. The roof was totally missing from the two pods farthest north, and those classrooms withstood substantial wind and water damage.

She was about to return to the makeshift offices they had set up in the center of the campus when she reached the Fordman classroom. It looked like all the others, except for the tree limb that had crashed through the window. The limb was lying across the special air-conditioning unit, which had obviously been destroyed.

Smiling broadly, Grace realized that she finally had another reason to call Parker McDaniel.

"Excuse me."

JoAnn had been half-asleep, but the sound of his voice snapped her back to reality. As he walked toward her, she wondered if her hair was as messy as she suspected, and she wished she had taken the time to put on some makeup. She flushed as she said, "Detective Kent, right?"

"No, Chase. I was working on the rescue at the school and came in with one of the kids. Since I had a few minutes, I thought I'd drop by to check on you. How are you feeling?"

"What rescue are you talking about?"

His gorgeous eyes widened. "You mean you haven't heard about this morning's tornado?"

She shook her head. "It's been quiet here all day. Come to think of it, it's been more quiet than usual.

No one's been in checking blood pressure and temps like they normally do."

"That's because the emergency room is swamped with people hurt by the storm. I'm sure all available nurses are helping down there."

"Was it bad?"

He nodded but added, "Not nearly as bad as it could have been. We were very lucky."

"It was nice of you to stop by when you're so busy. Has something new come up with my case?"

"No. I just had a question I wanted to ask you."

JoAnn smiled and said, "Fire away."

"After you're out of here, would you like to have dinner and maybe catch a movie?"

JoAnn blushed again. Her first instinct was to politely say no, but she caught the word before it spilled out. Instead, she took a deep breath and said, "I think that would be nice. I'll warn you though, I'm a hopeless workaholic."

"That makes two of us."

She glanced around the tiny hospital room as she said, "If you have a pencil, I'll give you my phone number."

He winked at her and said, "That's okay, I've already got it. If you'll excuse me now, I've got to get back to work."

"Thanks again for dropping by." JoAnn watched him slip out the door. She was overwhelmed by a sickening feeling of guilt, which she pushed down. Justifying her actions, she thought, *It's only dinner and a movie, and he may never even call. I'm not married to J.D., after all. Besides, he still sees other women. At least I think he does . . .*

"Parker McDaniel."

"Mr. McDaniel, the answering service said a woman just called who said it was urgent she talk to you. Her name is Grace Milliken. Should I call her back for you?"

"Go ahead." Several seconds later he said, "Grace?"

"Parker? Is that you? This cellular phone has so much static on the line it's hard to tell."

"What can I do for you?"

"Have you heard about the tornado?"

Parker bolted upright. He'd been in meetings all day, and no one mentioned anything about the weather, much less anything severe. "What tornado?"

"I'm afraid East Elementary was hit pretty hard. Luckily, no one was seriously injured. There was substantial property damage, though, including your air-conditioning unit. I'm afraid it was destroyed."

"We'll have someone come right over to pick it up. You let me know when things are back to normal and we'll arrange to install another one."

"I'm afraid that won't work. The National Guard isn't letting anyone on the campus. It doesn't make any difference, though. The classrooms probably won't be ready to use again until after Christmas break."

Holy shit. "Could you arrange for someone from our company to come by? We keep pretty close tabs on our inventory, and I'm sure our lawyers wouldn't want us to leave damaged equipment around. Someone could get hurt."

"I can try, but it won't be before Monday. They're worried about looting. I wouldn't worry about your equipment hurting anyone. It's covered by a tree, and it certainly doesn't pose any threat. Considering the other damage to the campus, it's hardly even noticeable. I just thought you would want to know."

"I understand." He hung up. *Holy shit!*

Parker McDaniel was pacing back and forth carrying on about what he called a disaster, which was beginning to irritate Gene Lemmond. He expected more than this gibberish from McDaniel, much more. "What do you mean we can't go and get it?" he barked.

McDaniel stopped in his tracks. "You heard me, sir, the National Guard has the place sealed off."

"What about the nursing home?"

"No damage on that end of town. Just a power outage. Our man has already checked the unit, reset the gauges, and made sure the battery backup is fully operational."

"And nothing has been done at the school?"

He slowly replied, "That's right."

"For Christ's sake, be creative. How am I ever supposed to retire if I have incompetent people running around in key positions? I expect you to have a solution to present whenever you come in with a problem. What would you have done if I wasn't here?"

"I was merely keeping you apprised of the situation, Mr. Lemmond. Since the Citrinol3 field tests will be drastically affected, I felt you should know as soon as possible. As soon as an opportunity arises, we'll be on it. I also thought you needed to be aware of the potential exposure this could be to TechLab."

"God damn it, McDaniel, there's not a serious exposure problem at this point. First of all, the whole affair is through the subsidiary, so TechLab's hands are clean no matter what. Second, the equipment is beyond the technical expertise of ninety-nine percent of the people running around out there, so even if they saw something, they wouldn't have a clue what it was. And third, we can still have this whole thing wrapped up in an hour, two hours max."

With a slight edge of sarcasm, he said, "How, sir?"

"If there's one thing I learned from the military it's how to get around the military. They won't unnecessarily endanger lives, civilian or otherwise. We'll get a couple of the goons Security occasionally uses for our discreet jobs. Have them go in as Public Service Company employees. They'll need uniforms, and one of those big green and white trucks they drive around in, but I'll bet coming up with those won't be too big a problem. We'll have them tell the guard that the power is about to come back on, and the electric company received a report of a line down that needs to be repaired so no one gets electrocuted. Got the basic idea, McDaniel?"

"Yes, sir."

"Then get the hell out of my office. And, McDaniel . . ."

He had turned to leave, and with his back still to Lemmond he answered through gritted teeth, "Yes?"

"Harper and his crew can handle the details. I'll have him get observation reports on all the kids in that class by tomorrow morning. If any of them were badly injured, we may have a few problems that you didn't think to worry about. Don't concern yourself anymore on this matter. I'll have him report directly back to me."

By four o'clock that afternoon, National Guardsmen were personally escorting the teachers out of the parking lot, since most of the children had been safely picked up. All traffic was routed away from the middle school, where rescue teams were still working. The fact that half the city was still without power made things even more complicated. Stacey had Jonathan beside her as they waited in line to leave, although he was so quiet she hardly knew he was there.

"Are your feet as wet as mine are?" she asked.

He nodded.

"Did you see that big truck the electric company sent? It was right by our classroom."

"Uh-huh."

"Pretty awesome, isn't it? They'll have the power back on before we know it."

"Yep."

"Are you cold? I can turn on the car's heater."

He shook his head.

"Worried about your dad, aren't you?"

He nodded.

"We're going straight to the clinic." They were a couple of miles from the school when she couldn't stand the silence any longer. "It looks like this part of town was hardly touched, except I know the phones are out since I tried to call your dad using one of the policemen's cellular phones. We'll be there in a couple of minutes, even without the benefit of stoplights."

He didn't answer. Instead, he turned and watched the scenery go by.

As soon as they pulled into the clinic, they knew exactly what the problem was. There was no place to park, so they pulled around to the back and double-parked behind Jess's Cherokee. Before she could even put the car in park, Jonathan had leaped out of the door and was running into the back door of the clinic. Stacey opened the door in time to see Jess come out of surgery, grab Jon, and bear hug him.

When he set his son back down, Stacey was shocked to see the blood-covered scrub clothes Jess was wearing, and that even the shoes he wore were caked with blood. She quickly realized what his day had been like. From the closed exam-room doors, she knew that several patients were anxiously waiting for Jess, and with a quick glance out front, she saw the reception room was overflowing as well.

"I'm so glad you're both all right. The police assured me there were no serious injuries at the grade school, but I've been worried sick about you two all afternoon." He walked to Stacey and carefully hugged her. "Thanks for taking care of Jon. I can't tell you how much I appreciate it."

"Is this chaos from the storm?"

"Yes. I've done six surgeries to stop internal bleeding, and there are at least eight more animals waiting with broken bones. I think one dog may end up blind from the glass fragments I can see in his eyes, but I can't tell yet. We've been absolutely swamped. I don't suppose you'd both like to help?"

Jonathan smiled from ear to ear. "Can I help you in surgery?"

"You bet. Without electricity, it's a little tricky. Can you hold a flashlight, tiger? I'm saving the lanterns until it gets dark."

Jonathan excitedly asked, "Do I get to watch?"

"If you can take it."

"Awesome. Wait till I tell my class!"

"Stacey, would you cover for Jill, my receptionist, for a few minutes? Even though the phones are out, there's plenty to do out there. The main thing is to keep the owners calm. Talk to them, offer them Cokes, but warn them the electricity is off, so they won't be cold. Tell Jill I need her to help prep Hershey, the Smiths' rabbit in Room 3, and then we'll take care of Kramer, the Olenders' cat in Room 1. If anyone else comes in, try to find their chart. They're in alphabetical order in the file cabinets on the north wall. If it's someone we haven't seen before, have them fill out a new client information sheet."

"Sounds pretty simple." This time it was Stacey who hugged Jess, but she didn't bother trying to avoid his bloody scrub clothes. "We're glad you're okay, too. We were both a little worried."

"I'm sorry, it's been a disaster area here." He was headed back for surgery. "Thanks for helping."

"It's the least I can do." Stacey almost started to cry when she went into the reception area. Dogs and cats wrapped in blood-soaked towels and blankets were everywhere. Half the people were standing, since there weren't enough seats for everyone. Although a few of the dogs barked when someone moved too quickly, most of the animals were very subdued. Worried owners swapped stories of how they'd come outside once the worst of the storm had passed, only to find their beloved pet pinned under a fallen limb or blown against the side of the house.

Four hours later the electricity flickered and came back on. The three people still in the reception room cheered. Stacey turned off the lantern and wearily sat back down. Much later, Jess found her with her head on the counter, sound asleep. He nudged her gently and said, "Come on, sleepy, it's time to go home."

She opened one eye and rubbed her neck as she stiffly sat up. "So soon?"

"It's past eleven o'clock."

"Really?" She looked around. "Is everyone gone?"

"Yes, and my other faithful helper is asleep, too. He's in the car waiting."

Jess had dark circles under his eyes, and his hair was a mess. Stacey stood up and hugged him. "Are you okay?"

"Just tired."

"Then let's go home." They headed for the back door. "I'm so hungry," she said.

"Me, too. I haven't stopped since breakfast, much less eaten."

Jess opened the door for Stacey, who immediately froze in her tracks and screamed, "Stop!"

He saw the man an instant later. He was dressed in black and had been shining a flashlight in Stacey's car. Now he was running across the parking lot at top speed.

Jess chased him down the block, then gave up. The guy had too large a lead and ran like a gazelle, plus

Jess was already exhausted. When he came back, Stacey was in the Cherokee beside Jon, with all the doors locked. "Everyone all right?" Jess asked as he tried to catch his breath.

Stacey whispered, "He didn't even wake up. What do you suppose that was all about?"

"Probably a car thief."

"Why would anyone want to steal my car? Never mind, it's obvious."

"I'm too tired to think. Why is it obvious?" Jess asked.

"First the apartment. Now everything I kept at school. That car is the only thing I have left."

"Bullshit."

"Excuse me?"

"That's bullshit. You have plenty left besides that car."

Her cheeks flushed, and tears rushed to her eyes. She was too tired to argue, so she simply got out of the Cherokee and went back to her own car. If there had been someplace else for her to go besides his house, she would have left instantly. Instead, she followed him home, never noticing the dark blue sedan that was tailing them at a discreet distance.

"We'll stop by your place first, so you can see if there's anything you need. The storm yesterday broke a few small limbs in your backyard, but nothing serious."

"Thanks, J.D. I've been worried about the damage from the burglary, I guess I should be grateful the storm didn't wipe out what was left. I hope getting things fixed will give me something to do while I recuperate. Wouldn't want to be bored, now would I?" JoAnn said.

J.D. reached over and squeezed JoAnn's hand. "I'd like to see the day someone with your energy and ingenuity gets bored. The main thing you need to do is get well. Are you in much pain?"

"It comes and goes. It's just nice to be out of the hospital."

They rode silently the rest of the way. JoAnn was surprised to see the black Lexus in the driveway when they pulled in. A flash of that horrible night ran through her mind, sending shivers down her spine. "I thought my car was impounded by the police," she said nervously.

"It was, but since it technically belongs to TechLab, we pulled some strings and got it out."

Shaking off the disturbing mental images she tried to do what she'd vowed to herself in the hospital—concentrate on the positive side of life. "Great. I promised to go see the Lawrence family this afternoon. Having my own car will make things so much easier."

"Are you allowed to drive already?"

"The doctor said I could as long as I'm not taking any pain medication. Luckily the Lexus is an automatic. Even so, learning to drive left-footed should be a challenge."

"Not to mention one-handed. I'll drive you wherever you want to go. I really don't mind."

"Sorry. I'm too independent to be chauffeured around. Besides, I have to get my life back to normal sometime. Might as well be now."

"That must be why I love you so much. You're stubborn and pigheaded, just like me." J.D. helped her out of the car and got the crutches out of the backseat for her. After slowly going up the brick stairs, he started to open the front door, then said, "Close your eyes, gorgeous. I have a surprise for you." He led JoAnn blindly into the entryway.

When she opened her eyes, she was sure there

had been a mistake. They weren't in her house, they couldn't be.

Everything was different. Her parents' comfortable Early American furniture had been replaced with sleek Danish modern pieces. The beige carpet was gone, in its place glossy bleached wood was scantily covered by brilliantly colored decorative rugs scattered here and there. Even her collection of watercolor landscapes was gone. An immense impressionist print hung over what she thought was supposed to be a sofa, but she wasn't sure.

"So, what do you think?"

"I . . . did you . . . for me?"

"I've finally found a way to show you how much you mean to me. Expensive, but from the expression on your face, I'd say it was well worth it."

JoAnn had a hard time holding on to her crutches, but she managed to work her way toward the kitchen. She was relieved to see it was still the same.

"My decorator says she can help you tackle the kitchen next. Once you're feeling better, of course."

"This must have cost a fortune." She hobbled back into the living room and headed for the den. Once again, she stopped dead in her tracks when she saw the room. At first glance, she recognized absolutely nothing. The second time she looked, she did recognize her mother's lead crystal vase perched atop a stark white desk that cut diagonally across one corner of the room. Hesitantly, she asked, "My rolltop desk?"

"Smashed beyond repair."

"My computer?"

He walked over to the desk and pushed a button. Two doors rolled into the wall revealing the monitor. He pulled open the top drawer to expose the keyboard. "TechLab's computer whiz kids managed to save most of your data even though the machine was in pretty bad shape. They've upgraded your programs and installed all the latest bells and whistles. Pretty slick, isn't it?"

"I can't believe it. How am I going to pay for all this?"

"I already told you, sweetheart. This is my get well gift to you. No strings attached." He came over to her and took her by the arm. "You look like you need to sit down."

"I can't let you do this, it's too much. Once I figure out what was stolen, my insurance company will reimburse me. That is, if I can remember what was here before."

"That won't be a problem. I had a professional photographer come in before anything was touched. We have pictures of everything for you to use to fill out your damage reports."

JoAnn felt as though she were going to be sick. After J.D. helped her into a chair she said, "Would you mind bringing me a glass of water?"

"Anything you like."

I'd like my life back the way it was. My own furniture. A healthy body . . . How am I going to get out of this mess? I think living at the YMCA might be more comfortable than living in this stuffy showcase.

J.D. handed her a glass of water. "My God, you've got tears in your eyes. Don't tell me you don't like it. You seemed to like my place so much, I thought . . . We can change everything back the way it was if you'd rather."

"It isn't that. I'm just . . . overwhelmed. I need some time to adjust. So much has changed so fast. It feels like I'm caught in a dream. Nothing seems real. Except the pain, believe me, it's real."

He pulled her out of the chair and kissed her. "Everything here is real, too, JoAnn. From now on, things will get easier. I've got everything arranged to make your life simple for a while. Everything."

Another tear ran down JoAnn's cheek. "I certainly hope so," she whispered, "I certainly hope so."

Chapter 12

Jess, Jonathan, and Stacey were all exhausted the next day. Jess disappeared at sunrise to go to the clinic and treat the injured animals that had been too ill to send home. Stacey and Jonathan had a quiet breakfast, then spent the morning cleaning up the yard and cooking. Just after Jess came home for lunch, Jonathan ran through the house screaming, "She's here! She's here! I saw her car from my window!"

"Who?"

"Ms. Rayburn! Did you forget she was coming over for lunch?"

Jess and Stacey exchanged knowing looks and smiled. Stacey said, "Luckily, I cooked enough for an army. I thought after yesterday, we could all use a good meal."

"Hamburgers and fries?"

"Wake up, Jess. You're dreaming again."

While Jess and Stacey went outside to help JoAnn in, Jon rounded up Rocky and Bell. It was a beautiful autumn day, so they settled JoAnn into a softly padded lounge chair on the back patio. Within seconds, the puppies were crawling over her, welcoming her as only they could.

Jess said, "Don't be shy, if you need anything at all, you just ask."

"I will. I haven't mastered the fine art of crutching quite yet, so I need all the help I can get. Looks like you all made it through the storm okay."

Stacey said, "Barely. It was quite an experience."

"Where will school be while they're doing the repairs?"

"They're setting up some portable partitions in the gym and cafeteria."

Jonathan ran up and breathlessly said, "You mean we'll still have to go to school? No way!"

Stacey mimicked him and said, "Yes, way. It'll take a lot more than a little tornado to close school. You may get a couple of days off, but it won't be long."

"That's not fair! We shouldn't have to go back so soon. It was a troubmatic experience."

"Traumatic experience. You don't look very traumatized to me. In fact, you look pretty spirited."

"Geez. Kids don't get any breaks." After kicking the ground, he ran off to play with the dogs.

"How does smoked turkey, green salad, broccoli with almond slivers, French bread, and a coconut meringue pie sound?" Stacey asked.

"Wonderful. I just wish I could help. I feel like such a burden."

Jess remembered all too well what kind of shape JoAnn's house was in the last time he saw it. "It's no trouble. Really. Have you been by your house yet?"

"I think so."

"You're not sure? Maybe you shouldn't be driving."

"Believe me, right now I wish my house was just a hallucination. Or better yet, a casualty of the tornado."

"The place was quite a mess when I saw it. We'd be glad to help you straighten up."

"That's the problem. There's no mess to clean up. My boss had his interior decorator redo the living room and den. Spotless doesn't even come close to describing it. Surreal pops to mind, though."

Stacey grimaced. "Isn't that overstepping the employer/employee relationship a bit? I'd be horrified if the principal of the school redecorated my apartment, even if she was only trying to be nice."

JoAnn's eyes watched her own hands work furiously, one fidgeting with the edge of the cast on the other. "This isn't the normal employer/employee relationship. He and I are, well, we're . . . involved."

Stacey slid under Jess's arm and hugged him from the side. "We understand. It's nothing to be embarrassed about. I really shouldn't be dating the father of one of my students, much less be living in his house. I take it from your reaction that his decorating taste doesn't match yours."

"That's putting it mildly. I live in the house my grandparents built near Swan Lake. It's a beautiful, quaint older home. Before my . . . injuries, it still had the furniture I grew up with, and now suddenly everything is chrome, glass, and leather. I know I should be grateful for all the work he had done, but I feel like a stranger there now."

Stacey said, "Maybe it will grow on you."

"I suppose. At least I have a while to get used to the idea before I have to live there. J.D., that's my boss, offered to let me stay at his condo for a while, since I wouldn't have to negotiate any stairs. Maybe by the time I go home, I'll have a better attitude. I suppose it could grow on me."

Jess said, "I'm sure it will, and if it doesn't, you can always change it. We'll be happy to keep the puppies as long as you want. Jon loves them."

JoAnn watched as the dogs chased Jon around the backyard. "And they love him," she said. "I wish I had more time to play with them."

"Maybe we'll come by after school once in a while when you're back in the swing of things. Meanwhile, I need to run back down to the clinic for a few minutes to treat the animals again. Will you ladies excuse me for twenty or thirty minutes?"

Stacey said, "Sure. Just don't smuggle any greasy cholesterol-burgers back with you." He pinched her and waved good-bye. She pulled a chair up next to JoAnn and said, "Jess tells me you have a fascinating job at TechLab, JoAnn. Chief of Research?"

"Yes. I used to think it was a great job. Now I'm not so sure."

"I read about the Shore woman's murder at River-parks. And wasn't there some kind of bizarre accident that killed another TechLab employee just recently?"

JoAnn sadly nodded and replied, "Yes, Amy White was trampled by a horse."

"Did you know either of them?"

"Hanna was my supervisor, and Amy was a tech in BioHazard. She was in my department."

"BioHazard?"

"There's an entire division of TechLab everyone refers to as 'BioHazard' mainly because we all share the same underground facility. All the top secret projects are maintained in our area, which is adjacent to the sophisticated laboratories used to monitor contagious diseases. That lab is actually the only one that's a true biohazard, but the name was applied to the rest of us. That way Security can keep an eye on all the potentially dangerous projects and make sure the corporate secrets are guarded at the same time."

"So you don't work with contagious diseases?"

"No, basically my goal is to retard the growth of cancer cells, possibly find a way to reverse the process altogether. The actual biohazard research is both interesting and terrifying, though. The scientists and techs all wear space suit-type protective garments at all times. If they somehow become contaminated, even by a pinprick, then the entire facility locks down to ensure the disease doesn't spread. A slip of a needle or a scalpel could prove to be deadly. I don't envy them."

"It's too bad it's so dangerous. Sounds like it would make a great field trip for my class. They'd love to see people working in space suits. It would be quite a thrill."

"BioHazard is off-limits to unauthorized visitors, but TechLab has an interesting tour of their pharmaceutical supply subsidiary. Lots of conveyor belts, fancy packaging machinery, and high-tech computer graphics."

"For the first time ever, I'm not worried about taking a class of first-graders on a field trip. This year, the kids started out pretty rowdy, but now they're like little robots. You should have seen them in the tornado, they did exactly what they were told to do."

"You sound as though that's a bad thing."

Stacey waved her hands and smiled as she said, "Don't get me wrong, they do everything I ask, when I ask, and I really appreciate it. But I've never had a class before where the majority of the kids just accept everything they're told without question. There's no spark in their eyes when they grasp a new concept. It's almost like they're memorizing everything and spitting it back out on command. I only have three kids who seem to be excited about learning. What's even more surprising is they're my special kids."

"Special?"

"Learning disabled. I have two dyslexic children and one little girl who has an auditory processing disorder. I hate the tags the system puts on children who are different, so I just call them special. I've always thought that as a first-grade teacher, the most important job I have is making sure every single child feels good about themselves. The academic work will fall into place if the children feel like they have something to contribute to this world."

"So special children are in regular classrooms?"

"It depends on the severity of the disability. Even extremely handicapped children are mainstreamed as much as possible these days, at least in large school districts. Children accept what they're taught. If they're taught that handicapped people just have different challenges in life, then they react to them as equals. It's really incredible to see how much love and attention children have to give to kids who are less fortunate than they are.

"Budget constraints make mainstreaming tough, though. The severely handicapped children need a full-time teacher's assistant with them. Otherwise, the teacher ends up spending a disproportionate amount of time with one child at the expense of all the others in the class."

JoAnn fleetingly wondered if she would ever even have children, much less be able to devote herself to their needs as much as someone like Stacey did. She warmly smiled at her and said, "The kids are lucky to have someone who cares as much as you do."

"I have a motive. I have a mild learning disability myself. I know how frustrating school can be for these children."

"Then they're even luckier than I thought. Your problems sound a lot like the budget problems I work with now that I'm considered management. Allocating funds between research projects is a real problem. We spend hour after hour in boring meetings listening to the different scientists pitch their pet projects. Of course, most of the money has to be funneled into the research that will benefit the masses. But researching treatments and cures for rare diseases is important, too. I guess no matter what you do for a living, one way or another you have to bow to the financial burdens that bind our society."

"When will you go back to work?"

JoAnn sighed and said, "I'm not really sure. A few months ago I would have already found a way to be there. I'd probably have snuck out of the hospital in the middle of the night just so I could get back in the lab and try a new twist in the molecular structure of my latest synthetic blocking agent, or I'd have been poring over trade publications looking for neuro-biological advances in other fields that might be trans-ferable to my research. But things have changed so much lately, I wish I never had to go back to TechLab again."

"You don't think your attack was related to your job, do you?"

JoAnn's eyes fell back on her cast, then she looked straight at Stacey. "I honestly don't know. I've had plenty of time to think lately, and I really believe I was just a victim of random violence. The guy was an ex-con and he'd only been out of jail a couple of weeks. I was probably in the wrong place at the wrong time. The trouble is, with everything that's happened in the last few weeks, it could very easily be connected to TechLab."

"Have you talked to the police about your suspi-cions?"

"I wouldn't dare. I know you don't know me from Adam, but I really need someone to talk to who's more objective than I am. Would you mind?"

"I'd be happy to listen, but remember, most of the advice I give is geared toward first-graders. Simple so-lutions for relatively simple problems. This sounds far from simple, but I'll help in any way I can."

JoAnn spent the next fifteen minutes going through the details of Hanna's murder, the mysterious warning Hanna sent, the calendar Rocky discovered, and Amy's sudden death.

When JoAnn finished, Stacey leaned forward and said, "I'm really glad we talked, JoAnn. It must be something in the air. Strange things are going on in my life right now, too."

"So your life has gone haywire, too?"

"I'll say. The night my apartment burned, I found a little silver thing inside one of my wall outlets. I didn't think anything of it until the fire department's arson specialist said it was a bug."

"A listening device?"

"Yes. They sent it to the FBI for confirmation, but he seemed pretty positive. He also says he thinks the fire was started by some sort of sophisticated incendiary device planted under my bed."

"That is scary."

"I've become super-paranoid. I even checked Jess's wall outlets to make sure his house wasn't bugged. I won't talk about anything important or unusual unless we're outside. Crazy, huh?"

"Not at all." JoAnn closed her eyes and felt the sun on her face. "I'm glad we had our discussion outside. With my luck, TechLab has bugged every house in the city to make sure I don't go AWOL before the project I'm working on is completed. I've always suspected our phone calls at work were monitored, but I wish I knew if my house was bugged."

"I'd be happy to check it out for you. I'm getting pretty good with a screwdriver."

"Would you? Jess knows where I keep the key in the flower pot out front. I'll leave J.D.'s number with you before I go."

Stacey rubbed her hands together. "It'll be fun. Like playing cops and robbers. Besides, I'd love to see what your house looks like now."

"I wish I could say the same."

"Does TechLab stand to lose much if you decided to find another job?"

JoAnn laughed. "Millions, maybe more. They've plowed a substantial amount of money in my work for the last ten years, and now that it's been upgraded to a top-priority project, the budget is virtually unlimited. I guess I can't blame them for being a little worried about my well-being."

"Then it makes no sense that they would be behind the attack. Unless, of course, someone else could pick up your research where you left off. Could they?"

"Yes and no. I've kept detailed technical documentation of every step of my research, so from that sense any scientist could pick up the pieces and forge on. The problem is, completing a project like mine is similar to raising a child. Both processes are a lifetime commitment and require total devotion. Most parents instinctively know which discipline to use and when to use it. A substantial part of perfecting a treatment protocol is skill, but part is a combination of blind luck and inspiration. Some people would call it intuition or even destiny. I've dreamed of nothing but finding this cure for the last ten years. I hope I can still do it, and I know that if I leave TechLab I can't. Legally, they own all rights to the work I've done under my contract with them."

"I'm sure you can still succeed. It may not be in the way you initially thought, but life has a way of working these things out. I hear Jess's car. Do you mind if later I tell him what you've told me? He might have some helpful ideas."

JoAnn leaned over and whispered, "Be sure to talk to him outside or use Morse code. Okay?"

Stacey laughed. "I'll either tell him in pig Latin, or I'll make sure the background noise inside is loud enough to drive whoever could be listening crazy. If someone does have this house bugged, they're probably comatose by now anyway."

"Why?"

"First of all, because we lead such boring lives; and second, ever since I became ultra-paranoid I play my nature tape constantly. Between the sound of the ocean waves and the singing whales, those poor eavesdropping fools probably are facedown in their beer nuts or heavy into yoga."

The women were laughing when Jess came through the house and stepped onto the patio. "Looks like I missed all the fun. Let me guess. Two single women laughing . . . you were probably male bashing."

They laughed even harder. Stacey managed to say, "Talk about paranoid," which doubled JoAnn over and brought tears to her eyes.

After highlighting their conversation for Jess, Stacey promised to fill in the rest of the details after JoAnn went home. Once they were finished eating, Jess helped Jonathan strap on his rollerblades and he joined an impromptu game of street hockey with several of his neighborhood buddies.

As she watched him skate away, JoAnn suddenly remembered the blood sample Jess had given her to test. "I'm sorry I haven't gotten back to you on Jon's blood test. I ran a few preliminary tests the last night I was at work, but I got some rather confusing results. To be sure they were accurate, I requested a complete workup by Pathology. I'm sure the results have been in my tube for days now."

"Tube?" Jess said.

"TechLab spares no expense. A computerized network of pneumatic tubes connects the various research labs with Pathology. It saves a great deal of time and ensures the samples being tested are confidential and safe."

Stacey said, "You mean like the systems they have at the drive-in bank windows?"

"The same basic idea, only much larger and more sophisticated. I'll be going in on Monday with J.D. for a little while."

Stacey said, "Are you sure that's a good idea?"

"J.D. wants me to talk to the lab techs who report to me. He thinks they need a pep talk, but I think they just need to see that it wasn't TechLab who did this to me and that I'm all right. I could tell when they stopped by the hospital to visit that some of them are getting pretty nervous, especially my assistant, Leanne. It won't take long, and I can grab Jon's test results while I'm there."

Jess said, "I took him to his pediatrician a few days ago. You'd have thought they shot him when they drew his blood, but somehow he survived."

"Did they find anything?"

"The hematology results were inconclusive. Since there were some abnormalities, but nothing specifically identifiable, the doctor wants to wait eight weeks and retest him."

"I'm sure he'll love that."

"I haven't told him."

"Smart man."

"From what little I've heard, I'd guess security is really tight at TechLab. Are you sure you can't get into any trouble for running the blood tests?"

JoAnn cringed as she remembered the strange similarities Jonathan's blood showed to her Citrinol3 test cases. With results like that, no one would believe it wasn't part of her project even if they did find out. "I'm positive," she said.

Stacey said, "I suppose they have all those high-tech identification systems like they show in the movies?"

"If you mean a machine that verifies who is entering by checking their retina, or one that does voice printing, the answer is no. Our corporate headquarters are in the buildings above the underground labs. Even though employees are always supposed to wear their identification badges, anyone can come and go as they please. It gets a little more complicated if you try to take the elevator down to the underground facility, though. You have to run your security card through an electronic reader or the elevator won't work. Then in order to gain access to the BioHazard wing, you have to punch in the code at the main door. Once you're inside the holding chamber you have to enter the security clearance code for that particular week to get all the way inside."

"The employees have to memorize a new code every week?" Stacey asked.

"That one is usually easy. No one is supposed to have noticed, but they always pick a number sequence that spells a color on the keyboard."

Jess said, "So if you were to need help from someone outside, there would be no way we could get in. TechLab sounds like it has all the odds in its favor. Maybe Hanna was right. Getting out before anything happens might be the best idea."

"I thought about that while I was in the hospital. Believe me, I had plenty of time for paranoid planning and dark thoughts. Leaving TechLab means throwing out the last ten years of my life. I don't know if I can do that."

"I wouldn't want to have to make that kind of decision without all the facts either. I'd feel better about the whole situation if I knew you could get help if you ever needed it."

"The problem is, even if I had a way to get someone inside, I'd never ask anyone to risk their life. Part of me feels stupid for even thinking such horrible things about TechLab, and another part of me is screaming—*run away, run away!*"

"If you ever do need help, I'd be glad to come."

"Me, too," Stacey added.

"It really is very generous of both of you to offer. I just wouldn't feel right about asking."

Jess said, "Listen, TechLab is one of the largest companies in Tulsa. If they're doing anything illegal, it'll impact all of us, not just its employees."

"I do know of a way that might get someone inside, but I'm not positive it would work. The calendar Rocky found had Hanna's identification codes inside. If Security didn't cancel them when she died, they allow access to all top-security clearance areas. Would you mind if I left the numbers with you? Just in case?" She jotted down the numbers and handed them to Jess.

"Not at all. Promise you'll call us if you need anything at all. Especially if something goes wrong. I can be there in ten minutes."

"And what will you say if the codes don't work and Security has you dragged off to jail?"

"I'll just tell them I got an emergency call about a sick lab animal. Your lab animals do get sick, don't they?"

"Unfortunately, most of them die premature deaths in the name of science. We have a staff veterinarian who handles illnesses that can't be related to the experimental treatments. I guess I could say he didn't answer his page."

"What kind of illnesses does he treat? I'm not exactly an expert on rodents."

"We have a wide variety of animals. Sure, there are quite a few rodents, but we have primates as well, monkeys, then some dogs, cats, and pigs. We usually call him to treat broken bones, cuts, and lacerations. Sometimes the animals get pretty violent as a side effect of different drugs. We try to restrain them, but it isn't always done soon enough and occasionally they hurt themselves."

Stacey grimaced in disgust. "Science can be so cruel."

"I guess I've gotten used to the idea. Testing on these animals makes it possible to jump from the test tube stage of an experiment to a living creature without endangering human life. They're a necessary evil. Like war." JoAnn suddenly smiled. "I have an idea. Why don't I talk to J.D. about having you be listed as an alternative veterinarian to call in emergencies? If he buys it, Security will do a thorough background check, then they'll issue you your own identification numbers. It might even be a good way to earn a little extra money. TechLab may have its share of faults, but paying its people fairly isn't one of them."

"I don't think it would be a long-term project I'd want, but for now I think it's a brilliant idea. How long do you think it would take for them to clear me?"

"Probably four to six weeks. They are very, very careful."

"Then it's a good thing I'm squeaky clean."

Stacey said, "Except that you have a strange woman living in your house."

He pulled her into his arms and said, "And I thought you were just a little unusual. Now that you mention it, strange does fit you pretty well . . ."

"When will your apartment be ready?" JoAnn asked.

"The landlord has no idea. He acts like I took a torch and burned the place down on purpose. I hate even talking to him."

JoAnn excitedly said, "You could move into my place. I won't be there for a while, but even when I am there it isn't for very long on any given day. I spend most of my waking hours at work, as well as most of the time I should be sleeping and eating. At least, I used to."

"That's very generous of you." Stacey hesitated, then tentatively added, "Have you ever had a roommate before?"

"No. Is that a problem?"

"I've tried having roommates share the cost of my apartment twice and so far it's always been disastrous. I tend to lean a bit too far on the neat side for most people. They would leave the kitchen stacked with dirty dishes and the bathroom looking like a mud wrestling team had invaded. It drove me absolutely crazy. I swore I'd never try it again."

"I know this sounds odd, but my house never gets very dirty. I'm not there enough to make much of a mess, and I have a woman who mows the yard and a cleaning lady who comes once a month and does the heavy-duty stuff. Speaking of which, I'd better call her before she walks in the front door and has a heart attack. Why don't you think about it for a week or so and let me know? I'll be at J.D.'s at least that long. Besides, this doesn't have to be anything permanent. It might be a good place to stay until next summer, then you could decide something more long-term."

"I'll definitely consider it. I've been thinking of buying a little house, and it would give me a better idea if I'm up to it. If you don't mind, I'll look around your place while I do that little deed we discussed earlier."

Jess said, "Uh-oh. What are you two up to?"

JoAnn winked at Stacey and said, "Stacey kindly offered to give me her opinion of the new furniture."

"I suppose she'll be wielding her power screwdriver while she scopes the place out for you?"

"Maybe."

"Paranoid. You're both totally paranoid." He smiled slyly and winked as he said, "Can I come along?"

* * *

"Is this what you had in mind, Mr. Cook? We've added this door to connect Ms. Rayburn's office to the vacant one next door, and we've moved all the things you had brought from her house in there. Looks pretty comfy, doesn't it?"

"You've done a fine job on such short notice. Did you install locks on both doors?"

"Just like you asked."

"I'll make sure your supervisor hears about your diligence."

"Thank you, sir. Do you need anything else? There's a toilet backing up on the third floor that needs my personal touch."

"Then I certainly wouldn't want to keep you a second longer. Thanks again." J.D. watched the maintenance man walk down the hall and turn the corner before he went into JoAnn's office. After closing the door and locking it he took the photographs out of his pocket and flipped through them once again. His hired friend had given him pictures of the latest in eavesdropping technology, everything from common bugs to fiber-optic cameras. Included were up-close pictures of the surveillance items found in his own house and planted on his car. He pushed down the surge of anger that always threatened to break through when he realized how much of his life the security guards had probably been privy to.

Once he was sure of what he was looking for, he began his search. After ten minutes, he was about to give up. He was lying on the floor peering up at the back of the printer stand when he saw the small object. A quick reference to his pictures affirmed his suspicions. He then went into the second office, and after a thorough search found an identical match under one of the tables that had just been brought from JoAnn's home.

Less than eight hours after its delivery, that son of a bitch had already had her things bugged.

Even though he knew better, he grabbed the small silver device, threw it to the ground, and smashed it. He then stormed back into JoAnn's office and scooted down where he was sure his message would be heard loud and clear.

"You can tell Harper that Ms. Rayburn is not a security risk and that any further attempt to invade either her privacy or mine will be taken up directly with Gene Lemmond. Her presence here is absolutely essential until the Citrinol3 project is back on-line. Understand?" He then snatched the small device, threw it down and crushed it under his heel.

Several floors up, the security guard on duty ripped his headphones off for the second time in two minutes. Harper was going to love this tape. He only hoped he could manage to hang around long enough after he delivered it to watch his reaction.

JoAnn watched the Sunday morning scenery, her mind a thousand miles away from work. J.D. had waited on her hand and foot, planned every second to seem more like a romantic vacation than a painful detour in her life. That morning he had made love to her as though she were a fragile doll, worrying only about her pleasure, her needs. Finally at ease, she vowed to push down all the nagging thoughts that were keeping her from finding happiness with J.D. After all he had done, he deserved a chance.

She glanced up to see a steady stream of people slowly emerging from a beautiful church as they passed. Suddenly she realized it was the same church she drove by every day on the way to work. Sitting up straight, she said, "J.D., we're not going to TechLab, are we? I thought we were just going for a nice ride to get out of the house for a while."

"I can't wait any longer to show you what I've done. I know you'll be as excited as I am."

JoAnn didn't respond; instead she mentally pictured his last surprise and wondered if this one could possibly be as bad.

Chapter 13

JoAnn hadn't really looked at TechLab's corporate and research facilities in years, since it was usually dark when she arrived at work and dark again when she left. As they approached the elegant buildings nestled in rolling woods, she realized how impressive the darkly designed structures truly were. English ivy cascaded over balconies on every floor. The landscaping was immaculate, with perfectly symmetrical dogwood trees lining the central entryway, each turning brilliantly red to welcome autumn. The summer flowers had all been removed, and bright yellow and black pansies blanketed the rows of flower beds that separated the visitor parking places from the road.

J.D. stopped at TechLab's main entrance and helped JoAnn out of the car so she wouldn't have to walk quite as far. At her slow pace, he parked the car and caught up with her before she even reached the main elevator bank.

"I don't have my purse, so I don't have my security card," she said.

"I'll show you the executive bypass if you promise not to tell a soul. Do you know your access number by heart?"

"Sure. It's 07 24 84 10 29 85." She didn't tell him that Hanna had shown her the override only two days after she came to work there, or that most of the employees used it whenever their cards weren't handy.

"I can't believe you can remember that long a

number. Mine is one of the original codes with only six digits, and I still have a hard time remembering it." He laughed, then said, "Once a friend of mine called to me when I was getting on the elevator. I stopped and talked to him for a few seconds, then I accidentally keyed in my number after I'd already used my security card. All hell broke loose."

"Why?"

"The system monitors duplicate entries. They probably thought someone else had found out my identification number and they were trying to sneak into the building."

"What happened?"

"When the elevator finally opened on Subfloor 4, there were three gunbarrels pointed at my chest. I didn't even breathe. Luckily one of them knew who I was and called off the other two."

"They wouldn't really shoot anyone, would they?"

"Trespassing is a serious crime, but I think that the infiltrator would have to be armed before they'd hurt him."

"Or her."

"Excuse me. I guess I need a refresher course in avoiding sexist language. We actually made all our managers take a two-day seminar a few years ago. It was called GNAT. You're supposed to be brilliant. What do you think GNAT stands for?"

JoAnn hesitated, then said, "Other than being a pesky little fly that bites, I suppose it means Gender-Neutral Administrative Terminology."

"You cheated."

"How could I?" She wasn't about to tell him she clearly remembered Hanna coming back from the seminar and complaining about all the sexist remarks the men had made the whole time, like a bunch of irritating gnats buzzing around. "Besides, what else could it stand for?" she added innocently.

He squinted his eyes and glared at her until they were at the entrance to BioHazard. "Since you're so smart, I'll let you use your access code."

"I wasn't here last week, so I don't know the secondary code."

"Aqua."

She punched in the long series of numbers and the first set of doors slid open. They stepped in and the doors closed behind them. When she entered the numbers that matched A-Q-U-A, the second door opened as well. "Do these security measures ever seem rather childish to you?"

"Never. The amount of industrial espionage is unbelievable. People think it only happens in James Bond movies because they don't read about it in the papers or see it on the news."

"I noticed there wasn't anything on the cleaning woman."

"There won't be."

"But how can you keep it quiet?"

"Let's just say Gene Lemmond has friends in both high and low places."

"A little palm greasing?"

"Not as much as TechLab's pull for adding thousands of jobs and millions in tax revenue. People reciprocate the favor TechLab does for the entire community in any way they can."

She thought, *Bullshit*, but kept her mouth closed. The crutches were getting easier to use, but she was already exhausted from the long hike down to the BioHazard wing. Besides the stinging spikes of pain crawling up from her ankle, her underarms ached, her broken finger throbbed, and she wished her head would either stop pounding or roll off her shoulders.

They were at her office door, which was closed, when J.D. asked, "Are you all right?"

"I've been better."

He slid a key in the doorknob and said, "This should lift your spirits."

JoAnn cautiously went in and sighed her relief when she saw that everything was pretty much the way she had left it. She glanced around, noticing the only change was a door that had been added in the far wall.

"This way, my dear."

She followed him over and stood behind him. Without realizing it, she closed her eyes and took a deep breath as he threw open the connecting door. When she opened her eyes, she thought she must be confused. She shook her head and looked again.

Her bedroom was right there in front of her. At TechLab. The bed, nightstands, and comforter were there. Her antique dressing table, cushioned rocker, and cedar chest were there. Even her curtains were hanging on each side of the bed as though there were windows behind them. If windows were behind those curtains, they would have to open to a wonderful view of solid stone. She walked over and pulled the satiny material away from the wall, half expecting to miraculously see her backyard as she peeked behind it. A blank ivory wall brought her back to reality.

What the hell are you doing to my life? she wanted to scream.

"Now you can come back to work tomorrow, or just stay today, if you like. Whenever you get tired, you just lock the door to your office and come in here. All this has been done after hours, so none of the other employees know this is here. Your doctor even thinks it's a grand idea. After I explained how important your work is to you, he was all for it."

Remind me to tell the bastard to mind his own goddamn business next time.

"Why don't you move in today? I'll bring your meals, or the company cafeteria will bring something down, and you can work whenever you feel up to it. No commuting, no long walks between the parking lot and BioHazard. It will save you an incredible amount of time and energy."

She tried to sound enthusiastic as she said, "And we can get the Citrinol3 tests back on schedule."

"I knew you'd understand. Well, what do you think? Maintenance did a great job, didn't they?"

I think you'd do anything to keep me under your thumb. "You have been a busy little beaver, haven't you? First my house, and now this. No wonder you were having a hard time holding down the fort."

"I did it all for you, JoAnn. You and that Nobel Prize you're going to win."

Kiss my fuzzy butt, you asshole. JoAnn started to laugh, as much at her own biting thoughts as at the extent J.D. would go to in order to get work done. *That's what all this is to you, isn't it? A job. I'm part of your fucking job. Or is it, fucking me is part of your job?* She laughed so hard, one crutch fell to the floor and she leaned against the wall for support.

In a few seconds the laughter turned to tears. As J.D. tried to kiss them away, JoAnn cringed. She felt as though she no longer had control over any aspect of her job or her life. J.D. carried her to the bed, and sensing she needed to be alone, he kissed her cheek and left her surrounded by the cold concrete walls.

JoAnn wondered if this was how caged animals felt—confined, abandoned, and incredibly frustrated.

A few hours later JoAnn dialed Jess Lawrence's number as she sat at her desk looking through the stack of work in her IN box. When Stacey answered she said, "Hi. This is JoAnn."

"How are you feeling?"

"Okay. I need to give you a different number where you can reach me for the next few weeks."

Stacey hesitated. "You mean you won't be at the number you gave us just yesterday?"

"There's been a slight change of plans. I'll be staying at TechLab."

"But . . . How can that be? Your doctor can't possibly have released you already. Maybe Jess and I should . . ."

"Wait, Stacey. Remember all we talked about yesterday? Especially that favor you're going to do for me, and being careful while I recover. I think those things are even more important now, and I wouldn't want to slow down the healing process."

"I understand. Does TechLab have some sort of living quarters you'll be staying in? Can we at least come by and visit? Rocky and Bell will expect to see you, not to mention Jonathan."

"My boss wanted to make it as simple as possible for me to work, so he had the office next to mine converted into a place for me to stay." Her voice became very flat as she added, "He even moved my bedroom furniture in so I'd feel at home. He thinks of everything, doesn't he?"

Stacey was silent for a few seconds, then she quietly said, "How can we contact you?"

"My direct phone line is 555-0108. If I'm not in, just leave a message on my voice mail."

"Can you get mail?"

"Just send it care of TechLab. I suppose I need to contact the post office and have all my things forwarded here for a while. Thanks for reminding me."

"Let me make sure I understand this. You're going to be working around the clock, aren't you?"

"I can if I want to. I suppose that's the beauty of this plan. I can heal, and at the same time my project won't fall any further behind schedule. From a purely technical, professional standpoint, it's a brilliant idea. I just need to get used to the concept. Considering how much time I've always spent here, my life won't be much different than it was before the attack."

Another silence. Stacey was obviously weighing every word. "I know how you must feel. Since we're going to be roommates soon, I'll need to keep in touch. Maybe you can figure out a way."

JoAnn smiled. "That was a pretty fast decision considering you haven't even seen the house yet."

"It's funny, but somehow it just feels right."

"I can't tell you how much I appreciate it. I'm here so much, having someone around to play with Rocky and Bell will make me feel less guilty. Besides, it'll be fun to have an actual person to talk to. The dogs are precious, but they really aren't great at giving advice."

"Since you'll be living at work for a while, can I at least come by and have lunch with you? I'd be happy to bring something."

"I'll see if I can get it cleared with Security tomorrow. Teachers don't have much time off for lunch, do they?"

"Normally, no. But this week is fall break, so I'm off on Thursday and Friday. Why don't we plan something for Friday? I can look over your house on Thursday and we can work out the details of my moving in when I come for lunch."

"Even if I can't get Security to clear it, I could still meet you somewhere. After all, I'm not a prisoner here. It's just a convenient solution to a very inconvenient problem."

"Right."

"Tell Jonathan and Jess hello for me."

"I will. Take care of yourself."

"Bye." JoAnn stared at the phone for several seconds, then rolled her chair back and hopped over to the door. Balancing herself, she pushed the button on the side of the small silver opening. It slid back, and she pulled out the cylindrical pneumatic tube.

Popping the top of it off, she withdrew the protective foam casing, removed the specimens and lab report, and returned the empty tube to its chamber.

After she hopped back to her desk, she began to read the report. At first, most of the results were normal, as she expected. Cholesterol, HDL, LDL, and triglycerides were all within expected ranges for a young, healthy child. But then her stomach turned as she read the remarks section under the title Cellular Structure/Function. For the last two years, almost every report on Citrinol3 had contained problems in this area. She knew what to expect and braced herself, although, logically, she knew it would be virtually impossible to duplicate Citrinol3's exact pattern of cell damage.

Logic didn't make reading the results any easier, so she read them again and again. "Irregularity and thickening of cell walls due to protein deposits ... oxygen absorption deficiency ... presence of beta amyloid in plasma and plaque formations on red blood cells."

Amyloid plaque. I must have confused the specimens somehow. This is totally impossible.

A stack of Priority One reports waited in front of each seat. Even though it was Sunday, an Executive Board meeting was scheduled to begin in five minutes. As each person arrived a seat was taken, the top folder was opened, and they silently studied the information at hand. When Gene Lemmond spoke, all eyes simultaneously lifted. "The status reports on Citrinol3 are quite interesting. I'm particularly impressed by the effects on the beagle."

Parker McDaniel picked up the top file folder from in front of him and said, "For those of us who haven't had a chance to read the report, could Cook fill us in?"

J.D. responded, "I'd be happy to." He looked around

the table, studying the eyes of the other men. "I'm sure you are all aware that the field tests of Citrinol3 are being conducted at two primary locations—River-Birch Retirement Community and East Elementary School. So far, the test results have been very beneficial, and we expect to narrow the drug's side effects tremendously from the information we've accumulated. The discovery made yesterday should be of vital concern.

"Some of you may already know that one of the patients at RiverBirch has a beagle. The beagle was a Christmas present to the old man from his grandchildren approximately three years ago, shortly before he entered the retirement home. Lucky for us, River-Birch believes in supporting their patients' mental health and encourages pets.

"The dog started showing signs of decreased activity approximately two weeks ago. Per our staff veterinarian, the normal onset of such a decrease is ten years of age. Since this dog is only three years old, we suspected the Citrinol3 might be a factor. It was tough, but we managed to obtain a blood sample to confirm our suspicions, and to prove that the beagle is developing symptoms that mirror the classic side effects of Citrinol3. As you all know, this is a very exciting advance. Finding an animal model at this stage is an incredible breakthrough."

McDaniel said, "How are you planning on explaining this to JoAnn Rayburn? She's been searching for an animal model for ten years."

"It's under control. One of our field research doctors, Gordon Sterns, is preparing the memo."

McDaniel seemed shocked. "But isn't he a botanist in our Mexico City office?"

J.D. raised one eyebrow and said, "I'm impressed by your knowledge of the international network. As a matter of fact, he is, but JoAnn won't know that. We should have a convincing report in house by tomorrow afternoon that details the discovery of beta amyloid proteins by several research groups in canines, specifically beagles."

"What if she tries to contact him? She will, you know. She's pretty rigorous when it comes to tracking down details."

"That's the beauty of my plan. He's leaving at the end of the week for a six-month stint with the Rainforest Coalition. He's screening plants for possible medicinal use, so he'll be in the middle of South America by the time she tries to contact him."

"How has the East Elementary site been affected by the recent storm damage?"

"As a matter of fact, it couldn't have happened at a better time. We had a long enough initial exposure time to study, and now we can resume the experiment in January and compare the results. In the lab, the drug took several months to clear the system. Now we'll have a good idea how long it takes in humans."

"So, for now, there won't be any additional exposure or testing?"

"As a matter of fact, McDaniel, we need you to arrange to accumulate some testing information. The same I.Q. tests we administered in September need to be repeated now, and again in January. Can you use the ITL cover and handle it?"

He smugly answered, "Of course."

Even though the clinic was closed, it echoed with the sounds of barking dogs, so Stacey raised her voice to say, "There must be something we can do. She sounded totally miserable." Stacey was cradling a small poodle in her arms as she waited for Jess to join her.

Jess finally managed to catch the collie that had been eluding him, and he slipped a leash around her neck. "You crazy girl, you usually love me. Why were you running away? Playing hard to get, aren't you?" he said as he followed Stacey outside.

"Are you talking to me or the dog?" Stacey asked.

"The dog, but now that you mention it, I suppose you're playing hard to get, too. I keep hoping to wake up and see you've crawled into bed next to me."

"Remember your son, my student? What would he think if he came wandering in?"

Jess pulled her against him, his lips grazing her ear as he playfully asked, "Isn't that why someone invented locks for doors?"

Stacey sighed, "We both know it isn't that easy. Once we cross that line, our whole relationship changes." Quietly she added, "I just want to be sure."

He started to reply, but his mouth snapped closed. After a few seconds he quietly asked, "Are you really going to move into JoAnn's house?"

He barely heard her say, "I think so."

Pulling her even closer he said, "I'd rather you stay with us."

"The temptation is too great. I'm afraid my will-power will be lost some night when I catch a glimpse of that hard body of yours. Those boxer shorts you traipse around in don't leave much to the imagination, you know."

He smiled friskily. "Thanks for noticing. I've noticed those long sweatshirt things you sleep in are pretty impenetrable. But don't worry, I have a great imagination."

"Thank God that guy invented door locks, huh?"

"Depends on which side of the door you're on. Seriously, I want you to know how much I care about you. If I tell you I've fallen madly in love with you will you run away screaming?"

Stacey pulled the poodle closer to Jess so she could kiss him. "Why don't you try me?"

"I love you."

She stood absolutely still while looking all around. "See, I'm still here."

"But you're still going to move into JoAnn's house, aren't you?"

"I think I have to. I need to be sure that all the things I feel for you aren't wrapped around your generosity at this horrible time of my life. I think I love you, but so much has happened so fast that I'm not sure what I feel. Maybe moving to JoAnn's house for a while will make things fall into place, give me some time to think."

"Absence makes the heart grow fonder?"

"Maybe. But mainly it's a personal hang-up of mine. I need to feel like I can do things for myself. I guess you could say I have a fear of being dependent on anyone besides myself. I've depended on you for so much since my apartment burned . . ."

"I understand. Really." He smiled and said, "I'll help you move your things."

Stacey laughed, too. "You mean all five outfits and my toothbrush? Really, it's so generous of you to offer, but I think I can handle it myself. For now, our main concern should be JoAnn. What are we going to do?"

He hesitated, then said, "She was evasive on the phone, so she must think there's a possibility they're monitoring her conversations. If they're watching that closely, I don't think we have many options. I know you won't believe me, but for totally unselfish reasons, I'm not sure it's a good idea for you to move out of my house right now. It could be dangerous."

Stacey was livid. "But that man has taken over her life! It's like she's a puppet and he's got the strings pulled as tight as they'll go without snapping. She just got out of the hospital and he's already managed to get her back to work. On a Sunday, no less. Besides, I thought you thought we were just being paranoid."

"I don't know what to think. So many odd things are going on. Plus, you have to realize that we hardly know JoAnn. What if she tends to be dramatic or deluded? Or worse yet, what if she really is in the middle of a game of corporate espionage? Then we're caught in the middle."

"Quit playing devil's advocate. I haven't known JoAnn for long, but she doesn't seem any more deluded than I am."

Jess grinned and tried to tickle her as he said, "And I'm supposed to take the word of a woman who comes to live in my house and checks the wall outlets for bugs? Then she insists on playing ocean songs and whispering half the time?"

Stacey wiggled away from him and said, "Maybe I just like to cuddle while I talk."

"And maybe this boss of hers only wants her to be comfortable while she recovers. JoAnn admits to being a workaholic, so he may think that she has to be at work to be happy. After all, he has gone to a hell of a lot of trouble from what she told us about her house and now her office."

"That's part of the problem. He's going way over the line of friendship. Even lovers don't take the extreme route he has. Why is he pushing this so hard? She's been working on this same project for ten years. What's a few weeks now?"

"You've probably just figured it out. There must be something going down in the next month or two that's critical. Maybe the project is up for review again, or TechLab's stockholders' meeting is coming up. Who knows? Whatever it is, it must be his responsibility to make sure the BioHazard work is completed on time. She told us herself that she's the only one who can really see the project through to the end."

"Wouldn't it be easier just to tell JoAnn what he's

up against? She'd do whatever it takes to get the job done."

"Maybe, maybe not. Some people work great under pressure. Others freeze up. If he thinks she'll perform better without the added pressure, then he wouldn't tell her, would he?"

"I guess not. It all seems really kinky to me. Bedrooms at work."

"I'll agree with that. And what are the odds of being attacked in a parking lot on the same day your house is burglarized? Especially in this town."

"Probably the same as a grade-school teacher finding a bug in her living room and having her apartment burn down twenty minutes later."

"The fire inspector still hasn't called you back, has he?"

"No. I think my fall break is going to be spent trying to get some answers. And I'm not going to give up on helping JoAnn, either."

He pulled her close. "I never thought you would."

At six o'clock on Sunday night, JoAnn's hand was shaking as she pricked the end of her finger with a small sterile razor. She dropped the razor in the lab's contaminated trash container and walked over to the counter near the microscopes and centrifuges. After smearing her own blood on several slides, she dug through the supply cabinet until she found a Band-Aid.

For several seconds she stared at the slides. If Pathology had made a mistake on Jon's blood sample, then maybe she could catch them in the act. Perhaps the Pathology department was short staffed and they sent a copy of an old report to the code they recognized as her office in order to save time.

But the codes are supposedly top secret and altering lab reports would destroy years of research. No one would do that. It could make all my work useless. She shivered at the thought.

Still, finding an error seemed like her only hope at this point. She'd spent the last two hours trying to rationalize the test results, but everything she thought of was so bizarre she knew it was impossible. Looking around, she realized how much she missed working out here. She closed her eyes and thoughts of Hanna rushed in.

Hanna had spent hours in this section of the lab. She always called it the loft, since it was a platform area that looked down on the floor below. The electron microscope was in the middle of the lowest area of Bio-Hazard. Its immense size and the vibrations it caused required it to be. Glancing over the rail, JoAnn could see it still had an OUT OF ORDER sign dangling from it.

Hanna used to joke that the loft was her favorite place to work late at night, since her office made her claustrophobic after twelve or fifteen hours, and the vibrations from the electron microscope kept her awake.

JoAnn moved to the edge and glanced down at the equipment below. She understood now why Hanna liked this part of the lab so much. It was the only place where there was open space. Space to think. JoAnn slumped into a chair and put her face in her hands. Since her surgery, she hadn't been able to think clearly. Her mind flitted from subject to subject, and prolonged concentration was almost impossible. Looking out over the open area, she tried to put the pieces together again, but they floated beyond her grasp.

Two hours later she hobbled back into her office as depressed as she'd ever been. The Pathology forms were already complete, so she slid two of the specimens into the protective casing and listened as they were whisked away. By Monday afternoon she should know more of what she was up against. For now, she needed to rest, and to plan what to do next. She stumbled into the makeshift bedroom, dropped onto the bed, and instantly fell asleep.

It was late Monday afternoon when JoAnn heard the unmistakable *whoosh* of the pneumatic tube arriving from Pathology. She quickly hopped over, withdrew the contents from the mechanism, and hopped back to her desk. Frantically she searched the hematology report on her own blood for signs of amyloid proteins, but the report only showed traces of the antibiotics and anesthetic she'd been given at the hospital.

The sharp rap on her door startled her so much that she dropped both the slides and the report. Without even waiting for her to respond to his knock, J.D. came barreling in. The glass slides had shattered on impact, and JoAnn stood staring down at them.

"I suppose that's my fault."

"You could call first."

"I was too excited. I've got great news." He lifted her up, sat her on the desk, and started to clean up the broken glass. "Citrinol3 has just been given twenty-five canine slots in the kennel division. Isn't that great?"

JoAnn was shocked. "But why now? Our search for an animal model has been under way since shortly after the first genetic engineering began ten years ago. Is this just a blind shot in the dark?"

"That's what's so great. I know it should have been you who read the report first, but while you were out, one of the scientists found a correlation between some studies being done at another research facility and our project." He laid the neatly printed memorandum down on her desk. "I just got around to reading it this morning. Lemmond pounced on it. Without an animal model, the jump from test tube to human is too unpredictable to bank on. This puts the Citrinol3 project in the lead spot. You're TechLab's current star. How does it feel?"

JoAnn ignored his question, her mind still confused. She'd been watching for reports of similar studies for years. How could she have missed this one? "What breed?" she mumbled.

"Beagles."

"Beagles?"

"Yes. Aren't you excited? This could be the lead we've been waiting for. According to this memo, beagles can be tested for memory alterations and have amyloid proteins similar to the ones you're working with. What a break!"

"Having amyloid proteins doesn't ensure compatibility. What about tumor incidence?"

He patted the memo he left on her desk and stood up to leave. "It's all in there. I've got to go now. I'm bringing a romantic dinner tonight at seven. Have the candles ready."

She sighed, "I'll be here."

❧ Jess grabbed the phone a few seconds after the receptionist paged him. "Jess Lawrence."

"Hi, Jess. This is JoAnn. I'm sorry to bother you at work. Can you talk?"

"Sure. Stacey told me about your rather abrupt change in plans. Are you sure there's nothing we can do for you?"

JoAnn was silent for a moment, then finally said, "Well, there are a couple of favors I need to ask. First of all, could you give Stacey a message for me?"

"Sure."

"Tell her that Security denied letting me have a visitor for lunch inside the BioHazard wing, but that I'd love to meet her somewhere for lunch on Friday."

"If I can be a little on the forward side, I'd like to

invite myself along. Why don't we pick you up in front of TechLab at eleven-thirty? Would that work?"

"Sounds wonderful. It will be nice to see the sky again."

"It's a good thing you're not claustrophobic."

"True. I have one more favor. It might be a little more difficult, but I think you can handle it."

Jess quickly replied, "Just name it."

"Remember the night you diagnosed Bell's coccidia?"

"You bet."

"I need another specimen from the ponophobic patient to use as a control. The hematology test results need verification."

Jess's mind raced as he tried to remember exactly what ponophobic meant. "Could you hold on for a second, JoAnn?"

"Sure."

After putting her on hold, Jess pulled out his medical dictionary and looked up the word. He read the definition aloud, "Extreme fear of pain or fatigue," and instantly realized she was referring to Jonathan. He pushed the button to reconnect her and said, "I can get another one for you, but the patient isn't going to like it one bit. I'll probably get bitten in the process."

"I know. I'm really sorry. Tell him I'll get him a nice juicy bone to make up for it. He's such a sweet little fellow."

Jess laughed. "I'm sure that will make it much easier. How can I get this to you?"

"Would it be too much trouble to drop it by some time tomorrow? If you'll just call, I'll be waiting at the entrance."

"Anything I should be concerned about?"

"Not yet. I just like having different specimens for comparison. I'm sure you understand."

"I'll call you in the morning."

"Thanks, Jess. I appreciate it."

"See you tomorrow." Jess hung up the phone. His stomach was knotted from the implications of the call.

I knew there was something wrong with Jonathan. Why the hell didn't I do something sooner?

"I've been holding for ten minutes for Joe Thompson. If he isn't in, could I please speak to his supervisor?" Stacey paced back and forth in the small teacher's lounge of the central administration building. Since the storm, all of the first-grade support staff had been moved, and personal phone calls were practically forbidden. Twice Grace Milliken passed by, both times glaring at Stacey so she felt like a three-year-old caught in the act of stealing a cookie.

"Ms. Fordman, this is Joe Thompson. Sorry you had to wait so long. We were in the middle of a drill."

"That's okay. Did you find out anything about the fire in my apartment?"

"The official report lists it as suspicious, but mainly because the point of origin is away from any common ignition sources and your statement indicates no flammable items were present just before the fire started."

"What about the wires you found?"

"They were sent to the FBI arson lab."

Stacey didn't like the insolent tone of his voice. "And?" she said bluntly.

He hesitated, as though groping for the exact words, before answering, "And when I called to check on them, they told me they never arrived."

"What?"

"I'm sure they'll turn up."

"What about the bug I gave you?" she asked.

"It was with the other evidence."

Stacey took a deep, calming breath before she asked, "So it's lost, too?"

"For now."

"Great."

"Sorry."

"You don't sound like it," she muttered.

"The damage is already done, Ms. Fordman. You'd be smart to just get on with your life. After all, dwelling on what caused the fire won't do you any good. Be thankful you are still alive and just forget it."

"Thanks for the advice. I don't suppose you could give me the address of the FBI arson lab so I can verify what you've told me?"

"Sorry, we're not allowed to give out that information."

"Then I guess your supervisor's name will do."

"Assistant Chief Coulderby."

"Thanks." She hung up the phone and took a deep breath. School was definitely not the place to lose control, yet she felt like screaming. Instead, she dialed Jess at the clinic. "Is Jess busy?"

The receptionist was a young, perky brunette named Jill who said, "I'll see if he's available. Stacey Fordman, right?"

"Right."

"Hold on."

Jess answered a few seconds later. "Hi. This must be important for you to risk calling from school."

"I needed someone to yell at."

"Fire away."

"Remember the arson investigator we met at my apartment?"

"Sure. He seemed like a nice guy."

Stacey took a ragged breath, trying to regain her composure. "Well, he's not. First he wouldn't return my calls, and now I finally get through to him and he tells me the evidence has all been lost."

"Everything?"

"According to him."

"That doesn't make sense," Jess said brusquely.

"I know! He made me feel like the fire was my own fault and I should just forget about it."

"He didn't accuse you of anything, did he?"

"No. It was just his condescending attitude. He's the one who lost the evidence and he has the nerve to talk to me like it's my fault. What a jerk!"

"I know how aggravating this is, but you really have to keep things in perspective. With all the storm damage and electrical problems in the southwest part of town, your case is probably one of the least important things he has to deal with right now. Besides, they haven't got any leads on arson suspects, and the property damage was all covered by insurance."

"Bull. Something else is going on. I can feel it."

"Are you implying he got rid of the evidence on purpose?"

"I don't know. I just find it hard to believe it would disappear."

"So do I."

Stacey glanced at her watch and realized recess had ended five minutes ago and her kids were probably wandering around the cafeteria disrupting the other makeshift classes. "I've got to get back to class. See you tonight. Thanks for listening."

"Anytime."

Stacey hung up the phone and dashed around the corner, nearly tripping over Mrs. Milliken who was standing just out of sight. "Excuse me. I didn't realize anyone was here. Are you all right?"

"Certainly. I believe your class is waiting for you, Ms. Fordman."

"Yes, ma'am."

JoAnn took a deep breath, then silently twisted the doorknob and poked her head inside J.D.'s office. She watched him for several seconds. He was obviously very interested in the computer printout he was studying. His hair was flawlessly combed to highlight the tufts of grey at his temples. The Armani suit was pressed to perfection, the matching tie knotted firmly yet precisely. If he were to look up, the eyes would soften, the perfectly curved lips would smile from under the groomed mustache, making his entire face seem compassionate, yet firm. All were management tools, she realized. Strategically deployed tools, well under control, and quite irritating.

Finally she quietly said, "Got a minute?"

J.D. threw his head back, startled by her voice. As he spoke, she noticed he nonchalantly closed the printout and slid it into his top desk drawer. "How did you get all the way up here?"

"I'm not an invalid, you know. I walked." She held up her crutches, then added, "Sort of."

He walked to her and said, "You should sit down."

"I'm fine, really. Using these things is becoming second nature. They actually come in handy sometimes."

"No kidding. When?"

"They're great for catching elevators at the last second and for beating off would-be muggers."

"Have you run across many muggers here at Tech-Lab?"

She pointed at her own head. "Only up here. I suppose it has something to do with victim psychology. I keep imagining how I would handle another attack. I have every move memorized, from every conceivable angle. These crutches could whack someone quite efficiently, don't you think?"

"Remind me not to tangle with you."

"Does that mean you'll do me a little favor to stay in my good graces?"

"Ah, a setup. You're much too clever to think you can pin me down so easily. What kind of favor are we talking about?"

"Actually, it's two different favors."

He sat back down in his chair and put his feet on his desk. "Try me."

"The reason I crutched all the way up here is that I'm beginning to feel like a prisoner in my own office. I talked to Security to see if I could have a visitor every now and then, but they turned me down."

J.D. cockily said, "Define visitor."

"Friends for lunch or dinner. Just simple meetings in my office, like you and I have. I'm so swamped, all I do is work. You know what they say, all work and no play . . ."

He smiled coyly as he said, "Some of our dinners get rather . . . heated. I'm afraid I'm much too possessive of your favors to allow other visitors of that nature."

"Come on, J.D. You know I'm not seeing anyone else." *At least not yet.* "I just need some time to visit."

"Ever heard of a telephone?"

"You're not going to give in, are you?"

"I'm afraid Security already contacted me on this one. As soon as you called them to ask permission, they called me to remind me exactly how strict the entry requirements for BioHazard are. That jerk, Harper, even read the pertinent section straight from the employee's manual so he couldn't be accused of misinterpreting the facts. I wish I could help you, but my hands are tied on this one."

JoAnn visibly softened her defensive posture and said, "I know how much trouble you went to so I could work whenever it is convenient, and I really do appreciate it."

"How's the research going?"

"Better than I would have speculated. I can work for a few hours, then go in the other office for a catnap. It really has been a lifesaver."

"And you're sleeping all right at night?"

"Now that I'm used to the noise the air purifiers and

pneumatic system make, I'm sleeping great. It's just at night, it gets so quiet in the lab that it's almost spooky."

He laughed and said, "I'd have never guessed you to be the type who could be spooked."

She shrugged as she said, "Up until a few weeks ago I'd have agreed with you. Now, I'm not so sure."

"After everything you've been through, that's understandable. What's your other favor? Maybe I can do better with it."

"I have a friend who is struggling to make his veterinarian practice succeed. I thought that maybe since the Citrinol3 project has been allocated kennel space, we could use him on a part-time basis. He's an excellent vet, impressive credentials, and very hardworking."

"What's his name?"

"Jess Lawrence."

"I'll see what I can do. You know he'll have to pass a drug screening test and the BioHazard background check Security does on every new employee, even though he would only be contract labor."

"I understand. He'll pass with flying colors. He's really a great guy."

"Sounds like I should be jealous."

"He's practically engaged. Besides, how many times do I have to tell you, I'm not dating anyone but you." *Actually, I'm not even sure I'm interested in you,* she thought, but instead added, "I'd really like to help him, J.D. Both he and his girlfriend have been very nice to me since the attack. In fact, besides you, they're the ones who have proven to me that there are good people left in the world. After what happened, I really needed to be shown again and all of you have been so kind to me, I want to express my appreciation."

"I'll pull some strings and get the ball rolling. It

won't be much, you know. He may only be called once or twice a month."

"That's fine. Anything would help."

"I'll walk you to the elevators. I need to stop by Human Resources anyway, so I'll throw your friend's name out for consideration."

"Thanks, J.D."

"No problem."

They walked as quickly as JoAnn could, and J.D. watched and waved to her as he stepped off the elevator and its doors slid closed. Instead of stopping in Human Resources as he said, he walked farther down the corridor and turned into Security. Harper was standing outside his office door when J.D. approached.

"I need to talk to you." J.D. motioned for him to follow him inside the office.

"What now?"

"Human Resources is going to request a background check on Jess Lawrence for a contract veterinary slot. I need the process slowed down, then rejected based on the background check."

"Is there some background problem?"

"His son goes to East Elementary. He's in the first grade. The Fordman class. We have his house under surveillance. Any questions?"

"Can't think of a one. I'll bet Lawrence has some old dirt we can dig up from high school or college. If not, we'll generate some."

"It needs to look legit. We don't need Legal pulled into this."

"Cook, when are you going to give other people some credit? We're not all the assholes you think we are."

"JoAnn Rayburn's furniture was bugged the same day it was moved from her house. I don't think you can claim that you're not an asshole, it's become more a matter of how big a one you are."

"Just doing my job."

"And I must admit, you do it quite well."

Stacey was almost standing on top of Jess as she murmured, "It is a little stark, isn't it? Pretty, but cold."

"Why are you whispering?" Jess asked, his voice echoing through JoAnn's house.

"You know why."

"I just don't agree with it." He pulled the electric screwdriver out of the back pocket of his Levi's and said, "Let's get this over with so you can relax."

"I'll see if the stereo works." She hunted around and finally found a CD player. It not only worked, it sent waves of classical music rolling in every direction so loud they could barely stand it.

When she returned, Jess had the first outlet's cover removed. "Feel better now?" he asked over the noise. He shined his flashlight in so she could see there was nothing suspicious.

"I suppose." She pointed to the den and said, "You keep looking, and so will I."

Jess had tried six different outlets when he heard Stacey call him from the kitchen. He screwed the cover back on as he said, "Coming. I suppose you found something. Women have all the luck."

When he entered the kitchen, Stacey was holding one finger over her lips, a clear signal that he should be quiet. As she led him to the window she said, "I don't think anyone in their right mind would describe either me or JoAnn as lucky considering how the last few weeks have gone." She pointed up at the ceiling.

Jess looked up, but couldn't see anything so he shrugged as he said, "You're both still alive and kicking. Considering the circumstances, that's pretty lucky."

She pushed his head over toward the window and he finally saw what she was pointing at. Tucked in the inside corner of the kitchen cabinetwork was a small silver device. Even though it was up high, it was apparent it was a close match to the one she had found in her apartment. "I don't think this place is right for me, Jess. I just wouldn't feel at home here. There's no warmth like at your place."

They headed for the front door. As soon as they were outside, he pulled her in his arms and said, "I'll bet you planted that there, didn't you?" He tickled her. "Come on, admit it."

"What? Why would I do such a thing?"

"So you'd have an excuse to stay with the wonderful Lawrence family. Admit it, we're hard to resist, aren't we?"

She kissed him. "Conceited, maybe. Besides, since when do I need an excuse? I thought I had an openended invitation."

"You do. And by the way, I'm man enough to admit when I'm wrong. You were definitely right, all along."

"About what?"

"You have good reason to be paranoid, and apparently JoAnn does, too."

"I know. The question is, now what are we going to do?"

"Who knows? I do have one thing I'd really like to know."

"What's that?"

"How in the world did they whip up that tornado?"

"I can't believe it's already Friday. Between cleaning up at school and trying to reorganize everything, this week has flown by. I'm really nervous about this lunch, are you?" Stacey asked.

Jess pulled into the circular drive in front of Tech-Lab and mumbled, "More than I care to admit. I've thought of a hundred things that I wish I knew, and a hundred other things I wish I'd done differently."

As she had promised, JoAnn was waiting for them by the curb, and Jess helped her into the car and stowed her crutches in the trunk.

"Where shall we go?" Stacey asked JoAnn.

"Somewhere noisy. How about the new Tex-Mex place on Harvard?"

Jess said, "Sounds great. You look worn out. Are things turning out all right at work?"

"Surprisingly enough, I've been so busy I haven't had time to think about it. I'm either working or sleeping. For now, I'm really glad J.D. arranged things so I can stay there. I've needed every second, and I don't think there's any break in sight."

"Is there some critical experiment that has to be completed in the next few weeks?" Jess asked.

"Not that I know of. I've spent virtually every second since Sunday afternoon working on a different dilemma anyway. Unfortunately, it concerns you."

They arrived at the restaurant and went inside. Once they were seated JoAnn said, "I know how hard this waiting has been on both of you. I think I'd better start at the beginning, so all this will make sense. Research is usually built on scientific facts and other scientists' findings. When I started my project, several scientists had already concluded through autopsies and other means that amyloid plaque deposits and neurofibrillary tangles were the markers of Alzheimer's disease. They determined that the buildup of these proteins was responsible for killing healthy brain cells and thereby destroying vital parts of the patient's memory."

Stacey glanced at Jess, who nodded reassuringly and said, "I'll translate into nonmedical terms for you later. Go ahead, JoAnn."

"When I began my research, I built my work around

a relatively simple theory. If we could isolate and control the type of cellular activity that makes amyloid plaque deposits so damaging to healthy brain cells, we could use them to attack and damage cancer cells instead."

Jess asked, "So you started with amyloid proteins and derived a compound that could be administered into a tumor to invade it?"

"No, we wanted to target proteins that would not attack healthy cells, only the cancerous cells, for general inoculation. I'm mainly concerned with a rapidly growing type of tumor that usually occurs in the brain. Most of the time, these type tumors are inaccessible, so direct injection would be very difficult, if not impossible."

"Weren't you worried about Alzheimer's disease being a side effect of the treatment?"

"Only at first. After a few years of genetic engineering, we developed a derivative amyloid protein that attached itself to a type of chemical tag generated by the cancerous tissue. Our main side effect of Citrinol3 has always been that for some unknown reason, microscopic particles of the compounds break loose and attach to healthy red blood cells, causing damage. In ninety percent of the test animals, there is some mechanism that allows these particles to break free, some threshold or trigger event that occurs approximately six weeks after the initial treatment begins. I don't know what it is. Every day I wish I did."

"And the other ten percent?"

JoAnn beamed. "Controlled tumors. Even complete reversal in some cases. For ten percent of the test animals, Citrinol3 is the cure for a deadly cancer."

"So you're trying to isolate the difference between the ninety percent and the ten percent?"

"Exactly. Unfortunately, there are so many contributing factors it's like looking for a needle in a haystack. Heredity, environmental influences, protocol deviation, and even microscopic chemical variations could be the problem. The catalyst may be something blatant, something so slight it will never be found, or a combination of hundreds of things. All we can do is keep trying to narrow the differences between the test groups until we discover the answer."

"Or at least increase the odds of success."

"Precisely."

"So what did Jonathan's second blood sample show?"

JoAnn frowned. "The exact same thing as his first. Amyloid proteins were present."

Stacey gasped and said, "You mean he has some kind of cancer?"

"No! Not at all."

"Then exactly what the hell does it mean?" Jess demanded.

Chapter 14

JoAnn wondered if the other people in the restaurant could feel the tension crackling in the air. Jess and Stacey were both stunned, staring gravely at her and waiting for her to speak. After taking a deep breath, she tried to explain. "I know that I'm probably the leading expert in the world when it comes to this type of blood abnormality. The only problem is, I haven't got a clue why Jonathan's blood is testing this way. I've checked and rechecked the results, praying that somehow the compound really wasn't there, but it is. I've spent most of the last four days with my head buried in medical books or on the computer researching the hematological incidence of these particular beta amyloid proteins being randomly identified in the bloodstream."

Jess spoke slowly, deliberately, "And what did you find?"

"Nothing. Absolutely nothing."

"Why doesn't that surprise me?"

Stacey took his hand. "It isn't JoAnn's fault, Jess. She's just trying to help us find out what's wrong with Jon."

He slammed his fists together as he said, "Damn it, I know. I just feel so damned helpless. My son is sick with something that supposedly doesn't exist except in laboratory rats. Plus, no one has a clue how he got it or how to treat it."

JoAnn touched his shoulder and said, "If it's the last thing I do, I'll find a way to help him. I promise."

They were all silent for a few seconds, then Jess asked, "Where do we go from here?"

"That's another problem. My research is not only top secret, legally it belongs to TechLab. I can secretly work on this without them knowing, but I can't openly provide any information to anyone outside, not even physicians." She saw the shocked look on their faces and quickly added, "If there was some way I knew to control the cell damage, I'd have already given you whatever it takes. There simply isn't anything a doctor can do except eliminate the source of contamination. With all we know about TechLab, I don't think it would be wise to let them know I've been discussing their secrets with outsiders. Do you?"

Jess said, "No. But there has to be something we can do."

"I have one idea. Get Jonathan out of here. There must be some environmental factor that is causing this. When Citrinol3 exposure is eliminated, eighty percent of the research animals show marked improvement in the incidence of red cell damage. In fact, most of it totally reversed within six months and all traces of the drug were gone within eight months."

"What happens to the other twenty percent?"

JoAnn mumbled, "They die. That's the problem with the inhalant protocol."

Jess stared out the window for several seconds, then said, "So you think he's somehow being exposed to this experimental drug you're working on?"

"There just isn't any other explanation. I've racked my brain for days trying to come up with something that makes more sense."

"Could the water supply be tainted?"

"TechLab has its own purification system. The facility isn't tied to the city water supply."

"Could some of the lab animals have escaped?"

"No."

Jess's voice rose again, "How can you be so damned certain?"

"We're in a BioHazard lab, Jess. They work with viruses so lethal it would scare you to death if you knew about them. Nothing can get in or out. I personally checked, and all the lab animals used in the Citrinol3 experiments are accounted for. I even checked the corpses."

"You keep the dead ones?" Stacey asked.

"We never know exactly what we're looking for, so the tissues are preserved for later tests. Not one Citrinol3 lab animal is missing. Dead or alive."

Jess said, "What about this amyloid protein you found in Jon's blood? Is it the type commonly found in brain tissue, or the genetically engineered version you created?"

JoAnn looked down and said, "The genetically engineered one."

"Then this has to tie back to your work at TechLab."

"Unless someone else has somehow gotten their hands on our data and reproduced our work in a less strict environment."

"But how could that happen? You just said nothing could get in or out of TechLab's security."

They barely heard JoAnn's voice as she said, "It could have been Hanna."

"The woman who was murdered at Riverparks?"

JoAnn nodded her head. "I've known since I was given her position that she may have sold out to the competition. I didn't believe it at first, and I still don't want to believe it. Hanna was a good person. She wouldn't have endangered people's lives."

Jess said, "But someone did, and she had access to the information, didn't she?"

"Yes."

Stacey was watching them both, her skin as pale as

the plate she was shifting her food aimlessly around on. "My class. My God, the tornado. My whole class."

"What are you talking about?" Jess said.

"The changes in the children. Not just Jonathan, but almost all of them. Tired, lethargic, too calm. When the tornado hit, the other classes were out of control, but mine was unbelievably calm. They've all been exposed, haven't they?"

Jess looked at JoAnn and said, "Is that possible? How is Citrinol3 administered?"

"Different ways at different stages of the experimentation. We've tried injections, capsules, ingestion, and even vaporized compounds."

"What version was being tested just before Hanna died?"

"Inhalant. I'd just developed the inhalant formula. I thought it would be less traumatic to administer, until a few of my lab animals started to die prematurely."

Jess said, "So if the children were somewhere and they breathed a little of this compound as it floated past, would they be reacting like Jonathan?"

"It's hard to tell, since humans are so different from rodents. I'd guess that even one heavy dose would have little effect on anyone. All our studies show that it takes six weeks of relatively heavy exposure, two to four times a week, to have the negative side effects. I accidentally got a whiff of it about a month ago and when I tested my own blood on Monday there were no signs of the amyloid protein whatsoever."

"So the children are being continuously exposed," Stacey said. "It would have to be at school, wouldn't it? I mean, how else could that many children be affected? They live miles from each other, and most of them only see their classmates while they're at school."

"But how could that be?" Jess said incredulously. "How could a whole class be exposed to a chemical and no one know? Is there any way this could be contagious? One person was exposed and now it's like a virus?"

"I don't see how. When you look at the hematology reports, the protein is attaching to red blood cells and free floating in the plasma. It isn't being carried on a virus, at least no virus our technology can identify. Plus, it doesn't replicate."

"That's not very comforting. What purpose would there be in exposing children to this kind of thing?"

"I don't know," JoAnn answered. "But I know we're going to find out exactly how it was done, and who is responsible. I have some slides in my purse. I was hoping I could get blood samples from both of you to see if either of you show signs of exposure."

Stacey said, "Sure. If Jon is being exposed at school, then I am, too."

"And if it's at home, mine would be positive," Jess added.

"Yet neither one of you is showing symptoms." It was obvious JoAnn's mind was racing through possibilities. "Have either of you felt anything strange lately?"

Stacey said, "I had a horrible headache just after school started. It lasted a few days, then it went away."

"Did you have any trouble breathing?" JoAnn asked.

"Come to think of it, I did get winded easily. Is that important?"

"I don't know. I do know that no matter what, testing your blood and Jess's should help us narrow down the possibilities. Meanwhile, is there anywhere Jonathan can go for a while?"

"I'll send him to stay with his grandparents in Minnesota. He'll have a great time playing in the snow."

Jess looked at Stacey. "Can you send his school work with him so he won't fall behind?"

"You bet." She turned to JoAnn. "How long will he have to be gone?"

JoAnn shook her head and shrugged. "Until we figure out exactly what is going on."

"What about the rest of the class? We can't just ship all of them off. Of course, having class in the cafeteria may help. If the classroom was somehow contaminated before, it certainly isn't now that the roof is gone."

"I wish there was a way to test a few more of them so we could be sure they were all exposed."

Jess smiled. "I know the perfect way. I was already scheduled to come tell them about being a veterinarian. While I'm there, we could show a few brave volunteers how to tell what blood type they are. I'll bring everything we need, and we'll do an extra smear for JoAnn to test."

"Great. How soon can you do it? Obviously time is not on our side," JoAnn said.

Jess looked at Stacey. "When would a good time be?"

"It's fall break right now, but the sooner the better. First thing Monday morning would be fine."

Jess said, "Stacey and I can go first to show the kids that having their finger pricked is no big deal. I'll bring the slides to TechLab around ten-thirty Monday morning."

"I'll be waiting."

Stacey said, "Shouldn't we call the police?"

JoAnn answered, "Not until we can prove what is going on. Right now, I'm the only one we know for certain is breaking any laws. If I end up in jail, we may never discover how Citrinol3 got out of the BioHazard lab. Could you two check the classroom for anything suspicious?"

Stacey said, "You mean what is left of the classroom? We can try, but I'm not sure the National Guard will let us in."

"Is there any way you can find out if the woman who was murdered really did sell out?" Jess asked.

"I have a feeling we'll know as soon as we pinpoint the source of exposure. I'm not sure which would be worse at this point."

"What do you mean?"

"If Hanna sold out, I've lost the memory of someone I truly respected, but at least we would know exactly what we're up against. Plus, we have TechLab's staff of lawyers and security advisors to stop them, and protect us. What I'm afraid of is . . . what if it wasn't Hanna? Then . . ."

"Then what?" they both asked in unison.

"Then TechLab is even more dangerous than Hanna's warning implied, and we're all in deep trouble."

Stacey leaned forward and said, "Wait until you hear this. We checked your house for listening devices, and we found one in your kitchen."

"You're kidding!"

"I wish we were. I think TechLab is behind this whole thing. My apartment, your accident, everything."

JoAnn shook her head. "It could be whoever Hanna sold out to. They could be listening, watching our every move, trying to find out our secrets. The only thing that doesn't make sense is why they would want to listen to me at home. I'm hardly ever there, and when I am, I certainly don't talk about my research. Who would I talk to?"

"Maybe that's how they keep track of where you are."

Stacey shook her head and said, "Then why bug a schoolteacher's house? I have no connection to TechLab at all."

Jess held up his hands. "Listen, ladies, none of this is getting us anywhere. We need some solid evidence, and sitting here isn't going to give us a damn thing. JoAnn, we'll take you by your house and show you what to look for. Then when you get back to work, you can check your office. We'll go over my house with a fine-tooth comb, too, now that we know they don't just use electrical outlets. Personally, I want to find the son of a bitch who is behind this and strangle him."

"Or her," JoAnn muttered.

"What?" he grumbled.

"Sorry, just trying to be politically correct. Besides, if it was Hanna, someone already beat you to it."

After they dropped JoAnn off at TechLab, Jess drove Stacey to East Elementary. Once the guard on duty checked her school identification, he let them pass through the roadblock. As they walked down the empty halls of the first-grade building, Jess was sickened by the destruction. "My God, Stacey. You and Jonathan could have been killed."

"Hundreds of children could have been killed. We were lucky. Very lucky." They reached her room and she dropped her keys in her purse. The door to her classroom had been removed and most of what had been inside was gone. "They sure work fast. I guess I should have spent more time trying to salvage things. It was all so wet, I thought I could come back after things dried out a little better. I guess it's too late now."

Jess walked over to where her desk had been. "Is this where the tree limb came through?"

"Yes. They cleaned it up already." She looked out the hole that used to be a window. "The air conditioner is gone, too."

"Air conditioner?"

"Don't you remember? I told you my class was being observed by the Board of Education this year to determine the adequacy of the curriculum. Some company called ITL donated a special air conditioner, since this room gets so hot in August and September."

"Doesn't that seem a bit odd to you?"

"Which part? The curriculum study or the air conditioner?"

"The air conditioner. Why should the kids they're studying deserve special treatment? In other words, if the test scores are going to be accurate, then the test children should be treated just like everyone else. Besides, how much could a few degrees affect their retention?"

"That's a good point. Maybe we should talk to the principal, Mrs. Milliken. She was the one who arranged the whole thing. I was just happy to be comfortable for once, so I never thought about questioning the logic."

Jess grinned and said, "Let me guess, none of the kids can stand the principal, Mrs. Milliken. Right?"

"Of course. She makes it very clear that she will not tolerate any misbehavior, so most kids live in fear of being sent to her office. She really has to grow on you. I think she just tries too hard. Deep down, I'm sure she's a nice person."

"I'll bet someone said that about Adolf Hitler once, too."

Stacey answered defensively, "She's not that bad. Personally, I think she's lonely. Rumor has it her husband died years ago."

"Or maybe she whacked him with her ruler once too often."

She swatted his arm. "Stop it, Jess. Like it or not, she's my boss."

"Will she help us find out where the air-conditioning unit went?"

"Of course she will . . . I think . . . Well, maybe she will."

JoAnn went back to her office, locked the door, and started to search. It was hard, since she kept bumping her bandaged ankle as she crawled around, but she inspected every place she could think of. By the time she gave up, she was exhausted. Sitting down at her desk, she looked at the stacks of work that were accumulating. Since she'd been back, she'd concentrated on only one thing—the amyloid proteins in Jonathan's bloodstream.

Picking through her box of memos and mail to read, she dug out the report on using beagles as the animal model for Citrinol3. The recommendation had come from Dr. Gordon Sterns. After thinking back to all her meetings, she never recalled meeting anyone by that name. JoAnn pulled open her desk drawer and flipped through the employee phone listing until she found his number and extension. It was an area code she didn't readily recognize, but she dialed it anyway.

"*Hola.*"

"Extension 371, please. Dr. Gordon Sterns."

"*Habla español, señorita?*"

"*Muy poco. Dr. Sterns, por favor?*"

"*No esta aquí. Esta en Brazil. Buenos dias.*"

JoAnn stared at the phone as she listened to the dial tone. *What the hell was that all about?*

"I don't want to go, Dad." Jon kicked a rock across the parking lot as they walked toward the airport's main terminal. "What about Rocky and Bell? They need me. Who will play with them like I do?"

"Jonathan, we've already discussed this. Your plane leaves in a little less than an hour."

"I hate flying. Remember last time when we hit that thing?"

"The air pocket wasn't that bad."

"Yes it was! It made my fingers and toes tingle like that awful roller coaster, Zingo. I hated it. And now you're not even going with me."

"That was just a rush of adrenaline. Besides, last time we had to fly through quite a bit of turbulence. I checked the Weather Channel, and there aren't any storms between here and St. Paul. As a matter of fact, the weather is beautiful there. They still have about six inches of snow on the ground from the other day, so you can sled as soon as you get there. You'll have a blast. Grandma and Grandpa are really looking forward to your visit."

He dropped his head to his breastbone and sighed as he said, "But I'll miss school!"

Jess hugged him and asked, "Since when did you want to go to school?"

"I like Ms. Fordman."

"So do I. She's sending your work with you so you won't get behind."

"But, Dad, this is weird. All the kids asked me why I'm going in the middle of the school year. Can't I wait until Thanksgiving or Christmas break?"

"Sorry. It's important for you to go right now."

Jon kicked another rock and looked up at Jess with tears in his eyes. "Are you gonna die like Mama did? Is that why you want me to go stay with Grandma and Grandpa?"

Jess stopped and kneeled beside him so he could look him straight in the eye. "I'm not sick, I promise. I wouldn't do that to you, Jon. We're buddies, aren't we?"

He nodded.

"I told you the truth. You've been too tired lately and I'm worried about you. I think going to Grandma and Grandpa's house for a while might make you feel better. Have I ever lied to you?"

Jon thought for a second and said, "Once."

"When?"

"You said the guy in that movie we watched last week said shucks when he got mad. That's not what he said. I snuck down after you were in bed and watched it again. He said the 'f' word you told me never to say again after Derek said it at school. You lied to me. I'm not a baby anymore, Dad. I've heard bad words and I know not to say them."

Jess had to smile. His son was growing up so fast. "You're right. I shouldn't have lied to you. But it wasn't a big lie, was it? Not something that really mattered."

Jon shook his head and said, "I guess not."

"From now on I'll try to treat you like you're a young man. Of course, that means you have to act like one."

"How do I do that?"

"You trust me."

"Okay."

"Be brave and fly to St. Paul all by yourself."

"Do I have to?"

"Yes, you have to."

Grace Milliken peeked nervously from behind her living-room drapes. She still couldn't believe Parker had called and asked her out to dinner. As soon as he pulled into her driveway, she dashed into the bathroom to dry her sweaty palms and check her lipstick one last time. When the doorbell rang, she counted to ten, then calmly pulled the door open.

"Parker, it's so good to see you again. Won't you come in?"

He glanced at his watch. "I'm afraid we're running on borrowed time already. I have a flight to catch in two hours. So, if you don't mind, I think we should be off to dinner. I made reservations at Molly's Landing."

"You have to leave so soon?"

"I'm afraid so. I just barely managed to squeeze in a visit." He pulled her against him and kissed her. "But a short visit is better than none at all, isn't it?"

"Much better."

They walked to the car and she slid into the passenger side. When he got in she asked, "Isn't this the same rental car you had last time? It even has the same parking permit. What do you suppose TL stands for?"

Parker was silent for a second as he pondered the TechLab logo, then said, "It isn't a rental. ITL has a small office here, and that's our logo—see, the 'I' and the 'T' are sort of blended together. This car is one of our fleet. That is, if you can call five corporate cars a fleet."

"Oh. You know, I must be going crazy. I thought I saw you the other day."

"Really? When? Where?"

"Last Tuesday. Driving south on Memorial. It's silly, isn't it? Sometimes you want to see someone so much you imagine things."

"Let's see, last Tuesday I was in Tennessee, so unless you have very good eyesight, it wasn't me."

"I know." She laid her hand on his thigh. "Just wishful thinking. By the way, did you get my message? I got clearance for your company to remove the damaged air conditioner."

"That is so sweet of you. We've already taken care of the problem, so don't give it another thought."

"How did you get past the guards?"

"I understand it was pretty easy. Our repairmen just showed them a copy of the work order and they let them through." He ran his hand up and down her thigh as he said, "I'll bet your life has been hell since that storm hit. I've been thinking about you constantly."

"It has been hectic. We lost so much, but we were very lucky no one was killed. What will happen to the test program now that Ms. Fordman's classroom has been destroyed?"

"I'm afraid we'll have to drag this into next semester. Assuming we can get approval from the Board of Education, that is. I'd like to ask you a personal favor, Grace."

"Sure."

He reached into the backseat and grabbed a large manila envelope. "These are the tests the children are supposed to take next week. I know things are crazy, but could you make sure they're still administered?"

"But if you're going to reschedule the testing until next semester, why bother?"

"We can still use any results from this semester to issue preliminary reports, with a truckload of disclaimers tacked on, of course."

"Do you want me to send them directly to you, like the last time?"

"That would be fine." He stroked her cheek and added, "By the way, how is Ms. Fordman holding up? It seems like she's having a rough year."

Grace leaned into his touch as she answered, "Her apartment burning was such a tragedy. She lost everything, you know."

"And now the tornado. I know this sounds really crass, but since I don't know her, I have to rely on your judgment. Is she handling her teaching assignments all right considering she's under such personal stress?"

"I've been keeping a close eye on her. I can honestly say that she's handling it better than I'd expected."

He brushed his lips across hers as he whispered, "That's great. You realize something good came out of the tornado, don't you?"

Grace could barely think, but she managed to ask, "Such as?"

"The project won't be completed so soon, and I'll have a good reason to keep coming back to town."

"I was counting on it."

"Mrs. Milliken, can I come in? I'd like to ask you a few questions about the special testing for my class." Stacey watched as Grace glanced over the top of her reading glasses and nodded.

"That's quite a coincidence, I was going to ask you to stop by today. I have the next set of tests we need to administer." She handed Stacey the envelope. "You need to give these as soon as possible and return them to me."

"But we're already so far behind because of the storm, and without a quiet classroom . . ."

"I know, but this is an expensive project, and the Board of Education is depending on the results."

Stacey nodded politely and said, "Yes, ma'am."

Mrs. Milliken raised her eyebrows and asked, "Did you want to ask anything else?"

Stacey nodded. "I was just wondering why a special air conditioner was installed for my classroom. Wouldn't the test results be more accurate if the children were treated equally?"

"Not necessarily. The concern was that your room was not indicative of the entire district. Not all the rooms are excessively hot, as yours is. The air conditioner was a hedge against any excuses that the results were biased because of the environment of the test room."

"They certainly removed it quickly."

Her eyes gleamed as she said, "The people at ITL are very efficient. Parker McDaniel has watched the project personally from the very beginning."

Stacey stood up and walked to the door. As she pulled it open she asked, "By the way, what does ITL stand for again?"

"Independent Testing Laboratory. Why?"

She shrugged and said, "I was just wondering."

Jess was examining the growing list of past due accounts on the computer in his office when Stacey came in the back door of the clinic. She leaned over him, nibbling his ear as she mumbled, "Hi, handsome."

"Like my licorice aftershave?"

She scrunched up her nose and said, "Is that what that is?"

"No, it's really elk musk they say will make any female alive rip off her clothes and attack whoever has it on."

"I suppose if it's being worn by an elk it might work." Jess turned toward her and she kicked the door closed before settling on his lap. "Personally, I prefer my men straight."

"As opposed to crooked?"

"No, without cologne, or aftershave, or anything else."

"I'll have to remember that, although I'm rather fond of the elk musk even if it does tend to draw flies. Did I win the bet? Did you find out anything?"

She smugly answered, "Yes, you won. I didn't find out nearly as much as we hoped for. All I know is that we need to check on a company called Independent Testing Laboratory. They call it ITL. The contact person there is a guy named Parker McDaniel. From the tone of Mrs. Milliken's voice, he must be able to croon old love songs while walking on water. You'd have thought I asked her about Robert Redford."

"So you didn't tell her what we suspect?"

Stacey adamantly shook her head as she said, "No. She got kind of glassy-eyed when she talked about this McDaniel guy. I didn't get the impression she would react very well if I implied he was some sort of mad scientist who was testing his latest experiments on unsuspecting children."

"Good point."

"They want me to give the kids another one of those tests this week."

"Did you bring one with you?"

Stacey pulled a manila envelope out of her purse as she said, "Yes. The one Jonathan would have taken. Believe it or not, they're numbered and have the kids' names on them when I get them. It's kind of spooky."

"Maybe that's how they're doing this. I'll get it to JoAnn so she can see if it's contaminated with Citrinol3."

"Good idea. Mrs. Milliken said they're going to continue the testing next semester since any results they get now may be skewed by the disruption of my class by the storm."

"At least we know whoever is behind this isn't planning on totally jumping ship. How much do you know about Mrs. Milliken?"

Stacey shrugged. "She's been at East Elementary for years and years. Since she doesn't attend any of the social activities, I don't think many of the teachers feel very close to her. I know I don't."

"Do you think she's in on it?"

"In on what?"

"The drugs, the testing. Maybe they paid her off so they could use your class as guinea pigs."

"Jess! The Board of Education approved this whole project. Besides, she wouldn't do a thing like that."

"How can you be so sure?"

Stacey glared at him and said, "I just am."

"What do you mean the Lawrence kid is gone? It was bad enough that he was the only one you couldn't confirm wasn't injured by the tornado. First you get chased away by his father the other night like a damned criminal and now this. Jesus Christ. Harper is gonna shit." The security guard on duty slammed the phone down and took a deep breath. He needed to calm down before he approached Harper. Make it sound like it wasn't any big deal. A few minutes later he finally had the nerve to knock on his boss's door.

"Come in."

"Sir, I have some news on Jonathan Lawrence."

"Yes."

"You know he hasn't been back in school since the tornado, don't you?"

"Yes."

"Well, we know for certain he wasn't hurt in the storm. Our man confirmed that he was healthy and playing in his backyard the day after the tornado."

"Good. So what's the problem?"

"He hasn't been to school the last two days."

"What do the house taps show? Is he at home?"

"No. I listened to the tapes myself. They play this weird music all the time on the stereo. It's strange, like whining waves. If the kid is at home, you can't tell by the surveillance tapes. Plus, our drive-by observations indicate no one is there during the day. The Fordman woman is teaching, and his father is at the vet clinic, so if the kid is there, he's either alone or with a babysitter. We haven't seen anyone else come or go, so we're almost certain he isn't there."

"Then where is he?"

"We don't know."

"It wouldn't be too difficult to find out."

"We didn't want to arouse any suspicions, sir. Especially after what happened the other night in the parking lot of the vet's clinic. If we start asking a bunch of questions and poking around . . ."

"I'll handle it."

"But . . ."

"I said, I'll handle it."

"Yes, sir."

"Grace, it's Parker. How are you doing?"

"Wonderful. I'm surprised to hear from you so soon. Thank you for the flowers. They are absolutely beautiful. All the teachers are green with envy."

"I wanted you to know how much I enjoyed dinner the other night."

Grace excitedly said, "I had a splendid time, too. Are you coming back to town?"

"Afraid not. I was wondering how the testing was going."

She tried to hide her disappointment, but her voice betrayed her as she answered, "Good. Ms. Fordman is administering them today."

"Great. I forgot to ask the other day, are all the children okay? Were any hurt in the storm or traumatized?"

"They're all perfectly fine. I went by just a few minutes ago and they're working away. I had them take over another teacher's classroom for the day so they could be tested. It was quite a chore, but I'm sure it's worth it."

"So all eighteen of them are there?"

"No. One little boy is out of town, but the rest are present and accounted for."

Parker hesitated for a second, then said, "Really? Isn't this a strange time to pull a child out of school? Why not wait until Thanksgiving or Christmas break?"

"God only knows. You'd be surprised at the things parents judge are more important than education. After all these years, you'd think I'd be used to it, but it still irks me."

"Which child is it?"

"The Lawrence boy. I understand he'll be keeping

up with his class work while he's gone, but in my opinion, being absent is still inappropriate."

"He scored high on our first test. It's too bad he isn't there. If you could find out where he is, maybe we could send the test to him. Otherwise, the results will be meaningless. Unless, of course, he'll be back in the next couple of days."

"No. I got the impression he would be gone for quite a while. Hold on, I'll ask my secretary." Several seconds later she said, "Parker?"

"Yes."

"He's visiting his grandparents in Minnesota. He may be gone for a long time. Do you need that address?"

"That would be very helpful."

"I'll see if I can get it for you. I'll call you back."

"Thanks, Grace."

"You're welcome, Parker."

McDaniel hung up the phone, then dialed it again. Since he knew every word was being taped, he used the codes agreed to almost a year ago. "I'll be late for dinner tonight. Why don't you meet me at the Spudder at seven. Fine." He hung up again, this time leaning forward to rub his aching temples.

In two months it will be over, and I can quit playing these asinine games.

"This isn't good." Gene Lemmond glared across his polished desk at the three men standing before him. Mike Harper, Parker McDaniel, and J.D. Cook stared back, all bearing the same grave facial expressions.

"There may be some perfectly logical reason why they sent him away. Maybe one of his relatives is dying or something. Personally, I don't think it's possible that they're on to us. But I'll admit it's odd that we haven't gotten any pertinent information from the

Lawrence house taps since the Fordman woman moved in," Harper said.

"Were all the devices in her apartment recovered?"

"All but one were retrieved early the next morning. And we recovered that one, as well as the other evidence collected at the scene, from the package intercepted from the fire department. We're stepping up our security on both Fordman and Lawrence by adding tracking and listening devices to both cars." He glanced at his watch. "They should already be in place. Plus, tonight we'll take care of the vet clinic."

"Good. Any recommendations, gentlemen?"

McDaniel spoke, "I think we should wait until the principal gets me the address where the boy is staying. It should be pretty easy to find out why he was sent to stay with his grandparents. If he was sent there because his father is suspicious, then we'll handle it appropriately."

"Be sure you do. Fordman, Lawrence and his son, plus the grandparents are all expendable. The last thing we need right now are any potential liabilities."

Chapter 15

Five more. Five more children. Stacey was right. The whole class must have been exposed. Or even worse, the entire school.

JoAnn continued to read page after page of lab reports. She cross-referenced each identification code to what looked like a Christmas list she had tucked under her calendar so she could tell whose blood tests she was reading. The sixth blood report showed no cell damage, and no amyloid proteins. She checked again to see which child had either not been exposed or not been affected. Meredith. JoAnn put a star by her name and went back to checking the report. The next child's blood showed amyloid protein damage again.

When she reached another negative test result, she stopped. After finding they were Stacey Fordman's, she reread the entire page and began to feel excited. Although there were minute traces of amyloid proteins present in her blood sample, they were free-floating in the bloodstream. None had attached to the red blood cells as they had in the other cases. The last test result was the same. Amanda Nichols had definitely been exposed, but cell damage had not occurred.

In spite of her disgust over the endangerment of innocent children, the results now fascinated her. If Stacey Fordman had been exposed at the same rate as the children, then for some biological reason, the Citrinol3 had not been toxic to her system. And better yet, if Amanda Nichols was also equally exposed, she might be looking at two cases in which Citrinol3 was successfully administered to humans. Of course, since neither had the cancer they were designed to treat, it was impossible to tell if the drug would have attacked cancer cells as intended. Still, isolation of whatever protected these people could eliminate the drug's negative side effects and cut years off the research time.

JoAnn suddenly felt nauseous. *Is this how they trapped Hanna? Money couldn't have done it, Hanna had everything she ever dreamed of. But did a promise of a miracle at her fingertips corrupt an honest, hardworking person? If only a few people's lives were risked, wasn't the big picture more important, the thousands who would be saved?*

Jess handed Stacey a steaming mug of hot chocolate piled high with tiny melting marshmallows as he said, "You realize that we're alone. Jonathan's gone. No one is here to interrupt or see anything."

She stroked the puppies who were sleeping beside her and said, "Except Rocky and Bell."

"I had a long talk with them. They promised not to tell a soul anything they see or hear."

Stacey placed her mug on the coffee table, then gently pushed Jess onto the soft cushions and started kissing him. She slowly worked her way up the roughness of his neck to his ear and whispered, "But what if they see something really, really exciting? Something so seductive and erotic that they lose all track of themselves. Then what would we do? We'd be responsible for the corruption of minors."

With a quick turn of his torso, he flipped over, pinning her under him on the sofa. His voice was husky as he said, "I'll lock them in the pantry. If they want to learn the facts of life I'll rent them a doggie porno tape. But not until they're older, of course."

Jess was gently biting every exposed bit of Stacey's skin as she lightly protested, "Is that how you plan on explaining things to your son? Rent him a porno tape?"

"He already knows. The week school started Derek gave him a lecture on sex so twisted and biased that I immediately sat down with Jonathan and explained everything."

She reached down and stroked him until he groaned. "Everything?"

"Well, not *everything*. But definitely the basics. He knows what goes where and why."

"Are you sure you explained it right? Maybe you've forgotten. You said yourself it had been a few years."

He was teasing her, caressing gently, then more forcefully. "You're a teacher. Teach me. That is, if you know how." His mouth covered hers and they heatedly explored each other until they were interrupted by the ringing phone.

"Ignore it," he muttered.

"It could be Jonathan. You told him to call whenever he wanted to."

Jess groaned and reached over to grab the phone. "Hello."

"Is this Jess Lawrence?"

"Yes."

"This is Mrs. Milliken. I'm principal of the first grade at East Elementary."

"Could you hold on a second?" He covered the phone and whispered to Stacey, "It's Mrs. Milliken." He leaned close to her so she could hear what was being said. "I'm sorry for making you wait. What can I do for you?"

"I'm calling about your son Jonathan's absence from school. Is everything going well at home?"

"Yes. He's visiting his grandparents for a while." He winked at Stacey as he said, "I'm keeping in very close contact with his teacher, Ms. Fordman, and she is providing all his work so he won't get behind."

"I understand that, Mr. Lawrence, but did she explain to you that he is part of a very special group of children?" Before he could answer she continued, "Ms. Fordman's class was specially selected and approved by the Board of Education to be reviewed. Your son, Jonathan, is one of only eighteen children chosen to represent the entire school district. I'm sure you'll understand that it is a very expensive, time-consuming project, and that since it is such a small group, the test results will be distorted by his absence."

"I'm very sorry, Mrs. Milliken, but he won't be back for quite a while."

"He doesn't have to come back, Mr. Lawrence. We can send the test to him. Once he completes it, he can send it back to us. All I need is the address where he is staying."

Jess's mind was racing. He had no intention of telling her anything about Jonathan. "I apologize, Mrs. Milliken. Someone is trying to get through on my call waiting. It could be a client with an emergency. If you'll give me your phone number, I'll call you right back with the exact address."

After a brief hesitation, she finally said, "Fine. My number is 555-6285. I'll be waiting for your call."

The tension in the air almost pulsed in the Security section of TechLab. Even though it was late, Mike Harper was still there. For the first time in months, he was personally observing the surveillance operation. The guard on duty had scurried around, finding an extra set of headphones so he could listen to the conversations in the Lawrence home "live" instead of waiting to hear the playback. The phone call from the Milliken woman had been an added bonus.

Harper pulled off his headphones and said, "I want

someone in Minnesota to check out every person over forty whose last name is Lawrence. Either send someone from here, or fax whoever we use any surveillance photos we have of the boy. Just to be certain, we need to act fast before Jess Lawrence has time to change his son's whereabouts."

"Is this still a fact-finding mission, sir?"

"For now. But tell whoever we use that if the facts they find are right, they have permission to eliminate the problem. Immediately."

"Yes, sir."

● Stacey was already up and headed out the French doors that led to the backyard when Jess hung up the telephone. He followed her out until they were in the middle of the backyard. The leaves were cold and crisp under her bare feet as Stacey turned to Jess, her anxiety apparent by her folded arms and stiff stance. Keeping her voice very low she said, "This is getting scary. Why would anyone need to know where Jon is staying?"

Through gritted teeth he growled, "Because they've used him like a goddamn laboratory rat and they want to know if he's chasing his own tail yet. There's no way I'm going to tell her or anyone else where he really is."

"Do you have other relatives or friends who live in St. Paul? I'm afraid if she doesn't already know where he is, she will soon. Jon told several of his friends where he was going and they've been talking about it quite a bit at school."

"No. But I can stall her for a while. I'll tell her they took him on a sightseeing tour of Canada and they won't be back until after Thanksgiving. That'll give us a few weeks to line up a different place for him to stay. When I was a kid, we used to vacation at a little resort called Farm Island. If they rent cabins in the winter, maybe my parents could take him there."

"You'd better call and warn them."

"I will, but not on this phone. I'll stop and use a pay phone on the way to work tomorrow."

"Good idea."

"I'm supposed to meet JoAnn for lunch. I think we'll have plenty to talk about."

"I hope she remembers to bring that test back. You can bet Mrs. Milliken will be on me like glue in the morning trying to get it. I told her this morning I'd left it in my briefcase at home, so I don't think she'll buy my stalling much longer."

"I'll drive you to work tomorrow. You can blame not having it on me."

"You still think she's in on all this, don't you?"

"Damn straight. And I want you to be very, very careful about what you say to her. If whoever is behind this thinks we're on to them, we may all be in trouble, especially Jonathan. I'm afraid it's up to you to convince her everything about his trip is on the up and up."

"Mrs. Milliken, may I have a word with you?" Stacey's hands were ice-cold. Even though she had practiced every word she was going to say all last night, visualizing it like a speech presented for thousands, she still wondered if she could lie convincingly enough. She wished she'd told Jess her plan, since right now her own judgment seemed questionable at best.

"Come in, Ms. Fordman. Did you bring the Lawrence boy's test booklet?"

"No. I'm afraid his father brought me to work this morning and it was in my car, so I don't have it with me. I promise, I'll bring it first thing tomorrow."

"That's what you said yesterday."

"I'm really sorry. I'm well . . . a little distracted right now." Stacey took a deep breath and said, "I've always thought you were a very fair woman, Mrs. Milliken. Can I confide in you?"

Mrs. Milliken sat back in her chair, looking almost shocked. "Well, of course. I'm always available to the teachers. Are you having a problem with one of the children in your class?"

"No. It's much more complicated than that."

"Really?"

Stacey nodded.

"Are you pregnant?"

"It's not that complicated!"

"Then what can I do to help you, Ms. Fordman?"

"There have been these rumors lately about how you . . . uh . . . the flowers . . . and you know . . ."

"No, I don't know. And from past experience I've found that most rumors are totally inaccurate. What gibberish is being spread around this time behind my back?"

"They say that you're involved with a very handsome man."

"Do they? How interesting. And what does that have to do with you?"

"Well, I'm involved with someone, too, and I was hoping you would understand since you may be in the same position yourself." Stacey blushed as she stood and said, "I'm sorry. I'm making a fool of myself. I shouldn't bother you with this."

"Sit down. It's no bother."

Stacey reluctantly slid back into the chair.

"Who are we speaking of?"

"Jess Lawrence." Stacey braced herself.

Very calmly, almost indifferently, Mrs. Milliken said, "Jonathan Lawrence's father. You're dating a parent of one of the children in your class?"

Stacey nodded, but continued to only make eye contact with a particularly spectacular pink rose in the arrangement on the corner of the desk.

"I talked to Mr. Lawrence just last night. He seemed rather distant."

"I know. I was there."

"How convenient."

Stacey finally looked her in the eye as she said, "You see, he was trying to protect me. He was afraid if you found out about the two of us that you would be upset with me and it would affect my work, if not cost me my job. But I told him you weren't that kind of person . . . that you would understand."

"Yes."

"He was vague about Jonathan's trip because in some ways it is because of me Jonathan left town."

"You're responsible for one of your children missing weeks, possibly months of school?"

"Not directly. His grandparents had promised to take him with them the next time they toured Canada, but under normal circumstances, I'm sure Jess wouldn't have allowed him to go in the middle of the school year."

"And because of your involvement with his father, circumstances at the Lawrence household are no longer considered normal?"

"I'm afraid not. We're at a crossroads of our relationship right now and we want to be sure we're . . . you know, really compatible before we make any long-term commitment. With Jonathan around all the time it was almost impossible to . . . address the physical aspects of our relationship."

With wide eyes Mrs. Milliken said, "Are you telling me Mr. Lawrence sent his son away so the two of you could spend time alone?"

Stacey stared at her hands and nodded her head. When she raised her eyes back to look at Mrs. Milliken, they were brimming with tears. "Things have been so hard lately. First my apartment, then the tornado. I'm so confused. I didn't want him to send Jonathan away, but I didn't do anything to stop him either. I don't know what I want anymore." Stacey took a ragged breath as she fleetingly wondered if she should have been an actress instead of a teacher.

"It's all right, Ms. Fordman. I'm not the wicked old hag everyone around here thinks I am. I learned a long time ago to separate my personal life from my professional life. Obviously, you haven't learned that lesson yet. I hope it doesn't turn out to be too costly for you."

Tears were rolling down her cheeks as Stacey said, "I think I love him. He's even talked about getting married. What should I do? How do you know when it's right?"

"I'm certainly not the right person to give advice on this subject. My own love life has been far from noteworthy, but I am glad you confided in me. It explains why Mr. Lawrence was so vague last night. Plus, now you have one less thing to worry about. There's no reason to sneak around behind my back. I'm not out to get you, or any of the other teachers who work here for that matter.

"I do have some advice for you, Stacey. Try to relax. Get some sleep. Life is too short to waste so much energy worrying about things you have no control over." She looked at the bouquet of flowers on the corner of her desk. "Sometimes you just have to enjoy the wonderful things that come your way and not ask too many questions."

Early morning light sparkled on the fresh snowdrifts lining the streets of St. Paul. As they drove, Jonathan drearily watched the slush splash across the road's fluffy white border leaving it marred with grime. He wished he were at home, then he looked at his grandmother, who was driving so slowly and carefully. She was always nice, almost too nice.

He finally said, "Why do you call Grandpa 'A.J.,' Grandma?"

"Because he likes it better than his real name."

"What's his real name?"

"Axel Julius Lawrence."

"I don't blame him."

She laughed and said, "And they call me Betty, because my real name is Elizabeth Patricia."

"Elizabeth isn't so bad. I thought they called you Betty because of the cartoon. You know, the Flintstones."

"I've been around a lot longer than that cartoon, Jonathan."

"But Dad even said you used to look like that Betty. He said you had pretty black hair when he was a kid."

"I did. Did Grandpa tell you that your dad left a message on our recorder this morning while we were out getting donuts? He said he's going to call back at lunchtime."

"Can I talk to him?"

"Of course. Did you like watching it snow last night?" she asked.

"It was okay."

"Has it snowed in Oklahoma yet this year?"

He shook his head. "It doesn't snow much at our house. Maybe once or twice a year. But it's better that way."

"Why?"

"Because when it does snow they almost always close school. They close everything in the whole town. It's really neat. Up here, things just go on like normal. Snow isn't special here like it is at home."

"We have snowplows here that clean the streets so the buses and cars can keep going. I don't suppose they have those in Oklahoma."

"Nope."

"Cheer up. You'll love the park we're going to. There are swings and things to climb on, and you can ice skate. I think it's so precious that you can wear your father's old ice skates. I'm glad I never gave them away."

"I miss Dad. And Rocky and Bell. And Ms. Fordman."

"You'll see them again before you know it. Meanwhile, you need to relax and have fun. I know I'm going to."

"Okay, Grandma."

◆ They parked and walked over to the ice-skating rink. After his grandmother helped him lace up the skates, he rushed onto the ice. Thirty minutes later he finally skated back toward her, practically landing in her lap as he breathlessly exclaimed, "I can do it! I remembered how to skate!"

"And you do it quite well. You must have inherited some of your father's athletic abilities. He was always speeding around everyone else, skating as fast as he could. A real daredevil."

"What's a daredevil?"

"A person who takes risks. They like to try new things and sometimes they aren't very cautious about how they go about it."

"My dad? Are you sure? He doesn't even like it when I climb up the tree in our backyard. I like to go to the very top, but when I do he yells at me not to go so high."

She laughed. "I'll bet he does. You'll understand when you have a boy of your own, it's all part of being a father. You know, it's awfully cold out here. Are you sure you're warm enough?"

"Grandma, you made me wear three pairs of socks, two coats, and gloves and mittens. I'm hot."

"It's twenty-one degrees outside and you're hot.

Would you mind if I wait for you in the car? I'm a little cold sitting here in the wind."

"You should have worn more clothes."

"Next time, you can remind me."

"I will. Can I swing now?"

"Sure." She helped him take his skates off, slip his snow boots back on, then walked with him to the swings. "If you need me, I'll be in the car. Don't swing too high, okay? And stay where I can see you."

"Okay." He knocked the snow off the seat of the swing and jumped on, pumping his legs as hard as he could. In no time at all he was flying back and forth. At the peak of one forward swing he let go of the chains, his body arching out and away before skidding across the snow as he landed on the cold, crunchy ground. "Awesome!" he yelled as he slid to a stop.

A man seemed to appear out of nowhere and said, "Wow. I used to do the same thing when I was a kid. I'll bet you could go farther if you tried."

"Sure I could." Jon hopped back in the swing and pumped even harder. The man watched as he flew through the air again, this time skidding five feet farther than he had the first time.

"Very impressive," the man said.

Jess looked at the man. He was tall and wore a leather bomber's jacket and new blue jeans. Jess noticed he had snakeskin cowboy boots on, the same kind his dad wore. He looked cold. His face and ears were red, and his hands were shoved deep in his pockets to keep them warm as he asked, "You aren't from around here, are you, son?"

"How can you tell?"

"Your accent."

"What's an accent?"

"The way you talk. You know, I'm pretty good with accents. I'd guess you're from Oklahoma. Am I right?"

"Wow! How'd you know that?"

"People from each state all talk a little different. What you have to do is listen very closely when they say things. It's like a game. So are you visiting St. Paul with your folks or did you move up north recently?"

Jon shook his head and started swinging again. He remembered what his kindergarten teacher, Ms. Fordman, and his dad had all said about talking to strangers. This man was nice, but he was still a stranger. Jon's stomach began to ache a little, that same ache that used to make him wish he could stay home from school. *Never talk to strangers. Never talk to strangers.*

"I'll bet you're staying with your grandparents. A little visit, right?"

Jon barely nodded.

"Where are my manners? My name is Bryan Peters. Nice to meet you . . ."

Jon flew out of the swing again, but this time as soon as he landed, he bounded to his feet and he yelled, "I have to go now." Running as fast as he could, he raced to his grandmother's car, afraid to look back. He slammed the car door behind him and locked it, then reached across and locked his grandmother's side as well.

After dodging his arm she said, "Goodness, Jonathan, you're in an awfully big hurry. Did you get cold?"

Breathlessly he begged, "Please, Grandma, let's go home. Right now. Please."

JoAnn was waiting on the curb of TechLab's circular drive when Jess pulled up. She slipped him a note as he helped her store her crutches in the backseat. As they drove off he said, "Nice weather we're having."

"I miss that sometimes. Never knowing if it's sunny or raining. I go for days now without ever leaving the

BioHazard lab. Lately, I've pretty much lost track of day and night, too."

While she talked, Jess read the note she had given him.

Be very careful. Don't mention anything in the car, it may be bugged. I'm sure my office is, and so is my phone. A noisy restaurant where we can't be heard would be great.

"Why don't we pick up a couple of subs and eat at LaFortune Park? It would be a shame for you to miss the chance to enjoy such a beautiful autumn day. Besides, you look like you should soak up a little sunshine. Have you considered taking vitamins? You're awfully pale."

"I think I'm just working too hard. There is so much to do, and even though there isn't a specific deadline, the pressure to complete the project I'm working on is intense."

To save time they bought lunch at a drive-up window and headed for the park. Once they were settled at a picnic table bathed in sunlight Jess said, "I'm glad you took the time to break for lunch. Everyone needs a chance to unwind every now and then."

JoAnn shook her head as she said, "Not at TechLab. They just wind you tighter and tighter. Sometimes I wonder if employees ever really quit, or if they are victims of spontaneous combustion and the cleaning crews sweep them away to make room for the next team of workaholics."

"I think the principal at East Elementary may be involved. She seems overly concerned about Jonathan's trip."

"At this point anything is possible. The blood tests confirm our suspicions. Jonathan wasn't the only one exposed. Of the ten blood tests I ran, two were totally negative—yours and that of a child named Meredith. Six of the other children's results were like Jonathan's— damage has been caused by amyloid protein deposits. And the last two—Stacey's and that of a child named Amanda—showed amyloid proteins were present, but, miraculously, they hadn't caused any cellular damage."

"Confusing results."

JoAnn was obviously at home discussing her work. She was noticeably more relaxed and confident as she explained, "Not really. I ran a statistical analysis, and they roughly coincide with the lab figures we've obtained. Of course, without testing the entire group exposed, it means nothing."

"Actually, it means we are dealing with ruthless bastards who would experiment on innocent children, and God only knows who else. Did you check the test packet I gave you?"

She nodded. "It's in my briefcase. No signs of any unusual chemicals. I even checked the ink. If they used the tests to expose the children before, they aren't doing it anymore. Do you know anything about the two children whose blood didn't test like the other children? Meredith and Amanda?"

"I know they're both, as Stacey calls them, special. When I went to talk to the class, Meredith missed the first half of my presentation because she goes to some kind of lab class every morning. I'm pretty sure Amanda and Sloan either go to lab classes, or an inclusion teacher comes in to help them, too."

"Sloan? Did we test his blood?"

"No. As soon as he saw the first skin prick, he lost all interest in knowing what type blood he had."

"Too bad. It might have been important."

"How's that?"

"The three unusual test results were from Stacey, Amanda, and Meredith. There must be some common factor they share. Assuming the exposure to Citrinol3 was in the classroom, my first guess would be that Amanda and Meredith spent less time there each day because they went to lab classes for their learning disabilities. Therefore, their exposure to the compound may have been minimized when compared to the other children. But that doesn't explain Stacey. She probably spent more time in that classroom than any of the children. I vaguely recall her telling me she had a learning disability herself, but it was right after I got out of the hospital and everything is a little cloudy. Do you know anything about it?"

"I don't mean to offend you, JoAnn, but I think we need to concentrate more on how to stop whoever these people are than on the importance of the scientific breakthrough at hand."

"Of course. I just don't know what else to do. My entire life's work is at stake, and so are innocent people's lives. I'm attacking this situation scientifically, since that's the only way I know how to deal with a problem. Any problem."

"I know how hard this is for you. But we have to find out who is doing this and stop them."

She grabbed her knees and rocked gently as she looked up at the sky. Finally, she said, "I'm scared, Jess."

"Me, too, but neither of us has any option at this point. Stacey said the company doing the analysis at school was called Independent Testing Labs. I have a client who owes me a favor. He said he'd check out ITL for me. Ever heard of them?"

"No, but I'll see if I can find out anything when I get back to TechLab."

"Do it carefully," Jess asked quietly.

"Believe me, I will."

"You told her *what*?" Jess asked, his mixture of anger and shock apparent.

Stacey matched both the volume and intensity of Jess's voice. "You heard me! When you cut through all the bullshit, I told her you sent Jonathan off to Minnesota so you could land me in bed. Uninterrupted sex for weeks on end. What part don't you understand?"

"Have you lost your mind? She could have fired you!"

"But she didn't. Don't you see, now she'll tell whoever she's working for that we wanted to get Jon out of the way awhile because he was cramping our sex life. That way, they won't know we're suspicious or suspect why we really sent him to Minnesota. Frankly, I thought it was a brilliant plan."

"A plan that makes me look like a sex-starved pervert who kicks his son out of his own house so he can screw his teacher. I'll never be able to show my face at that school again."

"What about *my* reputation? I have to look this woman in the eye every day. Now she thinks I'm a ditzy bitch who can't handle her own love life, not to mention a teacher who would hop into bed with the father of one of her students. Oh, yeah, let's not leave out the part where I'm responsible for keeping my student from getting an education."

Jess suddenly started to laugh. He leaned against the fence that lined the backyard of the clinic. After several seconds Stacey started laughing, too. Finally she managed to say, "What is wrong with us?"

"Everything."

"No shit." They broke back up, this time sliding down until they were sitting in the cold grass leaning against the fence. With tears in her eyes Stacey asked, "How are we ever going to get out of this mess? And better yet, how did we get into it in the first place?"

*   *   *

"Independent Testing Labs is a shell corporation owned by a whole series of other shell corporations. The trail ends with some Brazilian company. They have a phone number in Kansas City, but it's answered by a service. The service won't release any information on how the messages are forwarded. I also checked on the guy named Parker McDaniel. There is a Parker McDaniel who lives here in town. He's a bigwig at TechLab, I believe his official title is Vice President—Product Research. He has an unlisted personal phone number and drives a blue Seville with Oklahoma vanity plate TL-PM. It may or may not be the guy you're looking for."

Jess sighed. "It probably is. Thanks for the fast work, Tim. How much do I owe you?"

"I told you, Doc. This is payback for taking care of Lady. Besides, now that Lady is gone, I'm thinking about getting my wife another puppy for Christmas. I may be calling in this favor sooner than you think."

"I'll look forward to it. Just do me a favor. This time, bring the puppy in before your wife gets attached to it. Neither of you needs to go through the ordeal of having another dog with a congenital heart problem."

"You'll be the first one to see the little pest. I promise. Who knows, maybe I'll come to my senses and buy her a new washing machine instead. They don't pee on the carpet."

Jess laughed and said, "Think about getting one from the animal shelter, Tim. Believe it or not, mutts are usually healthier than full breeds and there are plenty that need a good home."

"Good idea. I'll check with them before I make up my mind."

"Thanks again, Tim." Jess hung up the phone and stared at the wall above his computer while he thought. *Either TechLab is involved, or whoever exposed Jonathan was smart enough to use the name of one of Tech-*

lab's top men to throw any suspicion back on them. Thank God Jonathan's safe and sound in St. Paul.

JoAnn picked at the dinner J.D. had brought to her office while she pretended to be interested in what he was saying. He sat across from her, enthusiastically eating the lukewarm Chinese take-out food while bragging about the latest contract TechLab had signed.

"Are you listening, JoAnn?"

She nodded and halfheartedly took another bite.

"This new compound is believed to be able to mutate certain proteins that control DNA replication. Do you have any idea how valuable that could be?"

She stared at him for a second and said, "J.D., I know precisely what the benefits would be. You're not talking to your mother."

"Well, excuse me, Miss Rocket Scientist. I was just trying to carry on a polite dinner conversation with you, but obviously your mind is on the proper mixture of fuel to use for your next liftoff. Besides, judging from the mood you're in, I'd probably be better off talking to myself."

"I think you're confusing me with someone else."

"Yes, someone who gives a damn."

He abruptly stood, but JoAnn quickly hopped up and gently touched his arm as she said, "I know I'm not very good company. I guess I'm just overly concerned about a friend of mine."

"Really? Who?"

"Jess Lawrence."

"Didn't you have lunch with him again today?"

"Yes. He's having a hard time right now."

"Is it anything that would affect his security clearance? They're still working on it, you know."

"No, nothing like that. He's worried about his son,

and whether the woman he's involved with is right for him. You know, pretty ordinary problems."

J.D. dropped his plate into the trash can and seemed much more interested as he asked, "Why is he worried about his son?"

She laughed. "You'd have to know Jess. He's such a meticulous man that he makes himself crazy over the littlest things."

"Like what?"

"His son is visiting his parents for a few weeks. They're taking the kid all over Canada to sightsee."

"And he's worried something will happen to him?"

"No. He feels guilty because the kid isn't here to take some crazy test at school. I guess the principal called him and made him feel like a rotten parent for letting Jonathan take a vacation in the middle of the year. Personally, I think the child will learn more from traveling around a foreign country than he would sitting in a classroom eight hours a day. Don't you?"

"That depends. Children need to know that life isn't doing whatever they want to do whenever they want to do it. I think taking them out of school for a long time sends the message that school isn't a top priority. I would never have allowed it with mine. Not that I would have been asked, mind you."

JoAnn was shocked. With wide eyes she said, "You have kids?"

He nodded rather nonchalantly as he replied, "Two."

"You've never said a word about them. And there aren't any pictures in your condo or your office."

"I know. They've lived with their mother since the divorce. They were only two and four when we split, so they never really knew me. Their stepfather has always been there for them, so I pretty much stay out of the picture. They think of him as their dad."

She gently touched his hand as she said, "How sad for you."

"Not really. You wouldn't believe how many nights I spent lying awake, wondering how they were doing. After a few years, you learn to accept it. Otherwise, one day you look around and you realize that the best years of your life are gone. Then it dawned on me—I was running out of time. I decided I wanted to reach certain goals before it was too late. Not seeing my kids is just part of the cost of attaining those goals."

"That's a pretty high price."

He threw back his shoulders as he replied, "They're lofty goals."

"So you never kept up with their school work?"

"Not really."

She shook her head. "Too bad. I was hoping you could tell me something about the company who's testing Jonathan's class. Jess is so worried, I thought it would ease his mind if I could let him know that it isn't any big deal. Besides the lab techs, you're the only person I see anymore."

"I can check around for you. What's the company's name?"

JoAnn looked him straight in the eye, never hesitating as she said, "Independent Testing Labs."

Several thoughts flashed through J.D.'s mind when he heard JoAnn say the name of TechLab's front company. To cover his agitation, he stood up and walked across the room as he thought.

She knows, and she's toying with me. Did Harper have them install new bugs in this office? If Security is listening to this, they'll be down my throat in a matter of minutes. Look at her! She doesn't know shit. She's stumbled into a hornet's nest that could get both of us killed and she hasn't got a clue. She's the goddamn genius, and I've got to cover her ass every time I turn around. Why can't women just do their jobs and keep their noses out of everyone else's business?

"So, have you heard of them?" she asked.

"Doesn't ring a bell. I know a couple of guys who work in Marketing who have kids that age. I'll ask them."

"How do you know how old he is?"

Shit! He hesitated, then nodded his head as he said, "I must have read it in Lawrence's preliminary security check. He's seven, right?"

"He's in first grade. Seven sounds about right. Really cute kid, too. He's going to be a real lady-killer when he grows up."

"I have to go now. I'll see you tomorrow."

"I thought you were going to stay for a while."

"I just remembered a report I have to get out before noon tomorrow. I'd better run home and get a little sleep, then get back here at the crack of dawn."

"Thanks for bringing dinner."

He walked over and kissed her. "Take care. You are staying here tonight, aren't you?"

"Where else would I go?" JoAnn mumbled.

J.D. walked slowly down the arched hallway toward the elevator bank. *A real lady-killer. I wonder if that's what my mother thought I would turn out to be.*

JoAnn watched J.D. leave, thankful he was finally gone. She was sweating so much, she knew if she moved at all, the pale satin suit she wore would instantly reveal how nervous she truly was. Looking around the office, she felt like a caged animal. There was no way to get out, but every instinct screamed at her to run away and never come back.

Even though J.D. had remained cool and calm, the instantaneous flicker of recognition when she said Independent Testing Lab's name had been unmistakable. There was no doubt in her mind that he had heard of the company. The question was, how? Was it connected with TechLab directly, or was he familiar with it through one of Techlab's competitors? And if he wasn't involved, why didn't he tell her what he knew?

Going into the makeshift bedroom, she changed into a sweat suit and began her nightly routine of Achilles tendon stretching exercises. As usual, the pain was excruciating, bringing tears to her eyes. But tonight the pain gave her something to focus on besides her own confusion and self-pity. Suddenly the anesthetic cloud she'd been wandering around in for weeks seemed to break, revealing a startlingly simple idea that just might work.

Why the hell didn't I think of this weeks ago? she wondered as she hobbled back into her office and settled in for a long night's work.

Chapter 16

In any other office, the black file cabinet's main purpose would have been to gather dust. But in an underground, virtually dust-free facility like BioHazard, it merely served as a place to stack more work to do. Since she'd taken over Hanna's position, JoAnn barely had time to keep up with the unending flow of current reports and memos, much less search through the historical data Hanna had maintained.

As she opened the first folder, she smiled. Hanna's immaculate, beautiful handwriting graced the inside cover. In her normal thorough style, the contents of the file were neatly written on the inside cover, complete with entry dates and descriptions. JoAnn eased herself into a cross-legged position on the floor and settled in for a night of reading.

The first drawer held files that were interesting compilations of budget meetings and staffing requirements. The second drawer was even more fascinating. It was full of research files on Hanna's own pet project, an antidepressant compound that was responsible for her success in the scientific community. It had been a brilliant achievement for such a young woman, and had paved the way for her giant leap from performing basic research into being the youngest, and only female, member of TechLab's upper management team. As she read the painstaking steps Hanna had taken, JoAnn felt a familiar ache for her mentor and friend.

At three a.m. JoAnn finally rolled open the last

drawer. In it were the files for the work done while Hanna was Chief of Research. The first files she read were very familiar. They contained memos, mainly from her to Hanna, regarding the status of the Citrinol experiments. The inch-thick file of memos brought back long forgotten memories of what a slow, meticulous process Citrinol had progressed through.

She flipped past memo after memo of familiar information, but the last entry puzzled her. It was dated two weeks before Hanna's death. Unlike the other computer-generated memos, it was merely a handwritten note that appeared to be a reminder from Hanna to herself about the project. It read:

Citrinol3 progressing well. Coach JoAnn on the vital nature of the project to help her come to grips with TechLab's lofty goals.

Schedule meeting soon on connections, network, and project's artificial ceiling. Also, emphasize the relative importance of correlative thought processes.

JoAnn reread the note, snagging on the strange wording once again. Stretching her arms, she shrugged off the odd feeling Hanna's handwriting always gave her and yawned. Grabbing the pile of files, she stuffed them all back into the drawer, then pulled out the set of files behind them. These were marked SynCur6. She recognized the name, and she closed her eyes, willing away her need to curl up on the floor and fall asleep. Where had she seen the name SynCur6 recently?

Opening the first folder, she scanned Hanna's log on the inside cover until she saw an entry for an intercompany memorandum marked "Proposal Summary." Flipping past the usual budget memos, she found the one she was looking for and quickly scanned it.

According to the project's specifications, SynCur6

was destined to be used in conjunction with a memory altering drug to provide an improved anesthetic agent that would yield little, if any, side effects. Alone, it provided the muscular paralysis needed for performing delicate surgeries, but, unfortunately, left the patient fully aware of the pain. With the memory blocking agent, the patient remembered no pain, yet regained consciousness very rapidly without grogginess, nausea, or headaches. In light of the increase in outpatient surgical procedures, TechLab expected the drug blend to be very profitable.

JoAnn read through memo after memo, but entire sections of work were missing from the file. She flipped to the front entry log and read the description of the entries Hanna had made. They all seemed routine. But if they were routine, why were they missing? She scanned the listing again, this time noting the date each entry was made. From start to finish, the entire project had taken only six years. That was an incredible rate of completion for such a major project. She stacked the files to one side and pulled out the next block.

These files were on the drug NiAl2. They, too, were missing critical sections of work. She scanned the timetable and noted that once again, this project had been completed in a remarkably short period of time.

The rush of adrenaline as she suddenly remembered where she had recently seen the names SynCur6 and NiAl2 jolted JoAnn. *Hanna's calendar.* She closed her eyes again, visualizing the pages and exactly what Hanna had written. Although she could clearly remember each entry, the dates were vague. She needed to get her hands on that calendar again. Now.

It was seven o'clock in the morning, and a fresh layer of snow was falling on St. Paul. Another four inches had already accumulated, and according to the radio, no end was in sight. The Lawrence household was in a state of chaos as Jonathan and his grandparents prepared to leave town. Even though the garage was connected to the heated basement, the cold air crept up the stairs and chilled the entire house.

They were all on edge, more from concern than from the bitter nip in the air. Even though it was early, they were already tired from going up and down the basement stairs so many times. At last, it seemed as though everything was finally packed and they could leave.

Jonathan had spent the last ten minutes staring out the window in the living room. He grabbed his grandpa's coat and tugged on it as he said, "Do you have any binoculars?"

"Yes. Should we pack them?"

"No. I'd like to use them now if it's okay, Grandpa."

"Why?"

Jon gripped A.J.'s coat and led him to the picture window. Wiping the condensation away from a small area, Jonathan pointed down the block. "See it?"

"See what, son?"

"That car. All the other cars have snow on them, but that car is almost clean. It only has a little snow on the back."

"Maybe whoever it is has been getting ready to go to work. They probably already cleaned it off."

"But it's been that way since we first got up. I've been watching."

"So?"

"So it might be *him*."

"Him? Who?"

"The creepy guy who talked to me in the park."

"It probably isn't anything to worry about, Jonathan. But if it will make you feel better, I'll get the binoculars and check it out. Nobody fools with a Lawrence, right?"

"Right."

"I want you to go get your pillow and wait downstairs in the car. Okay?"

"Okay, Grandpa."

A.J. rummaged through the hall closet and finally found the binoculars. They hadn't been used in years, but once he dusted them off and focused them, they worked perfectly. Although he couldn't see the man in the car clearly, there was no doubt there was someone sitting behind the steering wheel, and that the car was running.

Betty came up behind him and scolded, "For heaven's sake, what are you doing? We're supposed to be on the road today."

He pointed down the street. "Jonathan thinks the guy in that car parked in front of the Clarks' house is watching us. He just may be right."

"Then we should call the police."

"Jess said if those people think anything suspicious is going on that it could mean real trouble. Calling the police would be the worst thing we could do."

"Then we're stuck here. He'll follow us if we leave."

A.J. smiled as he ran his hand through his silver hair and said, "Not necessarily."

Harper's hand brutally squeezed the round stress ball as he asked, "So the kid ran away from you yesterday?"

Butler's scratchy voice exuded confidence as he said, "Yes, sir. I'm certain it was him."

"Why did he run? Do you think he knows something? Did he act like he'd been warned?"

"You know how kids are these days. Everybody harps on them about not talking to strangers. I don't think he distrusted me any more than he would have distrusted anyone else who said 'Boo' to him in a park."

"Did you follow him?"

"Yes. I've been watching the Lawrence house ever since."

"Are you sure you've got the right house?"

"Positive. I checked their mail yesterday. A.J. and Elizabeth Lawrence. According to city hall, they have a son named Jess Lawrence."

"Great. How do you plan to proceed from here?"

"I'm parked up the block. As soon as they leave, I'll wire the house and the phone. My partner is on the next street waiting for my signal. He'll tail them and attempt to make contact again, since I've been seen."

"Do you have an incendiary device with you?"

"A lightbulb conversion model. A little crude, but still effective."

"Install it."

"Yes, sir."

"I wish it were springtime."

Jess pulled Stacey a little closer as he whispered, "I thought you loved cold weather. I seem to recall you saying it always lifted your spirits."

Stacey looked at the eastern sky blushing pink and orange with the promise of the sunrise. Before, she would have enjoyed the sheer beauty of the moment. But now, her teeth were chattering and she huddled even closer to Jess as she said, "Cold never bothered me before, but I've never had to go outside half naked every two minutes either."

"Next time, grab a coat. And some shoes."

"I need to buy some winter things. If you'll remember, my wardrobe isn't exactly brimming with seasonal selections. I miss my mukluks."

"You had mukluks? In Oklahoma?"

"Sure. They were beautiful. I got them in Colorado last time I went skiing. Listen, we can talk about this nonsense in the house. What do you want to tell me that required dragging me out of bed and risking frostbite?"

"You didn't sleep very well last night, did you?"

"What was your first clue?"

"Actually, it was a toss-up between the circles under your eyes and that razor-sharp tongue of yours."

"I need some more makeup, too."

"We'll go shopping after I get home from work, then have a nice quiet dinner."

"I'm freezing my butt off, Jess. Cut to the chase, will you?"

"I called Dad a few minutes ago from the gas station. By now they're getting ready to go to Farm Island or some other little resort town. Jonathan said a man scared him in the park yesterday."

"Oh, no. Did they try to kidnap him?"

"No. He says the man was just asking questions. Still, if he made Jonathan feel that uncomfortable, there may be something to it. I'm glad they're getting out of St. Paul. If they have to, they'll move from place to place. Dad's pretty sharp. If he sees anything suspicious, he won't take any chances."

"How will we know if they're safe?"

"They're going to call my friend, Tim, from a pay phone every other day and leave a message on his machine. He knows what's going on, and if anything goes wrong, with his police background he'll know how to handle it. Plus, if things get settled here, we will know how to get a message to them that it's safe for Jonathan to come home."

"I wish we could just go to the police."

"And risk getting JoAnn killed?"

"I know. But we have to do something."

"We're going to. Unfortunately, right now, the ball is in JoAnn's court. She's checking things as discreetly as possible."

"How long are we going to sit around and wait?

You realize that something could happen to her and we'd never know."

"She calls the clinic every day to check on Rocky and Bell. If she misses a day, we'll know something is wrong."

"All this is making me crazy. These assholes burned everything I owned, drugged your son, and we're sitting around doing absolutely nothing. You're a trusting soul, aren't you, Jess Lawrence?"

Jess turned and walked away as he said, "Do I have any choice?"

The garage door seemed to clatter forever as it rolled open. Jonathan looked anxiously at his grandfather, who winked at him as he twisted around to back the Oldsmobile Cutlass down the snow-covered driveway.

Betty held Jon's hand and said, "Don't worry, son. Your grandpa knows exactly what he's doing." She glared at A.J. and said, "You do, don't you?"

"Of course I do." When the nose of the car cleared the garage, A.J. pushed the controller that sent the door rumbling back down.

Jonathan twisted his feet underneath him, squatting on his knees so he could see better. As they eased into the street he yelled, "Look, Grandma! That guy down the street can't see anything!"

"Get way down, Jonathan. Just in case he's not alone."

Jonathan immediately slumped down, laying his head on his grandmother's lap and whispering, "Did you used to be a spy or something, Grandpa? You sure know how to take care of bad guys."

"We old folks have a few tricks up our sleeves." A.J. smiled as he glanced at the rearview mirror while he quickly drove down the street. His old friend, Mac Clark, had come through for him again. The snowblower he was using to clear his drive was aimed directly at the parked car. The view from the windshield was completely blocked in a man-made blizzard of white.

Once they turned out of the neighborhood onto the busy street, A.J. ruffled Jonathan's hair and said, "You can sit up now, son. Remind me to thank Mac when we get back. Ever been ice fishing?"

"Can you hear me, Garner?"

"Loud and clear."

"Some son of a bitch is covering my goddamn car with enough snow to build a friggin' igloo. I need you to come around from the north and we'll switch positions for a few minutes while I clean all this shit off."

"Be right there."

Butler flung open the door to his car, in time to catch a fresh blast of snow from Mac's snowblower square in the chest. The impact made him stagger backward as he yelled, "What the hell are you doing?"

Mac was bundled from head to toe, and either didn't hear Butler or chose to ignore him. Butler ducked out of the path of the artificial snowstorm and charged to Mac's side, his fancy cowboy boots slipping on the freshly cleared concrete. "I said, what the hell are you doing? This coat is suede, and that last stunt you pulled probably ruined it."

Mac shut off the snowblower and said, "Sorry. I didn't realize anyone was in that car. Ya know you're parked illegally. Snowplow will be along in about half an hour, and they'll write you up faster than you can blink if you're in the their way. If they're feeling generous, they'll skip the ticket and just bury your ass under four feet of snow. Hope you have a shovel handy."

Mac started the blower again, and yelling loudly over its noise added, "Now, if you'll excuse me, I need to get my driveway cleared before the plow comes 'round. Have a good day."

Butler stomped back down the driveway, the whirling cloud from the blower sending stray ice pellets down the nape of his neck. As soon as he was back inside his car, he heard Garner's voice over the two-way radio saying, "Where the hell are you, Butler?"

"I'm back. What's your problem?"

"There are fresh tire tracks leaving the Lawrence house. Did you see which way their car went?"

"Hell no, I didn't see a damned thing. See if you can follow the car's tracks. I'll circle around and come in from the back side of the house, since Frosty the Snowman is keeping an eye on the front."

"Are you sure they all left in the car? Someone may still be inside."

Butler shivered as the ice melted and trickled down his back. Through gritted teeth he said, "What do I care? If someone is in there, then this isn't going to be one of their better days, is it?"

JoAnn paid the cabdriver and made her way up the stairs in front of her house. She was rapidly gaining proficiency at using her crutches, and she rested them against the familiar bricks and dug through her pocket until she found her key. Glancing around, she was warmed by the familiar surroundings and thankful that at least some things hadn't changed in the last few months.

She unlocked the door, took a deep breath, and let it glide open. Grabbing her crutches, she made an awkward dash to turn off the burglar alarm before it automatically summoned the police. She still didn't understand how the burglar circumvented the alarm system that night, and neither the alarm company nor the police had any reasonable explanation.

After catching her breath, she glanced around. Just looking at the new furniture gave her chills. Hobbling into the den, she wished her old rolltop desk were still there. She knew exactly where she had left the calendar. But, like everything else in her life, nothing was the way it used to be.

The new desk felt so strange, its curved surface cold to the touch, hard as marble but not nearly as refined. Drawers floated silently open with only a slight tug. JoAnn riffled through the few things perfectly stacked inside, but found little more than pencils, pens, and paper clips.

A gentle push made the cabinet doors somehow disappear into the adjoining walls. There was no doubt about the craftsmanship of the carpenter who built the desk, his work was impeccable. Inside the cabinets were computer manuals, boxes of diskettes, and even a note from TechLab's computer expert offering his assistance whenever she needed it.

She searched the entire den, then the living room and kitchen. Even though she doubted it would be upstairs, she climbed them one by one to check. When she opened her bedroom door, she gasped. Although she knew her furniture was at TechLab, it had never dawned on her that her house would be so empty without it. Most of the room was vacant. A few knick-knacks were still scattered about, but for the most part everything was at work.

She opened the bathroom door and saw J.D.'s razor lying alongside the other toiletries. Holding it in her hand she twirled it back and forth as she thought. *J.D. knows the burglar alarm code. J.D. came here after I was hurt to cancel my credit cards. The card numbers were on top of my rolltop desk, in my Rolodex. He could have looked in the drawers. He could have found Hanna's calendar, it wasn't well hidden. He could have taken it.*

Dropping his razor, she hurried down the stairs as quickly as she could. Thing were finally making sense, and now she knew exactly what she had to do.

"How could you have lost them? I thought you were an expert at surveillance." Harper paced back and forth, instantly breaking into a sweat.

"I am, sir. There was an unexpected interruption. Don't worry, I have contacts all over the state keeping an eye out for them. If they're around, we'll find them in no time."

"What if they're going to Canada?"

"That makes things a little more complicated, but not impossible."

"Did you wire the house?"

"Yes."

"Any problems?"

"None. In fact, I scored big."

"Meaning?"

"In their address book was a list of their credit card numbers. If we're lucky, they'll charge their gas. We should be able to track them without any problem."

"Good work."

"Thank you."

"Find them. Soon."

"We will."

"You do understand the consequences if you don't?"

"I do."

"Don't let me down again." Harper hung up the phone and grabbed his jacket, patting the inside pocket to make sure his canister of SynCur6 was still there. The Lawrence kid's disappearance was wrapped up in a few too many coincidences. It was obviously time he personally stepped up the Citrinol project surveillance.

* * *

The backyard was covered in leaves, and JoAnn's crutches sank into the moist ground with each stride. She'd never given much thought to the privacy fence that surrounded her property before, but now she realized that the cedar pickets were six feet tall and each one came to a rather nasty point.

Standing back, she stared at the fence, trying to determine a way to scale it in her condition. Carrying a ladder would be practically impossible, plus jumping down on the other side was out of the question. It seemed hopeless, yet she knew if she used her own telephone that TechLab's goons would know exactly where she was going.

Just as she decided to give up, she heard someone humming on the other side of the fence. Hobbling toward the sound, she pressed her eye against a knothole and peered into her neighbor's backyard. A pretty young woman was planting pansies in the flower bed that lined the fence dividing the two properties.

JoAnn excitedly said, "Excuse me. Could I possibly borrow your telephone? Mine seems to be out of order."

The woman's smiling face almost instantly appeared over the top of the fence, her dirty gloved hands gripping two pickets while she balanced on one of the fence's support rails so she could see over the top. "Are you JoAnn Rayburn?"

JoAnn shyly said, "Yes."

"I'm Alexa Adams. We've been neighbors for three years. I'm glad to finally meet you."

"I really don't mean to be unneighborly. I do tend to be gone most of the time."

Alexa laughed and said, "I'll say."

"It's great to finally meet you." JoAnn shifted her weight as she tried to push aside her embarrassment.

She smiled and said, "I've seen your children play out front. They are adorable."

"Thanks."

"If you don't mind my asking, have you ever noticed anything odd going on at my house?"

"You mean besides the herd of people who worked twenty-four hours a day that one week? I've never seen such an impressive renovation team. Your house must be quite a showplace. The furniture they were carting in was something else."

JoAnn shrugged and said, "You could say that."

"I couldn't believe you were robbed. I never saw or heard a thing. I'm so sorry about that and your . . . accident at the supermarket."

"It's all right. My ankle is getting better by the day. I can actually walk a little without crutches now."

"If there's anything I can do for you, just give me a call. I'm here most evenings. This week I'm on vacation, so I'll be around most of the time. These old houses sure require a lot of upkeep, don't they?"

"Yes, they do. Could I impose on you to use your telephone? I need to call a cab. I'm afraid I'm already late for work."

Alexa's face disappeared for a second, then reappeared. In one hand was a cellular phone, which she extended to JoAnn as she said, "I keep it with me all the time. Part of being a mother, you know."

"Thanks," JoAnn said. She quickly dialed the cab company's number. "This is JoAnn Rayburn. I need two taxies. One should pick me up as soon as possible at 2222 Swanlake Drive and the other needs to wait for me behind the drugstore at Thirty-first and Lewis. Behind it, not in front of it . . . Yes, both right now. Have the one behind the drugstore wait . . . No, I don't care if the meter runs the entire time, just make sure it waits in back."

JoAnn handed the phone to Alexa and said, "Thank you so much. It was nice to meet you."

"Likewise. Don't be such a stranger."

"Thanks again." JoAnn hurried back into her house. Chitchat always made her edgy, especially when there was so much to do. Her crutches left streaks of mud and grass on the living-room floor, but she didn't care. She went into the den and sat in the chair by the sleek white desk. This time she ignored the drawers and slid the cabinet doors open. Running her fingers along the neat row of books, she scanned the titles, then pulled out the old dictionary her parents had given her when she graduated from high school. Holding her breath, she grabbed the thick book by its binding and slowly shook it. With a sigh of relief, she watched what she had hidden float down to the pristine carpet.

The bastards didn't find everything. Maybe they aren't as brilliant as they think.

Chapter 17

Without being overly conspicuous, JoAnn tried to watch the cab's rearview mirrors as they drove away. If anyone was following the cab, she couldn't see them, but she knew that probably meant very little. The cabdriver pulled to the front of the drugstore and said, "Fare is seven bucks. You want me to wait while you shop, lady?"

"Sort of. I'll give you an extra twenty dollars to wait here for fifteen minutes. If I don't come back by then, leave without me. Will you do that?"

"Sure."

She handed him the money and slid out the door. As quickly as she could, she went inside the drugstore and headed for the rear exit, weaving in and out of different aisles. A short old man with a face like an English walnut caught her eye twice, but by the time she was at the back of the store, no one was in sight. She slipped out the rear door and into the other waiting cab.

"You J. Rayburn?" the cabbie asked.

"Yes."

"Where to?"

She pulled the envelope out of her pocket and read the address to him.

J.D. knocked a second time on JoAnn's office door, his patience wearing thin. It was hard to conceal the bottle of expensive wine under his coat. Suddenly it occurred to him she might not be answering her phone or door because she was sound asleep. Security had confirmed that she'd been working every night lately, usually past two or three o'clock in the morning. With his free hand, he dug his keys out of his pocket, flipping through them one-handed until he found the one to her office. Once inside, he noticed the door to the makeshift bedroom was closed, so he locked the outer door behind him and sat the bottle of wine on the file cabinet behind her desk.

If she was asleep, he knew the perfect way to wake her up. He popped a TicTac in his mouth and slowly opened the adjoining door, already stiffening with anticipation. The room was dark, but the light from JoAnn's office revealed enough of the room to clearly show there was no one there.

J.D. wasn't sure why he was instantly furious, he just was. He went back to JoAnn's desk and grabbed her appointment calendar. There were no entries recorded at all for the day. He angrily shuffled through the stacks of work on her desk, sending several files plummeting to the floor while carelessly mixing budget memos with her research notes. As he turned to leave, his foot caught the strap of JoAnn's purse, which was tucked under the corner of her desk, causing him to stumble. "Damn it!" he shouted as he untangled himself.

Storming across the hall, he burst into Leanne Caldwell's office and demanded, "Where is Ms. Rayburn?"

Leanne smiled and calmly said, "I don't know, Mr. Cook. I haven't seen her since this morning."

"What time was that?"

"Around ten-thirty or eleven. To tell you the truth, I wasn't really paying much attention."

"She didn't tell you where she was going?"

"No, sir. But then again, she usually doesn't. I'm not her secretary, you know. I'm just an assistant research scientist. Level 7, to be exact."

"I'm fully aware of who you are. Any ideas where she might have gone?"

"She did mention the other day that her physical therapist wanted her to buy a pair of cowboy boots. Maybe she went shopping."

"You're kidding."

"No. JoAnn said the high heel and extra ankle support would help her Achilles heal. Hey, get it? Heal instead of heel."

J.D. glared at her, obviously not amused, and said, "Just tell her to call me as soon as she gets back in. It's urgent."

"Yes, sir," Leanne barked, a little too stiffly.

J.D. half expected a salute to accompany the woman's curt answer. He made a mental note to dictate a memo for L. Caldwell's personnel file when he got to his office. TechLab didn't need sarcastic employees with attitudes. As he headed back toward the corporate offices, his next thought began to calm him down, and he smiled.

Security would know exactly where JoAnn was, since she was under Code 4 surveillance. What an excellent test of how efficiently Harper's department was performing. A test Harper will probably fail miserably. And with an Executive Board meeting in the morning. What a pity.

The neighborhood was old, lined with huge trees. Leaves were still falling, swirling in the late autumn wind before settling into their favorite nesting places. JoAnn paid the cab and carefully made her way up the concrete steps. She rang the bell, but no one answered. Even from the porch, JoAnn could hear the voices from the talk show on the television set. She rang the doorbell for the second time, this time adding a sharp knock as well. Finally, the door slowly opened, and she said, "Mrs. Shore?"

"Yes."

"I'm JoAnn Rayburn. I worked with your daughter, Hanna, at TechLab. Could I speak with you for a few moments?" JoAnn couldn't help but notice how much Hanna had resembled her mother. Although the years had left their telltale signs, the woman before her was still as beautiful as anyone JoAnn had ever seen, except for the overwhelming emptiness that filled her eyes.

"Please come in. Can I get you some tea or coffee?"

"That would be very nice, Mrs. Shore. If you don't mind, I'd like to speak to you while you prepare it. I'm afraid I don't have much time."

"Certainly, but please call me Louise. How can I help you?"

"First of all, I want to thank you for sending me Hanna's letter. It was very thoughtful of you and I know that it came at a difficult time."

"It was the least I could do. Hanna was a good daughter. Just like everything else in her life, her personal affairs were so organized. Her final plans were already made, simply written yet very detailed. All I had to do was follow her instructions. She was so young. Most young people don't think of writing wills and things like that." She shivered, running her hands up and down her arms as she added, "It was almost like she knew she didn't have much time left with us. They say some people just have a feeling about these things. Oprah did a whole show on it."

JoAnn felt a chill and she shivered, too, except she knew the basis for hers was borne in stark reality. "Do you know if Hanna was frightened of any of the people at TechLab?"

"We didn't discuss her work much. I'm afraid she probably thought I didn't care to hear about it, but that wasn't the case at all. I loved hearing her talk about finding the right molecules and twisting things until they worked. She came to life when she talked about her work, bubbling with enthusiasm and hope. She loved it, you know. But so many of the things she tried to tell me were over my head. I guess after a while she decided it was easier to not talk about her work than to have to explain microbiology, or protein crystallography, or whatever it was she was working on at the time to me."

"She spoke very highly of you. I know she loved you very much."

"She was a good daughter. Never in trouble. Always calling and helping."

"Did she act any different than usual last summer?"

"She did seem much more nervous the last few months she was alive. At first I thought it was because she had broken up with her boyfriend, but after I saw that show on Oprah, I figured she just had that feeling that her time was near."

"She was dating someone?"

"Oh, yes. A fine gentleman. One of the top people at TechLab, I believe. They dated for almost five years. I thought for sure he was finally the one for her. But then Hanna said he didn't turn out to be as nice as she first thought, so I guess it worked out for the best."

JoAnn's hands were icy as she asked, "Do you remember his name, or what he looked like?"

"Of course. He had dark hair, greying at the temples. His beard had very distinguished grey markings as well. His name was Dean something." Louise gazed out the kitchen window and said, "I'm sorry, JoAnn. I don't recall his last name."

JoAnn sighed with relief when she realized it wasn't J.D. Hanna had been involved with at TechLab. And now that she heard the name Dean, she remembered it being referred to in Hanna's calendar several times.

"Did she ever mention anything that might help me?"

"In what way? I'm afraid I don't really understand

what you're looking for." The tea was ready and Louise poured a steaming cup for JoAnn. "Maybe if you tell me what you need to know, I can be of more assistance."

JoAnn hesitated, weighing the wisdom of endangering this woman's life against her own seemingly selfish needs. "Hanna's letter implied there were things about TechLab that I should know. I just wondered if you had any idea what she might have been referring to."

"I'm afraid not." Louise closed her eyes and pinched the bridge of her nose as she thought. "The only thing I remember Hanna saying about you was that you were her best worker. And that you had the same lofty goals that she once had."

JoAnn almost dropped her cup of tea. Her hand was shaking, and the cup rattled as she placed the delicate china back on its saucer. "I have to go now, Mrs. Shore. Thank you so much for meeting with me. I can't tell you how greatly I appreciate your help. Could I please borrow your phone to call a cab?"

J.D. knew the answer would infuriate him before he asked the question, "Where's Harper?"

The secretary sheepishly shrugged her shoulders as she said, "I'm not sure, Mr. Cook. He left a little while ago and he didn't leave word where he could be contacted."

"Who's responsible for the surveillance on JoAnn Rayburn?"

"General duty."

"Meaning?"

"Whoever is on duty. The main surveillance room contacts the field personnel closest to the target. From then on, they keep in constant touch so different field personnel can assist. Hold on and I'll check on the status of Ms. Rayburn for you."

She walked away, and several minutes later when she came back in she said, "I'm sorry, Mr. Cook. Ms. Rayburn has been in the facility all day. Neither of her locating beacons has shown any movement."

"Where are they?"

She flipped to the front of the file. "Her Lexus and her purse. She's around here somewhere."

"Guess again. She's been gone since ten-thirty this morning. Her purse is in her office."

"Have you considered the possibility that she may be attending a meeting in a different area of the complex? Our devices would only indicate surveillance requirements if she left TechLab's grounds."

"She left. I know it."

"I can have Mr. Harper contact you when he gets back in if you like."

J.D. was quiet for several seconds, then smiled charmingly as he said, "No. Don't bother. You're probably right about the meeting. She would have taken her purse if she left the complex. I'll get back with Mr. Harper later. Thanks for checking for me."

JoAnn was surprised that the reception room of the clinic was vacant. She rang the bell on the counter, and when the pretty young girl came out of the back room she said, "I need to speak to Dr. Lawrence. It's urgent."

"I'm afraid he isn't in, Miss . . ."

"Rayburn. JoAnn Rayburn. How soon will he be back?"

"It will be several hours. He's assisting another vet in a rather complicated surgery. He asked me not to book any office visits until after two o'clock."

"Oh, dear."

"After all our phone conversations, it's nice to finally meet you, Ms. Rayburn. I'm Jill. I'd be happy to give Dr. Lawrence a message if you like."

"If you could lend me a piece of paper and a pen, I think I would like to leave him a short note."

"Sure."

JoAnn sat in the reception room and jotted a message that she hoped Jess could decipher. At this point, she couldn't risk coming directly to the point.

"Grace, how are you doing?"

"Parker?" she asked excitedly.

"You'd better be careful. One of these days you'll guess the wrong gentleman's name and really start an argument."

"So far, I think I'm capable of keeping all of my men straight. What can I do for you?"

"I was just wondering how the Lawrence boy's test was being handled. Did you get an address where we can mail it?"

"I'm afraid not. Apparently, he's touring Canada with his grandparents. His father didn't seem to understand the gravity of the situation."

"It is a shame. People these days have so little respect for the hard work of others." He hesitated, then added, "I'm going to be in town one day this week. Do you think it would help if I personally stopped by to talk to him about it?"

"Not really, Parker. I'm pretty sure the decision is out of his hands. If he had an easy way to contact his son, I know he'd do it. After all, he's involved with his son's teacher, Ms. Fordman. She's probably put in more than just a few good words for your program."

"Then he should understand how important his son's test results are better than anyone."

"True. You know, you can always stop by and see me if you have any free time."

"I'm going to try, but don't get your hopes up. These one-day trips are killers. There are so many things to do in such a short time."

"You could always spend the night, you know. Life is too short to rush through."

"I'm afraid I've sandwiched this trip between a Board meeting and a trip to South America. Otherwise, I'd take you up on your offer. If it was an offer."

"It was."

"Cruel woman."

"Why am I cruel?"

"Because all the way to South America, I'll be wondering which of those other men took my place."

"You're irreplaceable, so don't give it another thought."

"If you say so."

From head to toe, there wasn't one part of JoAnn's body that didn't ache by the time she got back to TechLab. Her broken finger hurt the most, throbbing from the strain of maneuvering her crutches all day. Still, she knew she couldn't see if she'd properly guessed the meaning of Hanna's clues until late, late that night.

Instead of going directly back to BioHazard, JoAnn very slowly made her way to the elevator bank that served TechLab's corporate offices. Seated to one side, the security officer on duty smiled politely as she approached, then went back to reading. "Excuse me," she said. "Could you help me?"

"I'll try to, Ms. Rayburn."

"I was in a meeting the other day and I met several of the executives. I can't remember one of the gentlemen's names, and I need to send him a copy of the memo I've written that summarizes the meeting. Are you familiar with most of TechLab's executives?"

"I've worked here for ten years. I believe I know everyone who comes and goes. What did he look like?"

"Dark hair, grey temples. Distinguished greying

beard. I think his first name is Dean, but I couldn't find anyone in the office directory by that name."

"Sounds like Mr. Cook." He smiled, then winked slyly as he said, "But I'm sure you'd recognize *him*."

JoAnn blushed and nodded as she said, "Yes, I definitely would recognize Mr. Cook. Any other ideas?"

"Not really. Let me look at my security clearance list. If he's an exec, he'd have top clearance." He scanned the list and laughingly said, "Nope. The only Dean listed is James Dean Cook. Sorry, Ms. Rayburn."

"Who is James Dean Cook?"

"You are tired, aren't you? That's J. D. Cook, remember?"

She tried not to show her shock as she casually said, "Just him again, huh?"

"You really look beat. Would you like to sit down for a few minutes? I could get you a drink if you like."

"No. I'll rest when I get back to my office. I have a lot of business to take care of."

Jess—I know that I wasn't much help the other day at lunch, but I think that very soon I'll be able to shed some light on the real problem you are facing. I expect to inherit an old friend's wisdom soon, and I feel it is what we have been searching for. I often think of the day you graciously invited me into your lovely home. I hope you have the same fond memories, for such precious times are rare. I'll call soon to check on Rocky and Bell. Intently, JoAnn

Jess was waiting outside Stacey's makeshift classroom when the bell rang. He pressed himself against the wall, avoiding the herd of children while he tried to suppress his overwhelming longing for Jonathan. Once the path was clear, he tiptoed up behind Stacey and kissed her on the neck, nipping his way up to her ear.

"Okay, okay. I'll give you an A. But next time you

have to earn it like the rest of the kids." She turned around feigning surprise and added, "Oh, it's you, Jess. I thought you were one of my children."

"How are they doing?"

"It may be my imagination, but they seem to be getting a little better. Judy Olender, the P.E. teacher, dropped by today to tell me she noticed a couple of them had a little spunk. She said it was about time, and I agreed with her wholeheartedly."

"That's great. I have something you need to see." He handed the small piece of paper to Stacey, then quietly waited for her to read it before asking, "Well, what do you think?"

Stacey said, "JoAnn's found something. Did she mail this to you?"

"No. She came by the clinic a couple of hours ago, but I wasn't there. I wish I had been."

"Did Jonathan ever tell you about the conversation he had with JoAnn about being smart?"

"No."

"He told her one time that he was one of the smartest kids in his class. She told him that being smart doesn't do a person any good unless they put it to use wisely. He told me she said he needed to practice by maneuvering and manipulating his environment. Of course, he didn't pronounce those words quite right, but I got the general idea."

"Wonderful. She's encouraging my son to be even more manipulative than he already is. How does that apply to this?"

"Jonathan said it meant he should look at life's different angles. Not accept the face value of what he sees and hears. Like those blasted 3-D pictures I can't see. She told him you always have to look deeper to find the real answer. I think that applies to this note. She's trying to tell us more than we think."

Stacey held up the paper and pointed as she said,

"Like this line that says 'I expect to inherit an old friend's wisdom soon.' I think she's talking about her friend, Hanna, who was murdered. I'll bet she found something Hanna left behind that's going to help us figure out who's behind all this."

"You may be right. Do you remember anything in particular that happened the day she came over for dinner? She must have mentioned it for a reason."

"Let's see, we talked about school, and she told me about her affair with the guy from TechLab while you were gone. After you came back, we fixed dinner and . . ."

Jess's eyes lit up as he said, "Photographic memory! JoAnn has a photographic memory. When she told us about Hanna, she wrote down Hanna's security clearance codes from that calendar she found. That must be what she wants us to remember. She thinks she might need our help getting out of this."

Stacey asked excitedly, "Do you still have the codes?"

"I hope so."

Her eyes widened. "You don't know?"

"I'm sure I didn't throw them away, at least not intentionally. I just haven't run across them lately. We can search after we hit the mall and have dinner."

She shook her head as she said, "I'd feel better if we search first and saved the mall for later."

"Good point. Just don't get all bitchy on me again and start whining about being cold because you don't have any winter clothes."

"Then stop dragging me outside half-naked."

"I could drag you somewhere else half-naked."

"Promises, promises."

Leanne practically ran into JoAnn's office saying, "Thank God you're back. I thought Mr. Cook was going to have a stroke when he found out no one knew where you were."

"You'd think I was a prisoner here. I suppose I need to call him?"

"I'd appreciate it. I don't think he was very happy with me when he left."

"When was that?"

"Around noon."

JoAnn glanced at her watch and slumped into her chair, "My God, it's almost four o'clock. He probably already had a stroke, called out the National Guard, and told Human Resources to start recruiting my replacement."

"I wouldn't doubt it."

JoAnn bent over and picked up the files on the floor as she said, "What happened in here?"

"I don't know. He closed the door when he came in, then slammed it closed again when he left. He has quite a temper, doesn't he?"

"I've only had the pleasure of seeing it once, and that was more than enough. I suppose I'd better check in like a good little employee."

Leanne glanced at the bottle of wine on the file cabinet behind JoAnn and was obviously tempted to make one of her offhanded remarks. Instead, she bit her tongue and said, "Good luck," then walked out, pulling the door closed as she went.

JoAnn laid her head on the desk for a few seconds, then took a deep breath as she dialed J.D.'s extension. It took all her energy to sound cheerful as she said, "I hear you've been looking for me, and I see you brought wine. Did you have something special in mind for tonight?"

"Where have you been?"

"Let's see. First I stopped by my house. You know, I really should do that more often. It gives me some distance from this place, some time to think. I'm beginning to lose my objectivity."

"Is that all? You spent all day at home?"

"No, I did some shopping, too. In spite of my utter devotion to TechLab, there are still a few necessities that the company doesn't provide."

"I'd have gone with you. I worry about you. You shouldn't go out alone."

"It was a spur of the moment decision. Haven't you ever been working and realized that if you look at one more report your head will explode?"

J.D.'s temper was cooling down, and he laughed as he said, "Mine has exploded many times. I just keep scraping the bits of brain tissue off the wallpaper and stuffing them back in."

"And I always thought whoever decorated your office just had bad taste."

"How could you go shopping without your purse?"

JoAnn hesitated, snatching the purse off the floor and emptying its contents softly onto her desk as she said, "It's too hard to carry while I crutch around. I just stuffed some money in my jeans. Men do it all the time, you know."

"Did you have any problems driving?"

She was still filtering through the pile of things from her purse as she said, "I took a cab. I didn't have enough energy to try the one-footed, one-handed, God-I-hope-I don't-kill-someone routine again. Once I get the cast off my hand, I'll feel more comfortable. At least I hope I will. To tell you the truth, the Lexus gives me the creeps. It still reminds me of that night."

"I'll see if I can get Fleet to issue you a different car."

Turning around, she grabbed a scalpel from her supply drawer. While slitting the silk lining of her purse, she said, "You don't have to bother. We all have to face our fears. It's time I learned to confront mine."

JoAnn didn't hear what he said next, she was too busy staring at the small, oblong device wedged carefully between the folds of black leather.

Harper watched the pair as they crossed from the sidewalk into the school's parking lot. His hand was on the small of her back, and their eyes held that extra moment when they occasionally met. He'd seen it all before. Even from a distance, it was clear they were like all people in love, eager to share their lives, create memories together. Yet somehow, when these two lovebirds were in a car, or at home, they had little to discuss besides the weather and what to fix for dinner.

His instincts were screaming loud and clear. They knew too much. It wasn't just the coincidences that had him worried. The warning signs were all there. He'd spent the last two hours listening to the surveillance tapes of the Lawrence house. Endless whale songs drowning occasional whispers. They never discussed anything important. Normal offhand remarks that people usually made were almost nonexistent, especially since the boy had left. From the tapes alone, you would swear these two people hardly knew each other, and that they damn sure wanted to keep it that way.

When he pulled some of the archived tapes from before the Fordman apartment fire, Harper knew he was right. Back then, Jess Lawrence and Stacey Fordman had conversations. Real conversations about real topics. Not the drivel the surveillance devices had been recording for the last few weeks. They knew something, he could feel it.

He watched as the Cherokee pulled out of the parking lot. His radio picked up their conversation, if you could call it that. After deciding which restaurant to have dinner at that night, only silence came through his earphone. Any other time he would have assumed the equipment was malfunctioning, but he was sure it was still working perfectly. They were giving him the silent treatment. Again.

The whale songs moaned in the background as Jess pulled Stacey into his arms. "Did you see that car?" he whispered.

She nuzzled against him as she murmured, "The blue one that went around the block, then parked about three houses up?"

"That's the one."

"Ever seen it before?"

"Nope. Must be a new guy. We'd better be extra careful while we search for Hanna's code."

"We could close the drapes," she said as she ran her fingers through his hair.

"Don't you think that would be a little obvious?"

Her lips barely touched his ear as she whispered, "Not if we were, let's say, romantically engaged at the time. He'd think we just wanted our privacy."

Jess smiled as he whisked Stacey into his arms. He carried her into the living room and stopped where he knew any voyeur in the neighborhood would have a spectacular view. Holding her in his arms, he kissed her passionately until he bent his knees and they sank as one to the floor. Rolling over, he grabbed the cord, yanking the drapes closed before slinking back over to Stacey's side. Folding her back in his arms again, he whispered through urgent kisses, "What was it we were supposed to be looking for?"

"I haven't got a clue."

JoAnn locked her office door, then dug through the file cabinet until she found what she was searching for. After shoving the other door shut behind her with her crutch, she spread Hanna's file open on the bed and stretched out beside it.

Closing her eyes, she realized how desperately she needed rest, and that this was not going to be the night to get it. For a fleeting moment she had the urge to throw the damn file away. Forget anything strange was going on, pretend life was normal. But she knew it was too late for that now, in more ways than one. She couldn't go back, even though she desperately wished she could.

Rolling over, JoAnn flipped through the Citrinol file. She read the last memo Hanna had written once again, even though it was already etched permanently into her memory.

Citrinol3 progressing well. Coach JoAnn on the vital nature of the project to help her come to grips with TechLab's lofty goals.

Schedule meeting soon on connections, network, and project's artificial ceiling. Also, emphasize the relative importance of correlative thought processes.

Lofty goals. Artificial ceiling. Correlative thoughts.

JoAnn rolled over, stretching across the bed to bury her face in the pillow. Hanna had hidden something, something very important. Whatever it was had cost Hanna her life. It was in the loft, probably the ceiling of the loft. All she had to do was find it.

And manage to stay alive long enough to do something with it.

Chapter 18

"I seem to recall having your personal guarantee that you could find them, Butler."

"Our electronic surveillance network is one of the best in the country, Mr. Harper. Under normal circumstances, we would have located them hours ago."

"So you only work well under normal circumstances. Seems to me that in your line of business there is no such thing," Harper said sarcastically.

"I've never run across a case before where the people didn't use the credit cards they have. Normally, we'd have snagged them the first time they stopped to fill up with gas." He hesitated, then continued, "At any rate, we've checked every credit card company. A. J. Lawrence hasn't used his Visa, MasterCard, Discover, not even any gasoline credit cards in years. Apparently they aren't into living beyond their means."

"Which is not surprising for a retired couple in their late sixties. You should have tagged their car."

"There was never a chance. I even did my IRS agent number at the bank yesterday. The teller said they are just good people, nice customers to work with. She was shocked when I fed her a story about how the IRS was going to be seizing their assets for tax evasion. She did tell me that their account records don't show any automated teller activity, and that they've never been assigned a Personal Identification Number. So, they can't get any money by computer, and they aren't charging things. They won't be gone long."

Harper was obviously losing his patience. "Not necessarily. It could mean either they took cash, or they're staying somewhere that won't cost much and isn't very far away, possibly with friends or relatives."

"Sorry, sir. Finding them will still be like looking for a golf ball in a snowstorm."

"Then we need to even the odds. We'll make it a fluorescent orange golf ball."

"How's that?"

"Torch their house. Bad news always travels fast. It will find them, and so will we."

The building was deserted. Each step they took echoed off the walls. "Look," Stacey whispered. She pointed at a sign above a white telephone and read it aloud. " 'After hours and weekends—dial TechLab Security at extension 6585 for assistance.' Sounds easy enough."

Before she could finish dialing the number, a security guard came around the corner. They both jumped, his booming voice startling them as he said, "May I help you?"

Jess answered, "Yes, please. We'd like to see JoAnn Rayburn."

"Ms. Rayburn works in a secured area. She isn't allowed visitors."

"We won't stay long. We just want her to know someone cares. She's had a hard time lately, you know."

"I know, but rules are rules."

The puppies were black balls of energy trying desperately to free themselves from the confinement of Jess's jacket. They squirmed in his arms, managing to poke their heads out as they scratched and whimpered. He looked at the guard and said, "Listen, I know this is an unusual request, but last time I talked to her she seemed really depressed." He pulled Rocky and Bell completely out so the guard could see their adorable faces. "These are hers. Couldn't you make an exception just this once?"

"Listen, I wish I could. Ms. Rayburn looked pretty miserable when I talked to her late yesterday afternoon, but no one is allowed in BioHazard without a security clearance. No one, not even God."

Stacey said, "You have security clearance, right? You could take the puppies to her for a little while. Just a couple of hours, then we'll come back and get them. Come on. You look like a nice guy. She's lonely."

Jess added, "We're not asking you to break any rules. Just stretch them a little. That is, unless they make you run security checks on all the lab animals, too. Wouldn't want a couple of tiny dogs spreading the company's top secrets around, now would we?"

He laughed. "Sometimes things around here seem that crazy. I'll tell you what I'll do. I'll call Ms. Rayburn and see if she wants to come up here. There are park benches on the grounds. She could play with her puppies for a while outside. Some fresh air might do her good."

Stacey laid her hand on the guard's arm, her eyes sincere as she said, "That would be wonderful. Thank you so much."

The guard dialed the phone and said, "Ms. Rayburn, you have visitors at the main lobby entrance. Can you come upstairs?" He nodded, hung up, and said, "She'll be here in about ten minutes. It's a pretty long hike, and the crutches slow her down."

Stacey glanced around. The main entry was all marble and smoked glass, embellished with a veritable jungle of potted plants. "This place must be enormous."

"It is, ma'am."

"Have you ever gotten lost?"

He chuckled. "Not in the last few years." Reaching under the desk, he pulled out a leaflet. "We give these to visitors so they won't get lost."

Stacey opened the glossy tri-folded paper. On one side was an overview map of the facility, showing each of the buildings, the parking areas, and the grounds. The other side listed where each department was located and the extension to dial if assistance was needed pinpointing a particular office. "Would you mind if I keep this?" she asked. "I'm a schoolteacher, and I'm planning on bringing my children on a field trip here in the spring."

"Sure. I've got hundreds of them."

Jess was having a hard time controlling Rocky and Bell, so he said, "Could you tell JoAnn that we're waiting outside? I'd hate to be responsible for a puppy puddle on this beautiful marble floor."

"No problem." He stood up and walked them to the door. "If you'll just turn right when you go out, there are benches under the trees by the water fountain."

"Thanks." They headed out, and when they were a safe distance away from the building Jess set the puppies down as he said, "So far, so good."

"I don't think it could have gone any better."

Rocky and Bell strained at the end of their leashes, sniffing every blade of grass in their path as they pulled Jess and Stacey along. Jess winked at Stacey as they both noticed the surveillance camera mounted in one of the trees.

It didn't seem like long before they saw JoAnn heading their way. She let her crutches fall and gently swept the dogs into her arms. For the first few minutes, the licking, wiggling creatures did what they did best. They loved her.

Finally, Jess said, "We thought you needed some visitors."

"I did. Your timing is perfect." She shivered. "It's cold out here."

Jess took off his jacket and insisted JoAnn wear it. Stacey held the puppies while Jess helped her slip the coat over her injured hand. "Are you doing okay?" he asked, then whispered, "Careful. There's a surveillance camera in the tree."

"Yes. I'm just tired. I spent the day running errands, so now I'll be up all night working."

"Maybe you should just get some rest for once."

"I'm on the verge of a major breakthrough. Even if I wanted to sleep, I couldn't. My mind doesn't work that way."

"I know how you feel. When I've got a tough case, I lie awake at night trying to decide the best way to treat it. Dogs and cats are like people. What works on one may not work on another." He winked at JoAnn and smiled. "It's like breaking a code. Once you find the right one, your troubles are over."

JoAnn understood and smiled as she said, "You should have gone into research. Our lives are spent breaking codes and unraveling genetic clues so we can find the source of the disease. Although sometimes a scientist will get lucky and a cure just sort of falls in his lap."

"I don't think I could take being stuck in an underground lab, much less working through the night most of the time. There are other things besides work, you know."

"Really? I hadn't noticed."

"Why don't we all have lunch tomorrow? It's Sunday, so you shouldn't have to work. We'll pick you up. One o'clock all right?"

"I may not be very good company."

He swept Rocky and Bell into his arms as he said, "Then we'll just have to bring these guys with us. No one could be in a sour mood with them around."

Stacey said, "I'll pack a picnic lunch. It's supposed to be clear but cool, so dress warmly. We can lie in the sun, stuff ourselves, and rest. Sound good?"

"How can I refuse? Thank you both for everything. I'd better get back to work now." They all walked back to the entrance together. She slipped out of Jess's jacket and handed it to him saying, "You two are life-savers."

"We do our best."

JoAnn disappeared through the black glass doors.

"We'd better get these two fur-balls home," Jess said.

"And build a fire?"

"You bet."

"And roast marshmallows?"

"If you insist."

"I insist. I'll show you the right way to do it."

He pulled her to him and said, "I can't wait."

Once they were back to the Cherokee, Jess picked up Rocky and Bell, unfastening their leashes as he handed them to Stacey. When he walked around to the driver's side, he slid the leashes into his coat pocket, his hand grazing a peculiar, cold edge. Running his fingers along the small square of folded paper, he smiled.

JoAnn never ceased to amaze him. She had slipped a note in his coat pocket.

The fire crackled and popped. Jess and Stacey were sitting a few feet from it, looking at the note JoAnn had left them.

I'm sure I'll find what we've been looking for tonight. If I need help, I'll call you. Come only if I say "My work is over-whelming. I think you should keep Rocky and Bell for good." I'll use the week's color code in the conversation, so listen carefully.

From the main entrance, go straight west, turning north at the end of the hall. The elevators to BioHazard will be dead ahead. When the doors open, punch in Hanna's code and press the button marked "Sub 4." Follow the red stripe to BioHazard. Enter Hanna's code again, then at the green light, enter the color code I've given you when I call.

I can't imagine needing you to come here, but it makes me feel safer knowing you're out there. Be very careful, JoAnn

Stacey silently opened the map of the TechLab facility and traced the route to the elevators with her finger. Jess nodded, then tossed JoAnn's note into the fire. They moved closer together, watching the words blacken. It was going to be a long, long night.

Outside, Harper himself was watching the Lawrence house. He intended to put an end to this nonsense Monday morning at the Board meeting. One way or another, their time was up. He just needed a way to prove it, or maybe not.

JoAnn was faithful to the routine she'd fallen into in the last few weeks. She did her physical therapy, agonizing through the stretching exercises until she finally sat down and cried. Although she didn't retain a word of what she read, she filtered through the pile of incoming memos on her desk. Finally, at midnight, she lay down on the bed and spent three hours staring at the ceiling.

At three a.m. she purposely kicked her crutch as she rolled out of bed and said for the sake of the security crew, "Damn it! There's no point trying to sleep when there is so much to get done." She pulled on a pair of blue jeans, a sweatshirt, and a lab coat. After going to the rest room, she made her way slowly through the lab as every muscle in her body screamed for sleep.

As usual, it was eerily quiet. The constant hum of the electronic equipment in the background suddenly was very irritating, making JoAnn wish she could jerk every plug as she passed. To be careful, she forced herself to run two different Citrinol3 tests. She then carried the paperwork from the tests to the loft, where she flipped on the lights, spread her notes across the countertop, and sat down. The security camera was directly over her head, and she knew that its angle prevented her from being seen as long as she stayed along the far wall.

She'd thought of nothing but this area for hours. By mentally picturing this section of the loft, she had already eliminated possible hiding places. JoAnn had come up with only one logical place Hanna could have used to hide anything that wasn't in view of the surveillance camera. Only one place where cleaning crews and other scientists or technicians wouldn't routinely come across whatever it was. Although it was killing her not to know, she couldn't risk rushing at this point. As best she could, she began working on the Citrinol3 test results.

Thirty minutes later she nudged her pencil off the counter's far end and watched it roll across the floor. Hopping with one crutch, she worked herself behind the largest piece of equipment in the area and began to search. The space was tight, but big enough for her to easily fit in. Looking up, she saw the ceiling was different in this area than the rest of the lab. Two-foot-square acoustic panels lined the entire area, probably to help absorb the vibration of the electron microscope on the floor below.

Using her crutch, she gently pushed on one of the ceiling tiles. It easily moved upward, revealing several feet of empty space overhead. Even if she weren't hurt, JoAnn couldn't have looked up into the ceiling without a stepladder. Hanna had been a few inches taller, but she would have needed assistance, too.

JoAnn took a deep breath, trying to clear her mind. There was no way Hanna would have risked bringing attention to herself by dragging a ladder or a chair over. JoAnn stared at the walls, then concentrated on the large machine beside her. It was taller than she was, and about six feet long. She ran her hand along the side and smiled as she felt a seam in the metal. There wasn't much light, but she could see that directly above the seam were the words "Maintenance Door 6A."

After unlocking the hinge, she eased the heavy metal door open. It was exactly the size of the narrow space between the machine and the wall. When fully open, the door hung parallel to the floor, about three feet above it. JoAnn leaned on it, and the heavy metal barely moved. It would probably hold her weight. She glanced inside the machine, hoping to end her search early, but only a hollow space under a mass of wires was inside.

Using her crutch, she pushed herself up onto the door, half expecting it to break under the pressure of her weight and send her sprawling to the floor. After several seconds she relaxed a little and stood up, concentrating on the ceiling. She pushed back the tile closest to the wall and eased her head into the open space.

After a few seconds her eyes adjusted to the dim light and she looked around. A few feet away there was a large silver tube, approximately two feet wide. It snaked along the far wall and disappeared. The ceiling was suspended with a symmetrical series of wires, about six feet apart, but a kind of makeshift floor had been laid under the silver tubing. JoAnn was about to give up when she saw it. A slim, black briefcase was barely noticeable lying on top of one of the tiles. And of course, it was just beyond her reach.

Damn it, Hanna, I'm not that tall! She could almost hear Hanna laughing at her. It was an old jogging joke they shared. Closing her eyes, she could see Hanna's long legs carrying her effortlessly along, while JoAnn ran beside her, taking twice as many steps, breathing twice as hard, struggling to just keep up.

"Relax," Hanna would say. "Roll through it. You're making it too hard."

JoAnn tried to relax now. She rotated her head slowly around, then looked again. As always, Hanna's advice made things seem so easy. JoAnn ducked her head and replaced the tile she had removed. She inched a little farther toward the corner and lifted up the next tile. Now the briefcase was well within her grasp.

Her fingers closed around the handle, just as a rapidly approaching noise sent shock waves of terror down her spine.

It was four o'clock in the morning when the phone rang. The CD player still echoed romantic music in the background. Jess and Stacey had fallen asleep on the floor in front of the fire, which had long ago died. Jess shook himself awake as he crawled to grab the phone. He mumbled, "Hello."

"Is this Jess Lawrence?"

"Ya."

"This is Mac Clark. Remember me?"

Jess was instantly awake, memories of his childhood neighbor flooding in. He had grown up two doors down from the Clarks'. His first love had been their daughter, Jeanne. "Of course I remember you. What's wrong?"

"Don't worry, your parents are all right. I mean, I guess they're all right, I don't really know where they are, or what they're . . ."

Jess interrupted, "What is it, Mac?"

"It's their house. The fire department tried to stop it, but everyone in the neighborhood was asleep, so no one called until . . . and with this Northerner blowing in and all . . ."

Jess rolled over, slumping onto the floor. He rubbed his eyes as he slowly said, "It burned down?"

"Afraid so. I'm really sorry. Do you know how to contact your folks? All they told me was that they were taking little Jonathan sightseeing. He's a great kid, Jess. You've done a fine job with him."

Jess almost answered with the truth, then caught himself and said, "They went to Canada. I really don't have any idea where they might be."

"How long were they planning on staying gone?"

"A few weeks. Is there something I can do from down here?"

"I don't know. I suppose the fire department can tell me what needs to be done and I can call you back. Right now, it's just a mess. Looters would probably be the main concern."

"Is there anything left to steal?"

"Can't tell yet. There may be some things in the basement and garage that can be salvaged."

"I hate to impose on you, Mac, but would you check it out? I'll pay a moving company to come in and take things to storage if there's anything left. Mom and Dad can sort through everything when they get back."

"Maybe it's for the best. They could have been killed if they'd been here."

And they still may be. "Will you call and let me know?"

"Sure. I'm sorry, Jess."

"I know, Mac. Thanks for being there." Jess hung up the phone. Stacey was beside him, and he pulled her next to him and held her fiercely. In her ear he whispered, "Those low-life bastards burnt down the house I grew up in."

Stacey was silently crying, her tears hot on his neck as he clenched his fists in her hair and muttered under his breath, "They're going to pay for this. For your apartment, for what they've done to the kids, and now this. I'll kill them myself if I have to."

Instinctively, JoAnn jumped down when she heard the approaching noise. Landing on both feet, she crumpled against the wall as excruciating pain shot up her leg, but she didn't cry out. In only a second, the noise drew closer, then whizzed over her head. Too late, she realized it had come from the large silver tube in the ceiling. Someone must have sent something pneumatically to Pathology. Or Pathology was already sending out morning lab results.

At four-thirty in the morning? You're here, stupid. There must be other people as crazy as you are. Nuts who work all hours of the night. People who don't have a real life. Now get off your butt and get out of this mess before someone wonders where the hell you are.

She looked around to orient herself, then up. The briefcase was half dangling from the hole in the ceiling. Turning up the end of her jeans, she ran her hand along her injured Achilles tendon, feeling the rough edges of a fresh tear. That side of her ankle was already knotted and swelling rapidly. Using the open machine's door, she pulled herself up, careful to keep all her weight on her good leg. Grabbing her crutch, she sat down on the door, balanced the crutch overhead, and hit the briefcase with its wide end.

The briefcase fell down, and JoAnn practically tumbled backward off the door as she leaned to catch it. Setting it aside, she tried to use the crutch again to move the ceiling tile back in place, but it was hopeless. It had been pushed too far to the side, and she couldn't snag it with the rubber handle.

With all her determination, she twisted around and

pushed herself up. Crawling up, first she kneeled on the cold metal, then braced herself against the wall as she stood completely up. Pain was making her sick to her stomach. She slowly slid the ceiling tile back in place, then leaned back to catch her breath. With one hand against the wall, and the other against the machine, she slid down until she was once again seated on the door. Using her crutch, she managed to hop down without catching her foot.

After pushing the door closed and securing it, she leaned over and grabbed the briefcase. It was too large to conceal between the files she normally worked with, so she pushed it out of sight against the back of the machine and hopped back out to the chair by the counter so she could think.

How can I get it out of here? She thought of her friend again, picturing her in her mind. *How did you get it in here, Hanna? Help me.*

The loft was a narrow circle built above the floor below. It was an unassuming place, with only the long work space where JoAnn was seated and two relatively simple machines. Below, enormous pieces of state-of-the-art laboratory equipment were scattered about, shrouded in shadows cast by the dim illumination of the lights around the loft. JoAnn stared down, concentrating over the pain.

Pieces. Break complicated things into pieces.

JoAnn worked her way back behind the machine and eased herself onto the floor. Her hands were shaking as she laid the briefcase down flat and clicked open the small locks. She eased the top up as though she were opening a radioactive sample and reluctantly peered inside.

The briefcase was packed with files and memos. Along one side were two things carefully wrapped in scraps of white cloth. As she unwrapped them, JoAnn instantly recognized them as test tubes of top secret compounds. One was marked SynCur6, the other NiAl2. Along the other side of the case were two small copper canisters that were equipped with spray nozzles. She carefully picked them up, examining them for labels. Both were unmarked, but appeared to be pressurized containers designed for chemical dispersal. She resisted the urge to squirt them, then realized they were identical to the one J.D. carried with him. He didn't carry pepper gas and Mace for protection, he had something much more powerful, and probably more dangerous than she cared to imagine.

With utmost care, she rewrapped the chemical compounds and slid them into her lab coat pocket. She slid the canisters into her other pocket and picked up the stack of files. Closing the empty briefcase, she tried to slide it under the machine, but it was no use, it wouldn't fit. She would have to put it back in the ceiling or take it with her.

The thought of putting it back in the ceiling made her want to cry, but she knew she had no other choice.

Stacey jogged along beside Jess as they headed around the block. "It's cold," she said.

"You'll warm up fast enough. I used to jog every day at five o'clock in the morning. It's a great time. The air is clean and crisp. No traffic to speak of. And best of all, it's quiet."

"And dark. Very dark."

"So?"

"I'm scared."

"I always figured criminals were too lazy to be up at this hour. Besides, judging from the talents these guys have, among them arson and murder, I don't think we're in any more danger out here than we are inside the house."

"Unfortunately, you're probably right. Slow down a little. This isn't the Olympic trials, you know."

He shortened his strides and fell into an easier pace. "We should do this more often."

"I'll make you a deal. If we get out of this mess in one piece, I'll run with you every day."

Jess nudged her as he said, "Promises, promises. I'll settle for three times a week."

Stacey glanced over her shoulder and said, "I'll bet they're having a heart attack trying to figure out how to follow us without being seen."

"Serves them right. I'd like to beat them all senseless, then torch their houses with them inside."

"I'm really sorry about your folks' place, Jess. Believe me, I know how they feel."

"I know you do. How's my sweat suit fit?"

"Surprisingly well. I just have to keep it from falling down. Why are you so sure the fire wasn't an accident?"

"First your place, then my parents'. Don't you think that's an awfully big coincidence? Especially in such a short time?"

"I suppose so. How are we going to talk to JoAnn at lunch today without them around?"

"I have an idea that should work."

Both of them saw the car coming toward them at the same time. Although its headlights were on, it was moving too slowly to be part of the normal neighborhood traffic. They held their breath as it passed.

"Could you see anything?" Stacey asked.

"Damn windows are tinted so dark I couldn't see a thing. Could have been Dracula at the wheel for all I know."

"Let's hope so. At least he'll leave us alone as soon as the sun comes up."

* * *

By the time JoAnn hobbled back into her office, she was certain she was going to faint. She dropped the files on the floor and slumped down beside them. Glancing at the clock on her desk, she realized she didn't have much time, yet the pain from her ankle made it difficult to think about anything else.

JoAnn crawled to her desk drawer and riffled through her personal things. Grabbing the bottle of prescription pain medication left over from her surgery, she snapped open the childproof lid, then moaned when she tilted it and nothing fell out. After scattering things everywhere she realized there was nothing in her office she could take to ease her suffering, not even an aspirin. As she collapsed against the desk, she was losing hope. Tilting her head back, she took a deep breath and tried to calm her nerves.

They'll find me with this and kill me, just like Hanna. Why did you do it, Hanna? Why did you sell out? She wiped a tear from the corner of her eye and leaned her head back. The bottle of wine J.D. had brought was still on top of the file cabinet. *A drink will calm my nerves. Maybe cut enough of the pain so I can find a place to hide these things.*

She pushed herself up and grabbed the bottle and a wineglass and sat at her desk. Glancing down at her foot, she could easily see swelling on the outside and back of her ankle. Another surgery, plus God knows how many more weeks of the excruciating torture the doctor so blandly calls physical therapy were undoubtedly ahead.

After opening the bottle, she poured a full glass and gulped it down as fast as she could. Coughing, she poured another glass and set it on the desk. Easing herself down, she crawled around on the office floor, gathering Hanna's papers. Even though it was Sunday, she took out a few of her Citrinol3 files and stacked the papers and records inside them in case anyone came in early.

The second glass of wine went down easier, and as she poured a third, she smiled as she looked curiously at her hand. It wasn't shaking nearly as much. Opening one of the files, she scanned the first page. It was labeled "Priority One—SynCur6—Executive Board Only." JoAnn had never seen a Priority One report before, she'd never even heard of one. She turned to the first page and began reading. Her hand started to shake again as she realized that Hanna hadn't sold secrets to another company. TechLab was responsible for everything.

In a state of shock, JoAnn drank more wine as she read about secret test sites, surveillance procedures, project expenses, and scores of unethical experiments that were performed to speed the research process along. Nursing homes, schools, they certainly hadn't discriminated. Flipping past page after disgusting page, JoAnn was even more shocked when she read the specifications for the chemical. What had started out as a valuable surgical anesthetic had been twisted into a sick weapon. Is that what they had in mind for Citrinol3?

JoAnn suddenly remembered the coroner's report on Hanna's body. Multiple stab wounds, yet no signs whatsoever of a struggle. *Hanna knew the bastards who killed her. They drugged her with SynCur6 and then slashed her to pieces knowing she could feel every single cut. She tried to warn me, but I wouldn't listen.*

As she read more and more, she realized exactly how grave her situation was, yet she began to feel uncannily calm, almost giddy. In fact, the entire evening had to have been a bad dream, nothing more than a nightmare. Real people weren't greedy enough to risk the lives of innocent children and elderly cripples. They wouldn't do the things she just read only to

make money. It was inhumane, it was sick, it was nau-
seating.

Pouring another glass of wine, she gulped a little
more, and then held on to the edge of the desk as she
hopped toward her makeshift bedroom. She stared at
the ridiculous sight for a second, discovering the sick
humor of it all. *A bedroom at TechLab. J.D. must have
been thinking with his dick when he came up with this idea.
Then again, he screwed Hanna, too. Maybe that's the only
way he knows how to think.*

Smiling and humming, she hopped back into her office and grabbed a scalpel. *For centuries, people have
been hiding their valuables in their mattresses. Maybe it
will work one more time.* As carefully as she could in her
condition, she pulled the mattress to one side and
sliced through the bottom of it. She took the sample
compounds from her pocket and slid them inside,
then pushed the mattress back in place.

The stack of files was tougher, since there were too
many to hide in the mattress without it bulging. Instead, she sliced open the back of her pillow and
pulled out part of the stuffing. Once she surrounded
the files in fluffy white, she replaced the pillowcase
and made the bed. She laughed as she thought, *Who
says you can't sleep on your work?*

Making her way back into her office, she straight-
ened the things on her desk and sat down to think.
*There must be a way to handle this. It's Sunday morning.
People are going to church soon and I'll be sitting here
stinking drunk trying to figure out how I got into this mess.
Hanna says the samples and maybe even the Priority One
reports are tagged with radioactive isotopes. If I take them
out of BioHazard, they'll catch me. Of course, they'll catch
me either way. They're watching every move, listening all
the time.*

JoAnn finally knew the answer. It was time to die.
She giggled at the thought, then mentally chastised

herself. Although death was nothing to be taken so lightly, pure physical exhaustion and fear made it impossible to think clearly. Tipping the wine bottle again, she generously poured the deep red liquid to the rim and stared at her own reflection in the glass . . .

Chapter 19

Jess looked at his watch again and stared at Stacey as he said, "It's almost one-thirty. JoAnn has never been late before."

"Maybe she forgot about our lunch appointment."

"Then she won't mind if we go inside and have the security guard check on her, will she?"

"I wouldn't think so. What if she got hurt? No one would find her until Monday." They pulled through the circular drive, parked in the visitors' lot, and went inside. Stacey immediately walked to the white phone on the wall and dialed the extension listed for Security.

"Yes."

"We're in the main lobby. Our friend, JoAnn Rayburn, was supposed to meet us here for lunch half an hour ago. We're worried about her. Could you check to see if she's all right?"

"In case you haven't noticed, lady, it's Sunday. We're closed. Come back tomorrow."

"Yes, I know it's Sunday, but Ms. Rayburn spends practically all her time here. Would you just check for us?"

"I'll call her office. Stay where you are and answer the phone when it rings."

As Stacey hung up, she said, "Obviously good manners aren't one of the job requirements around here." Several minutes later the phone rang, its hollow sound echoing in the spacious lobby.

"Hello."

"Ms. Rayburn isn't in today."

"Do you know where we can find her?"

"Sorry, lady, I just came on duty."

"Thanks. Sorry we bothered you."

They walked back outside, got into the car, and drove off. Neither said a word, since they both knew their unspoken questions might best be left unanswered for now. Besides, they had too much to do, and apparently not much time left.

"I'm not going to school tomorrow," Stacey said adamantly before they went into the house.

"Yes, you are, my dear," Jess replied with equal conviction.

"Do you have lab coats at the clinic like the one JoAnn had on the other day?"

"Yes, but you aren't going."

"Afraid I am, Mr. Lawrence. Quit being ridiculous," she said as she blocked the front door.

"Why should we both end up in jail?"

"Go ahead, say it—or dead?" Stacey asked.

"And I thought dealing with my first-grade son was a pain in the neck," Jess sighed.

"Where do you think I learned all my tricks? Seriously, Jess, we should both go. If we wear lab coats and look like we're discussing the theory of relativity or something we won't look so obvious. Besides, you know as well as I do that with JoAnn on crutches, it will take both of us to get her out of there in a hurry. By the way, where are we going to take her where they can't hurt her?"

"To the Police Chief's office. I'm going to call all the major television networks and have them waiting on his doorstep for an announcement. That way, when we turn over the evidence, no one will be tempted to ignore it, plus JoAnn can be given immediate protection."

She hugged him. "You said 'we,' you know. Does that mean you aren't going to try to sneak out of here and leave me behind?"

"We'll see."

"Are you sure we lost them?" Stacey glanced around the mall. It wasn't even Thanksgiving yet, but early Christmas shoppers were out in full force and the place was a madhouse.

"I know I lost the one who was tailing me. What about you?"

"There isn't a man alive who can look inconspicuous while surrounded by aisles of bras and panties. I hit six stores, making sure I spent plenty of time circling and going out different exits. By the time I finished in Victoria's Secret, I'm sure I was alone."

"What if it was a woman following you?"

"I don't even want to think about it."

"Where's your friend's car supposed to be parked?"

"Just outside the food court." She wrapped her face with a muffler and pulled a stocking cap over her head. "Like my new things?" she asked as she slipped into a long black leather coat.

He tore the tags off her sleeve as he said, "You look gorgeous. That is you in there, isn't it?"

"I'll get the car and pick you up on the other side of the mall." Five minutes later Stacey pulled up in her friend's two-toned Ford Explorer, complete with a stuffed cat hanging on for dear life to the back window.

"Nothing like being conspicuous," Jess said.

"So my friend loves stuffed animals. Is that a crime? Besides, it was nice of her to loan it to us."

Jess nodded and said, "True. When is she going to pick up the Cherokee?"

"Not until eight or nine o'clock tonight. She has a

red blazer just like the one I have on, and she's going to wear a hat and muffler."

"Is she worried about spending the night at my house alone?"

Stacey laughed and said, "Not at all. She's been studying kick boxing for a while. I think she'd be more than happy to test her skill."

"Did you give her the tape of our argument?"

"She's going to play it nice and loud as soon as she walks in the door. Followed by a dose of whale songs, of course."

"Perfect. Where to first?"

"The studio. I talked to my old boss and he said I could borrow one of the cameras and a zoom lens from the studio. When we're done, he said I can develop them in his lab."

"What if this guy never leaves his house?"

"Then we're going to have a very, very boring day. But look at the bright side."

"What's that?"

"There are a couple of guys watching your Cherokee in the parking lot of the mall who are going to have an even worse time than we are."

J.D. was staring out the window of the hospital room when he heard JoAnn moan. He walked over and sat on the edge of the hospital bed. Taking her hand, he said, "Hello, Sleepy."

JoAnn groaned and begrudgingly opened her eyes. "Could you turn off the lights?"

J.D. switched them off as he said, "How is it?"

"What? My ankle or my hangover?"

"Why didn't you call me when you fell?"

"I didn't want to wake you up in the middle of the night. Besides, I had no idea the damn thing was torn again. I thought it was just stretched a little."

"Shit. Is it hurt as bad as the first time?"

"No, the doctor says only the stitches along the outer edge of the tendon tore this time." She rolled her eyes and added, "Whoopee. Maybe we should celebrate."

"It's not too bad. At least the whole thing didn't rip back apart."

"J.D., he still has to repair it."

"So you're going to be stuck in the hospital for another week?"

"Not yet. I promised I'd stay completely off it. Once the swelling goes down, then he'll decide exactly how much damage was done and what to do about it." She stuck her foot up. "He put this cute new cast on for me. It's supposed to remind me to slow down. Not only is it heavy, I'm sure in a couple of days it's going to itch like crazy."

"You scared the hell out of me this morning, you know. I came in with breakfast and found you sprawled on the floor with that broken bottle of wine beside you. I was afraid you'd committed suicide."

JoAnn raised her hand to her head and rubbed her eyes. "I wish I had. I definitely had way, way too much to drink."

"Am I putting too much pressure on you? I don't mean to, you know. I just want what we both want."

She kept her eyes closed and laid her head against the pillow as she said, "And what would that be? A million-dollar mansion and a Ferrari?"

He cocked his head and stared at her. "No. To see Citrinol3 become the effective, powerful new drug that we both know it can be."

JoAnn remained still for a while, then yawned and tried to sit up. "My throat is really sore. Could you get me some ice? The machine is just down the hall."

"Certainly."

As soon as he left, she grabbed the telephone on the nightstand and dialed Jess's number. His answering machine picked up, so she said, "Sorry I missed lunch. I'm at the hospital, but I won't be staying. I fell last night and tore part of my Achilles again. I've given it a lot of thought, and I want you to keep my puppies. It's been a very long night and I'm feeling pretty blue, so I'll think about it today and decide for certain in the morning." Just as she hung up, J.D. came back in the room and handed her a plastic cup of ice.

"The nurse said you can leave anytime."

"Then let's get the hell out of here."

"Where do you want to go?"

"I want to go home, but I *need* to go back to Tech-Lab."

"You *need* rest."

"How do you expect me to make us that million dollars and buy us matching Ferraris if you won't let me work?"

"I would be the last one to stand in the way of your work, my dear. I just want you to be careful. Lab mistakes can cost millions if they aren't discovered."

"I don't make mistakes."

"You don't usually work with a hangover."

"I'll take a long nap first."

"What is suddenly so important?"

She sounded excited as she said, "It's against my better judgment to tell anyone before I'm absolutely certain, but I think I'm on to something. It's very, very promising. That's why I fell. I was in a hurry to get back to double-check the test results."

"What is it?"

"I don't mean to insult you, but it's too complicated to explain in layman's terms."

"There's an Executive Board meeting in the morning. They've been really pushing me about this project. At least give me enough to tell them what direction you're going."

JoAnn thought for several seconds, then said, "Tell

them we may be able to start field-testing in the next few months. I've found a way to eliminate Citrinol3's major side effect. We may even be ready for Citrinol4."

J.D. eagerly asked, "How?"

"Simple. I created my own pharmacological weapon. I exposed a test animal, then made a synthetic derivative of the antibodies its body formed. Once I encapsulated the Citrinol3 compound in a kind of protein overcoat, the maverick proteins no longer threatened the red blood cells. In a way, it's just like working with a virus. What I've done is created a kind of vaccination. The beauty is that because the chemical defensive wall around the tumor cells is different than that of other body cells, the amyloid proteins still attack the tumors, but leave the red blood cells intact." JoAnn smiled at J.D., who obviously believed every word of the nonsense she'd just rattled off.

"That's fantastic. Is this why you've been working so many late nights?"

She nodded.

He pulled her off the bed and hugged her. When he stepped away, he handed her crutches to her and added, "Let's get you back to the lab."

"Under one condition."

"Name it."

"I need time alone. My mind is working on every step of this process, even while I sleep. I don't mean to push you out of my life, but for now, I really have to be by myself."

Jess was unaccustomed to the red light of the darkroom and the smell of chemicals. "How much longer?" he asked.

"Just a couple of minutes. Watch. They're coming out now."

The images slowly appeared. Crisp, clear close-ups.

"They're great, Stacey. You're a very talented lady."

"Thanks." She held the eight-by-ten black and white glossy photos up and examined them. "They're pretty good if I do say so myself." She finished the developing process and cleaned up the area. Grabbing the pictures, she opened the door, and as they walked out she said, "Now to see if we've wasted our time."

Jess rushed to keep up with her. After they were inside the car he quietly asked, "Are you sure this is a good idea?"

"Positive," Stacey said.

"What if she's in on the whole scheme?"

"She's an elementary school principal, Jess."

"So?"

"So, people don't go into elementary education unless they love children. Anyone who loves kids could never be involved in anything this sinister."

"Maybe she's changed. Years of frustration can have some pretty devastating consequences."

Stacey was silent for a while, then finally said, "We have to trust someone, Jess. I've worked with Grace Milliken for years, and even though she can be difficult at times, she's always been fair."

Jess took Stacey's hand and squeezed it as he said, "You're right. We can't do this alone."

It was a short drive to their destination, but they circled and twisted through two extra neighborhoods to be certain no one was following them. When they pulled up in the drive, they sat and waited for several minutes before going to the door.

Grace Milliken seemed shocked as she pulled open her front door. "Ms. Fordman, what are you doing here?"

"I'm really sorry to bother you, Mrs. Milliken, but it's urgent that Jess and I speak with you."

"Then by all means, come in."

"If you don't mind, we'd prefer you come outside. We have something in the car we'd like to show you."

Grace hesitated, then slipped on some shoes and followed them to the Explorer. Stacey and Grace climbed into the backseat and Jess slid into the driver's seat, started the engine, and said, "I'd be more comfortable if we're on the move. Is that all right with you, Mrs. Milliken?"

"Quite frankly, none of this is all right with me. You are both acting quite odd. Would you please tell me what you're doing?"

"Do you know anything about the exposure of my class to experimental drugs?"

Grace gasped. "What are you talking about?"

Stacey pulled out the photographs and handed them to her. "Do you know this man?"

"Of course. It's Parker McDaniel."

"Do you know where he works?"

"Independent Testing Labs."

"Where does he live?"

"In Chicago. What exactly are you getting at?"

"Mrs. Milliken, this man lives here, in an estate on the outskirts of town. He's a top executive at TechLab. We believe he's involved in a very criminal scheme, and that he's been using you. Independent Testing Labs is a front company being used to test experimental drugs on unsuspecting children."

"Then why haven't you gone to the police?"

"It's very complicated, Mrs. Milliken. We know for certain one woman has already died because of this, and a close friend of ours is missing. TechLab has connections, the kind millions of dollars can buy. We can't risk going to the police until we can nail them to the wall. Understand?"

"Yes, but what do you want from me?"

"We need your help. Tomorrow morning, we're going to try and help our friend get out of TechLab. Hopefully, she's still alive."

"Are you sure you're going to be all right here all alone?"

"Really, J.D., I'll be fine." JoAnn lay back against the pillow, instantly realizing Hanna's files had not been a figment of her imagination as she felt the strange hardness against her head. "I'm going right to sleep. Would you lock my office door as you leave?"

"Sure. Want me to bring you dinner or breakfast?"

"I'll probably sleep straight through. I think I'll just get something out of the vending machine when I get hungry. It's nice of you to offer."

"You'll call this time if you need anything?"

"I promise."

He backed out of the bedroom, closing the door to her office as he went. She heard the outer office door close as well, but stayed very still for twenty minutes to be certain he was gone. With her new cast, it was easier to be quiet crawling than walking, so she slowly made her way into her office. J.D. had laid her lab coat over the back of her chair when they came in. She grabbed it, thrusting her hand in the pocket. Nothing.

She flipped it over and grabbed the other pocket. Her fingers closed around the two copper canisters. J.D. hadn't found them. Thank God.

Grace pulled back the dingy curtain of the motel room and peered outside. It was starting to get dark. "Don't you two think you're overreacting?"

Jess answered, "Not at all. We know for certain our house is bugged, and yours probably is, too. The cars must have some sort of homing device on them. Otherwise, they wouldn't be able to follow us so easily without being seen."

"You mean they know where we are?"

Stacey said, "I borrowed a friend's car. They don't know we're here."

"But why do I need to stay here tonight? If I go home, I won't say anything to tip them off. I promise."

Jess said, "I'm sorry, Mrs. Milliken. We just can't risk anything going wrong at this point. I hope you understand that your sacrificing one night and being a little inconvenienced may help put these bastards in jail. Did we mention they were the ones who burned Stacey's apartment?"

Stacey added, "And after we sent Jonathan to Jess's parents' house, it mysteriously burned down as well."

Grace slumped into a chair as she said, "Oh, my God. What have I done?"

JoAnn had no idea where she was when she woke up. After several seconds, she turned her head, which painfully objected to being moved. The clock on her nightstand glowed three thirty-nine a.m. When that information soaked in, she bolted upright. It was already early Monday morning. She'd slept for more than twelve hours. She reached over and turned on the light.

Suddenly terrified that Hanna's files were gone, she grabbed her pillow. Relieved, she tugged on the pillowcase and pulled them out. Her head ached, but her mind was sharp again. The words she'd scanned in her drunken stupor now held more meaning. Hanna had documented enough criminal activity by the TechLab Board of Directors to put them all away for the rest of their lives. The corporation would be destroyed. Thousands would lose their jobs.

In the middle of the formal documents was a handwritten diary Hanna had maintained for the last few years. JoAnn read each weekly entry, seeing herself mirrored in Hanna's writing in so many ways. Hanna had started out naive and wide-eyed about corporate politics. She'd fallen hopelessly in love with James Dean Cook, who treated her as though she walked on water, professing to be her best friend, someone who cared about her long-term well-being. But Hanna never felt her affection was returned. She began to suspect his true motives, just as JoAnn had never felt quite certain about the man she knew as J.D.

When Hanna first joined the Board, they were illegally field-testing the compound called NiA12. Originally, she'd been outraged that innocent people were being victimized. But the Board's explanations and logic ran true, at least in the case of NiA12. She'd been told the testing was done strictly on afflicted volunteers, who were paid handsomely for the privilege. They were people whose lives had been devastated by disease both emotionally and financially. They were virtually guaranteed death using the medical treatments available at the time. In exchange for their secrecy, TechLab gave them hope and financial stability for their loved ones. Hanna had believed their lies, and gone back to concentrating on running her department.

It was SynCur6 that jolted Hanna's confidence in TechLab. As it was developed, she watched each step Redman, the scientist who invented it, took toward achieving a promising anesthetic agent get twisted by the Board's profit motive. Hanna never believed Redman committed suicide, although watching his life's work be turned into a weapon could certainly have been considered sufficient reason. Most of the Syn-Cur6 tests were run on poor South Americans. Entire villages were subjected to the chemical by low-flying aircraft. The first test resulted in widespread death from an unexpected side effect. Luckily, contagious virus samples from the BioHazard group easily explained the deaths. By the fourth trial run, they knew they had struck gold.

Hanna had stolen two canisters of SynCur6, which she planned to take to the police, along with documentation on the other illegal tests. The main problem was going to be getting the samples out of BioHazard without the radioactive isotopes triggering the alarms on the exits and pneumatic system. Although the sub-floors' elevator bank and stairs were the only direct way out, Hanna had hand-sketched a map of her anticipated escape route. JoAnn recognized exactly where it started—inside the ceiling of the loft. The route followed the pneumatic system's piping up four levels to an intake vent on the north side of the building.

Hanna had one more piece of evidence she was waiting for before she deserted TechLab: the plans for the latest drug to be field-tested—Citrinol3. She was worried that JoAnn would be victimized, as had Redman. Hanna had hoped to steer the Board away from JoAnn by planting lies in her personnel file. Announcement of the East Elementary test site had been the final straw for Hanna. Nothing was worth risking the lives and futures of an entire class of children. Nothing. The last entry was written two days before her death.

JoAnn felt incredibly guilty as she read Hanna's final pages. They described the brutal warning issued by the Executive Board, which she knew they would enforce without hesitation. They made it clear that Hanna's mother's life would be the price of betraying TechLab.

She wished Hanna had confided in her. Together, she was sure they could have made it, but with her ankle in a cast, there was no way she could do it alone.

*   *   *

"Gentlemen, we need to get the Executive Board meeting started. I'm sure Mr. Harper will be joining us as soon as his busy schedule allows." As usual, Gene Lemmond was in no mood to wait. He sipped from his mug of steaming coffee as he said, "Take the next few minutes to review the Priority One reports in front of you. I'm sure you'll all be as pleased as I was with our financial statistics."

Each man flipped through page after page of statistics until Lemmond said, "As you can see, our profits are up considerably over the last quarter. This can be directly attributed to the FDA's early approval of NiA12. Projected year-end bonuses for the executives will run between one hundred fifty thousand to over a quarter million. Plus, our top-level managers are expected to receive between twenty-five and fifty thousand each. Not a bad Christmas present, if I do say so myself."

Harper slid in the conference-room doors and crawled into his seat.

"How nice of you to take some of your precious time to join us, Mr. Harper."

"I'm sorry I'm late. We seem to have a few abnormalities occurring in our surveillance of the Citrinol project."

"Abnormalities?"

"Yes, sir."

"Would you care to explain?"

"It's probably nothing to worry about, Mr. Lemmond. I just like to make sure we're protected at all times."

"I'll decide what is worth worrying about. What's going on?"

"Well, first of all, the Lawrence boy has still not been located. We're working under the assumption he is traveling in Canada with his grandparents."

"Go on."

"Yesterday, his father, Jess Lawrence, and the Ford-man woman went to the mall. They split up and we lost them. But we caught up with them later. She drove his car home last night about eight o'clock. We don't know how he got home, but he was there when she arrived."

"How do you know?"

Harper laughed. "They were arguing. It was a whopper, too. She called him an insensitive bastard and he said she was a raving bitch. It was really quite entertaining."

"We're all glad you enjoy your job so much, Harper. Anything else?"

"The Milliken woman has been awfully quiet."

McDaniel looked up from his report as Harper continued, "She normally calls her aunt every night. Tells her every stinking thing that happened each day. Last night, there was no call, and no one answered her phone. The damn thing practically rang off the wall. Drove the tech crazy. We had a man go to the door. There wasn't any answer."

McDaniel confidently said, "She may have been working. I can try to contact her at school. She'll tell me what's going on."

Harper shifted nervously as he said, "To be quite honest, I'm not very comfortable with this project any longer. There are too many coincidences."

J.D. leaned back and threw down his pen as he said, "Let me guess, you want to knock off Jess Lawrence and Stacey Fordman and let's not forget his son, Jonathan. Oh, yeah, and while we're at it, let's hit the Milliken woman. Why not kill JoAnn Rayburn, too? And the other seventeen kids in the class? Plus the twelve people in the nursing home. You've been awfully quick to rack up a body count lately considering half the time your staff doesn't know where the people are they're supposed to be watching."

"What's that supposed to mean?"

"The other day JoAnn Rayburn left this complex at ten in the morning and came back at four. Security thought she was in her office the entire time, because she didn't take her purse, and she didn't drive her own car. Not exactly what I would classify as expert surveillance. Considering the exorbitant budget for Security, I'd expect more. Wouldn't you?"

Harper stood up and glared at J.D. as he said, "Listen, Cook, I've kept your ass out of the fire more times than I care to remember. You should show a little more respect."

"My ass. You're only looking out for one person, and it certainly isn't me. You've wanted us to shut down the Citrinol project for weeks. Now, just as JoAnn makes a breakthrough that will guarantee the success of the project, you're trying to convince the Board to cut its losses and run."

Lemmond interrupted, "Explain the breakthrough, Cook."

"It's very technical. But I do know that it's the work of a genius. JoAnn has devised a way to coat the genetically altered protein so that it's no longer attracted to healthy cells. It will target the cancer and eliminate it. Our side effect problems are gone. We'll make millions."

Harper stood up and shook his head as he said, "Or maybe she's filling you with a bunch of shit to keep you off her back."

"Why on earth would she do that? If JoAnn suspected anything she wouldn't have come back to the lab yesterday after I took her to the hospital. She was eager to get back to work. Her drive was back, I could feel it just being near her. Her dream is about to come true, Harper, and I don't intend to let you stand in her way."

"I won't. *She's* well under control. It's Lawrence and

Fordman I'm worried about. I think we should take them out."

"And what impact do you think that would have on JoAnn's work?"

"She doesn't have to know."

"We don't have her locked in a cage, you know. She's free to come and go. She listens to the radio. After Hanna and Amy White, do you really think she'll buy another accident? The techs discuss the news. She'd find out. Besides, Lawrence is taking care of her puppies. She checks on them every day."

The intercom buzzed and Lemmond pushed the button and said, "This better be good."

"There's an urgent call for Mr. McDaniel. The woman says it's extremely important that she speak to him right now."

"Put her through. McDaniel, I think we'd all like to listen to this one."

Lemmond pushed the speaker phone button and McDaniel said, "Hello."

"Parker, it's Grace Milliken. I'm sorry to bother you while you're in a meeting, but it's urgent. Stacey Fordman and Jess Lawrence know what's really going on."

Chapter 20

Jess and Stacey blended well with the other people filing into the TechLab complex. Most of the employees were in their twenties and thirties, anxious to build a career and thrilled to work for a corporation so generously involved with the community. It was a little before eight o'clock on Monday morning, and they chatted casually about the approaching winter storm as they walked into the building behind two men and one woman who were arriving for work.

Keeping their faces tilted down, they followed the others through the main entry. The men headed for the corporate offices, while the woman went around the corner to the bank of elevators that led down to BioHazard. Jess and Stacey walked into the elevator right behind her as if they knew exactly where they were going.

She ran her identification card through the security device and glanced quizzically at them as she said, "Are you new?"

Jess answered as the elevator started down, "In a way. We've been temporarily transferred here from the Chicago division to help Dr. Rayburn."

"Really?" She held out her hand. "I'm Leanne Caldwell, Dr. Rayburn's assistant. She didn't mention that we'd be getting help, but God knows we could use it."

"I'm Jay and this is Lacey. JoAnn sounded really exhausted when I talked to her on Saturday. I'm sure it just slipped her mind that we were coming today. She says the work on the Citrinol project is progressing nicely. Slow, but steady."

The elevator opened and they stepped off. Jess and Stacey tried not to act too impressed by the massive underground structure as they followed Leanne. She said, "It really is a long painstaking process. We keep hitting dead ends. JoAnn tells me all the time not to worry, that one day it will just work out, but it gets so frustrating. You'd think after fifteen years in this business, I'd know better."

"This is quite a facility. How far underground are we?"

"Right now, four stories. BioHazard goes another floor deeper than the rest of the building. The sensitive equipment, you know."

"Of course. JoAnn told me everything here is state of the art. I'm looking forward to being able to use such an advanced facility."

"Really? I thought all the TechLab facilities were kept up. Have they let Chicago slide?"

"A little."

"How long are you supposed to be stationed here?"

"Two months."

"Over the holidays? You poor souls."

Stacey smiled and said, "I'm sure our visit will be quite an adventure. We've been looking forward to it."

They came to where the red stripe ended at a large metal door and Leanne said, "Here we are." She punched in her security code and stepped inside the first door. When Jess and Stacey tried to follow, she said, "I'm sorry. Security would have my job if I let anyone inside on my code. Rules, you know. You'll have to use the codes they assigned each of you."

McDaniel's voice never wavered as he said into the speaker, "Calm down, Grace. What in the world are you talking about?"

Harper flipped over his report and scribbled, "How did she get TechLab's phone number?" He held it up and McDaniel shrugged. Harper scribbled, "I'm putting a trace on it," and ran out of the room.

Grace said, "They thought I was on their side. They explained everything to me about who you really are and that you work for TechLab. Right now, they're trying to prove that you used the air-conditioning system you donated to the school to test an experimental drug on the first-grade children."

"Really? How do they plan to do that?"

"I'm not sure. They told me they were going to prove your company was responsible for Ms. Fordman's apartment fire, too. They wanted me to help them. Don't get me wrong, Parker. I'm on your side. I will help *you*, not them. Parker, I love you."

"Do you actually believe all this nonsense, Grace?"

"I didn't at first, but they showed me pictures. Apparently they've been building evidence for quite a while. Dr. Lawrence may be a veterinarian, but he knew that his son's illness was caused by some sort of toxic exposure. That's why he sent him away."

"Don't you see, Grace? They're crazy. Pretty soon they'll convince you that I managed to have a tornado hit the school as well, just so I could destroy some stupid air conditioner. They're living in a fantasy, and they're trying to pull you into it."

"Then why did you lie to me about where you live and where you really work?"

"I was afraid to get involved with anyone again." Several men rolled their eyes as McDaniel continued, "You were too much of a temptation, Grace. I needed some distance."

"What about Independent Testing Labs? Ms. Fordman says they have proof that it's a cover corporation, and that TechLab owns the subsidiary that owns it."

"That part is true. TechLab is a very large conglomerate. We have interests in more than twenty corporations, some of which own other corporations. All that is public record, Grace. Anyone can find out if they just follow the chain of ownership. But Independent Testing Labs is a real, active corporation. We've done numerous studies for public school systems across the nation. Fordman and Lawrence don't know what they're talking about, and I can prove it."

McDaniel looked up as Harper stuck his head back in and gave a thumbs-up sign indicating they had successfully traced the call. "Listen, Grace. I'll come over right now and we can talk this whole thing out. Just tell me where you are and I'll be right there."

"Alone?"

"Alone. I promise."

"They only gave us one security code, Leanne. Will it work if Lacey and I both come through the system at once?"

"I swear, Security hires the most lazy, worthless people. I suppose it will be all right. Just be careful. You only get one try before they come and shoot you." She saw their shocked expressions and tapped Jess on the shoulder as she laughed. "Just kidding. It takes about thirty minutes, then the computer automatically resets. It's mainly just a pain in the ass."

"Thanks for the warning." The outer door slid closed and Jess punched in Hanna's security code from memory. It slid back open and they both stepped inside as it sealed behind them. "Piece of cake," he said as the green light came on and he entered the numerical equivalent for "blue." The inner door popped open, and they both sighed.

Leanne was waiting for them. She pointed at an archway to the right and said, "The rest rooms are through there. Sometimes on Mondays, there are donuts near the coffee machine down that hall. And if you'll just follow me, JoAnn's office is right across from mine. It's so exciting to have new people to talk to, even if it is only for a little while. JoAnn and I are the only ones in the entire sector today and tomorrow. Everyone else has to attend the annual safety update classes." She glanced at her watch and added, "They should be losing consciousness from extreme boredom any minute now."

Jess said, "I hate those classes. How'd you manage to get out of it?"

"Corporate politics." She laughed. "No, seriously, JoAnn invoked a little executive override on my behalf. I've worked here for six years, and five safety classes are more than enough. If I were any more careful, I wouldn't be able to leave my house in the morning."

"We really appreciate all your help, Ms. Caldwell."

"Leanne."

"Thanks, Leanne."

Leanne rapped lightly on JoAnn's office door and said, "Are you in?"

"Sure, come in," JoAnn called back.

Leanne brightly announced, "Look who's here!"

JoAnn was visibly shocked, but before she could say anything Jess said, "You didn't forget we were coming today, did you? I know, I know. The project work order was approved ages ago, but we had to wait for executive approvals."

JoAnn stammered as she said, "Why, of course not. I just lost track of what day it was again. I do that quite often lately. Come in. We can go over the project specifications. I have most of the information right here in my office."

Two floors up, in the main surveillance room, the shit was hitting the fan. The Executive Board had just issued a Priority One Security Alert. Every on and off-duty guard's pager had just sounded the emergency code, and Harper was barking commands to ten different people at once.

The guard assigned to monitor JoAnn's office had laid his headphones down and was too busy listening to his boss scream obscenities at his colleagues to hear anything else.

Lemmond pushed the button on the phone, disconnecting Grace Milliken's call. "She said she was at school. Where did the call come from?"

Harper answered, "The East Elementary switchboard."

"McDaniel, can you bring her in?"

"No problem."

"Security will be backing you up, of course," Harper said.

"Of course." McDaniel looked at Harper and said, "Where should I take her?"

"Not here. Take her to your house. Leave the alarm system off and we'll come in and wrap everything up properly."

"How soon?"

"It won't take long. Believe me, if you'll just sweet-talk her for a few minutes, we'll come in and finish things before you know it."

McDaniel left as Harper called a backup team to follow him. By the time he hung up, the only one left in the conference room with him was Gene Lemmond. Lemmond said, "Do them both."

"McDaniel and Milliken?"

Lemmond nodded as he said, "Carefully. McDaniel may try to run."

"Don't worry. SynCur6 will make sure they cooperate. They'll be naked in bed when a fire starts from a carelessly laid cigarette. It will be quite a scandal, I'm sure."

"What about Lawrence and Fordman?"

"Our team says they haven't left his house yet. When they do, they'll have a little surprise."

"It can't be too obvious. No car bombs. No suicides. Once it's done, every inch of that place needs to be searched, and check out that clinic of his, too."

"Of course. I was thinking more along the lines of a car wreck or possibly even something as simple as exposure."

"Exposure?"

"That cold front blowing in is supposed to drop the temperature down to twenty tonight. Their car could break down outside of town, and with a little SynCur6 to keep them perfectly still, it probably wouldn't take long for them to freeze to death."

JoAnn asked, "Where will you be working today, Leanne?"

"I've got some crystallography work to do, so I'll be over in the far west wing."

"Would you like to join us for lunch?"

"I'd love to."

"Meet us back here at noon. Okay?"

"Great."

As soon as she was out of sight, JoAnn held a finger to her lips and locked the door as she said, "Leanne is my best employee. She's always willing to help and is quite bright." As JoAnn spoke, she took out a pad of paper and wrote. "How did you get in?"

Stacey wrote, "Hanna's code worked!"

JoAnn rolled open her file cabinet and pulled two copper canisters out from underneath the top drawer. She peeled the tape off them and wrote, "This is SynCur6. It TOTALLY IMMOBILIZES anyone who breathes ANY of it for two hours. I think they used it to paralyze Hanna so they could kill her." She handed one to Jess and one to Stacey.

Stacey handed hers back to JoAnn and wrote, "You need this more than I do."

JoAnn nodded, then motioned for them to follow her. She led them into the adjoining makeshift bedroom where she tossed the pillow to Stacey. Next, she pushed the mattress aside so she could retrieve the hidden drug samples. Jess tucked both vials into his pocket as Stacey ripped open the pillow.

JoAnn wrote, "These compounds will set off the alarm if they are taken out of BioHazard via the main elevator bank or emergency stairs." She pulled the sketched map out of her pocket and handed it to Jess as she wrote, "Hanna left this. It must be the way she had planned to get the samples out."

Jess wrote, "I can do this. What about you two?"

JoAnn answered with, "We can just walk out the normal way."

"What about the files?"

"You can take the Priority One files. The others won't trigger the alarm. This map shows you'll end up at a vent near ground level on the east side of the building. We'll figure out a way to be there to help you."

"Then let's get the hell out of here," he whispered.

Stacey handed Jess the two special files, then opened her coat, tucked the other files into her blue jeans, then pulled her shirt down over them. When she buttoned the white lab coat, she looked a little chunky, but normal enough to pass without catching anyone's attention.

JoAnn motioned for Jess to follow her, and for Stacey to wait in her office. Jess walked down the hall beside JoAnn, casually asking, "Is TechLab responsible for all this . . . great equipment?"

"Yes, they don't have any outside partners. Everything is researched and tested in-house. Everything."

"I understand." They rounded the corner and JoAnn led the way into the loft area. Jess looked over the edge at the expanse of equipment and remarked, "Unbelievable. They certainly spared no expense."

"True. We've been having a little trouble with this one machine though. Follow me, I'll show you." She led him past the lab equipment to where Hanna had originally hidden the briefcase. After she opened the maintenance door on the back of the machine, she pointed up and handed him the map.

Jess tucked the files inside his shirt, hugged JoAnn, then slowly stood on the door, making certain it would hold him. He then used both his arms to push himself up onto the top of the machine, where he easily slid a ceiling tile aside. He winked at JoAnn and disappeared into the crawl space, replacing the tile behind him.

She closed the machine's door and said, "I've got that report in my office. You just stay here and work and I'll bring it right back."

JoAnn's heart was pounding as she made her way back through the lab. She abruptly realized that no matter what happened now, she would never work in this place again. Even though TechLab's methods were totally unethical, she would miss having the opportunity to work in one of the best facilities in the world. More than that, she knew for certain that her dreams to see Citrinol overcome cancer would never come true.

JoAnn was moving slowly now, her crutches were suddenly heavy, and the cast on her ankle felt like an enormous burden. When she finally stepped into her office, she stopped dead in her tracks.

J.D. was standing with one hand clamped down on Stacey's shoulder. In the other he held a knife, which he waved at JoAnn as he said, "Nice of you to join us, JoAnn. Come in, come in. We have so much to talk about."

Jess didn't move for several minutes after he replaced the ceiling tile. It was dark, and when his eyes finally adjusted he tried to use the roughly sketched map to determine which way to go, but it was so dark he could hardly see anything. An approaching sound made him freeze. The noise drew closer, then whooshed past him. He realized it was from the pneumatic system, and that if he followed it, it would lead him to the main system control.

The large silver tubing ran in both directions, and he followed it to the right, moving inches at a time. He couldn't risk falling through the tiles, so each step had to be placed very carefully near a brace with most of his weight borne by hanging onto the ceiling beams. Holding on to the tubing, he moved along until it started up a gentle incline, but the ceiling remained flat. Inching along the ceiling, he quickly realized that he had reached a solid, cold, concrete dead end.

"Where is he, JoAnn?"

"Who?"

"I'm not in the mood for games." He pushed Stacey over next to JoAnn and said, "I know Fordman didn't come alone. Where's Lawrence?"

"She came by herself, J.D. I needed someone to talk to."

"Bullshit. You might as well tell me. It won't be too hard to have Security check the entrance videotapes, now will it?"

"Please, J.D., Stacey hasn't done anything wrong. Let her leave, and we can talk about this."

"How'd she get in here anyway?"

"TechLab security isn't as tight as everyone would like to believe. She used my codes."

"Then you breached your contract. I believe that is grounds for dismissal, at the very least."

JoAnn's lip trembled and she was on the verge of tears as she said, "I wanted some company. It gets lonely down here."

"You know, if I hadn't just heard Grace Milliken spill her guts to McDaniel, I might actually believe your little act. It's too bad you couldn't just do your friggin' research and keep your nose out of things. Believe me, it would have been much healthier for all of you."

A loud siren blasted three times and J.D. slammed both women against the wall. He shoved the blade of the knife under JoAnn's chin as he muttered, "What the hell is that?"

"A Level 4 lockdown."

"What!"

"You heard me. It's a BioHazard lockdown. No one can get out of the entire BioHazard sector now. Not even you."

Jess had eased his way back to the large silver pneumatic system tubing. Straddling it, he worked his way up to the top of the next level, and was crawling along when the sirens blasted. He had no idea what they were for, but he knew it was nothing good.

Briefly he considered going back to help Stacey and JoAnn. His right leg was touching the outer concrete wall, and the other leg hung numbly over the cold tubing. His fingers were raw and bleeding from feeling his way along. Below him was a three-story drop. He only had one more floor to go. If he could get out and get rid of the evidence, he could come back with help.

He nudged a little farther up the tube, and prayed.

* * *

J.D. slammed JoAnn harder against the wall as he shouted, "What the hell instigated a lockdown? How did you do it?"

He was hurting her, so she muttered through her teeth, "Either someone in the Level 4 BioHazard lab was just exposed to a lethal contagious virus or the alarm at the main BioHazard entrance was manually activated. I didn't do it."

"When can we get out?"

JoAnn smiled and said, "Depends."

J.D. lowered his knife and clinched his fingers around her neck as he said, "I asked you when we could get out of here."

Suddenly Stacey saw her opportunity and rammed her heel into his foot, then brutally clawed his face. When he bent over in pain, she brought her knee full force into his face, instantly shattering his nose. Blood poured over his mouth and beard as he screamed and staggered backward, dropping the knife.

J.D. shook his head and lunged toward Stacey, sending both of them sprawling onto the floor. His hands closed around her neck, and he viciously pounded her head against the floor as he tightened his grip.

From behind him, JoAnn's crutch came crashing down at the base of his skull. J.D. crumpled and fell beside Stacey. He never heard JoAnn say, "That was for Hanna, you worthless, egotistical, manipulative son of a bitch."

Harper glanced at his watch and smiled. By now, he was certain McDaniel and Milliken were toasted to perfection. It gave him a warm feeling, imagining that soon they would be paralyzed, unable to scream as their flesh blackened and then cracked away from

their bones long before they were spared the misery
by death.

He slid his hand off the BioHazard lockdown alarm
and pulled a canister of SynCur6 from his coat pocket.
Harper looked around the empty lab. Twelve hours.
He had twelve hours to take care of JoAnn Rayburn
and cover his trail. It was going to be a long, lingering
process this time. Much more fulfilling than Hanna
Shore's tortured last moments in silent agony.

JoAnn wouldn't be so lucky. She'd live long enough
for the SynCur6 to wear off. Or maybe he wouldn't
use any at all.

Parker McDaniel walked confidently into Grace Milliken's office. She was seated at her desk, working diligently, so he tapped her desk and said, "Grace. Why
don't we go somewhere and discuss all this nonsense?"

He jumped as he heard her office door close behind
him. Two police officers were standing against the
wall. The taller man said sharply, "Mr. McDaniel,
you're under arrest."

McDaniel innocently turned back to look at Grace as
he said, "What's this all about? I swear, I haven't done
any of the things those people say I have."

Grace smiled politely and said, "Then you don't
have anything to worry about, do you, Parker?"

"But, Grace, I thought you trusted me."

"I did, but all the pieces of the puzzle fit together
after I talked to Jess and Stacey. What you haven't realized is that you've actually helped them succeed."

"How could that possibly be?" he asked as the police led him out.

Grace grabbed her coat and said as she ran down
the hall, "You were our diversion. We were counting
on your Security people worrying more about me than
what was happening right under their noses. By now,

Jess and Stacey have all the evidence they'll need to shut TechLab down. Forever."

"Get the hell out of here, Stacey. You can probably catch Jess if you hurry."

"I'm not leaving without you."

"Yes, you are. Don't you see?" She pointed at the cast on her foot and held up her injured hand. "I can't get out of here, but you can. You two are my only hope. Find a way out, then bring help. It's the only way."

"They'll kill you."

"The minimum time for a Level 4 lockdown is twelve hours. No one is going to get in or out of here the normal way for at least that long." She dug the canister of SynCur6 out of her pocket and said, "If he does regain consciousness, I've got this. It will keep him in line, even if I can't."

"But . . ."

"Go down the hall and turn left. Go straight until you have to turn to the right. The loft is a circular walkway that looks down over the lower level. In the far corner is a machine about six feet high. Go behind it and open the maintenance door. Stand on the door to get on top of the machine, then push a ceiling tile out of your way and crawl in. Maybe Jess will be able to hear you if you call him."

"I hate this. It just doesn't feel right. If J.D. didn't instigate the lockdown, who did?"

"Probably Security. This place has cameras and listening devices everywhere. Either that or somehow Jess triggered it."

"Then maybe I shouldn't follow him. He could be on his way back here, or they may have caught him."

"Let's hope not. Either way, staying here won't help. Twelve hours from now when those doors open, we need someone to keep them from coming in and declaring there was some kind of horrible accident that killed us all. You have to get out and bring help."

"I'll do my best." Stacey headed down the hall and turned. She quickly passed several rows of work-stations and was about to turn when she thought she heard something behind her. She froze and whirled around. Nothing.

She walked slower now, listening every second, barely drawing in her own breath. Following the path JoAnn had described, she was about to step into the loft area when the lab's lights blinked off. The rooms behind her were thrown into blackness, but the lights from the loft area were still on.

Stacey walked cautiously onto the narrow pathway. The machine JoAnn had described was only a few feet from her, but she turned and watched the dark door-way, which she knew was her only certain way back out, instead of going on. When nothing moved or made a sound for several seconds, she made her way behind the machine and tried to calm down.

The maintenance door opened easily, and Stacey crawled onto it. She effortlessly pushed herself up and climbed on top of the machine before she smelled the peculiar scent of vanilla and heard the sickest, most terrifying laughter of her entire life.

Jess could hear the muffled sounds of people below him. As best he could tell, he was above the ceiling of the first underground floor. The pneumatic tubing came to an end at a solid wall, and there was no way around it. He considered backtracking, but the ex-treme darkness would be the same hindrance it had been all along. Without being able to see, Hanna's map was useless. Plus, he had only a vague idea how he had gotten to where he was, and he didn't have a clue where that might be on her map.

Very carefully, he eased himself down and pried up

the corner of one of the insulating ceiling tiles. Below him, he could hear people laughing and talking.

Aren't you glad you aren't the one who got exposed?

Shit, you couldn't pay me enough to work in BioHazard. I always knew it would happen someday. Poor sucker. I wonder what disease got him.

I just hope their lockdown works. Ever thought about it? We'd be the first exposed if one of those viruses ever got loose. Not my idea of a fun way to die. How are those CBC's coming? They came in STAT. Like anything we do here is STAT. When I worked in hospital pathology, now that work was STAT. Half the time the damn surgeon was waiting with a patient sliced open. Too much pressure. The pace here is so laid back. This place is like heaven . . .

Jess slid the ceiling tile back and poked his head through the hole as he said, "Excuse me. Could you tell me where I am?"

Both men looked up from their microscopes and gawked at him.

Jess laughed and said, "I guess I do look rather odd up here, don't I? I'm working on the pneumatic system and I seem to have taken a wrong turn. I can't seem to get back to the central processing unit." Jess wondered if there was such a thing, and hoped these two didn't know any more about the equipment than he did.

"Boy, you are lost. You're in Pathology. I think the place you're looking for is by Radiology. It's on the other end of the floor."

"If I can manage to get out of here, can you show me where it is?"

"Sure."

Jess eased himself slowly down, his feet coming to rest on the countertop. He slid the ceiling tile back in place and hopped down. "I really appreciate this, guys. I'm new at this job, and I'd be in hot water if I told them I left my blueprints in the office."

"I hope you aren't planning on bringing the system down. I've got sixteen tests to get out of here in the next two hours."

"It's just a slow leak somewhere in the subsurface tubing structure, but it's definitely in your best interest to help me get it fixed. You never know when you'll lose enough air pressure to bring the whole system to a standstill. When that happens, it takes a hell of a lot longer to find the leak."

"How long have you been up there? You're a mess."

Jess looked at his clothes. His jeans and the white lab coat were covered with grease, and his hands were smeared and badly scraped. "To tell you the truth, over an hour. I really didn't want to have to admit I couldn't find my way back. What was that siren I heard a few minutes ago? It scared the hell out of me."

"That's a BioHazard lockdown. It means the fourth and fifth subfloors have been sealed closed."

"It's not a radiation leak or anything like that, is it?"

"No. More than likely someone pricked themselves with the wrong needle."

"Does it happen often?"

"First time since I've worked here. That's eight years. Here we are. This is the Radiology wing. I think the room you need is at the very end of this hall. If it isn't, just ask for Charlie Jenkins. He'll know where you need to go."

"Thanks again." Jess walked confidently down the hall, passing several empty offices along the way. As a veterinarian, he was more than familiar with radiology, and felt he could confidently bluff his way out of the department if he had to. When he came to a door that had the black and yellow insignia for radioactive material on the door, he smiled. Peeking inside, he saw the familiar X-ray equipment. He slipped silently into the room and easily found exactly what he needed.

* * *

JoAnn rolled J.D. over and kicked him with her cast while holding the canister of SynCur6 at the tip of his nose. He didn't move; his head only lolled to one side from the momentum of her blow. She crawled under her desk and disconnected an extension cord, which she wound tightly around his wrists, tied to the leg of her desk chair, then knotted.

Leaning against the wall, she wondered what she could do. Reaching over, she tried the telephone. It still worked. She could call the police, but that would risk bringing the entire Security department down on Stacey and Jess. Her computer hummed in the background, but she was sure any messages for help would have the same negative effect on their chances of survival. She could send a pneumatic message to Pathology, but what good would it do?

She sighed, feeling totally useless. Then she noticed the hallway outside her office was dark. Grabbing her crutches, she walked into the darkness, wondering why the lights were off. The light switches for the lab area and hallways were near the front door, next to the emergency lockdown alarm. She inched her way to the door, grasping her canister of SynCur6 in one hand while using her crutches to move along.

The red EXIT sign glowed over the main doors. JoAnn moved closer to it, suddenly sorry she hadn't stayed in her office and locked the door. She reached one hand out, running it along the wall until her fingers touched the switches. As she flipped them up, she heard Harper's voice directly behind her.

"Do you believe in poetic justice, Ms. Rayburn?"

Chapter 21

JoAnn whirled around, raising her hand as her finger frantically pushed the spray nozzle of the SynCur6 canister.

"First you illuminate me, and now I will eliminate you. Clever, aren't I?" Harper nodded toward her hand, which was still uselessly pushing the nozzle on the canister as he said, "It doesn't work. The two canisters Hanna thought she so cleverly stole won't work until the propellant is added." He smiled wickedly as he added, "You're shooting blanks, my dear."

JoAnn threw the canister at him as she asked, "What do you want?"

"I've heard for months how brilliant you are. Surely you have figured this out by now."

"You killed Hanna, didn't you?"

"Of course. Your boyfriend, Cook, doesn't have the balls to keep his women in line." He leered at her as he added, "It seems that task keeps falling in my lap, so to speak."

"And Amy?"

"Not personally, but I more than happily made sure the order was carried out." Harper shoved her toward her office and said, "Let's go."

"You bastard," she said as she grudgingly moved down the hall. "I suppose you were responsible for my attack in the parking lot, too?"

"I'm very good at what I do, Ms. Rayburn. Like you are. If I had been in charge of it, you would not have survived. But, unfortunately, I believe that was just a bit of bad luck on your part." He laughed. "And it seems what little luck you had left is quickly running out."

"Yours will, too."

"If you are referring to getting assistance from your friends, I don't believe I have much to worry about. It was unfortunate that Ms. Fordman took such a nasty spill onto an electron microscope a few minutes ago. I was looking forward to having a little fun with her as well, but limp bodies aren't nearly as entertaining as those that struggle. Hanna taught me that much. I assume Mr. Lawrence is hanging around here somewhere, too. As soon as I get you situated, I'll make sure he has an unfortunate accident. What exactly is he doing up in the ceiling, anyway?"

JoAnn just glared at him.

He searched for his radio as he said, "I could notify a security team right now. Of course, I'd rather wait a little longer. The fewer people involved in wrapping up this whole nasty episode, the better. With all of you dead, there won't be much corporate exposure from all this. A little negative publicity due to a few unfortunate accidental deaths, maybe, but we'll survive quite well." He glanced up and added, "Your friend lurking around in the ceiling will probably be back soon. I think I'll take care of him personally."

"He's long gone by now, Harper."

"Really, where did he go?" He nudged her when she didn't answer and said, "You'll tell me soon enough. Pain is a very effective tool in my business. And while you're literally spilling your guts, you can explain how Lawrence and Fordham breached my security system. Then I'll notify the rest of my department and Mr. Lawrence will be killed trying to steal top secret compounds."

She glared at him and smiled as she said, "The police are already on the way, Harper."

"Oh, I'm so scared. I'm stuck in a BioHazard lockdown for twelve hours and the police are going to be waiting at the door when it opens. Even though I sincerely doubt that will happen, I wonder how they would like a few of the viruses down here spread around the city. Think that would buy me a little time?"

"You are sick."

"Amusing, isn't it? I've had the perfect job, and now I'll be able to start a new life somewhere else with TechLab's wonderful technology paying the bills. I'm sure it won't be hard to find buyers for fatal viruses, or the SynCur6 compound, or even Citrinol3 for that matter."

"No one would want to buy Citrinol3 in this stage of its development. It does more harm than good."

"It's such a pity. You supposedly brilliant scientific minds have no imagination. Plenty of people would love to have Citrinol3, just as it is. Think about it. A little Citrinol3 in the air ducts of enemy camps would make the soldiers tired and listless, but not kill them. Then they could easily be retrained by our side. Whole countries could be persuaded to our way of thinking.

"Even here at home it could work wonders. A covert program could improve our public schools by administering it to the class troublemakers. They'd turn into obedient, calm students. Schools would no longer be a war zone. The kids who want to learn wouldn't have to sit through the disruptions caused by the handful who don't give a shit. The possibilities are incredible."

"What about the side effects? You don't care who you hurt, do you? Long-term exposure has never been tested, at least not legitimately."

"Long-term goals are not a problem with the type of people I deal with, nor are your so-called 'legitimate tests.' You get in and out, make your money and run.

As long as the short-term goal is met, nothing else is important." He shoved her through the door to her office and started to laugh at the sight of J.D. still unconscious on the floor, his hands bound by an extension cord to a chair. "It would appear Mr. Cook couldn't even handle a scrawny woman on crutches. I always knew he was a worthless bastard."

JoAnn recognized her opportunity. In one swift motion, she dropped one crutch and swung the other at him as she screamed, "That seems to be a common trait among the TechLab executives."

The crutch hit his right shoulder, sending the canister of SynCur6 flying against the wall. JoAnn was thrown off balance, but lunged toward her desk, desperately trying to grab a pair of scissors from its top corner before he reached her.

Harper bumped against the wall, but quickly recovered. He pushed himself forcefully off the wall, giving him plenty of momentum. Springing toward JoAnn, he grabbed a fistful of her hair as he laughed and said, "Nice try." He easily jerked her upward, and pulled her with him by her hair as he leaned over to grab the canister from the floor.

"Let go of me," she muttered, her face twisting in pain.

He shoved her away as he released her hair. "No more cute little stunts, Rayburn. Understand?"

She was rubbing the back of her head as she replied, "No. Remember, we brilliant scientific minds are a little dull sometimes."

"I suggest you shut up and get your butt in there." He pushed her toward the makeshift bedroom, but she stubbornly stood her ground. "Use the brain, Rayburn," he said. He thrust his wristwatch near her face. "Eleven and a half hours of lockdown left. The residual effects of SynCur6 last approximately two hours, depending on the victim's intrinsic metabolic rate. Unlike yours, my canister works quite well, at least it did on Hanna, and your nosey friend, Stacey Fordman. That means I can give you a whiff now and wait until you loosen up in two hours to finish you off." He shrugged and added, "Or you can just cooperate now."

JoAnn glared at him and sneered. "What difference does it make? Either way you're going to kill me."

"True. But with SynCur6, you won't have a fighting chance. Your body will be totally paralyzed, but your mind will feel every single thing I do to it. And I can guarantee you, I have some very unique things planned for you." He laughed as he said, "Without the SynCur6, who knows? Maybe you can overcome me like you did Cook." He kicked one of her crutches toward her. "Second try might be the charm."

JoAnn's mind was racing. Either way, he was going to torture her and kill her. "What if I make a deal with you?" she asked.

He smiled. "You don't seem to be in a very good position to strike any kind of deal."

She confidently held his gaze as she said, "Actually, I think I'm in an excellent position to negotiate."

He cocked his head and stared at her, then finally said, "We've got twelve hours. I suppose it wouldn't hurt to hear you out."

"I made the breakthrough on Citrinol3 two days ago. It will make a fortune in the legal drug market."

"What kind of breakthrough?"

JoAnn wondered how much, if any, technical knowledge Harper had, and quickly opted for a relatively safe, nonscientific explanation. "I solved the absorption problems. The main side effect has now been eliminated."

Harper appeared to suddenly be very interested. He leaned toward her and said, "And what good will that do you now? Will they carve on your tombstone that you *almost* made the scientific breakthrough of the century? I doubt it."

"Fine. Then kill me. You obviously aren't as financially motivated as I thought you were."

"Actually, I'm probably more motivated than you'd ever imagine. Go ahead, tell me your little scheme. I've got all day."

She thought for several seconds, then took a deep breath and said, "The way I see it, there are two ways today's lockdown can turn out. First, TechLab will crumble from this scandal, and we'll all be out of jobs. Or second, there could be someone to back up your version of what happened in the BioHazard lab. Someone to verify how the others were killed by a tragic accident, so TechLab isn't destroyed."

He nodded his head, instantly seeing the positive side of having someone else survive. "Go on."

"If TechLab comes through this intact, we could wait until the air clears, then sell the information to another pharmaceutical company. I haven't documented my findings yet, so by the time I get things all checked and verified we'd probably be able to find a buyer."

"And what about TechLab?"

"TechLab would go on, with or without Citrinol3. We'd have to both leave, of course. I could tell them I just can't work here anymore, after losing Hanna, Amy, and now J.D. I'm sure you could come up with a suitable excuse, too."

"What about the other option? The one where Tech-Lab is no longer in the picture?"

"Seems pretty obvious. If I die, the perfected formula for Citrinol3 dies with me. It's worth my life to give you half the money. All you have to do is take me with you."

Harper was quiet for several seconds. Finally, he

smiled at her and said, "Interesting proposition, Jo-Ann. Just imagine, you and I partners."

He lowered the canister and stepped slowly toward her.

In the surveillance room, Gene Lemmond sluggishly pulled off his headphones and tossed them aside. For several seconds he sat very still, then he stood up and briskly walked out.

Jess slipped the sample vials out of his pocket and laid them between two flexible lead shields used for protection from exposure to radiation. He shrugged off his filthy lab coat and stuffed it in the trash, then pulled the two Priority One files out of his shirt and crammed them between the shields as well. Grabbing a clean lab coat from a rack on the wall, he slipped it on and smoothed it down. He ran his fingers through his hair, took a deep, cleansing breath, then tried to decide what his next move should be.

Searching the room, he found a cardboard box filled with X-ray plates, which he emptied. The lead-shielded samples and files fit easily inside, although the shields made the box heavy and awkward to carry.

Glancing out the door, Jess made certain the hallway was clear, then walked confidently down it. A woman entering Radiology held the door open for him and he smiled at her and said, "Thanks."

On the way from Pathology, he had passed the main elevator bank, which he headed for now, nodding silent greetings to the few workers he passed. His arms were already starting to ache, partially from the weight of the box, but mainly from his long climb through the pneumatic system.

The elevator arrived quickly, and Jess held his breath as he stepped on. After several seconds the door slid closed, and the elevator began to smoothly climb upward. No alarms sounded. The only thing Jess could hear was the pounding of his own heart.

An older man was already standing inside the elevator when Jess had walked in. Jess glanced at him now and smiled. For an instant Jess was certain there was a flicker of recognition in the man's eyes, but he quickly decided he was just being paranoid. He cheerfully said, "Good morning."

Gene Lemmond gruffly laughed at him as he replied, "Not really. As a matter of fact, this isn't going to be a good morning for you at all. We've got your son, you know. We'll kill him and your parents if you don't cooperate fully."

When Harper was standing directly in front of JoAnn he said, "Partners," and laughed as though it was the most ludicrous idea he'd ever heard. His hand raised suddenly and in an instant he squirted SynCur6 in JoAnn's face while he backed away, carefully holding his own breath.

JoAnn fell to the ground, where she was helpless at his feet. After a few seconds, when he knew it was safe to breathe again, he said, "First of all, I don't believe for a second that you've made any scientific breakthroughs lately. You've been too damned busy trying to plot your revenge against TechLab with Lawrence and Fordman. Second of all, if you have made a breakthrough, I've got plenty of time to find the paperwork and sell it myself, since I know you would have recorded the information. You're much too good a scientist to not document your findings."

He kicked her, rolling her roughly on her side before he continued speaking. "Then, why would I need you? Oh, yes, and let's not forget the most important reason for ending this whole affair now. I've been looking forward to watching your slow demise for months."

Harper dragged JoAnn into the bedroom and threw her on top of the bed. Taking both pillows, he thrust her torso cruelly up and spread her legs, carefully tilting her head so she could see everything he did to her own useless body. He bent down and pushed up his trouser leg, sliding out a long stiletto knife from a leather case strapped to the outside of his calf. To make sure she could see it, he held it in front of her face and said, "Don't worry, I sharpened it after I finished with Hanna. The cuts will be flawless." He ran the cold blade smoothly down her cheek leaving a thin trail of blood springing from its path.

It only took a few swift slices of cloth to expose JoAnn's flesh. The sound of the material ripping seemed to echo from the walls. When he slashed through the lace of her bra, she felt her breasts fall free and tried to block his image from her mind.

But it was impossible. Harper stood back, his eyes glazed as though he were admiring his own work of erotic art. For a while he merely stared at her, then he moved closer again. He ran the cold, flat edge of the knife over her breasts and down her legs. The sound of his ragged breathing filled the room.

It was when he laid the knife down that JoAnn began to wish she were already dead. And after all the months of wondering, she finally knew exactly what Hanna had been through.

A thousand things raced through Jess's mind in the moments that followed Lemmond's remark. *Who is this guy, and could he be lying? Do they really have Jonathan and my parents? If they did find them, were they already dead?*

In a wave of fury, Jess's eyes hardened and he merely said, "Bullshit."

Lemmond lunged at Jess, knocking him off balance as he tormented him by saying, "Your father made one fatal mistake, Lawrence. He used his calling card to leave you a message."

The weight of the box shifted as Jess hit the wall, and he struggled, heaving it back toward Lemmond. "Then I guess it's your turn to die," Jess said through gritted teeth as he hurled his entire body at him. The double impact slammed Lemmond against the opposite side of the elevator. As the box overturned and fell to the floor, one vial escaped from its lead prison, coming to rest against Jess's foot.

The elevator came to a jolting halt while the security alarm's screeching sound filled the air.

Harper backed away from JoAnn then, standing up so his free hand could unzip his pants. In disgust, JoAnn watched him grope himself. She tried to concentrate on something else, anything else, but he carefully stayed directly in her line of sight. He stepped toward her, the knife held like a scalpel. She felt his leg touch hers, felt his hand against her flesh, felt a drop of blood trickle down her cheek and fall just below her collarbone.

He hovered over her for what seemed like an eternity. Just as he began to lower himself onto her, Harper suddenly stopped. His wicked smirk instantaneously transformed into an expression of gaping horror. His body fell across hers, and JoAnn inwardly cringed at the sight of J.D.'s knife protruding from his back.

The alarms stopped ringing as suddenly as they had started, throwing the elevator back into stark silence. The impact from both Jess and the box had thrown Lemmond against the side wall, knocking his breath out. He tried to stand up, but Jess thrust his right foot forward, catching Lemmond in the jaw and snapping his head against the back wall of the elevator.

Lemmond groaned as he rolled to one side and withdrew a copper canister from his jacket. He pointed it at Jess, but a second swift kick sent it flying. Jess reached down and pulled Lemmond up by his lapels until he was eye to eye with him. "What did you do to my family?" he demanded.

Silence. Lemmond smiled as he said, "What difference does it make now? You'll never get out of here alive."

Jess slammed him against the elevator wall hard enough to shake the entire car and said, "I don't know who the hell you are, but I'll kill you right now. If I remember my anatomy class correctly, the bridge of the nose can be slammed quite effectively into the brain causing immediate death. Shall we see if it works?"

Lemmond growled, "You aren't the type who'd kill anyone."

Jess brought his knee up, landing a vicious blow to Lemmond's groin. As he doubled over, Jess caught his jaw with a forceful upper cut. "I asked you about my family," he growled.

Blood was pouring from Lemmond's face as he mumbled, "Two men are supposed to take out all three of them. It's probably already done."

Jess closed his fingers around Lemmond's neck as he slammed his head against the wall. "What are their names?"

"Butler and Garner."

His fingers clenched even tighter. "Where are they?"

"Hinkley. A dairy farm outside of Hinkley, Minnesota."

Jess released his grip, then curled his arm back and struck Lemmond as hard as he could in the cheek. His entire fist burned, but he didn't care. Lemmond's head hung limply to one side and blood flowed from his mouth, staining his imported navy suit as he slumped to the floor.

With clenched fists, Jess was ready to strike again, but Lemmond didn't move. He knew he didn't have much time. He took the canister of SynCur6. Grabbing the box, he dumped the lead shields on top of Lemmond and tucked the vials in his pocket and the Priority One files inside his shirt. He dragged Lemmond's limp body directly under the escape hatch in the ceiling of the elevator, then used him like a step stool.

Standing on top of Lemmond, Jess slid the hatch open, then bent down and sprayed him with the SynCur6. "That'll make sure you don't tell anyone anything for a while," he said as he pulled himself on top of the elevator.

He glanced around. So far, there was no sign of Security. The elevator shaft held two cars. Next to him, the cables from the other car extended down to the lower subfloors. Jess guessed the other car was probably stopped on either Subfloor 4 or Subfloor 5.

He knew he couldn't go up, since they would surely have the ground floor secured by now. Jess slipped the lab coat off and turned it backward. He worked his hands halfway into the sleeves and prayed the material would be thick enough to act as a makeshift glove. He held his breath and jumped to grab the cables of the other elevator.

The lab coat caught as he wrapped his arms and legs around the cables. It began ripping as he slid rapidly downward, the slick metal cables making his descent much faster than he'd anticipated. His hands were burning from the intense friction, but he willed himself to hold on. Suddenly he crashed onto the top of the elevator below, the impact sending him rolling off the side of the car toward the empty space below the elevator Lemmond was still in.

Jess would have fallen to the lowest subfloor, but one sleeve caught on the metal frame that encased the elevator leaving him dangling. Even though his hands were mangled, he reached to his right side and managed to grab the top edge of the elevator. His shirt ripped and his full weight was hanging for several seconds before he saw the safety ladder a few feet away.

Jess edged along until he could swing to the ladder. He climbed down, searching for a way out as he went.

Behind Harper's lifeless body, JoAnn could see Leanne standing, every muscle in her body ready to fight. She was waiting, her eyes enormous and sharp as though her job might not be quite finished. Those eyes stared only at Harper's still body, a silent challenge to him. Leanne seemed to want him to spring back up, to lunge at her again so she could have the satisfaction of killing him one more time.

Harper never moved. Minutes passed in silence until Leanne callously kicked Harper's body off JoAnn. He rolled roughly off the bed onto the floor, his face showing no sign of life when the knife twisted and plunged deeper into his flesh as his back hit the floor.

Leanne carefully positioned JoAnn so she would be more comfortable, then covered her with a blanket. She sat quietly facing her on the side of the bed while she pressed a washcloth to her cheek to stop the bleeding.

Finally, she held JoAnn's hand and said, "I don't know if you can hear me or not, but I heard some of what Mr. Harper said to you. I'm not sure what all this is about, but I know he was evil and he deserved what I just did to him. I found Lacey below the loft, the woman I think he was calling Stacey Fordman. At first, I thought she was dead. Her eyes are glassed over just like yours. I can tell she has a broken arm from the fall, but she seemed to be breathing all right. Hopefully she'll be okay once this drug wears off."

Leanne held up Harper's can of SynCur6 and said, "I'll take Lacey, or Stacey or whatever her name is, a pillow now and try to make her as comfortable as I can, but I'm taking whatever this stuff is for protection. I hope there aren't any more surprises waiting out there. I think we've had enough excitement for one day."

When she was at the door, she turned and added, "I'm going to spray Mr. Cook with some of this stuff just to make sure he doesn't bother you while I'm gone. The next few hours are gonna be the longest wait of my life, but I have a feeling the explanation will be more than worth it."

Leanne poked her head back in and added, "It's too bad you didn't kill Cook. I never have liked that arrogant, manipulative son of a bitch."

Jess saw the metal grate a few feet above the opening for the lowest subfloor. Holding on to the ladder, he swung around as hard as he could, his feet crashing into it. It dented, but not much. The sound echoed around him, and he was certain everyone in the building could hear him. He tried again, this time making a little more progress. On his fourth kick, the metal vents finally broke, curling inward. A few more kicks left an opening large enough for him to get through.

Swinging over, he caught the hole with one hand. With every ounce of effort he had, he worked his legs and torso up to the side of the wall until he could push his body inside. Once there, he caught his breath and tried to figure out where he was. With the little light streaming in from the elevator shaft, he could see that a few feet away there was a sharp turn in the air duct. He crawled over and realized it went straight up.

Knowing he had nothing to lose at this point, he lay

on his back and kicked the joint in the duct as hard as he could. Only his legs seemed to move. He kicked again, and this time he felt one edge pull free. A few more kicks and the metal gave way.

Crawling out of the duct, he felt his way in the darkness. At first, he was helplessly lost. But then, his hands felt the large, cool metal tube. He instantly recognized he had found part of the pneumatic system and sighed. Kneeling down, he scooted over and pried up one of the ceiling tiles. Below him were large pieces of machinery.

He froze, listening. Not too far away, he could hear a woman's voice. Leanne's voice. He jumped down, landing awkwardly on top of a piece of equipment as he softly called Leanne's name. Like a rat in a maze, he worked himself around what he now recognized as Subfloor 5. But Leanne wasn't answering.

Suddenly she was behind him. She screamed, "Freeze! Move one muscle and you're a dead man."

Without moving an inch, Jess calmly said, "Leanne. What are you doing?"

"Making sure you aren't one of them."

"If you mean a TechLab goon, I can guarantee you, I'm not. Are JoAnn and Stacey all right?"

Her voice was still suspicious as she said, "How do I know you're not one of them?"

"Remember how happy JoAnn was to see us this morning? She gave us Hanna's old security code so we could help her get out of this mess. Hanna had evidence that would prove TechLab was illegally testing their drugs. JoAnn found it. I have it in my pocket. I was trying to get out of here with it when all hell broke loose."

"Let me see. Move slowly."

Jess turned around. Leanne had a canister of Syn-Cur6 pointed directly at him. With two fingers he pulled one of the vials out of his pocket as he said, "I have some files inside my shirt, too."

Leanne lowered the canister and sighed. "I think JoAnn and your friend are going to be all right. What is her real name, anyway?"

"Stacey, and mine's Jess Lawrence."

"Stacey is over here." Leanne pointed up toward the loft. "She must have fallen over the rail of the loft and landed on the electron microscope."

Jess started to run. "Where is she?"

Leanne followed him. "I didn't mean to scare you. I don't think we should move her. Mr. Harper said that stuff in the can wears off in about two hours. When she can move again, we can see how she is. I started to put her head on a pillow, but if she has a spinal injury, even that could be bad." They had reached the machine, and she led Jess to the other side. "You can crawl up this way," she said as she navigated her way upward using a combination of nearby machines.

Jess gasped when he saw Stacey lying helplessly. He, too, immediately noticed the obvious break in her right arm. He gently ran his hands over her, checking for other injuries. With his face just above hers, he said, "You're going to be okay. I have to try to get word to my parents that they know where they are. I'll be back just as soon as I can."

He turned to Leanne and asked, "Do you know where JoAnn is?"

"She's in her office. He got her with this stuff, too. Just like Stacey."

"Who did this?"

"Harper. He was head of security. Now he's dead."

"Dead?"

Her eyes narrowed and she flatly said, "Dead."

"I need to notify the police. Is there a phone around here?"

"We can try. Follow me."

Jess snaked through the machinery behind Leanne. They made their way to a stairway and walked up to Subfloor 4. "You can try my phone or JoAnn's. Mr. Cook is in JoAnn's office, but he won't bother you."

Jess scanned the scene inside JoAnn's office and reached for the phone. There was no dial tone, so he asked, "How do I get an outside line?"

Leanne said, "That's her direct line. Is it dead?"

He nodded.

"I'll try mine." She disappeared for a moment and returned shaking her head. "They must have cut off the phones. Let's try the computer."

They did, but the computers had been shut down as well. Both began pacing. Finally, they heard a strange sound. It was coming from near JoAnn. Jess walked in first, cautiously scanning the makeshift bedroom. The sound was coming from the dead man.

Jess reached into Harper's coat pocket and pulled out his cellular phone, which immediately stopped ringing. He held it up so both JoAnn and Leanne could see it as he said, "Thank God for small miracles."

He quickly dialed a number. "Grace?" he said.

The connection was bad, but he could barely hear her say, "Is everything okay?"

"No. We're trapped inside the BioHazard lab."

"I'm with the police, Jess. We're parked about two blocks from the TechLab complex. What do you think we should do?"

"How many policemen are there?"

"The entire Special Operations Team, plus a few dozen more. The media showed up, just like you said they would. It's going to be quite an event."

"What a woman. Be sure and tell them we're in the BioHazard Lab. Subfloor 4. We'll need at least three ambulances. And, Grace, this is most important. I need you to get word to the police in Hinkley, Minnesota. Tell them to go to Fritz's dairy farm outside of town. It's an emergency. These bastards are going to kill my family."

"My God, Jess. I'll get the police to call right now."

"Thanks."

He hung up. Fatigue had suddenly overwhelmed him. He turned to Leanne and said, "Why don't you stay here and I'll wait with Stacey?"

Leanne nodded. As Jess headed back down to Sub-floor 5, he prayed they could get word to the police in Minnesota fast enough. They had to.

Chapter 22

Jonathan was watching huge snowflakes float past the window of the small A-frame cabin when he saw them. "Grandpa!" he yelled. "Someone's coming!"

A.J. ran to the front window and grabbed the binoculars. He watched as two men on snowmobiles pulled up to the fence line and stopped. After several seconds they dismounted and began hiking through the deep snow toward the cabin. A.J. said, "You and Grandma do what we planned in case a stranger showed up. Okay?"

"But, Grandpa . . ." he pleaded.

"Now, Jonathan." He looked at Betty, who wrapped her arm around Jon and hauled him toward the narrow stairway. "Go ahead and call, Betty. But do it quick," he added nervously.

A.J. pulled out his pistol, checked to be certain it was ready to fire, then slid it in the pocket of his jacket. His finger rested anxiously against the trigger, but he willed himself to stay calm. A long, slow minute passed, until finally there was a loud knock at the door. A.J. took a deep breath and shouted, "Who's there?"

"Police. Your son, Jess Lawrence, told us we could find you here. We need to talk to you about him."

A.J. hesitated, then slowly pulled the door open. "Let's see some badges."

The men stomped their feet, knocking most of the snow off their boots before they walked into the cabin. The taller of the two said, "My ID is in my pocket." He pulled off his gloves and reached very slowly inside his jacket, leaving his ski mask covering most of his face. Meanwhile, the other man took advantage of the distraction by quickly raising a copper canister of Syn-Cur6 and spraying it in A.J.'s face.

In horror, Betty and Jonathan watched silently as A.J. collapsed to the floor. He had fallen hard, and was now completely motionless, his eyes wide open. They were in the loft of the cabin, looking down from two tiny holes they'd cut in a large Indian blanket draped over the stair rail. One of the men said, "Find the other two, especially the boy."

Both men started to move toward the kitchen, but Jonathan shifted to the end of the loft farthest from the stairway, then jumped up, waved his arms, and shouted, "I'm up here!" Both men froze, then smiled at each other. They took two steps toward the stairs, then dropped in their tracks. Their bodies sprawled backward, riddled with holes from the two shotgun blasts that caught each one square in the chest.

Betty broke open the sawed-off shotgun, pulled out the two empty hulls, and dropped in two more 12-gauge 00 buckshot rounds. She snapped the barrel back down and pulled Jonathan beside her as she said, "Don't look, Jon. Wait up here."

"What? I can't hear you, Grandma, my ears feel funny. They're kinda ringing."

She turned his face toward hers, literally pulling his stare away from the two bloody men at the foot of the stairs. Slowly, loudly, she said, "Wait by the bed. Understand?"

Jonathan nodded, but as soon as she let go of his chin, he looked back down at the bloody men. Betty stood up, pushing him toward the opposite corner of the bedroom as she said, "Call 911 again, Jon. They should have been here by now."

Betty raised the shotgun to her shoulder and moved

to the top of the stairway. She stood guard there, steadying the gun on the rail as she carefully aimed at the two men, her finger ready on the trigger. Even as the police cars began pulling up outside, she held her aim steady. And waited.

Epilogue

A.J. Lawrence picked up Jonathan and whirled him playfully around as he and Betty both said, "Happy Thanksgiving!"

Jonathan hugged him back, excitedly asking, "Grandpa, are you and Grandma really going to move to Tulsa?"

A.J. smiled and answered, "You bet. I think your grandma and I have both had enough Minnesota winters. It might be kind of nice not having to shovel snow every day for months." He pulled his grandson close and whispered, "Do you think you can help me with all the spare time I'm going to have on my hands? You know how it is. Grandma'll drive me crazy if I hang around the house too much."

Jon wiggled free. "I'll teach you how to climb trees and use walkie-talkies and play video games and . . ."

Betty interrupted, "Hold on, I think finding a new house will be enough to keep Grandpa busy for a little while. You two can have a great time, but I don't think I'll let Grandpa climb any trees, Jonathan."

Jonathan said, "I'll go get my surprise!" As he bounded up the stairs, Jess, Stacey, and JoAnn came into the entryway.

Jess slapped his father on the shoulder and hugged them. "Welcome home," he said. "I'd like you both to meet two very special women." He quickly introduced everyone.

A.J. turned and held his hand out to Stacey as he said, "It's nice to finally meet my future daughter-in-law." He hugged her and added, "Welcome to the family." Turning to JoAnn, he smiled and said, "You know, of course, that Jon has fallen in love with those pups of yours. You may have to work out some sort of joint custody arrangement to keep that boy from moving in with you."

JoAnn lifted one crutch and said, 'That's a great idea. It would certainly come in handy having a *trust-worthy* male around the house, especially one with two good legs." She nudged Jess and begged, "Can I take him with me? Please? I lead a very calm, peaceful life. Really I do."

Jess laughed and replied, "If you call the last few weeks calm and peaceful, I'd hate to see what you think is exciting."

She shrugged as she said, "Good point, but if he turns up missing anytime soon . . ."

A.J. smiled at Stacey. "Let me see that rock of yours, young lady."

Stacey blushed and extended her left hand. The one-and-a-half-carat solitaire ring glittered delicately. Stacey said, "It's so beautiful." She smiled warmly at Betty and said, "Mrs. Lawrence, I can't tell you how much we love your mother's diamond. It was so generous of you to . . ."

Betty interrupted. "First of all, my name is Betty, not Mrs. Lawrence, and secondly, that diamond looks like it was meant for you. The setting you chose is perfect. I hope you're as happy to wear it as I was."

Stacey hugged Jess and said, "Believe me, I am."

A.J. asked, "How's that arm of yours, Stacey?"

She held up her cast. "Better every day. Only four more weeks and I'll be free of this thing."

Jess gestured toward the living room as he said, "Come inside. We've got hot apple cider by the fireplace and Jon's dying to demonstrate his marshmallow roasting abilities. By the way, we're expecting a few other guests for Thanksgiving dinner. Grace Milliken, Leanne Caldwell, and Chase Kent should all be here any minute."

A.J. said, "You'll have to refresh my memory. Leanne works with JoAnn at TechLab, right?"

JoAnn answered. "Yes. Leanne Caldwell is my assistant. She saved my life that horrible day."

"Then I can't wait to meet her. What exactly do you do at TechLab?" Betty asked.

"We've been trying to find a cure for certain types of cancer, and you'll be happy to know something good did come out of all this. The tests I ran on Stacey's blood have helped locate a marker on the DNA. It's the breakthrough I've been searching for all these years. I'm very excited about the drug's potential."

Stacey chimed in, "Lucky me. I think I've given her half my blood to test, but I suppose I shouldn't complain."

Betty laughed, "Why not? I always complain when I have to have blood drawn, and I've heard Jonathan hates it worse than lima beans."

"How are the other children in his class?" Betty asked.

"They all seem fine. Unfortunately, they'll have to be monitored for the rest of their lives even though they weren't exposed for a long period of time," JoAnn answered.

A.J. asked, "I don't mean to change the subject, but who's Grace Milliken?"

Stacey answered, "She's the principal at East Elementary. She helped us get safely out of the BioHazard lab after the lockdown." She added playfully, "She's my boss, so let's all be on our best behavior."

Jess said, "And Chase Kent is a detective with the Tulsa Police Department. He was assigned to JoAnn when she was first attacked in the parking lot. He's spent most of the last few weeks working with the FBI to wrap up the TechLab case." He winked at JoAnn as he said, "He and JoAnn have become pretty close lately."

JoAnn blushed, but didn't argue.

Stacey said to Betty, "Wait till you see Chase. Every year the police department makes a calendar to raise money for charity. Chase is Mr. February this year."

Betty smiled and said, "I'll have to put one of those on my Christmas list. After all, the money goes to a good cause."

"Stacey, quit corrupting my mother," Jess said. "Besides, what am I, dog meat?"

Betty laughed. "Well, you may be an August or September, but you're definitely not a February, son."

Jess shook his head and said, "I don't even want to know what that's supposed to mean."

A.J. said, "Smart man. What happened to the guys from TechLab who masterminded all of this?"

Jess answered, "McDaniel turned state's evidence. In exchange for admittance to the Federal Witness Protection Program, he's telling everything about TechLab and their main competitor. It seems McDaniel is afraid both sides will want to kill him. He had already arranged to sell TechLab information to the other side, so he has enough evidence to incriminate the ringleaders in the industry."

"Nice guy. What about Lemmond? Wasn't he the one who sent those two goons after us?"

"Yes. Once he got out of the hospital, he was thrown in jail without bond, along with his buddy, J. D. Cook." Jess smiled and said, "I broke Lemmond's jaw in eighteen places. Stacey relocated Cook's nose for him and JoAnn gave him one hell of a concussion."

Betty said, "Too bad you two didn't use your dad's sawed-off shotgun like I did. It would have saved the taxpayers a lot of money."

Jess shook his head. "Mom, you never cease to

amaze me. I have to admit, I was pretty impressed with what you did. And very grateful."

"I'd never fired a gun before in my life, and I hope I never have to again." She winked and said, "But I will if anyone messes with A.J. Someone's got to protect the poor man."

A.J. chuckled and said, "Next time we'll use *you* as bait, my dear."

Jonathan came running back in, his arms filled with squirming puppies. "This is Rocky and this is Bell. They're JoAnn's dogs, but I've been taking really good care of them."

A.J. squatted to pet the puppies. Bell peed and ran to hide behind Jonathan, while Rocky rolled over so A.J. could scratch his belly. In his best grandfatherly whisper, A.J. said, "Maybe you should ask for some pups of your own for Christmas this year, Jon. I think you've shown how responsible you are by taking such good care of these little guys."

Betty shook her head and lightly kicked A.J. as she cleared her throat. Jess glared at his father, but he didn't have the heart to turn Jonathan down again, especially since he knew of a litter of puppies that would be weaned the week before Christmas. When Jon looked away, he winked at everyone and said, "We'll see. Meanwhile, let's concentrate on all we have to be thankful for . . ."

If you enjoyed reading *Deadly Company*,
turn the page for a tantalizing preview
of Jodie Larsen's next thriller,

DEADLY PORTRAITS

Coming soon to your favorite bookstore.

As he jogged through the serene Savannah park, Evan Peterson evaluated the cool October day. A westerly breeze rushed over the lush jogging trails, sending the few remaining clouds toward the ocean. Following the path, Evan twisted through a thick grove of trees, brushing strands of Spanish moss out of his way as they swayed in the gentle wind. Although another man would have relished the abundance of nature's blessings, Evan merely tabulated the effect the pleasant weather would have on the work ahead. When he emerged at the edge of the park's vast playground, he slowed to a brisk walk, then quickly counted the children playing in the area.

Sucking in a deep, cleansing breath, he felt the last shreds of nervous energy being replaced by a familiar thirst. It was a powerful feeling, the need to dominate, to prevail at any cost. In a matter of seconds he could change the destiny of any of the children before him. Smiling, he knew once again that he was still invincible, a predator among his prey.

Evan hardly noticed the striking young woman leaning over the double stroller that blocked the path ahead. It was the object of her attention that caught his practiced eye. The baby. A perfect baby. In a second he unconsciously tallied the toddler's attributes: large blue eyes with thick, dark lashes; brown curls; plump, healthy body. The mother's soft Southern accent seemed to float in the wind as she pulled the child out of the stroller and into her arms.

He could have easily touched the girl's silky hair as he passed by, but he resisted, content to memorize her features instead. As his eyes probed her face, she visibly tensed, as if she knew the threat he posed. An involuntary shudder ran through him. He was certain he must be imagining things. The child could not have possibly sensed danger, yet he was sure he had seen an instinctive flash of fear cloud those big blue eyes the instant before she turned away.

The jogging trail ended at the adjoining parking lot, where Evan stretched and discreetly watched. He could see the little girl struggling to be free, until finally the woman yielded and set her daughter on the ground. Without a glance in his direction she ran away, launching a full-fledged assault on a nearby array of heavy ropes precisely knotted to form a gigantic man-made spider web.

Even from a distance Evan could hear the child giggle as she clutched, swayed, and pulled herself to the center of the web. He found himself tempted to turn around and stare again, but the vision would have to wait. His very existence depended on being unseen, overlooked—another face in the crowd.

Without hesitation he opened the car door and slid in the front seat beside Tony Montegra. Tony did not acknowledge Evan's arrival. After a few silent moments he flatly said, "My package didn't include the specs."

Unfolding the paper, Evan read aloud the target information. "Caucasian. Blond hair. Blue or green eyes. No sex preference. Under two acceptable, under four months preferred."

"Business as usual?" Tony mumbled.

Evan nodded as he tossed his spare set of keys to Tony, and deposited the set he received into his own pocket along with the spec sheet. The extra keys were insurance against this park's chief disadvantage—parking lots on each end of the tangled stretch of playgrounds.

Even though Evan and Tony worked together on jobs only two or three times a year, they communicated silently and efficiently. Over the past fifteen years they had learned to understand the slightest glance or hand gesture. Where every aspect of Evan's life was controlled and precise, Tony preferred to wing it, to attack challenges as they came.

The men were opposites in every way, from their backgrounds to their appearances. Born and raised on a struggling farm in Iowa, Evan had watched his parents work themselves to death—literally. When he was left alone at eighteen, he sold everything, moved to Manhattan, and swore he would never live in poverty again. After only a week his destiny was set when a friend introduced him to Tony Montegra.

Tony was a dark, brooding young man who had a similar hunger for a better life. The oldest of five children, he had been like a father to his brothers, helping his single mother as much as he could by prowling the streets of Los Angeles with his friends. She never asked where he got the money he gave her, she only cried and hugged him. When he was seventeen, a store owner shot his best friend. Tony escaped with a bullet-grazed shoulder, and a valuable lesson. That night he left L.A. for good.

Tony learned how to survive first in Chicago, then in Manhattan. He quickly turned his street sense into a livelihood, alternating his crimes between the two cities. His reputation for discretion and solitude landed him several "positions," including a chance to be on the ground floor of an elite organization where minimal work held the promise of maximum wealth. Within the first year he realized the complex nature of the assignments required he work with a partner once again. The thought turned his stomach until he met Evan Peterson.

As they stepped out of the car, in unison Evan and Tony reached behind their backs, switching on the small battery packs that powered their more formal line of communication. Voice-activated, state-of-the-art mini-microphones were concealed under the collars of their jogging suits. The risks they took demanded the best equipment money could buy.

Evan casually walked away from the car knowing Tony would remain behind to scrutinize the light settings on the camera for several minutes. Perfection was essential. Crisp, bold colors with sharp images comparable to professional studio portraits were the only acceptable product. If the negatives weren't perfect, they had wasted their time and energy. Wasted time meant someone else might get the job. Losing the job meant losing ten thousand untaxed, unrecorded dollars a month. Each.

Evan lengthened his perfectly tuned body into a runner's stretch until he heard Tony's voice in his earphone say, "Program one engaged."

Striding easily into a soft jog, Evan muttered, "First pass underway." He rolled through each step, his footfalls practically silent on the winding path as he passed the children snagged by the spider web. None of them seemed to notice him. Relieved, he continued on, graciously nodding at each passing jogger and waving to children as they played on the vast array of nearby jungle gyms and swings.

Less than five minutes into their operation, Evan and Tony found their first target. A perfect match. Sitting alongside the jogging path near a redwood picnic table was a young mother.

As she gently pulled and pushed a side-by-side double stroller, she talked quietly to a friend.

In the double stroller were two children facing each other. The little girl giggled and played, thoroughly entertaining the baby boy. Both had blond curls and light eyes. Years of experience led Evan to estimate the girl's age between twenty and twenty-five months and the boy at two to three months.

A convenient row of bushes provided perfect cover as Tony eased himself into position. He slid the lens cap off and focused the camera. Beside him a photography manual was open to the section titled "Capturing Earth's Treasures." To any passersby Evan appeared to be casually photographing nature. But in reality the powerful telephoto lens on his camera pulled the children so close to his eye, he would have sworn he could jerk their precious blond curls with a twist of his fingertips.

Ten minutes and three rolls of film later, Evan and Tony began their wait. The second phase of the game was always more dangerous, but a lot more fun. Most of the people lounging in the park were enjoying a relaxed morning, but Tony's patience was wearing thin as time crept slowly by. Finally, he whispered, "Phase one is really dragging. Are you still clear?"

Evan answered, "Yes. Everything okay with you?"

"Doing great. Just bored stiff. How long do you think they're going to sit on their butts and talk?" Tony muttered.

"One of the brats will throw a fit soon. Just wait. We've been in position over an hour. I'm sure the little linoleum lizards won't make it much longer."

Tony flexed one leg without visibly moving. He was resting on a park bench, his face covered by the magazine on photography. "I hope you're right. I'm not sure how much longer I can stay this way. My friggin' back may break."

Snickering, Evan softly said, "Looks like we're in luck. The little girl just smacked her baby brother."

Both men discreetly watched the two women hug, then push their strollers in opposite directions down the sunlit path. The woman Evan and Tony were following stopped several times, pointing at birds and flowers as she identified them for her children.

"They're heading right at you. Sit tight," Tony whispered.

Evan listened to Tony's calm voice as he saw the woman pushing the double stroller approach his new location. Even though he was wearing a wig and stage makeup, he turned his face away, leaning into a long cat stretch as they passed. He knew this particular path wound through two small hills and another playground before it ended at the parking area. After watching them crest the first hill, he cut across a grassy knoll, then sprinted to his car.

Two minutes later, Evan was behind the steering wheel of a rented blue Caprice. The hat was gone, a different wig was in place, and a shirt and tie had appeared from under the jacket of the jogging suit. When the mother and her children walked within inches of him, Evan appeared to be exactly what he was—a professional.

Dropping in behind her as she pulled her minivan into the busy street, Evan was close enough to clearly see the mother's reflection in her rearview mirror. *Such a perfect little world she lives in . . . If she only knew,* he thought. *Would she run? Cry? Offer herself in place of her kids?* The last thought nearly made him laugh out loud.

Using their radios, Evan and Tony expertly tailed her by alternating streets, literally tag-teaming their quarry. When she stopped at the grocery store, Evan jotted down her license plate number so they could run a check on it, if necessary. Fifteen minutes later, they saw her emerge from the store balancing the children and a sack of groceries. As she headed back to her car, they moved into position.

Traffic had picked up slightly at noon, making it a little tougher to negotiate Savannah's busy streets. Both men were relieved when she finally turned into a newly constructed neighborhood. Brightly colored flags, marking model homes and vacant lots, were sprinkled near the entry, but the minivan didn't slow until it approached a block already filled with new houses. Toys were scattered on porches, and several children stopped on their bikes and trikes to wait for the cars to pass.

"She's pulling in," Tony said.

"I'll get the address. You get the name on the mailbox, if there is one," Evan said.

As he drove past the two-story colonial home, Evan noticed everything—flawless new landscaping, crisp white paint against hunter green shutters. Maps and plans would be prepared later. *If* an order was placed.

Stopping around the corner, he closed his eyes to commit the scene to memory. Every detail of the house was clear in his mind, and he would bet the second-story front windows were the children's rooms. Evan opened his eyes at the sound of Tony's voice.

"Did you see it on the mailbox? Nelson. Their names are George and Mary Nelson."

"I love it when they make it easy," Evan laughed. "So easy."

Six hours later, a taxi rolled to a stop outside the sleek Manhattan office of Paradise Promotions. Evan quickly paid the scrawny driver, unlocked the office doors, and dropped his luggage inside. He immediately relocked the door, even though it was well past time to open. After traveling all night, he was in no mood to handle questions from ignorant tourists.

He glanced around. Everything looked normal. Waving stripes of lavender neon bordered the slate gray marble of the countertop. Scattered about the room were meticulous displays of brochures, pamphlets, and stickers. Vacuum trails in the plush emerald carpet and the sparkle of the crystal tabletops were the only evidence left behind that the cleaning woman had come and gone.

Walking to the back of the suite, Evan unlocked the door to the darkroom by keying in the disarming sequence on the keypad. Smiling, he thought of the surprise unauthorized visitors would receive if they were stupid enough to try to enter this room. Initially, he thought the level of security designated was ridiculous, but after so many years he was used to the extreme precautionary measures. In fact, he wouldn't have it any other way.

Evan's movements could easily have been choreographed. His fluid motions were precise yet graceful. Experience flowed from his fingertips, reflecting his personal need for perfection in every act. In only a few minutes, the negatives were processed and seventy-two close-up pictures of two rosy-cheeked, happy babies hung drying. He washed his hands thoroughly, started to leave, then stopped. Moving slowly, he was drawn to one particular picture of the baby boy. Against the soft Georgia landscape he appeared to be smiling at a wispy cloud above, dreaming of a better life.

In the darkness of the room Evan greedily caressed the child's cheek. There was no doubt about it. The boy would sell quickly. A second trip to Savannah would be on his agenda, soon. He could bank on it.

"Nick Hunter."

"You sound more like some conceited old windbag than the Beagle Hunter I knew in college."

Nick's deep, reserved voice instantly broke into laughter as he slapped the desk and leaned back into his leather chair. He sounded much more relaxed as he said, "Jim! You old son of a gun. That was my high-priced, kiss-my-rich-ass lawyer voice."

"I heard you sold out, but I didn't actually believe it. What happened to all those lofty goals of working for the good of all mankind?"

"All mankind repossessed my car. Then they threatened to kick me out of my apartment. Court costs were eating me alive, and you know as well as I do the homeless people of Little Rock couldn't afford to pay." Running his hand across the top of his elegant mahogany desk, Nick glanced around. It was still hard for him to believe the large office was his. Thick burgundy carpet, flame-stitched wingback chairs, and original oil paintings were a far cry from the hole in the wall he'd worked out of just a few weeks ago. Sighing, he added, "Jim, I was damn lucky a firm as profitable as Kellars & Kellars would even give me the time of day, much less offer me a chance to work into a partnership."

"Top of your class probably didn't hurt your chances. I don't suppose you're allowed to do favors for old friends? Freebie, of course. Unfortunately, some of us are still wallowing in it, so to speak."

Rolling the chair back, Nick stood and walked to the edge of the floor-to-ceiling window as he hesitantly answered, "Depends on what you need. I had to sign the standard agreement when I came to work here. I'm not allowed to represent any cases, or even give legal advice to non-clients, without approval of the senior partner."

"Let me guess. The receptionist said you're with Kellars & Kellars, Attorneys at Law. The senior partner wouldn't by any chance be some hotshot named Kellars, would it?"

Nodding, Nick nervously stepped away from the window. "Will Kellars. He started the firm umpteen years ago. Runs the place like the Gestapo. He must be pushing sixty, but he still eagle eyes everything that goes on here."

"He must be a real publicity hound, too. I've seen some of those commercials of his when I travel. At least they've got style, but when you lick the chocolate coating off, the stench is still there. You get brownie points for ambulance chasing?"

"I thought you wanted a favor," Nick grumbled as he plopped back into his chair and spun around.

"I do. Peg asked me to call you. Sometimes I think she still has the hots for you, old pal. Her eyes kind of glass over when she says your name."

Nick knew asking for anything wasn't easy for Jim. He was the kind of guy who preferred to keep his problems to himself. When he finally spoke his voice was lower, tightly controlled as if the words were scratching their way out. "The last five years have been hell for us, Nick. Peg and I've seen every infertility specialist within a thousand miles, gone through hundreds of tests, Peg's had two surgeries. We've burned up every cent we'd ever saved, and then some, trying in-vitro fertilization plus every new procedure you can imagine. Nothing's worked."

He sighed. "I'm really sorry, Jim. I know how much the two of you want children. Peg would make a great mother."

"Which is where you come in."

The leather chair squeaked as Nick craned his head around, making certain the door to his office was still closed. Rubbing his forehead with his free hand, he sighed, "Oh, no. You're not gonna try to rook me into any kinky donor-fatherhood-by-test-tube deal, are you?"

"Hell, no! You think I want my kid running around looking like Stretch Armstrong? I can just picture the poor child. Seven feet tall with a mane of blond hair and that lady-killer smile of yours. We'd be beating off basketball coaches and women all day long. Don't worry, your gene pool is safe. We need *legal* help."

Nick was obviously relieved as he said, "I'm only six foot six, not exactly considered a giant these days."

"Which is a foot taller than I am, remember?"

"We can't all be born to greatness," Nick joked. Nick grabbed a pencil and began tapping nervously on the stack of files waiting for his attention. "Seriously, what kind of legal help do you need?"

"Peg's found a woman who says she'll have our baby for us. We have seven embryos still frozen at the Midwestern Fertility Center, but the doctors won't implant into another person, much less an unrelated person. Too many legal loopholes, they say."

"I can imagine."

"That's what we need you for. First, to get the center's attention. Those are *our* frozen babies, not theirs, and we should be able to control their destiny. Second, to handle the paperwork on the surrogate. We don't want any complications down the road."

Tossing the pencil down, Nick clutched the phone tightly as

he said, "When you ask for a favor, you don't pull any punches, do you?"

"I hate even asking, Nick. It's just that we're already broke. We're both working two jobs, trying to accumulate enough to pay the medical bills all this will run up. We just want a chance."

"Listen, I understand, and I wish I could help. But you're talking about a huge amount of time. The firm's time. Billable time."

"But it might be a highly visible case. Kellars will love the free press coverage. This case could be a media extravaganza if it's handled properly."

Nick sighed, "Or a media nightmare. I'll ask. But don't hold your breath."

"That's all we're begging for. We'll understand if you can't. Really."

Nick yanked at his tie and tugged open the collar of his crisply starched pale blue shirt as he said, "I'll give it my best shot. By the way, I don't chase ambulances. I don't handle quickie divorces and workman's comp cases. Strictly litigation, criminal and a few high-dollar civil cases. You can spread the rumor back home that I didn't sell out. At least not totally."

"My faith in mankind is somewhat restored. We'll be waiting to hear from you."

After punching the speaker button on the phone, Nick leaned back and listened to the silence around him. He stretched his long legs onto the corner of his desk. Memories of college seemed like only yesterday. Jim and Peg were always there, along with his other buddies. Studying, working, and rushing to classes had all blurred into an exhausted, driven lifestyle with only one goal in sight.

Nick swung his legs back down and roughly combed his fingers through his thick blond hair. After college, he followed his conscience through rough years where goals were constantly interrupted by harsh financial realities. The chance to make his own mark in the legal world had fallen in his lap, and he had no intention of failing. Yet after only a month at the firm he hated the thought of asking Will Kellars to take on a pro-bono case. Actually, he hated the thought of asking Will Kellars anything at all.

Angela Anderson crouched on the floor of her office at Kellars & Kellars, her head almost touching the underside of her desk. As usual, she wished she had on jeans and tennis shoes instead of a silk suit. It was virtually impossible for her to work in the cramped space without hiking her skirt to an indecent level. On the floor beside her were her personal tools. Nestled in small plastic pockets, each wrench and screwdriver had its own special place. She slid a tiny screwdriver back in and reached for the more powerful electric screwdriver on the carpet beside her.

In less than five minutes, Angela took the cover off her computer and spread its various parts neatly across the floor of her office. She carefully opened the box containing her latest system upgrade, took out the processing board, and snapped it into the belly of the machine. After admiring her handiwork, she acted with practiced precision to begin reassembling her machine.

Just as she was tightening the last screw, a deep voice in her doorway muttered, "Damn!"

Bolting upright, Angela's head thudded painfully against her desk. Frustrated, she gently massaged the new bump as she leaned back and called, "Who's there and what the hell do you want?"

Crawling out from under her desk, she twisted around to see an incredibly tall, handsome man sheepishly say, "Sorry about that. Are you okay?"

For a second after she saw him, her breath caught, then she cleared her throat and muttered, "Luckily, I have a very hard head." She pointed under the table. "I was adding a new chip that will double my machine's processing speed."

Following the man's admiring gaze, she glanced down at her skirt. As her cheeks tingled, she self-consciously tugged the short, tight silk of her black suit, coaxing it down her thighs. Touching her hair, she realized the French knot that had held it in place now sagged at the nape of her neck. At once she pulled out the confining pins and shook her head, freeing shoulder-length auburn waves. "I'm usually not such a mess, really . . ."

Nick extended his hand as he said, "I shouldn't have barged in. By the way, I'm Nick Hunter. I've been working here for a couple of weeks now. I was beginning to think Angela Anderson was a figment of everyone's imagination."

"Believe me, even though I've been gone, I've heard all about *you*, too." Angela's official title was director of public relations. A fancy name for someone in charge of writing advertising copy and handling press releases for the law firm as well as its larger clients. Officially an outside consulting firm, Compu-Corp was in charge of all computer operations, but everyone in the office knew Angela could troubleshoot problems. "I was attending an advanced management course, Public Relations in Mass Communications, in St. Paul," she added.

Raising his eyebrows, Nick said, "Sounds intriguing."

Angela cocked her head and eyed him, trying to decide if he had a sense of humor or not. Smiling coyly, she said, "You really should get out more if you actually believe that." She rubbed the growing bump on her head. When she looked up at him, his blue eyes reflected genuine concern. Moving closer, she tilted her face as though she were looking at the noon sun to see all of him. "Don't even think it," she said.

Smiling, he innocently asked, "Think what?"

She smugly replied, "You were wondering why they let kids work here, or who I'm kidding wearing high heels. Believe me, I've heard every vertically challenged joke there is."

"And I've heard them all on the other extreme." Easily staring at the top of her head he asked, "Are you sure you're okay?"

Ignoring him, she answered, "Believe me, it would take more than a little blow to the head to keep me down. Let me guess. You need an urgent press release. Which congressman got hauled in for DUI this time? Or did some socialite break a fingernail?"

He laughed. "Nothing that easy. My computer's gone crazy. Can you help me?" Nick asked.

"I'll try." She moved next to him and whispered, "Unofficially, of course. I believe proper procedure is to contact Compu-Crooks, or whatever that price-gouging firm's name is."

As she walked beside him toward his office, she noticed the air of confidence in Nick's quick stride. For once, the rumors she had heard had been true. He actually was young and good-looking. To keep from staring up at him, she consciously tried to notice things she had taken for granted for years. Even the halls of Kellars & Kellars were distinctive. Crimson crown molding lined somber gray walls that displayed a variety of original Native American artwork. Angela unconsciously smiled when they passed her favorite painting, a watercolor of a young squaw kneeling at a riverbank.

Approaching his office, they could hear the steady beeping from several yards away. "Is that your machine?" Angela asked, obviously puzzled and slightly amazed.

Nick meekly answered, "Unfortunately. I must have hit the wrong key. I ended up on the WKE screen."

Turning to him, she asked, "The *what*?"

"The WKE screen. That's what it said. I didn't know what it was, but it looked interesting. So I sort of . . ."

Grinning, she asked, "Tried to get in it?"

Nick sheepishly nodded his head.

As they entered his office, Angela suddenly stopped.

"What's wrong?" Nick asked.

Hesitating, Angela stammered for a second, then said, "Nothing. Really."

"I know. It's a little overbearing, isn't it?"

Staring at the room, she said, "I . . . I just wasn't expecting you to be in Rick's old office. It just threw me off for a second, that's all."

With raised eyebrows he asked, "Rick? As in Rick Kellars?"

She nodded. "Kellars must really like you. No one has had this office since his son died." Walking to the far wall, she admired a beautiful oil of an Oklahoma field ablaze with Indian paintbrush. "I don't remember this painting. Is it yours?"

"Yep. My grandmother painted it." Walking to his computer, he asked, "Can you please make this thing be quiet?"

Angela looked at the ominous message: *Access Denied—Password Investigation Underway.* She smiled and said, "No problem."

"Really?" he asked, obviously impressed.

Sliding into his chair, she reached over and gently pushed the Power button on the base processing unit, turning the machine instantly off. The screen faded to black as the electronic whine spiraled down to silence. The beeping stopped. Everything stopped. She waited about ten seconds before pushing the Power button again. The setup program whirled through its system checks before Nick's normal sign-on screen appeared. With a flourish worthy of a magician's assistant Angela exclaimed, "Ta-da!"

Nick's brows furrowed in mock disgust as he mumbled, "I could've done that myself."

"And next time you will. Let's see if we can recreate the problem. What were you trying to do?"

"I wanted to check for any outstanding or recent cases the firm has handled involving adoptions or the use of surrogate mothers."

"So you went into the Main Office Shell, then selected Caseload Directory?"

"That's what I did, or rather, it was what I was trying to do."

Expertly she typed the entries needed. Together they scanned the listings, finding nothing in either area. Angela stood and looked curiously at Nick. "You know, considering the Kellars family history, I doubt if the firm handles any cases in those areas."

"I don't suppose you'd care to expand?"

She lowered her voice, saying, "Not here."

Nick glanced at his watch and said, "I think I owe you lunch. Why don't I meet you at the elevators in five minutes?"

Angela hesitated for a few seconds, then called over her shoulder as she walked away, "Sounds great."

"Wait!" he said.

Stopping in the doorway, she twirled back around and gazed at him.

"Sorry, never mind . . ."

"Afraid we'll look ridiculous together?"

Shaking his head, Nick answered, "Of course not. I was just surprised to finally be having a business lunch with someone from the firm. Since I came to work here, the other lawyers have been rather distant. I was beginning to wonder if I had B.O. or something."

Angela laughed, but was too embarrassed to tell him the real reason why people were avoiding him. Instead she said, "It probably has more to do with this office than anything else. Mr. Kellars wouldn't have put you here if he didn't have some serious longterm plans for you. The other lawyers are probably just jealous." And after having met him, she realized they had good cause to be worried. Nick seemed to be brighter, wittier, and more persuasive than all of them rolled together. Even if he was a little different.

Rolling his eyes, Nick muttered, "Great. Should I be flattered or worried?"

Turning to leave, Angela smiled and said, "Probably a little of both."